LOVE'S GRAVITY

LOVE'S GRAVITY

by

PER WÄSTBERG

Translated by ANN HENNING

SOUVENIR PRESS

CONTENTS

'Do you know there is hidden treasure in the house next-door?'
'But there is no house next door!'
'Then we shall have to build one.'

MARX

I

OUT OF VISION

RENEWED DESCRIPTION

Someone must describe Jan Backman again.

There is not much to distinguish him from other people. There is no point in trying to indicate the existing differences – that would assume similarities. Who decides that people are all alike? Some of them look like each other, but that is another matter.

Initially he is, like everybody else, a foetus without a name. Then he is given a name and becomes a separate personality. He is given more and more papers for his identity. Later on, when he becomes an adult, he will notice a certain feeling of disintegration. Some facts he will readily accept: the passport evidence regarding hair, colour of eyes and height. He stopped growing at a certain height. Since then time continues alone.

His social security number has another figure added to it, thus implying that society is growing – or improving. Tick what is not applicable.

He gets it into his head that he may be a different person from the one described on the papers. The foetus could have had other names which have been forgotten, spoken a different language, or had its citizenship withheld.

Has he then been cheated of his rights? Yes – in secret ways. He might as well leave everything aboveboard. Some time in life he will still start again searching for the unknown.

There is a photograph of Jan Backman at the Water Palace. He is moving, slowly on his way out of focus, probably ignorant of the fact that someone is, at that moment, taking a photo of him. A still photo without depth. He is in its undefinable centre, looking vacant.

Some people who have met Jan Backman – or JB as his fellow students in Uppsala named him – say that the unusual, somewhat annoying thing about him is a certain lack of neurosis, tension and ambition. He is aware of time but of what time? He has varied knowledge, but no defined course.

Is that so? Some people say it is. Ask them again!

These people are his holds on reality. They are his yard-stick for perspective, proximity and distance.

To his mind's eye figures appear which are not easy to dispel. He invents questions for them and they bind with their answers and their silence.

However carefully you carve a figure, there is still another hidden in the wood.

A profile out of focus, Paul Gauguin said, but the eyes are of bone and volcanic glass.

Portraits preserved of James Cook, the seafarer, differ so much that they could be of entirely different people.

One day, looking through the telephone directory for Greater Stockholm, he finds that the people calling themselves conjurers fill up almost one column in the yellow pages. In the Arlanda area alone there are two. These magicians and drawing-room swindlers all perform under assumed names, names which they have been free to choose for themselves. He envies them, but not their livelihood. He has left behind all these children's parties.

His own profession is chief air-traffic controller at Arlanda Airport. He has changed his Volvo for a Peugeot 204, Arctic Ocean Blue according to the description, in other words grey. He has a flat in a house that is to be demolished in Uppland Street in Stockholm, and shares an inherited summer residence on the northern side of the island of Värmdö.

Jan Backman goes to work with dutiful precision. His profession is not suited to show and extravagance. It consists of trained manual exercises, figures and words to be received without hesitation or demands of modulation. That is why he longs to escape into the margins of the ill-defined and unfinished, to vaguer notions and free physical movements on an open space of land. That is when he sees his job as a kind of asceticism, where every invention has to be stopped, every whim checked.

He sometimes feels violent or lawless, ecstatic or obsessive, but is unable to register these feelings. His profession does not approve of them. Every action outside the framework and every gesture that is not recognized and learnt from the start risks lives and cuts off a chain of prepared actions.

He often touches the bottom of his chair with reluctant

expectation; his fingers hoping to find a secret message there. It is a habit he has kept from childhood. He finds only other things, grained or tough, which do not tell him very much.

Around him he can see people who have set up ingenious machinery to get through life quickly and easily. He fears that he too has moved fast where he should have lingered.

He is looking for a point of view. A weevil in the spring-time will watch from inside a dandelion ball yellow butterflies being born and dragonflies sidling up towards the end of narrow green leaves; the starting posts of life.

He believes that, given enough time, he will notice that not even the lions on the plinths of the statues are petrified. They exchange glances. They roll balls of stone to one another.

But on his instrument panel in the control tower the bulbs blink incessantly. He interprets them and answers the calls. He is in charge of things. Planes wanting to fly at the same altitude must leave at ten minutes' intervals and be three hundred metres apart as they move away towards the check-points at Trosa, Boda and Svappa.

Over Arlanda there is a sharp afternoon light; the light fore-boding thunder. Yet thunder is seldom heard in November. The sun appears through a distant haze. Low pressure creates a feeling of menace and claustrophobia.

It is an early winter's day, with nothing much happening. The landscape is a large waiting-room, but you cannot hear the railway signals any more. Most trains have stopped going in Sweden.

But aeroplanes take off. From a high altitude pilots can look down into the deep waters, provided they are still clear, and see the glimmer of our sunken treasures: the drowned loads of mercury, the chests of nerve gas, and plimsolls filled with hydrogen sulphide and radioactive ashes. Down there they await the deep-sea divers and sea archeologists of some future date.

The areoplanes take off with the sun shining on their wings.

JB reads in an advertisement for a travel agency that Turkey is no further away than your own telephone. Nothing is far away if you have got money and the right outlook. He looks out over the clay fields of Uppland: nothing grows there, but nearby, a few inches beneath the surface, a new crop is beginning to emerge.

Jenny Jeger cannot be far away either, but he does not know whether she is in London or Strasbourg. She has not been in touch with him – nor has he had word from Gertrude, his half-sister, who arrived in Botswana some days ago.

On his desk there is a reminder about a delegation. He is to show some Dutch people around Arlanda, one of his tasks being to explain the idea of this still unfinished place, which will hopefully one day turn out well. In any case there is space enough, provided Märsta does not spread too far over the flight paths. He is going to tell them about the flights of migratory birds in the area, and mention some historic flying attempts from Leonardo to Baron Cederström.

He recently read Leonardo's description of the parachute as a textile tent, with which one can 'jump from any height without contracting injuries'.

Moreover – this is how he thinks he feels himself. His love for Jenny and Gertrude is that parachute. It is fully developed and holds him still.

The time before Jenny . . .

He then sees before him a scene from the Gröna Lund in Stockholm during the mid-sixties. Dixie Blandy, yet another man with an assumed name, is swaying at the top of his mast. He has contact with the audience on the ground by telephone and a hose. When the Gröna Lund closes, he has a bed, books and whisky for his solitude. It is a cold summer, he is feeling well. As the days pass, they are counted on a blackboard. He is trying to beat a loneliness record that interests some people, as it is before the time when people float weightless in space. Dixie is not yet a pig living entirely within himself, rooting in himself, indifferent to calls, amorphously asleep, because he has adapted himself to achieve his extrinsic purpose, his mad ambition. Only the expectation prevailing between the ground and the top of his mast gives him shape, before he too fades away: an image of the period among many others, the last revolution of a record before the mechanical arm of the juke-box applies another.

When the banana skins are falling, I'm sliding back to you . . .

Jan Backman has a notion that the ideas of an epoch are so closely connected with its material expressions that, placed together properly, they should indicate connections that explain and illustrate each other. They should not have to be interpreted but appear obvious to everyone.

The connection will be seen between the Olympic Games, the Stock Exchange Index, the speeches on May Days, the deep freeze counters, the subjects of A-level compositions, the napalm bombs, bingo, the hijacking of aeroplanes and protest songs. Discarded letters, disposed posters, refuge in bins and sacks, rubbish incendiaries on the outskirts of cities, salvage washed up on the sea-shore when the wind is blowing inland – all this forms a picture whose appearance is not predicted.

Somewhere and some time, he imagines, words and events, ideas and experiences coincide for everybody. A hymn-book has been left open on its stand in Botkyrka Church; some Sundays have passed and other hymns have been played; but to one piece he has added an extra note or rest, you do not have to know which; and neither is it necessary to notice a slight change at a certain passage in the music. What Then Can Satisfy My Soul?

I shall follow your trail, the detective promises. Reality keeps silent so far. Leave me alone the victim mumbles, pays the cloakroom attendant and disappears out into the traffic. The plot is simple: a tie-pin, a belt, some pomade, and rubber bands to keep a windy existence under control.

JB looks out over an unwritten horizon. The spotlights will soon be lit over the Arlanda area. Night descends on the Swedish mail-order country.

Jan Backman is thirty-seven – the age when Sherlock Holmes stopped growing, although he went on living, actively engaged in new stories of varied interest.

THE MINUTE AFTER TAKE-OFF

One early winter's day Jan Backman drove through the gate to the so-called operational area, where he parked his car. The dampness on the junipers on the other side of the fence had frozen and looked like grey fur-coats, and the frost stretched the telephone wires between the posts. He left his coat in his office and took the lift up to the tower to relieve Jansson who went downstairs for a shower. He sat down behind the green glass and looked across the denuded areas. In August they would be red with rosebay, but now they were black.

'Anything special?' he asked Eklund, the meteorologist, who came up from the meteorological stage below.

'No sig,' said Eklund, 'And you?'

'No sig.'

Always the same thing: no significant change. Where did the days in the tower go to? What he remembered were the outlines, the limited actions, but not the things that led into each other.

'Tell me about something,' JB asked.

The meteorologist was ready:

'At the Lyall glacier in California they found a dead but well preserved mountain beetle. The species has been extinct for half a century. The mountain beetle was two hundred and fifty years old, and had fallen into a chasm. The last of a large family.'

'The frozen message of history,' JB said. 'One day we will be the ones they find.'

'Unless they melt the Polar icecapes. Are many of your relations alive?'

'My father is living in Brazil.'

'Nasty country. Right now, at least.'

'It's my father's speciality. But I don't know how things are with him.'

He did not mention Gertrude in Botswana. He seldom spoke about her at work. Nobody knew they were brother and sister.

Over the western sky an exercise plane dived, dragging the noise of its engine along. He watched it as if it were on a television screen – as though it were a film showing a plane different from the one that had in reality taken off. It had now been filmed, and would disappear on the cue 'cut'. Maybe that was the intention of whatever showed anything else, of all imagination, films and television programmes: that nothing should have to happen seriously.

At the post office he found a letter from Sten Tidström. Their long dialogue continued:

16

'I've never pretended I'm free. On the contrary : in Stockholm I could feel free, get involved with various things, talk
to you and other people and do business rather at random. A
multifarious life. But – now I can see it – I never felt quite real.
Here in Africa I feel more genuine but less free. I don't feel
I've got much choice : my life has narrowed, I've got enough
to do till I die.'

And further on, he finally read :

'Gertrude arrived and I have settled her in at the school.
She seems to be her usual self, only more on guard. What has
happened to her ? Maybe she will tell me before I hear it from
you.'

What has happened, he thought, has hit us from two directions. That's why she must tell her version.

He suddenly longed to be at Taheiti, that forgotten cape.
He could see Sten putting his arm around Gertrude on the
night when they celebrated his departure from Sweden. They
had talked about the past and those things that could be preserved and verified. The wind blew around in invisible power
circuits. Spring emerged from the end of the winter tunnel
into a stale cold clear daylight. And the world that day,
or perhaps that night, as they sat on Klas Lundin's veranda
consuming Akvavit and herrings, had looked like an abundant
vegetable garden and an ingenious workshop with each tool
in its place.

JB wanted to return to that emotional memory, as though
his happiness depended on it. But it was gone – like a shoal
of fish reaching shallow water and then turning back in a
flash.

Christina brought up the coffee thermos. It was not part of
her duties, but it was her nature to be like that, and JB had
got used to her always being at hand somewhere in the building. She was wearing dark brown trousers with a white polo-
neck sweater. A young face with blue eyes, a snub-nose and
in her hair a streak of grey that had nothing to do with age.

So much lust lying in wait, like sea-urchins under the
sand.

They come out and leave their light imprints before disappearing down into mazes and catacombs.

'Why don't I suggest that you come with me into town for
dinner ?' he said all of a sudden.

17

He was alone in the tower, and it was the first time he had ever suggested anything like that. He was filled with a new-found warmth, and for a moment he believed it could exist on its own without receiver or transmitter. He thought that he had discovered something new which everybody wanted to participate in.

'No thank you,' Christina said. 'I can't.'

He understood: she did not want to. She looked surprised. No warm breeze from the air-traffic control reached her. Her engagement ring was a glittering warning.

He thought Stockholm was far away. At Arlanda he worked at the point of intersection between arrivals and departures. Two-and-a-half million people, almost a third of the population of the country, would pass through in one year. Often the same people.

The radar control at the bottom of the tower signalled.

'Can Iberia take off?'

'Yes, at its own risk and after the Aeroflot has landed,' he replied.

A pilot came in and handed him a visiting card from Hong Kong:

'Have you forgotten me? I wish you'd drop me a line. We met when I visited Arlanda as a student. Lee Yang Tong.' At first he saw nothing, then he saw the face of a girl with short, black hair. He had sat next to her at a luncheon in the Jetorama restaurant. He had told her about the Swedish winter: trains delayed by reindeer herds, ships smashed to pieces by ice, nothing but catastrophes. But he could hardly remember her. He wished Jenny would drop him a line. Had she forgotten him? What was she doing whilst studying in Strasbourg? What was the Department of the Environment doing these days except letting rivers and fjords be polluted?

The Aeroflot plane was beginning its descent, and had assumed an altitude somewhat lower than agreed. Nothing to worry about. It could be due to the fog blowing in, which would soon be as dense as the steam in a laundry.

JB pressed the microphone button.

'Tower to Aeroflot 231. Runway three clear. Turn left to zero three one.'

The signal OK came at once. Two thousand metres above Arlanda the Russian plane banked. It seemed to the passengers

18

as though it would dip its left wing into one of the bays of Lake Mälaren.

'Bye now,' Christina said. 'I'm off. You know where to find me.'

'Fine,' he said.

But he did not know.

And he thought of the Russian air hostesses whom he occasionally saw leaving their planes: stout, often middle-aged, with red hands that seemed just to have cut birch twigs for the sauna. They wore their hair in a little bun with a lump of dough in it. They had a motherly security about them: one could vomit in their hands.

The Iberia DC8 took off. It had something wrong with one of its four engines and was returning to Zürich with crew only on board. The company did not have an agreement with SAS and thus would not have the engine repaired at Arlanda.

Every minute the fog became denser. No other planes were in the air channels. JB thought of Christina. He had tried to surpass a boundary; that was silly.

He was in contact with the pilot when the DC8 rolled off on its three engines.

'Good luck,' he said, in addition to the routine code language.

After a short while he was questioned by ground control:

'Can you still see the plane? It has not appeared on the radar.'

'I can't see it. Visibility is only a couple of hundred metres. It sounded as though it made a sharp turn to the right immediately after take-off.'

'Has the snow been cleared off all the runways?'

'Yes, as well as the emergency roads and the reserve runway beyond the main road.'

'We can't get it on the radar. If it had turned to land again it ought to show.'

'The fog is dense. Could it have left Sweden at an altitude of one hundred metres?'

It was a joke. The radar was blind at that level. Jan Backman's imagination did not work in the wake of catastrophes. He had experienced punctured tyres and belly-landings, but hardly anything serious.

The voice from the radar control sounded reproachful. 'I'll wait fifteen seconds. Then I'll apply the alarm.' The alarm was raised. Bulbs blinking SOS. It was real, not a misconnection.

For JB it was the first time. He felt suddenly he had a double who called the fire brigade, the ambulance service, snow-ploughs and emergency staff. But he did not know where to send them. Due to the roar of the Aeroflot's engines, no one had heard where the Spanish plane had gone.

He called the military aviation reconnaissance at Barkarby, but they could not take off. The airfield was fogbound. That was the usual thing. Sweden was unprotected, out of function.

He heard cars driving out into the fog and returning. He could not leave his place. He was shut up in the tower, en-veloped by cloud.

The fire brigade was ready by the runway. Red lights rotated on the cab roofs, and men in their gear were at their posts with ladders and hoses.

It was announced that landing was prohibited. A plane from Copenhagen was halted over Norrköping. One hour passed with no news. Nothing like it had ever occurred in the history of Arlanda. JB called on all possible wave-lengths. Eventually he heard a weak radio transmitter :

Help, help!'

'Where are you?'

'I'm an air hostess from the Iberia plane. We've crashed.'

'How many are alive?'

'Five are dead. One is badly injured.'

'We're sending help. We can hear you well. Have you got any distress rockets?'

'Can't get to them. Everything has been destroyed.'

'Okay. We have an ambulance ready. Where are you?'

'Near you. Very near you.'

'Indicate your location.'

'In the forest. We can see cars and lights in the distance.'

'What direction did you go in when you left the starting-point?'

'Don't know. We're near the airport. Search for us! We're cold!'

'We're coming, but you're beneath the radar.'

'We can see spotlights, but they are pointing in the wrong direction. We're quite near you.'

'Give a more definite location. Are you surrounded by forest?'

'We can see you. We're stuck. Help!'

The contact with the air hostess ended with a weak cry of distress.

A shiver went through him. From the ground control he heard that no smell of fire had been reported. It was a miracle that the plane had not caught fire. A helicopter was hovering over the area. Spotlights were lit, but they rebounded off the fog. He felt like pounding his way out of his glass cage.

He could feel Jenny's body against his out on the forest path near the runways. It was spring and an empty barn was attracting the first light of the day. And now dead people, ripped seats and exhaust pipes were strewn over the moss.

No sig – the time before Jenny. In the air-traffic control tower nothing unexpected was allowed to happen. But now it had, and what should have been cleared up in seconds, took many hours. Although he was the chief air-traffic controller, he was nonplussed. The military forces, the fire brigade, the Air Traffic Department and all the other protection authorities were helpless. A woman with a radio transmitter by a crashed passenger plane could not be located, although she could see lights from the cars on the main road.

Jan Backman was like a cog in a malfunctioning machine. He felt like a schoolboy at the beginning of term who had made a bad start. If you had a bad result on your first test paper, things continued to go wrong. He had put too much trust in the system.

There was a gap, some dangerous seconds between visual communication and radar, between senses and mechanics. And into that abyss a plane had fallen, with people on board.

Still there were many alarm signals at Arlanda. It was a well-equipped place. Disasters occurred in most places without the slightest warning.

Turkey is no further away than your own telephone. The crashed plane was out of reach in the Arlanda forest.

The fog spread like a blanket over the world. Time was full of loopholes.

Finally the crew of a helicopter caught sight of the wreck in a forest that was not penetrated by roads. It lay near the path where he had taken Jenny. The plane had ploughed up a three-hundred-metre track. The wings had severed the forest like a saw. One of the fragile fire-warden's watch towers, which are left unmanned in the Crown forests and usually burn first, had been dragged down. It had been hidden among pines and firs, but from it one got an extended view of the world : the corners of lakes, which were invisible from the ground; empty cottages hiding in overgrown glades.

Both the helicopter and the police-car reported to the tower. JB sent the tape down to the control room, where it was played to the airport management. The reproduction of sound was considered good. The tape began with JB singing a test tune to check that it was working. It was a pop song he had learnt from Jansson :

'This is ground control to Major Tom. This is Major Tom to ground control. The stars look very different today.'

He asked them to erase that part, but nobody dared. He told them that this part was irrelevant to the ensuing conversation, but the airport management answered that everything so far was relevant, regardless of whether the connections were technical or accidental.

The dead, covered by grey blankets, were taken by ambulance to Stockholm. The exhausted air hostess was interviewed by the press and television reporters after the doctors had seen her. She said she had been thrown out of the plane when it crashed, and had found the radio transmitter in the snow. The worst part of all, she said, was when she could see the searchlights so near her, and yet was not found.

Gradually the fog lifted. The runways which extended for many kilometres, were wet and black as musselshells; the sky appeared a similar colour to the inside of these same shells. Then the weather and the light changed : the runways became like mirrors, reflecting the steel blue sky.

A little later on, JB drove alone towards Stockholm. Jansson stayed behind. The tape was sufficient evidence. The car was going smoothly, but as he came to a bumpy, frost-damaged stretch of road, he noticed some vibration. He thought that this might be due to his own agitation, and slowed down to see whether the trembling would stop.

The car was still. It was he himself who was shaking. He realized what it meant to have no control over your body. He leant his forehead against the steering-wheel, murmuring Jenny, Jenny, Jenny. But nobody could hear him. The tape with the air hostess's cry of distress was replayed over and

22

over again. He wished that he could obliterate it from his mind.

Driving on, he saw himself in the rear mirror. He could not recognize the expression in his eyes. On his forehead the steering-wheel had left red marks, which looked like knuckle marks.

In Stockholm there was nobody waiting for him. The accident would soon, in different ways, be known. He wondered whether anyone would like to hear his version.

THE WINTERS IN PRAGUE

Jan Backman was walking alone in Stockholm, thinking of his love and of the air crash, which he had recorded and regarded as his own, although he had not witnessed it.

He had left his car in a garage in Kammakar Street. It was afternoon. His watch in the tower had ended at three. In his pocket were the key to his flat in Uppland Street and the key to Jenny's flat at Nybro Quay: both places were empty, so he could choose between them.

It was almost freezing. In the hard light people's faces appeared older than they were. Dusk fell along with the barometer hand. Tonight, he thought, the frost will come with its silent needle to etch ferns on the windows. Gertrude could stay up for hours watching the foliage design being created. She was the kind of child to whom parents will say: 'don't sit there dreaming.' Or maybe, in an attempt to console themselves: 'she may turn out to be a scientist one day.' But Gertrude's parents had had neither demands nor expectations concerning her.

It was Jan she had spoken to over the years; it was him she had enticed and seduced, guided to be driven in circles around herself. Eventually he had been the one to comfort and protect her, and he allowed her to stay quite close to him.

Their father had been less interested in Gertrude than in Jan. He had assumed that his children would be all right. They were educated and looked after by Mrs Tapper, the house-

23

keeper. They had the Water Palace and were not left out in the woods. When Adolf Oscar moved abroad, he was unaware that he left them to themselves. They joined the family together and became each other's parents. They moved in under the same roof to be able to breath the same air.

They did not hear very often from their father. One day a form arrived from the Foreign Office Library concerning some books which, according to their records, were on loan to their former envoy A. O. Backman. It had been discovered during stock-taking that these books had been taken out by him years ago.

JB did not know where the books were. One was the biography of Chiang Kai-Shek by Sven Hedin, and the other was called *The Sun-God's Tears*, an account of Mexican colonial history.

JB sent the note on together with a brief letter to Adolf Oscar in Brazil. When he did this, he thought of how little his father meant to him. He was like an out-grown suit, discarded in the wardrobe. His father was cast aside from his thoughts – seldom present even in his dreams. They had cut themselves off from each other. At an early age JB had been told that the world was rotten, but he had never had the opportunity to discuss with his father whether it was rotten in the flesh or at the core.

Mainly for fun, but with no real conviction, Jan could imagine that Adolf Oscar Backman had been driven away to South America, to such a great distance from Sweden and his past, for a very personal reason; it was a kind of madness he felt related to: like diving from a great height into deep water without worrying about the water holding the breath back, or like staring into the fire until you could sense an imaginary freedom and could think no more of equilibrium, security, routines . . .

Something in his father had wanted to challenge the accident, and out of spite or vindictiveness had distorted the image other people had of him as a dutiful servant. JB was afraid of learning too much about him.

He noticed that he was walking along the street where Sten Tidström, before his departure to Africa, had shown him a mural on a fire-proofed gable, which he had not known of before. The door to the courtyard was open. The house had

24

been rebuilt and replastered. He saw that they had painted over the mural. The summer breeze was restrained by thick yellow slimy paintwork. The vertical garden had disappeared, like everywhere else in Stockholm, where they could not afford to save the trees, as nobody would sweep under them. Here the large paint brushes had swept away the leaves for ever.

Sten and Jan had walked round, asking all the residents of the house what the painting meant to them. Many of them had not even seen it. Others were tired of its temptations. But to some people it was part of life. How easily it had been deleted. Not even a fragment remained. Somebody had given himself the right to say: it's my wall, and I don't want it to show anything but a wall.

JB walked up to the wall, but he could not find the line which had once marked the sea-floor. A document had been cleared out of the archive.

He passed the snack bar in Uppland Street but decided not to have any of its Polish sausages and Indian rice. Suddenly he was standing outside Stoll's home-furnishing shop. He was relieved. Surely Christian Stoll would like to hear about the air disaster. JB regarded Stoll as one of those old men who like Jules Verne in Amiens carried in his body a spaceship wanting to get away but grounded. Occasionally Stoll would start eagerly telling a story, but it never had time to develop. Most of them were about the old Prague, about things that have disappeared, been covered in paint or demolished.

At first JB could not discern Stoll among the things in the dim light of the basement. Only a pair of ears, as thin as paper and almost transparent, could be seen, with a benign smile suspended between them.

Stoll did not expect Jan to buy anything, except possibly a dish-cloth or a wooden spoon.

After some introductory chat Jan Backman said:
'I've just experienced an aircrash.'
'Oh? Well, that's to be expected in your profession. I had a burglary last night. Not very much was stolen. But I told the insurance company that the sentimental value exceeded the real value.'
'And how much was that?'
'Nothing, according to the insurance inspector. Only old rubbish nobody would have wanted to buy. My yearly turn-

over is too low. And things put up for sale, he said, could not have sentimental value. So they just mended the door and the window for me.'

JB refrained from commenting. The world seemed so strange when Stoll talked about it. Full of bureaucratic whims obviously inexplicable, like certain kinds of mad impulses appearing only during long Church holidays.

'A Spanish plane disappeared in the fog at Arlanda.'

'Yes, the weather is really bad. So much snow for November. Just look at it!'

In the Vasa area the cars were moving slowly. The sky was low with diffused violet light. People seemed half asleep.

'Like the winters in Central Europe,' said JB.

At last Stoll paid attention.

'My God,' he said, 'where can I find a place these days that serves rice pudding and prunes like they did in Prague?'

'I don't know,' JB said. 'Perhaps in some café near the harbour.'

'There's always somebody waiting round the corner,' Stoll said unexpectedly. 'They just leap at you and turn your life upside down. Like my relative for example, from Vienna, who appeared a month ago. Talked about Jewish solidarity during hard times. All he did was scrub these pipes in the ceiling, which made the place smell, and I found new cracks in the wall. The caretaker is after my blood. He's an old colour-sergeant who's taken to drink. He's the representative of the world, he says. The enemy is ready.'

He made a gesture, sweeping a saucepan on to the floor.

'Eventually chaos will win the game,' he told JB. 'It's the same thing in every life.'

'Have you heard from the city authorities?' Jan asked.

'I received a printed note, informing me that my writ had been received on a certain date.'

'Of course that won't prevent things from happenings.'

'I don't want to move. I've had enough. They should let you have your own place. At least the pidgeons should have time to get to know you.'

The whites of Stoll's eyes were reddish. He blinked often and wiped off the excess water. He seemed to have seen too much of the world too well. Now it appeared blurred and confusing to his gaze. He lived under the pressure of a huge conspiracy; he held on to the house and his basement premises like a mushroom at the edge of a deserted wheel track.

'If the commercial situation is bad here, I am the one to notify the authorities, not the other way round,' Stoll said.

'A passenger plane crashed today,' JB said. 'You probably haven't yet heard about it on the news.'

'No,' Stoll said. 'Better to know nothing. I feel so old I ought to stop talking.'

'Why not?' JB said.

'I've said what I've got to say, and nobody ever listened.'

'The plane ploughed up a three-hundred-metre path.'

'If I keep quiet from now on, people might eventually start listening to me.'

Stoll laughed, which was very unusual. The furrows on his face grew deeper, like streams making their way through moraine. Light appeared in his wintry eyes. Thoughts dawned on him. JB realized that he would never be able to make him listen to any account of the disaster. Stoll was also sending distress cries from somewhere. He held on to the caretaker, the insurance man, the cracks in the wall, although something else was at stake.

'Were the winters in Prague any more severe than those in Stockholm?' Jan asked.

Stoll was silent for a while, as if the mere comparison between the two cities was improper. Then he gave such a comprehensive answer that JB forgot what he had originally asked him about. The picture he described could very well have been Stockholm some decades ago, before JB ever knew the city.

In the springtime there was the sound of roller-skates on the pavements. On the dry summer days the dusty roads were sprayed by watercarts. Waitresses in black dresses wiped the table tops of the pavement cafés. In the autumn the wood in the iron stoves rattled with the poker. On the sideboard there was a bowl of hazel nuts, picked while they were still green to cheat the squirrels. Nobody left the house without turning back in the hall to check that the gas tap was properly turned off. In the cellar root vegetables went mouldy. In the winter the linen-drapers had their windows misted up.

Stoll talked about a middle-class existence, where the sauerkraut and Sunday roast marked the passing of the weeks, and the children's school badges glittered like stars on a Jacob's ladder towards a better future.

But when Jan Backman asked him why he had a basement shop in Stockholm, he was told that the reason for this would be disclosed on another occasion. Stoll's destiny was to be a refugee from the inter-war period. One could sense in his past a shattered illusion: a shabby entrance to a courtyard with cobblestones painted blue. The cabs were small and square with their spare wheel on the outside and red hubs. During twilight the sounds of the tattoo came across from the barracks of the garrison, which was there to protect the monarch and the capital.

They did not succeed: the monarch fell, and the capital was conquered and plundered. Some people only just escaped from being taken away, piled into heaps and burnt, from becoming bone-ash and passing into oblivion. Stoll was one of these. He never spoke about it. He managed to make his way to another country where nobody had yet plundered, and where people lived peacefully piled into heaps in multi-storey blocks. There he was, watching the progress: he could get hot water from a tap and stir powdered cream into his coffee. But he remained an immigrant in modern times.

In Prague the snow kept falling. Frightened music teachers moved stealthily along the streets, as if the pavements were rag rugs placed diagonally across the vast rooms in which they lived. Disaster soon struck again, and devoured them like a hungry wolf.

What Stoll was saying – apart from what he did not want to talk about – was projected with unreal clarity: like when JB stayed up late, though he was sleepy, to watch old films on the television. Under the glossy surface of fresh paint all the horrible and wonderful things remained, but they would stay invisible for a long time, as nobody wanted to be reminded of them.

Just as JB turned to go, Stoll said unexpectedly:

'Perhaps you'd like to hear the seven o'clock news?'

The broadcaster read out a report about the air crash. The part of the tape with the air hostess's cry of distress was played: 'We're quite near you. We can see you. Help.'

Stoll shook his head slowly and looked at JB as if he was finally prepared to listen.

28

'Turn it off,' JB said. 'There's no point in listening to it all. It's over now.'

Stoll immediately turned off the wireless.

'I hardly ever listen to the news these days,' he apologized. 'As you grow older, you go to pieces. People die, one by one. That air crash . . .'

'Yes I know,' Jan Backman said. 'There's nothing more I can tell you about it.'

A woman came in and asked for china soap-dishes with holes in. It was still afternoon. JB sent his regards to Mrs Stoll and then said goodbye to Mr Stoll.

THE HORIZON OF THE CITY

On Observatory Hill later in the day, as evening approached, Jan Backman could see Stockholm extending in three directions. He noticed that the lakes had shrunk and the ridges had been smoothed down to enable the cars to go up without effort. He saw the leafless forests of television masts.

This was where he had stood when he was locked out of his flat – in a world that belonged to him and Gertrude. He had come back when Jenny made her mark on him, saying:

'I don't need you. In spite of that I love you.'

Every era has its lives which have to be lived. The street light shone on the people in the street below like some new kind of cosmetic.

As soon as JB left the control tower at Arlanda, he felt like a man without any defined skills, doomed to improvise his way through life, following variable land-marks and contrived morals. Something glittered : a coin found by a sunbeam. Then it disappeared. Over the mountain, where astronomers and meteorologists had once observed low pressures following high pressures and climate changes, the sky was a vault without stars, blackened by soot and exhaust fumes. An umbrella of minerals and chemical compounds covered the city these days. A twin engine Metropolitan en route to Bromma Airport blinked its warning lights.

To the West, a red light-ship was stranded in the bay. Nearby, in the marshland of small industrial estates, the Department of The Environment had been silted up on its own doorstep. Jenny had taken her briefcase and gone out into Europe. She was on a committee dealing with a resolution regarding the prohibition of refuse disposal in European lakes and seas.

Further north, between Brunns Bay and the motorway, he could see the outline of the Academy of Science next to the steep-sided lantern of the National Museum. Someone else now sat at Gertrude's desk. The index cards with her handwriting on would be there until the catalogue was next revised. Few people would know who had written them.

Could he be alone and trustful of this new world he had been given? He could sense its enigmas and potentials like a rise in his body temperature. Jenny had taught him not to be afraid of people and to be happy exploiting himself. The edges of the test picture trembled. He felt the uneasy relief that usually follows a slight temperature.

What they inflicted on each other could only be judged by themselves. Measured by other people's values it could seem evil or good or silly. Whatever he did assumed its characteristics only when it bounced on another person.

His love had wanted to be a foetal membrane round both Gertrude and Jenny. But these two women he had seen almost go to pieces. All three of them had turned the pattern of love inside out and been horrified at all the knots and tangles on the other side.

They had talked through the days of the autumn.

At the Lövsta rubbish dump Jenny had stood with one foot over the edge, angry about love, which was like a disease, for although it brought well-being, it was also an injustice which did not diminish, even if justice was being done. Shady intervals had suddenly appeared between their moments of happiness. He had wanted to relieve the darkness inside her, to bore a lot of breathing-holes inside her to allow freedom to reach her from all directions.

They themselves could destroy their love. No one else was strong enough to untie it.

But deciphering love did not mean destroying it.

Gertrude had gone on her antipodal journey to save her feelings for him. She had known other men before, but with him everything fell into place. Adventure and peace no longer seemed opposites. Finally death was as unobtainable as it could be in one's lifetime. She extended herself in the calmness of their family relationship. That was how it was for her but not for him, as he did not grow in her soil and did not get all his nourishment from her.

Gertrude went away to avoid becoming a suspicious wife who could not be fooled. She feared that a thin membrane would grow over her body and make her hard-hearted. She refused to succumb to his will, although she thought he wanted her to. There was some feeling of rebellion about it, a decampment. He did not know whether there was also a desire for liberation.

'It's too late to leave you,' she had said. 'It was too late from the start.'

'You can leave me,' he said. 'But I don't want you to.'

'But can't you see that I've left already? You are still in the same place. I'm pregnant. I shall be compelled to change my life. Still I'm telling you : to leave you completely and seriously is too late.'

And she had looked at him from the depth of her soul, through the keyholes of her pupils.

Now Jenny and Gertrude had gone in different directions. Before, he had lived between them and had not had to make a choice. But what if they had both left to avoid choosing him?

Or were they helpless, just an hour away? Radar does not work on certain levels.

The city was growing dark on the horizon. After the rush hour the noise of the traffic subsided to a lower key – like a bee who tires itself out buzzing on the floor. Eighty-five decibels was the noise level in Stockholm during the day, which was twice as high as the sighing of the forest and the singing of the birds.

A coat of snow covered the climbing-frame in the playground. The pigeons flew from statue to statue, leaving white memoranda.

When JB descended Observatory Hill, he saw a man in a

31

sand-box. He was lying with wet newspapers spread out under him. Next to him was an empty unlabelled bottle. Jan got hold of him under his arms to get him to sit up. He was heavy. Suddenly he opened his eyes but did not say anything. JB was not sure that he could see him.

He had been lying there whilst Jan Backman wrapped up in a lined brown raincoat had been considering his fate nearby. What had happened to the man earlier in the day? Something had not worked out and had probably never done so: the weather, society, or even his immediate surroundings.

The man did not wake up properly and would not be moved. JB ran downhill to the police station in Kammakar Street.

'It's a cold night, almost freezing. Arrest him, at least.'

A pile of parking-tickets were heaped on the counter. The constable on duty appeared absent-minded.

'What did you say? I was watching television. There's been an air crash at Arlanda.'

'I know,' JB said. 'You must take care of that man. I couldn't move him.'

'We'd rather leave him. We're shortstaffed.'

'He may freeze to death.'

'Five people died at Arlanda.'

Uniform coats hung on hooks smelling of damp wool. The policeman turned to the inner room. A couple of constables were watching television there.

The tape with the air hostess's cry of distress was broadcast again by the mass media. JB saw these tapes, labelled and filed away, until they could be erased after the prescribed time: the daily routine bulletins. He wished he could have an identical tape; plus an unofficial one, with his private orders. And then a third tape, recording the other two, explaining them and taking away their enigmas.

'What did actually happen?' the constable said.

'What?' JB said, confused.

'Well, up there on the hill. Do you want to report him for disturbing you in any way?'

'I suppose I'll have to.'

'So what did he do then?'

'He threatened me. He wouldn't leave me alone.'

'What were you doing in the park?'

'I didn't go there to sleep in a sand-box. I was looking at the view of the city. It's an observation spot, as the name implies. I was standing there, and then I saw him right next to me. There was nothing I could do.'

'And he threatened you?'

'Yes.'

'We'll have to fetch him in then. But the residents of this house complain about the noise from the cells.'

Continuing on his way, Jan saw lights on at an exhibition hall in Drottning Street. He stopped to look at a plastic dog, and then saw a man who was eagerly waving to him from indoors. It was Klas Lundin.

'Come in for God's sake.'

'What are you doing here?' JB exclaimed.

'You know my love for the arts. I thought for a while that advertising was an art too. But not any more.'

'You still work in advertising.'

'People exposed to a lot of advertising are not so easy to deceive. They've got used to everything. That's the good thing.'

'Excuses,' JB said. 'I just saw a man half-dead in a sand-box. Up there.'

He pointed.

'Bloody hell,' Klas Lundin exclaimed. 'So much happens these days.'

Klas took him into the exhibition. This evening it was open for a private view. On a long table there were plastic cups and paper plates, bottles of cheap red wine and dishes of roast beef and potato salad.

'And today I had . . .' JB started.

But he stopped himself. Nobody asked him to continue.

It was very lively in there. JB carefully stepped over parts from old hoovers. They were like stiff intestines on the coarse fitted carpet, and had been reserved for a possible sale to the City Industrial Association.

He was introduced to an author whose name he had heard of. A collection of his poems, called Landscape with Absent Figures had been published, and he had founded a literary group named The Turning Stage. Recently an excerpt had been printed from his novel The Man Who Built Ruins.

'An allegory of the inoffensive quality of art,' the writer explained. 'The less free our society is said to be in my book, the freer our society will seem when it allows the book to be published and perhaps even be praised. By criticizing society I elevate it for its measure of free speech.'

'Is that your opinion?'

'Not at all. The book will be edited – disarmed by the printing procedure. I wish we had censorship. Sometimes I think of giving it all up. The same thing with this poor artist, who . . .'

'What about him?'

'He's just as powerless. The colours he uses are so beautiful that you want to go up to them, lick them up and leave the picture empty.'

'That can't be what he intended.'

'No, exactly. And what do you do?'

'I'm an air-traffic controller at Arlanda.'

'Oh. Isn't most of that computerized now? Untouched by human hands. Alienation.'

'It's a long time since aeroplanes were started manually with a handle. I like it. Especially if not too much happens.'

They were interrupted by somebody delivering a speech to the artist at the long table:

'We have to maintain what's human. Everywhere being human is referred to as being weak. It's human to err, they say. Or: that's human nature. What kind of slander is that? Beyond this clique nobody may understand it completely . . .'

JB missed what this was about. Klas passed and handed him a cup of red wine. It was strange to see Klas again. JB had not met him since Gertrude told him that she was pregnant by Klas. The child would make Klas one of his relatives. But Klas knew nothing about this.

Jan was chatting with the author, and could see Klas mingling with the other guests. Then he suddenly felt a hot flush and a pain in his belly. He wanted to go out and be sick. He could hardly understand this reaction. He should have been more jealous when John, the English architect, was staying with Jenny at Nybro Quay. Klas was only a friend who had comforted his half-sister, because he, Jan, had made her unhappy.

He looked at Klas's large freckled hands. Your seed is growing in Africa, he thought. He was calmer again. Gertrude was at the Swaneng Hill School in Botswana. Maybe she was not pondering about either him or Klas.

34

The exhibitor came up to JB.

'What can't be shown in a clear light doesn't exist,' he said strictly. 'That is my starting-point.'

'An appealing philosophy for work,' JB said. 'But doesn't it limit your motives? In very obvious things there is no movement.'

'So much the better. There's been far too much movement. Look at this one. Something from my figurative period.'

'A loaf of bread immersed in water,' Jan suggested.

'Of course not. Can't you see? It's Jutland like an erect penis at the bottom of Sweden.'

'A permanent condition?'

'Naturally. Where would we be otherwise?'

He looked around with quick-sighted glances, as if he wished to discover a picture thief among his friends. It was a time when international gangs were active in the large art museums. Maybe one of them would want to come to this out-of-the-way gallery on a night like this.

One painting confused JB: a girl inclosed under an inverted glass bowl. In front of the bowl on the ground lay dead bees. There had not been enough air for them. Inside the glass, and only there, was it still possible to live. The girl sat there with a fixed smile – a smile painted in such a way that you knew it would never change into a laugh or a straight face; and you knew just as well that the bees would not start to fly.

What was the picture about? Perhaps the pollution of the atmosphere, or the few remaining nature reserves? Then JB remembered the man in the sand-box, and decided that he was being taken care of by people who knew better how to handle him.

He ate a slice of roast beef, finished his wine and left at the same time as Klas Lundin. They said good-bye outside on the pavement, but it was not until they were a few metres apart that Klas said: 'Give my love to Gertrude.'

'She's in Africa,' JB replied.

Klas laughed, assuming it was a joke, but soon added:

'What did you say?'

'She's in Botswana,' Jan said. 'I thought you knew.'

By the light of a street-lamp he saw Klas's face become shiny and vulnerable. Then Klas turned round and walked away.

He himself walked down Drottning Street towards his house

some distance away in Uppland Street. He could hear footsteps behind him and turned round. It was a pale-faced young girl with long hair, who had also been to the party.

'Going my way?' he asked.

'To the Old City.'

They walked together for a while, then he took her hand and she let him do it. She looked down at the asphalt, which was thin and scraped like the phosphorus side of a match-box. Cars were parked everywhere. Her raincoat rustled against his.

Her name was Marie. She worked as an architect's assistant. He could imagine her in a room in an Old City alley, curled up on a couch, reading a book on batik and eating fish paté on crackers.

'What work are you doing at the moment?'

'Suburban.'

'Would you like to come up for a cup of tea?'

'Okay.'

He tried to open the door. It seemed as if the key had never been in the lock before, and he blamed the dim light on the stairs. A trunk which Gertrude had taken down from the attic but never used, was still in the hallway.

'This is where I live,' he told her. Then he closely observed the everlasting flowers in the jug and the record-player beneath its shimmering blue plastic cover. These items belonged to him and Gertrude: items they had bought together.

Marie made no comment about the place. She replied monosyllabically to his questions. She was wearing a khaki shirt and had gaps between her front teeth. She looked like Christina in the control tower and was much younger than Gertrude and Jenny.

He made the tea and offered her some crispbread, cheese and plum jam. Later he tried to kiss her, but she escaped from his lips. Quickly he bent down and kissed her knee. She laughed at this totally unexpected gesture. But their eyes did not meet and she only smiled slightly.

'You're worried,' he said.

She did not reply.

'Don't complicate things,' he said. 'Things happen. Then you keep them as experiences. They may benefit other people.'

Nothing but clichés. But he wanted to console her. It was an unusual night when nothing significant had to happen.

They knew nothing about each other. It was like being in a strange city. He tried to feel solemn about the fact that they might never meet again.

'Would you like some more tea?'

'No thanks.'

'Shall I turn on some music?'

'No, it's too late.'

However, she did not get ready to go. At the same time she avoided him – as if she wanted no lasting impression of their meeting. He started to wonder when he would get rid of her.

She was sitting quite still on the couch next to him. Longing to get closer to her, he slowly touched her breasts with his fingertips. She did not move but with a quick laugh looked down on his hands. He leant back and began to feel sad. A bold venture with no boldness. Nothing he did would change her; she knew it, and that was why she laughed. Caresses must have precision to be accepted. In desire there is will, the will to legitimise your infatuation. But his desire was insufficient.

At last she looked him straight in the eye and said:

'Is this just the way things turn out? Or was it planned?'

He did not know how to reply. Her voice had not sounded reproachful. Somehow something important had happened without his noticing it. In her silence she had perhaps experienced something he had missed. 'I've got to get up early,' he said in a tired voice, as if he was the one who had to leave.

'Yes, it's late.'

He saw her go down the stairs: an enigma with narrow shoulders. With a sweeping gesture she wrapped a flimsy, hand-knitted muffler round her neck.

He was worried and hungry but fell asleep presently. The city at night stayed at the back of his mind like a shimmer. The next morning the papers would be full of articles about the Arlanda air crash, unless something else had happened to overshadow it.

The next morning he shaved with the glass of the window as a mirror. He then shook his electric razor over the passers-by in the street. Some hairs of his old beard were carried away by strangers.

LANDING PERMIT

Jan Backman's office in the morning, situated in a long build-ing extending from the control tower. JB, his colleagues and some volunteers were discussing shorter shifts and other relief measures. Nobody had neglected his duty at the air crash but it accentuated certain problems.

The five victims were flown to Spain in coffins. At the site of the crash the investigating committee collected bits and pieces, studied the trees that had been mown down, and looked at the bark and moss that had been ripped off. They wanted to clarify the whole sequence of events and get a distinct picture of what had happened during those seconds when neither radar nor human contact had functioned.

Christina brought in the mail and coffee in paper cups. She stopped and listened to them. There was a letter from Jenny. JB thought it loomed large and white on his desk. He covered it with a sheet of paper. After a while he could see it again. He noticed Christina saw it too.

He felt like taking the letter and going out to the gents, but he would not have to wait much longer now.

'Let's see if the Pilots' Association has any complaints,' he said. 'In other words, we'll wait and see.'

The others left. Christina brought in a vase with Michaelmas daisies and golden rod. The last flowers of the year.

'The frost will take them otherwise,' she said.

'How kind of you,' he said in surprise.

She had done this occasionally in the past; she wanted him to be happy.

'We could have a cat here,' she said. 'There are people here most of the time.'

'There was a lot written about the air crash today.'

'Yes. We made sure there were none of today's newspapers on the planes. Instead they'll give the passengers the weeklies and yesterday's Herald Tribune.'

'They'll know anyway.'

At last JB was alone so that he could read Jenny's letter from Strasbourg:

'I'm staying in a crescent. At night the rectangular shape of my window moves over the wallpaper as the lights from the cars pass. My quilt is yellow silk and more flexible than myself.

The Council of Europe are discussing Greece. I've read Mangaki's letters from prison: the humiliation he experienced when the dictatorship was proclaimed and he was no longer considered worthy of being responsible for his life; and the girl in the cell next to his who refused to betray her fiancé who died on the first day of her trial and whom she will never see again. Every night she sings about him in her cell.

In this city Olympic Airways announce: 'When there is love in the air it usually comes from us. More smiles per hour than any other airline. We look after you with all the warmth of Greece.'

It has rained a lot in Strasbourg. The puddles never have time to dry up. The sulphurous fog smothers you, it's like living underground.

Nothing but meetings all day long.'

She wrote about other things as well:

'I've got to tell you all this as if you didn't know already. I promised you I wouldn't turn and run away. Yet I have written you several letters and torn them up. They were about desisting, about protecting Gertrude. Then I remembered your words: I am not to present you to her, I haven't got you on contract.

'I love you. If the choice is all or nothing I choose all. Stockholm is waiting. A thousand chats and excursions.

'The time we share never feels wasted. I know we only borrow what we have, but it's really nice to be allowed to borrow it.

'Do you ever pass Botkyrka? None of the warmth of our bodies has stayed in the stone walls. It's only me who get warm when I think about it. You are like sediments at the bottom of me. You whirl through my body when I move. It all feels unconsumed. Even when we're lying next to each other like well-adjusted jigsaw pieces, the pattern on the whole is unexplored and greater than our ability and our imagination can grasp.'

Jenny finished:

39

'My dearest joy! Take this jumble of words, screw it up into a ball and throw it far away. I'll land on Friday, in case you'd like to know.'

The letter was a caress from afar. His penis stretched to get closer to Friday.

He believed what Jenny wrote because he loved her, not because she wrote it in a convincing manner. Without loving her he could not have sensed that her words were true.

They were prepared to question everything: they were each other's guinea pigs. When he experienced something dangerous, he also became wary of things he did not heed. Earlier on in life he had feared that nothing would ever happen to him. But Jenny had changed him, more than he had thought possible. She had broken through to the most vital part of him. It was difficult to show this to the world around, but he could easily feel it. Like a spider, he travelled with his lifeline coiled up inside him.

He emptied his office waste-paper basket, tidied up his drawers, threw away the newspapers with headlines about the air disaster, cut his nails short and plucked out some hairs from his eyebrows and nostrils. All this in a rush to relieve himself of unnecessary ballast.

He gave himself time to go out and reflect on the letter. He had no watch until later on; the morning was to be devoted to office duties. By the gate he ran into the photographer of the Air Traffic Department. He had taken a couple of films at the scene of the disaster.

'Looked bloody awful. I'm surprised anyone survived. Quite a miracle.'

There are always systems to hide in. But JB wanted to be seen and not sneak away. The plane had been too low for the radar, it was not his responsibility. He had given permission for take-off. The condition of the plane was somebody else's concern. He had informed them that the runways were free. They led to nothing.

He was an expert: a link in a safety chain. He looked after an instrument panel and thought he could predict the results. That was the stipulation of his professional activities. Also he had other kinds of experience in different fields. These were to be used for events he could not foretell. There were no conclusions to be drawn but shapes to develop.

He crossed the football ground outside the operational area. It was neglected and seldom chalked out. In summer it was covered with white clover; now it was soggy under his feet.

If he could manage to make a résumé of his future life and summarize the events that had not yet happened, what would they be able to achieve, he himself, Jenny and Gertrude, linked together like the three dishes of a balance? Was he strong enough to make them both happy?

November: the landscape varying from lowland brown to highland green. Some space between possibilities. Far away, out of vision, a twin-engined aeroplane buzzing like a bee let out of its hive in winter.

At the edge of the wood, under a spotlight indicating the way towards runway number three, he found a dead pigmy owl. It was only the size of his fist, grey-brown and lying on a bed of still green sorrels. These might survive the winter undamaged, as they contained a large amount of sugar and resisted the frost if they were covered by snow. In the springtime they were still green, but the leaves were replaced by smaller leaves with stronger growing powers. The owl would be eaten long before then by foxes or voles.

A lot of the forest had been felled around Arlanda for the sake of the air-traffic. He came to a denuded area and saw the fading red colour of the heather and the rosebay with its waddy fruitage. Shaggy crowberry bushes grew between the boulders. The end of the runways lead into fields where the stubble dried up in the mud.

On the ground a light grey vehicle got off to a grunting start, leaving a dusty cloud of paraffin fumes trailing behind it. Jan Backman walked into the forest alone. The air in the Uppland forest in November was asleep under the trees. All activity was quietly ceasing. He noticed a flock of silent crows on a pine. It was time for them to leave the holiday reservations and settle down in the chimneys of densely populated areas, where they could choose the railway or the rubbish dump for this winter's work.

The thin air was gently inebriating. So was his happiness over the letter. He was whistling out of sheer happiness. He could whistle on other occasions as well; he found it a way to get rid of thoughts, anxieties and associations. It was like listening to radio one: an emptiness that worked.

He tasted the sloes. They were in season : they were sweeter after the frost and shrivelled up like finger-tips in the cold. He spat out the skin. The waxy agarics of the late autumn were wet and covered with pine-needles. When he hit the trunk of a birch, a beetle came out of a chink in the bark, inconceivably alive.

This was a world that could be touched before it disappeared. Nothing much to talk about, nothing much to worry about, and yet it absorbed him. On all sides and everywhere he was engulfed by air, but he could not feel it. He wished that everything could be sensed at the same time or almost the same with total concentration : like notes in a musical composition.

The letter had taken him to a watercourse with a strong current. Things that had only bounced on him the day before now got a hold on him. His life was like shooting with ball ammunition instead of dowels. A jay flew like a blue flash between the junipers; yesterday he would not have noticed it. On the electricity cables, golden balls glistened as a warning to low-flying aircraft.

Jenny had given him freedom and physical contact. The control tower, the forest, mere existence were no more his than hers or anybody else's. The public rights proclaimed that no one was interchangeable, but the world could be shared with many other people.

After the rain in the night the moss was again a clear green. JB met nobody. Dry brown excretion showed where a hare had rested. An echo from the motorway – like the soughing silence in a cathedral, inside a Gothic whale skeleton. This was how the ancient explorers had entered their forests. Suddenly they were eye to eye with other people, discovered, recorded, even addressed.

The periphery of the European flight net cut through Arlanda's woodland. In a hill some distance away from the International Hall and the glossy oil cisterns lay King Östen with lank grass on his tomb. Stone Age people had hunted there in the company of buzzards and gulls. Now DC9's from Bangkok and Kiev landed : they flew along the ancient amber and silk routes. And down on the ground the lichens crept over the stones at the same pace as they had in the Bronze Age. But the quarry had disappeared, and former petty kings had become county councillors.

Jan Backman walked in the trailing November light, touch-

42

ing the letter in his pocket. He could remember the cobble-
stone square at Riddarholmen, the strokes of the riveters at
Finnboda Wharf, the shadow under St Eric's Bridge amid the
oppressive air from the chocolate factory. Inside the gasometer
at Sabbatsberg, which had now been pulled down, he had seen
the water frozen to black marble – the largest floor space in
Stockholm. Jenny had been with him.

Several small farm-houses near Arlanda had been evacuated
because of the noise. One man with good hearing but very
poor eye-sight still lived in his red-painted cottage with white
weatherboarding. Jan had come across him when he was
writing an article about Arlanda's cultural environment for
his company magazine, The Wind Gauge. He saw the old age
pensioner on his cottage steps.

'I am Jan Backman, chief air-traffic controller at Arlanda,'
he said, as he knew the man had difficulty recognizing him.
'We've met before. I remember you had to sign a form stating
that you had no complaints about the noise.'

'If I hadn't they'd have given me a bedsitter in Märsta,' the
old man said. 'But why don't you come inside?'

There were pine-branches in front of the door, where he had
left his wellingtons. His birch firewood was piled in the shed.
The house was very tidy; a begonia in the window, a cat with
a striped coat, a loaf, Hamilton's snuff mixture and light ale on
the table.

'The grocery van comes from Märsta once a week,' he said.
'I buy instant mashed swedes, mince, sausages and bread. They
sell all sorts of things.'

A couple of decades ago he had driven wood sleighs along
the same road, which in those days had been narrower, and
the horse had steamed with sweat, as it plodded many kilometres through the forests, before getting its nose-bag round
its muzzle. Now Märsta library sent him recorded books. He
listened to Swedish biographies whilst aeroplanes enveloped
his chimney with clouds of paraffin smoke.

'My weathercock blew down,' he said. 'What a noise! I
thought it was the tail of an aeroplane. In the middle of the
night. I found it later.'

'Did you hear about the air crash?'

'I actually heard the plane crash, but I dared not go out in
the fog and I'm not on the telephone.'

43

'I see,' said Jan. 'Well, nothing could have prevented the disaster. But if we had found the place earlier we might have been able to save some more people.'

'I heard about it on the radio. But why does it crackle for me? Is it something to do with your transmitters?'

'Unrelated disturbances. Our frequencies are entirely different.'

There were many recluses who in spite of the Health Authority's edict still lived in the area. The Air Traffic Department knew about them. They had been swept under the noise carpet. Their lives were pervaded by take-offs and landings.

'Let's see how long the snow will stay away,' the pensioner said. 'We've had some sleet, but that's all. Tomorrow I expect the hard frost will be here.'

'Have you had plenty of whortle-berries?' Jan forgetfully asked.

'I don't know, I can't see them. Nobody has talked about lingon-berries this year.'

JB walked back to his job. It was a day when the seasons seemed to balance each other. Winter delayed its revenge. The landscape caught its breath.

The clearing-up force was still working. Aeroplanes landed, supervised by other people. Trucks went out with trays of roast beef and clean towels.

JB thought of Sweden as it had evolved: sawmills and Bethesda chapels, suburban gardens and municipal houses, camping sites and holiday camps, incinerators and steak houses, pornographic cinemas and petrol stations, open prisons and motorway approaches. And in between sparsely situated farms, pastures for tamed animals, sinking water reservoirs. The different versions of togetherness. The positioning of duties and necessities in columns, and at the same time the searching for co-ordination to keep it all together.

To live in constant reciprocated motion – that was the compulsion or the advantage, depending on how it was used. There was no alternative. He could hear Jenny's voice between the firs, see Jenny's body, the creases in her armpit, the shading under her knee-cap, her pubic hair, thicker in the middle. But only in glimpses: the echo of a visual impression and a voice.

He found it impossible to see someone face to face for a long time: he was interrupted by SOS signals, the girl called

44

Marie, Klas Lundin and a winter's evening in Prague which was there, inside him, although he had never seen it. These faces and apparitions and impulses passed like a merry-go-round while he himself was still, watching. He tried to stop them and impress them, but they pushed each other out of his circle and were rumpled by his self-reflection. He did not want to change them. He wanted to be the cement between them, and the flame melting the wax.

He was prey to fleeting thoughts, a plaything for cosy hours, influenced by things near and at hand. Without his compulsive routine at the tower and his immense love for Jenny he would feel like a semi-finished product: a transparent jelly-fish floating on other people's waves. Jenny had eventually made him discern his own map, which began with an index of symbols.

He lived in the margin of the Milky Way, ignorant of what new worlds might be born a cosmic mile away. Walking through the forest, alone and hidden by the tree-trunks, he still thought that the world was suspended like a cloth in the wind. With no more secret places.

Jenny was a mobile dot on his radar screen. He decided to go and meet her. As soon as he had made this simple decision and arranged for a staff ticket, he felt inebriated and light-footed, as if he could take off without the help of engines. He postponed a dinner date with a friend from the SAS and advised his colleagues that he had to go to Copenhagen.

Would Jenny's eyes look tired? Would the corners of her mouth be moving? In the plane he tried not to think of her. He looked down on the Limhamn chimneys: there was smoke from the limestone quarries and the ships were being loaded with quicklime. The plane flew in over the Saltholm marshland. A report containing thousands of pages about Öresund Airport came before his eyes – it had been sent from one Scandinavian Air-Traffic Department to another.

He approached her on a kicking-bicycle in one of the long passageways at Kastrup where the planes taxi up to the different entrances, so that the passengers do not have to cross the tarmac. She came out of a numbered entrance. She was alone. The bicycle fell over and hit her leg. She screamed. He held her tight and felt the need to be comforted for what had happened to other people.

'You heard about the air crash at Arlanda?'

'Yes. Was it your watch?'

He nodded.

'I was hoping all the time that you didn't have to be there,' she said.

'I couldn't prevent it. But the voice of the air-hostess is haunting me, since we couldn't help them fast enough.'

So he had finally been allowed to talk about the disaster. For a while he felt relieved of its echoes. He released her and booked a seat on her flight. After take-off he ordered champagne, but they only had apple juice on board. She told him about Strasbourg and her long meetings:

'So much talk about consideration, prestige and methods of action, and so little about the contents of the resolution and its consequences. Now I don't remember much about it. Nothing will remain of the things you leave behind and you're of no importance yourself.'

She leant her head against Jan's shoulder and told him that one day she had sneaked out to go to the zoo. The park was melancholy in November. The polar bear had its blue eyes open and a grey tongue looking like sand-paper. She was told that he was almost blind. He could not see the children by the fence. A parrot repeated the same brief phrase day and night. The orang-utan wandered about in an eternal depression with his arms dangling. It could have been a meeting with the Council of Europe.

A Capucine monkey had finally taken her hand in his own bony hand; a secretive little semi-man, polite but reserved. He had looked at her in the same way as children look at adults, wondering what will come next.

Jenny fell asleep in the middle of a sentence. They were carried through the air and nothing much had been said or done. Jan thought of experiments where people were shot out of the earth's atmosphere and, although they were gone for a long time, had only aged an hour or so on their return.

He wished his feelings could take trips like that. But he knew that at the moment when Jenny opened her eyes, they would again be consuming their happiness. It must be used in order to exist.

He sat still in the roar of the engines, so as not to wake Jenny. He hardly noticed they were travelling.

46

II

PRAISE TO WINTER

THE WHITE SCREEN OF TRUTH

Jan and Jenny made a winter journey.

Chance had it that the two of them had agreed to lecture in the provinces, and they managed to co-ordinate their appearances during one week. They would lecture in different premises in the same places or in their vicinity. It was the first time they had left Stockholm and its surroundings together.

They travelled through a version of Sweden where Coke had banished the fairies and Kavli whey butter had silenced all shepherds' pipes. The tansy flowers along the railway tracks had faded, there was little traffic these days on the rotting sleepers, and the signalmen's cottages had been sold to artists, hermits and handy pensioners.

They experienced a kind of everyday life – day and night, not just the delicatessen shop open all night.

'There are probably more than four seasons,' Jenny concluded.

For it was December with a breath of spring in the air and barely any snow on the ground. The great tit had been fooled into singing his March song, and the anemone stems lay waiting in coils under layers of mouldering leaves.

They were sitting opposite each other on an express train. Jenny was wearing a fur-lined jacket with a tweed skirt and thick tights. The railway signals could be heard a long way off on this still frosty morning.

'That's one of my mountain ridges,' she said, pointing.

It stretched from east to west like a pea-pod.

Jan thought of the long line of winters which nobody bothered to number. This winter or that . . . nobody remembered. They mingled together. Yet the summers came distinctly to meet you; you held them by the hand. The countryside in winter was timeless: the tough birds stayed and rustled around in the bare bushes, and the ducks lightly imprinted their traces on the first powdery snow. The plain extended, and the barns were dim with the half torn down posters of last summer's circus.

'We'll have to go and see Veronica in Kristianstad,' Jenny said. 'I often miss her.'

When they went for walks together in Stockholm, she would point out the house where Veronica used to live when she worked in one of the Law Courts.

So far they were on their way to Hallsberg. Suddenly a bag fell down off the luggage rack, and all the contents upset over the floor. As the owner was not around, JB started to put the things back in the bag. Then a man with a thin, stern face appeared.

'You have taken my bag down,' he said disapprovingly.

'It fell down.'

'And now you're going through my luggage,' he continued.

'There were so many things,' JB said. 'The whole floor . . .'

'Couldn't you have let me pick it up myself?'

'You weren't here.'

'I could have been on my way. Wasn't I?'

An unpleasant atmosphere was building up. Somebody had to leave the carriage. The passengers regarded them as thieves. They went to the restaurant car.

'I saw nothing suspicious in his bag,' JB said.

'But you were keen to look through it,' Jenny retorted.

They stopped between two carriages. Standing on the rocking iron attachments, they groped for each other. The train rattled and whistled. The leather sides moved like bellows.

He took Jenny's hand and pressed his lips to her palm. He had done this before, a long time ago, at one of their first meetings. She had sucked his fingertips warmly, so intensely that he was heavy with lust. Now it rose again within him.

Jenny kicked off her shoe in the restaurant, and put her foot up against his stomach under the table. The waiter served a shrivelled fig-leaf, looking like plaice. With it came a slice of lemon in a plastic packet with a red band to pull to open it, like a cigarette packet.

'We're so similar,' Jan said contentedly.

'You think so?' Jenny replied, pressing with her foot.

'I mean it's nice that we enjoy the same things.'

'We can't be sure of discovering any real differences between

50

the sexes until they are treated equally. Till then you have to suspect that the differences are connected with our social rôles.'

Jenny's face was serious but not her eyes: they were in a whirling dance. His penis supported the arch of her foot. The waiter inquired whether they wanted coffee. JB replied something in a hoarse and absent-minded voice.

'No thank you,' Jenny said, laughing.

JB had to take a look at the passing countryside to become a little less conspicuous, before he could get up.

They booked into the Grand Hotel in Örebro. At the reception the hysteria about marriage had lessened: only one of them had to register. In air-traffic it was still necessary to have the same family name: wives had a fifty per cent discount.

'We're only friends,' Jenny assured him in the lift.

The room looked out on the grey castle in the river. Across the sky was a ski-track from an air force squadron nearby. JB thought of the Arlanda tower, of other people sitting at his panel. Just as well. SAS had approved of this official journey.

They ate herrings and sausages at the Freemason Hotel, a summer restaurant used in the winter as a canteen for typists. One helped oneself to buttermilk, coffee and five different kinds of Swedish bisquits from a table in the middle. One nodded with a little smile and let other people jump the queue.

'What do you dislike most?' JB asked.

'Hot milk. And a kind of milky soup with bread and leeks that we had during the war. There are other things as well, but then I'd have to think and I'm saving my brain for this afternoon.'

Jenny had been invited to a college some miles over the plain. Under stifling clouds of smoke from a shale refinery she was to talk about precautions against air pollution, about the responsibility of the state, industry and the individual.

He walked with her to the bus station. Örebro was a town with an old-fashioned aspect. A sign announced: Carpenter. Orders accepted. Anything within the profession. A café had two rooms, one for just lager and stout, the other for sausages, black pudding and pea soup.

'I prefer to talk to students,' Jenny said. 'They haven't yet

51

invested in families and cars and property. They understand that only a corrupt and sterile society can strip the developing nations as revenge. Ecology teaches that we are all responsible and guilty. If you realize that, you are able to break the alienation between the individual and his environment. When you destroy part of your environment, you must comprehend that you're destroying part of yourself. In that way I try to relate local observations to the general principles of ecology.'

'Don't go too far,' JB said, 'No scenes of destruction. Powerlessness often becomes an alibi for indifference.'

Jenny disappeared in a yellow bus with condensation on the windows.

JB walked around Örebro in the wet slush. A department store had swimsuits on sale. Sun all year round in the Canary Islands, a poster proclaimed. That was just another advertising lie – the sun was not up at night. Sun for a maximum of half the year would sound less tempting, but then nobody would feel cheated by this poster.

On a well-trodden meadow, next to a comprehensive school, there was a prayer meeting in a tent. JB sat down on a bench by the exit, and was handed a printed hymn-sheet. The tent was bulging like a cocoon, out of which the salvaged man would presently emerge. There was a cross draught. The Lord himself was loose. Elderly women had gathered under the naked light bulbs of truth in the hope of catching Him. They gave evidence, some quietly, others wailing in a way that could turn into jubilation. Loosen my bonds, oh Jesus, take me away on your tidal wave! Come sweet as honey of the bees, I have always kept my kitchen door open to you!

What was imagination, what was truth? The poster in the department store . . . or these events in the tent, verbalized by human contact . . .

It would soon be time for him to talk to the people who had decided to come to the sombre High School assembly-room. Surprised and curious he lingered for a while longer in the tent. And the canvas vault lifted up like the canopy of Heaven, yes, like a triangular milk carton with the milk of eternal happiness.

His lectures were arranged by the Tourist Authority together with SAS. His theme was the same as Jenny's: the glory of the Earth. But he warned only en passant of its fragility. Instead he pointed out the hidden oases, in these days quite accessible to charter passengers who, thanks to the Globetrotter scheme, at a reasonable price could go almost anywhere by scheduled flights. Also this was easier to arrange than the trips to Heaven advocated by the preacher.

JB felt hesitant about his task. Was he cheating them? No. But perhaps those who were not there. Or the Earth it-self. He had a pathetic feeling that he was going off at a tan-gent, that he pushed relevant facts aside instead of taking advantage of the opportunity he had been given. He had given talks many times before; he had acquired a certain flexibility and was not bound to written texts.

There was a national athletics competition on television that evening followed by a musical. One cinema showed Dracula, and they played bingo in all the others. But some people had arrived and sat down on the benches at the back and in the middle. Later on they agreed to move a bit further forward.

He did not mind speaking in public. Quite the contrary: he liked being on a rostrum with his face towards a silent crowd. He had been shy as a child. Now he had cultivated this shyness in such a way that he would show anything rather than that. His task was to discuss why, where and how one should travel. He did not advise anyone to go to Spain, Portu-gal or Greece. He expressed his surprise that the Mediterranean on almost all sides was surrounded by states governed by dictators. The coastal terraces were only eroded forests, and the triumphal arches had weathered through centuries of defeat. The bath water was impure, and the oil slicks drifted fatally towards the private hotel beaches. He advised them to choose flights which took them beyond this misery on their doorstep.

'That's a political view,' a middle-aged man interrupted.

'I thought such views were commonly held these days,' JB replied. 'But I do agree, I was giving my personal opinion.'

'If Portugal isn't good enough, you shouldn't talk in favour of Sweden either.'

'I haven't mentioned Sweden. This is where we live. The Globetrotter scheme helps you leave Sweden for a longer or shorter period on favourable terms.'

He had brought some colour slides with him, but he seldom

53

used them. He felt the pictures illustrated and destroyed; they pinned down conditions in constant motion. He had only seen pictures of these countries himself. Should he show them again, without even transposing them into words? Usually a fly would walk across the lense and become fearfully magnified on the screen, just as he showed the national dish of the Philippines: meat-balls with diced cucumber and aubergine salad. Seeing the photo again was like putting a knife into a soft object.

So he relied on his words, and told them about the pictures he would not let them see. He made the following up about the Philippines:

'A typhoon named Susan suddenly hit the yacht club, and the white plastic boats gathered like egg-shells in the boiling water. Further away the wind lifted the house roofs as lightly as entrance tickets. An earth-tremor shook the asphalt, which the heat had made pliable enough not to swallow up the pedestrians.'

He stopped. Should he have used the present tense rather than the past, if this was to be a true picture of the Philippines? Wasn't it too drastic to tempt anyone to go there? On the other hand, what did it matter if nobody ever went there?

He flew to Japan in an SAS plane and groped his way along the chasm between old and new:

'The temples in Kyoto are scattered like glistening mussels in the clay . . . The new culture has given a rusty coat to the old, and slowly erodes it . . .'

The audience this evening shifted a little. One girl was eating cherries from a paper bag. An old lady had a fit of coughing and had to go out, followed by an anxious friend. On the front bench was the assistant head-master with his arms crossed and dull-polished shoes. He was a leisurely gentleman whose success was assumed, and whose failures were unmentionable. JB decided to look at him during the rest of his lecture.

He did not hide from his audience that there was a certain nostalgia about travelling, a yearning to return to an environment which in these places had been preserved. Many people seemed to have enough of the threatening, different and unknown things at home.

'We'll meet again in Petersburg, as if the sun had been buried there.'

He encouraged them to travel to let the knowledge of the home street enrich their experience of the strange boulevard. The Svartå river was the source of Okavango, and Kinne Hill the base of Mount Kilimanjaro.

Upset by the coughing and cherry-eating, JB enacted the old phrases in the travel guide. They depicted a more difficult era, when hotels were evil peep-shows, and trains were packed with contagious germ carriers and dogs without muzzles. He gave an impression of the traveller in the guide-book half a century ago, misunderstood, assaulted, crying in vain for justice and the station manager, always subject to insults: 'We do not accept your fake coins.' And when he replies: 'Please give me implements for writing, I wish to contact the Embassy of my country', he is thrown out into the street, the misty European highway.

So the traveller gets stuck in the trap of his own phrases, in suspicion and complaints and the inclination to save money:

'It looks like honey. It should be free of customs duty.'

'I said Charing Cross. You have driven me around in circles.'

'Conductor. I think my passenger is out of his mind. His nurse got out at G.'

Afterwards JB jumped down from the stage. Somebody took him by the hand, thanked him and asked questions. It was a strange moment. Earlier on he had had some kind of rapport with his audience by words and gestures. Now, standing on the same level, they looked each other in the eye, and he thought he did not have much more to teach or recommend. It occurred to him that his authority had come from his position in the room, some decimetres above the audience, where he had been placed without any reason and by unreasonable chance. The cashier came up, motioned him aside and gave him some bank-notes, which looked as if they had spent a long time under different people's mattresses.

'I don't mind fragments of the Dead Sea scrolls,' he joked, but the cashier blew his nose, not understanding this witticism.

Then coffee, politely, but in a rush. Yet another man accused him of being an unsolicited propagandist; and then he was asked about inoculations.

'What a pity you didn't have any pictures to show,' a lady said.

He wanted to leave. He felt like a big-mouth who had cast no new light over his subject but merely verbal ashes enough to bury Pompeii without the aid of Vesuvius.

He was alone when he came out of the large concrete institution. The school-yard had cracked asphalt and stiffened coal-dust. The smell of boys, many years old, lingered in the air. His own memory of smells was that of wellington boots, gauntlets and golf trousers. Somebody had torn the belt from a trench-coat to lash him. The prong of the buckle drew blood from his throat. He got hold of the belt, and in a blind rage, with unexpected strength, knocked down his assailant and ran away, afraid of his revenge.

Far away in the bygone days of Jan Backman's childhood, there was a feeling of irrevocable disaster, an awareness rather than an experience, because the experience was more concerned with moments of blind fear, when he had to escape at the speed of light without knowing where to.

These black streaks in his life made his heart jump at the unprotected moment when he awoke. In contrast to this was the happiness of walking with his raincoat and briefcase in the first snow in the provincial town, alone, among other people, past a chapel, a garage . . . The blue neon light of the shoe factory flickered against the sky. He walked along a street with ugly rainy streaked name-plates on houses which had once been red, and there were Christmas lanterns in their windows and geranium plants shading the rooms. The lorries roared past, and a wild cat climbed the sooty fence around the railway area.

He was on his way back to the hotel where he was staying with Jenny. He could feel security at the thought of everything changing. Opinions slowly crumbled away, idioms became dated. Maybe his conception of society as a wolf could be diminished, and the barriers of family egotism overcome. But the houses could stay there. They did not have to represent the past. They should be there to receive new lives in the future.

Jenny had come back, and was waiting for him. She had been discussing ecology for a couple of hours at the college, and then had their early dinner of vegetable soup and poached haddock, before taking the bus back. Her cheeks were rosy, and she smelt of smoke.

56

'I quoted,' she said, 'one of the Swedish UN speeches: "The physical, social and spiritual well-being of man is to a great extent dependant on his immediate environment." The wind blew, the stench of shale oil penetrated the class-rooms. Some councillors were there. They smiled slightly, but didn't lift the eyes from next year's preliminary budget. We're exposed to various kinds of pressure, they said, we must consider it. In other words, we'll have to press on and on and never give up.'

'You're very useful,' JB said. 'I'm doing the publicity for a semi-nationalized company. I ask people to leave their immediate environment for a while. The more people travel, the cheaper; more equality, that is. But my excuses are inspid.'

JB was still wearing his coat and, as they were in a strange city, they went out again. Jenny told him about her day. There was a slow movement in the city: people went to bed, made love, did not make love; they were overtaken by sleep or fatigue which was never restful; the houses jerked, their eyelids drooped, and a window open on the ground floor let out a smell of coffee and steamed potatoes or maybe damp ironing; a child was crying without being answered; something was going on behind the plaster.

'We could be two companions touring all over the country to gather material for a comic libretto about Sweden,' Jenny said.

'And this is the Örebro backcloth.'

'It reminds me of where I went to school, Västerås, the County town with a couple of industries supporting it. For a while I had an idea that I should walk home from school backwards. I stuck triangular bottle-labels on the shop-windows – I got them from the brewer's daughter in my class. Shake the bottle carefully to spread the fruit particles, it said on them. Miss Lundbom, my drawing teacher, found me out and wanted to report me. I gave her a label. She made winding movements in the air. I thought she was painting something she saw before her. She was a small woman, the rest was her hair-do. Once in primary school I caught her sitting on the loo with her hair down. I was frightened; I told the others there was a legendary creature in there, probably a mermaid.'

They could talk about everything. It was enough to know that this was possible, as there was not enough time. He told her about the prayer meeting in the tent. His relation to

57

religion and for a long time also to death had been uncompli-
cated. He went to the northern cemetery with Mrs Tapper to
put a hyacinth by his mother's tombstone. On a heap of
leaves he found purple ribbons from funeral wreaths: Rest
in peace. This is a nice scarf for Edith, he said to Mrs Tapper,
who had looked after his childhood.

In the Lilljan Woods a boy caught a yellow butterfly, and
wore it pinned alive on his sweater. To object was unmanly
and bad companionship. JB kept quiet, but asked God to punish
this cruelty with long-term torture in hell. For he loved
animals, brought home frozen ants to thaw out in the winter,
and visited the pet shops, in those days hidden in basements
in city centres, before they moved to suburbs where more
children live.

He got through puberty half-indifferent, half asleep. His
penis showed him the way. He trotted after it slowly. The
landmarks of purity and religious brooding pointed in other
directions: he did not see them. The nearest he got to a
religious feeling was listening to spiritual songs on the radio
before leaving for school in the morning. That music filled
him with vitality and extravagance. 'He's got the whole world
in his hands,' was a jubilant American Salvation march.

And to Jenny, on a pavement in Örebro, he sang:

> 'Truly sweet is the lot
> Such a fisherman's got,
> Taking out evangelical nets,
> Before the golden sun sets.
> His kind of net is the best,
> Take yours out, do not rest.'

He was not even a Sunday fisherman in the fjords around
the Water Palace, which had so many herrings in them. What
he credited God for was that he apparently kept secrets con-
fided in him. But so did Gertrude. JB did not wish to have
someone to live for, he only wanted something to live in.
God never succeeded in seducing him, so he avoided a lot of
temptations. Maybe that was why he never became a complete
human being. He took the plunge from childhood to adult-
hood without changing his skin. There was something clear,
as opposed to clarified in his way of looking at things.

He missed the fruitful confusion of puberty. But he saw its

symptoms all around him: the schizoid division between producers and consumers, intellect and feeling, passivity and infinite expansion. Too often there were partitions and boxes, seldom connections or bridges. Society had hidden the key: neither fish nor fowl.

Örebro by night. The last cafeteria had its lights turned out. The city was so quiet that the ticking of the traffic-lights for the blind could be heard.

They went to bed and were soon asleep, ignorant of each other. Asleep each one has his own quarters. But they were woken up by the music from the hotel restaurant.

'Why lie awake when we can dance?' JB said.

Jenny got out of bed and started to dress quickly. They told the head waiter they were looking for a friend and did not need a table.

Then they started to dance on the floor. Jenny looked at him and laughed.

'I've only got my dress on.'

'I can feel that,' JB said.

Their faces were still drowsy. All around them other faces were moving, with their expressions fixed in other states of mind. Nobody noticed Jan's fingers against Jenny's collar-bone, the back of his hand against her neck. Her body was alive under the thin material. There was a secret place between them. He thought they moved in obscurity, created by all the other people in the room.

A little later they were asleep again as after a shared dream.

FATHER UNKNOWN

Their hotel in Norrköping was small, situated near the theatre. A lot had been demolished in the vicinity: workshops and small factories, as well as tenement buildings built in the 1880s when people streamed in from the countryside to work in the cotton spinning-mills and wool-mills.

Their room was modest, mainly decorated in PVC and polyester. They were warned against leaving their shoes in the corridor – they should be polished with paper dusters. From their window they could look down into a patisserie, where ashtrays were emptied and cakes put into the fridge, as soon as the cinema next door commenced. A neon lighted sign for an insurance company shone in onto their bed, and the lettering of the National Farmers' Union crowned a distant castle-like grain silo.

They were happy there. They had got out of the bus on the plain between Linköping and Norrköping at a church mentioned in a tourist-guide-book. The portal had a naïve painting around the edge: 'This is the gate of heaven'. A happy and undoubted pretence, which also suited their room. Like Bonnard, who in a picture could make the standard heating system of a French bathroom look like the gateways of paradise. 'Arthur Carlsson, in his early years a farm-hand, later a stoker,' JB read.

They had stopped by a tombstone outside the church with the portal. Carlson seemed to be useful still, to be on duty.

'Jan Backman, a former air-traffic controller, now a globe-trotter,' Jenny said. 'One who has neither flown nor travelled.'

'That makes it easier to talk about it. Experience limits you.'

'Yes, if you really know about something, you don't talk about it,' Jenny said. 'I have a terrible suspicion this is so. And we talk so much!'

They cuddled each other on the burgundy bedspread under the etching of Moonshine over Brå Bay. Their fingers flew low and quick over well-known landscapes. Then they went off to the duties that had called them to the city.

Christmas was about to descend over Sweden, heavy like a glacial stage, entangled in garlands, calling everyone's attention. People looked past each other absent-mindedly.

'I'll come and listen to you tonight,' Jenny said. 'I want to hear the tales you tell them.'

'Well, you haven't visited the future you paint to your audiences in such sombre colours,' Jan said. 'And all those who give talks about André's flight, Swedish sledge records or Frederick the Great – have they been through more than I have?'

Yet another hall with faces scattered about in the rows of

seats. The local newspapers and the Tourist Board had arranged it, and he had a larger audience than he got when the educational associations were hosts. The proceeds like Jan Backman's fee would buy blankets for India. His voice sounded strange to him. He tried not to look at Jenny.

Suddenly he was in Japan, not for the first time:

'The smiling bow – varying in inclination and length but always more courteous than the one we see in this country, even at court and in period films – is Japan's answer to our formal handshake. These ceremonial rites of an acquired code make the stranger feel inhibited and insecure like being in a monastery, the first day at school or in a new job . . .'

He did not notice any informal expressions on the front benches, but Jenny had a broad smile on her face. He felt that they had been together in Japan. The first question afterwards was prepared beforehand. Then people became more willing. Finally one of the arrangers came up to thank JB. He introduced himself as Harold Engblom; had been a bank manager in the city until his recent retirement. He mentioned to JB that he had known his father. JB beckoned Jenny to join them, and in the end they went back to Engblom's home for a late night snack. He had a penthouse flat with a view overlooking St Olaus' Church on one side, and the harbour on the other. His wife had silvery hair and a face as blithe as milk and strawberries.

The apartment had needed maids, but they had learnt to enjoy their old age in the modern Swedish manner, looking after themselves as well as they could. They talked about this: the troubles of life and how they were still well off.

'We have a life insurance policy,' Mrs Engblom said, 'we're all right. But sometimes I do silly things. Like yesterday, when I couldn't find my large white hat. It had gone by mistake to the jumble-sale in aid of the Save the Children fund. Then, the very same afternoon, when I was having my coffee here by the bay window, I saw a lady passing, wearing it.'

She disappeared out into the kitchen, and the other three went out on the balcony. The snow flakes were as large as children's mittens. Norrköping: mail order, bed linen and the International Harvester. But now it was quiet before the harvest time, an intermediate time with the dull waiting for the government departments to come. Darkness rose from the stream by the Holmen Works. Far out in the harbour the outlines of cranes could be seen, lit by sodium lights. An occasional mast shimmered, Neapolitan yellow.

The dining-table was huge. On white linen table-mats they were served mussels and mushrooms on toast, rosé wine to drink, followed by sponge cake and tea. They sat so far apart that their voices hardly carried. Mr Engblom told them about the administration of the city, a bribery scandal, the merger of the brewery and a larger company, the problems of the new airport, and the empty factories. His wife said: 'Tomorrow I'm going to shop at the market. You ought to come with me. But the row of farmers has gone. Some people used to stick their fingers right into the butter to taste it. The jeweller's wife had an egg-spoon, the vicar's wife a penny to dig into it.'

'Do you often hear from your father?' Engblom asked. 'An excellent man.'

'There are several different opinions about my father,' JB said hesitantly. 'Many people have a negative view of him.'

'That is unfounded, and due to misunderstanding,' Engblom replied curtly.

A little later the host in a gentlemanly way led JB into his study, seated him on a leather upholstered chair, and pointed to a photo of a large sailing-boat.

'This is the *Indra*. By the wind, sheeted home. That's the easiest way to photograph a boat. This is my wife, Indra's daughter. And that is A. O. Backman, your father, in front of the foredeck. He's holding the stay. A really splendid man, with a rough surface but upright, not for our lenient times. You couldn't treat him just as you liked.'

'What did you do together?'

'Enjoyed ourselves. Sailed from Stockholm to Västervik, stopping on the way to fish for flounder. Sailing, he was his true self. But he didn't really understand children. There were quite a few things he didn't understand.'

He was silent. JB got up, as he was drowning in his chair.

'What happened to little Gertrude?' Harold Engblom suddenly asked. 'I can see her in that open car next to a housekeeper your father had. I guess she had come home for the Easter holidays.'

JB was watching the brown volumes of the encyclopaedia,

A – Anund, Ö – Öändan, high up by the ceiling stucco. He took some time replying.

'She's in Botswana,' he said. 'In Africa.'

The bank manager looked at him as if he did not believe him. JB for a moment could not meet his eyes. He tried to recall to mind the times when his father had said to some stranger:

'This is my son Jan. This is my daughter Gertrude.'

Had he ever said this at the same time? Maybe not – Gertrude was usually away.

Suddenly he could smell the scent of his father's hair: Watzin's Keratine.

'I'm off now.'

The room was dark. The night train was waiting at the station. JB had gone to bed. The scent was there.

'Do you have to?'

'Yes.'

'When will you be back?'

'Soon. Good-bye.'

He heard footsteps in the room upstairs, the click of the front door, and some other, less familiar sound. He decided to stay awake to listen, but a large feather fan of colours lulled him further and further away into sleep. As he got up in the morning, the house was empty. Mrs Tapper had gone out shopping or something. He got himself some corn flakes and milk, and listened to the news and the weather forecast on the wireless, just like his father used to do, his father who had just left. In those days he sometimes imagined that there was something to tie them together, him and A. O., but even then he hardly believed in that feeling.

'I see you haven't got a ring,' Harold Engblom said, looking at Jan's hand.

It went through his head: Did Engblom know about him and Gertrude?

'Possibly you're not a mason after all? Well, your father was a very loyal member of the freemason fraternity. As I told you, we had a lot of fun together. He was a man of honour.'

'I didn't know he was a freemason.'

'I suppose it was his interest in the secret stamps that attracted him to join.'

63

When Jenny came in, the bank manager changed the topic of conversation and said he had been to the City Theatre to see Two Men And One Woman, and an ignorant country person in the audience had got up from his seat and waved his clenched fist towards the stage, screaming:

'Tell that female she's wrong.'

He then told them about a round-shouldered physics teacher, who had studied too hard. He had watery, dreamy eyes and courted teenage girls. The one he loved most was called Eva, and she died at seventeen. He sent a wreath with a sash saying To My Love, and demanded to help carry the coffin. Spotting her boy-friend in the church, the teacher spat on his trousers. For weeks afterwards he wore a white scarf. Then he was found dead in a garden, wearing thin clothes, frozen to death in the snow. After his funeral they had coffee and a completely white cake with a white marzipan decoration on it, inscribed Eva in black chocolate letters. Nobody ever knew who had ordered it.

'That man was misunderstood. Nobody dared mention the girl's name. Except the one who wrote it in chocolate.'

'You haven't got another photo of my father?' JB asked.

'I don't think so.'

He opened the doors of a huge cupboard and rummaged through it.

'I coughed once too much at an auction once and came back with this cupboard. But it was cheap. No, I can't find one. There was one of us standing outside the Palace; there were trams passing and snow on the ground, and in the middle of the square was the Goddess of History with her bronze plate, you know; it looked like a white piece of paper in the snow.'

'So you worked for the Foreign Office too?'

'In the mercantile department. I left it for a private enterprise. I was afraid of ending my days in Jakarta or Quito, or being dismissed.'

'What were his duties in those years when you knew him?' Jenny asked.

Harold Engblom looked at Jenny, seemingly hesitant to reply.

'Contact matters. Information. We played bridge. He was of a reticent nature. But as a mason he gave certain confidences. Many of them, however, of little consequence.'

64

'So you had much to do with each other?'

'At the beginning of the war. We were poorly prepared. Now you can see better what it was like. A time of suspicion and confusion. Everybody was considered untrustworthy in some way, too Finnish, too Russian, too English, or too German.'

'What was my father?'

'He had several friends in the German Embassy. He knew the lists of the Swedish Secret Service. He favoured Germany, but hated the Nazis. He realized what German victory would bring. He destroyed, on his own accord, a German card index, one of the most important we had. I remember I heard him say: "The greatest factor of insecurity in this country is the Secret Service". There were people who wanted a revenge. Some people in the Secret Service spread rumours that he was a Nazi.'

'It must have been a strange period,' Jenny said. 'All the espionage trials . . .'

'The Foreign Office officials had a lot of power. The prosecution gave the papers to the Foreign Office to determine what could threaten Sweden's friendly relations with a foreign country. If these were considered threatened, they prosecuted. There was many an injustice that will never be cleared up. Oscar wouldn't compromise.'

Jan Backman saw a new Adolf Oscar Backman rising like a figure-head over the horizon in the West. But he could not get rid of his childhood impression.

Engblom continued: 'Many things were never known. The Ministry of Defence sent out capsules of cyanide to policemen, custom's officials and public prosecutors along the Norwegian border. Many people helped the Norwegian couriers. They were recommended to swallow the capsule if tortured.'

'Why did he leave Sweden?'

'I think he applied to be discharged when he realized the Secret Service lists could be abused. Sweden would give up some of its best people if the Germans gave orders for it. He could not bear to represent that nation as an envoy.'

'But then, how can he bear to live in Brazil?' Jenny asked.

'He may believe there is some freedom in the disarray,' Engblom said. 'Our computerized registration here he would probably detest as well as mistrust.'

'Did he ever speak about us?' Jan asked.

At that moment he felt afraid of himself. Was he giving away Gertrude, and their love?

'No.'

They looked out of the windows over the roofs, valve caps sitting on the chimney-pots like sleepy cats, and the black memorial runners of the Virginia creeper over plastered walls. In the distance lay a plain which was once a marsh for trilobites, wet fallow for the future. Jan Backman thought time was running alongside of himself, occasionally catching up with him, throwing him onto the wagon, and releasing him again. They had known each other such a short time, he and Jenny, and yet for so long. A. O. Backman had been gone for so many years and been missed so little.

'He needed no one,' Engblom said. 'That's the impression he gave. Maybe others needed him, I don't know.'

What the son remembered about his father was mainly distorted morality which said you should be adjustable and adjusted in suitable measure but at the same time not succumb to unmanageable demands. He knew that music; a steady drumbeat like that on the soldiers' parade, which they could hear from the flat in Brahe Street, the mounted Life Guards going down Sture Street towards the Royal Palace, followed by the number ten tram with its angry clink.

At the bottom of Adolf Oscar's soul there was probably a frozen spring. It would thaw at celebrations, and the Foreign Office afforded many such opportunities: hoisting the flag, national anthems, deputations and proclamations. Then his voice would break, and give it a pathetic quality, reflecting his deeper sentiments which habit, environment, and moral demands had not managed to cover completely with ice.

JB had no access to his father. In his memories the father moved jerkily as in films showing only one picture at a time. Jan had not seen any photos of him since his departure, and so his father had not aged but was there on the film which had been almost effaced. A few places were in the light, but the rest in shadow. He disappeared out of sight through lack of knowledge and dimensions, slid away out of focus. It became necessary to invent him.

But talking about his father brought Gertrude to mind. Jan remembered that as children they had wondered at the way

66

adults find a stranger to join, throwing themselves into the unknown. They themselves had hesitated to take that plunge.

How could he speak to Gertrude now about what their life, had been and make her see what he saw? Truth was hard to ascertain, held by pincers of untruth. He would sometimes make unclear statements, because his unclear perception was being true to himself, but in a muddy, uninteresting way. He felt more truthful when, by words or by aid of his senses, he could pass on to another person an experience he would not have liked to be without.

The truth about Adolf Oscar Backman came too late. The picture of him was imprinted. Had the truth about Jenny come too late for Gertrude? He realized that nothing was what it appeared to be. Gertrude was another person, and so was he, and even Jenny.

Escape from reality : escape to reality. But he did not know the direction.

'We'll say good night to your wife,' Jan said, as they decided to leave.

'That's not necessary,' Harold Engblom said.

But there was a light on in the kitchen, and they found her there reading The Golden Notebook by Doris Lessing, getting up rather embarrassed, leaving her glasses to mark the page. The kitchen was different from the rest of the flat with an unpainted table and red checked curtains.

He had misjudged her as well. It was a dark flat, but in a lighted square she was sitting happily – like opening a little door on a boring Advent calendar to find that inside it is nice and merry.

Then they were out in the empty street. Sleet was falling on the pavement, melting. The snow had disappeared again, except for the icy footprints here and there where the snow had stiffened under people's soles. They looked like white footprints painted on the pavement to lure people in to a sale.

'At first you introduced me as your friend from university,' Jenny said. 'When we left you took my hand as if we'd got engaged with your father's eyes upon us.'

'I don't care what they thought,' Jan Backman said. 'I'm more amused by your thoughts.'

Inside a glass door of a new construction, a couple were kissing, indistinct like fish in an aquarium. At a tobacconist's some motorcyclists were meddling with the cigarette machine. A police patrol car drove up, and a young blond bearded constable opened his window:

'Beat it, Lenny. Why don't you go home now?'

The policeman seemed to know them. If he arrested one of them, he would leave him with his mother. It was still a small town in a small country.

Jenny's lips were cold from the night. He tickled her ear, and took a light strangling grip round her neck. She pressed herself against him; he felt the bone where her stomach ended. She sneaked her hand inside his belt to caress his rising penis. Her finger-tips could see in the dark.

He longed for her in the uncompromising manner he had only felt with her: the yearning to run towards her, to walk for miles to get closer to her, to catch a glimpse of her at a street corner and rush at her as if the speed would help him penetrate her.

But Jenny released herself and buttoned his coat up. The stars were high in the sky, and did not sting. The sunset earlier on that day had been streaked with lemon over the Holmen Works, and bare branches scattered like iron filings over the sky.

'You hardly knew your father,' Jenny said.

'No. I don't know if he could walk on his hands or tell a ghost story. I used to take the Sunday newspaper from the letter box in the morning and take it to him while he was asleep. I was frightened by his large lonely face. I didn't know what to do: whisper, scream or touch his cheek carefully.'

The streets were empty and people were asleep, except the shift-workers in the wool-mill and in the harbour. In the gutter a vodka bottle sailed. In their hotel room with the plastic azalea and round white tiled stove they undressed, and Jenny put her hands on the farther side of his thighs: bark getting harder towards his trunk. She marked his boundaries. She laughed her sunny laugh, calling him out onto the smoothest ice, where he slipped. Her body was a hand groping for his.

He took her hand, stretching her fingers. He saw her movements which he could not control: muscles, nerves and intentions in a body that was not his. But another part of him let itself be influenced by her gaze.

His lips slid down her body to rest at her naval. He carefully bit into her pubic hair. His tongue reached soft play-mates. Jenny pressed her legs lightly towards his ears. He could not hear what she was mumbling over there. But with the tip of his tongue he was in contact with an unheard language, soughing in their conduits, reaching its destination without an interpreter. Waters mixed. He did not know what came from his mouth and what came from her vagina.

Suddenly everything changed. The film was cut off, the thirst quenched. For an icecold moment he perceived a fissure between his hand and the buttons of the instrument panel. He saw her knees, and did not know what they were demanding from him.

He slowly turned round.

'Jenny . . .'

He put his head on her arm, stroking her hard with his hand along her ribcage, as if trying out the strength of skin and bones.

Their eyes met. Clear and undisguised. She held his balls in a warm grip. A smile spread from the corners of his mouth down over his body. Hollows filled with lust and worry. Some third person had them in his grip and gently joined them together.

THE SON OF THE BEAR HUNTER

'I wonder who he was,' Jan Backman said.

It was morning in the Vänersborg Museum. A field vole was watching them with a stiff gaze. It rested on a bed of sand in a glass case edged in brown wood. It had a withered leaf and a slim mungo for company. There was an old school smell in the hall, and the animals were crowded.

'Who?' said Jenny.

They were the only visitors. The names of the species were written on labels in brown sepia ink.

'Axel Ericson,' Jan said. 'He died only seventy years ago.'

'A predecessor to Sten Tidström,' Jenny said reading a sign. 'It seems he came to South Africa exactly a hundred years before him.'

'The whole museum consists of his collections. I've never heard of him. I could write to Sten. Find out all you can about Axel Ericson from Vänersborg.'

'Guess what Sten would reply.'

'That there is seldom factual information on the spot. It's not in Botswana that they know of him, but in Vänersborg. This is where it began. The past of Botswana is confined in other places.'

'The exciting thing may be what he did in Vänersborg, and why he decided to leave town.'

'This is Cinnyris Ericsoni, Ericson's sun-bird. There is a lark named after him too. And there are only four stuffed examples of Ericson's honey-bird. That's what the sign says.'

JB looked at the sun-bird. It said nothing about the hunt, or the sunlight between the leaves on the day it was caught. Like going past children in a playground not knowing what captivating expedition of love preceded their conception. A dusty bird within the glass of a case tried to remind them of an experience. The quarry cheated the hunter.

He thought of Gertrude returning home from Africa with a child, the way Ericson had returned with the honey-bird.

'He discovered birds,' JB said. 'That's all we know.'

'Here is someone we can ask,' Jenny said.

He saw Jenny smiling to a man passing through the hall. 'I forgot that you work here,' she said.

Jenny told him who JB was. The other man was called Sven Trubleus, the museum official. He had been to school with Jenny. She had run into him at a couple of ecology conferences in Stockholm. Sweden was a small country.

'Ericson was afraid his collection might be eaten by termites, or plundered by adventurers, so he donated twelve hundred samples of four hundred and fifty species of birds to Vänersborg. They started to raise money here for a museum. The rifle-corps arranged dances in the ballroom of the Town Hall.'

'They weren't allowed to shoot the birds, just dance to build a house for them,' Jenny said.

'The honey-bird is tucked away,' JB said.

'You can't imagine how many birds he sent home. It was an amazing time in the town's history. Huge packing-cases arrived on the canal boat from Gothenburg. They were unpacked and stored in the Town Hall cellar. The school-children were taught the names of the birds. The custom's officer didn't know what to do about it, since they were not edible.'

'We haven't got a zoologist here,' Trubleus continued. 'The animals have been left in their cases, and will remain there for ever. You have to look for the honey-bird, like you had to in the old days. Ericson was the first man to spot it, and one of the last.'

The official took them to the next room.

'This is the spinning rod of Llewellyn Lloyd, the bear hunter. He caught salmon in the river, and shot snipe in flight. He lived in a garret in this town, and kept his clothes for immediate use under a British flag. He would sit in his dressing-gown among bears' skulls and stuffed salmons with a glass of brandy and water on the table. He shaped Axel Ericson's life.'

'Was there any correspondence, inherited possessions, or papers?' JB asked.

'We've got some letters and old newspapers, as well as some annual volumes of The Vänersborg Fraternity Journal.'

Trubleus got out what he had. It filled a whole hard-backed file, whose covers were dotted like African birds' eggs. Black cotton ribbons kept the documents of a lifetime together. The official left them between a Kaffire cat and a sugar cane rat. Hours passed. The unknown Ericson assumed greater clarity. There was a photograph of him with a dark beard, looking like many men of that period. He had children, but how many and by whom was not said. Maybe they were still living in Vänersborg. Occasionally they heard the traffic: a lorry passed the school and the church, making the glass cases shake. JB found a cutting from the local newspaper, November 13th, 1884: '. . . birds from the inner regions of Africa, parts of which white man has never visited, have a strange appearance . . .'

Axel Ericson shot about a thousand of these, and sent them in the skin to another Swedish hunter, Gustaf Kolthoff, who was a curator in Uppsala and organized a zoological museum there, before founding the Biological Museum in Stockholm. Kolthoff studied the birds. The yellow-breasted black magpie exists only in a few samples in the whole world, and the knife beak buzzard with a mouth like a night-jar, a beak like an owl, and wings like falcon, is extinct.

To entice wild animals, Lloyd bought scraps from a butcher in Vänersborg, Anders Ericson, who sent his son Axel to deliver the meat to the bear hunter's house. Soon Axel was allowed to go shooting with him, and he was taught how to stuff animals. He attended High School. In the summertime he would wander around in the countryside, and be seen as far away as the Hornborga Lake, where he made his way through the reeds. For hours he would watch ruffs, black terns, sedge-warblers and loons. He had potatoes, bread and ginger beer in his knapsack.

The bear hunter had sons by different women. One of them had the surname Anderson, like the housekeeper, with whom Lloyd lived for many years. His first names were Charles John. It was not until he was as famous as his father, that he was permitted to take his father's surname. He refused.

Lloyd taught Axel Ericson to examine and label all the wild animals, and when suitable conserve them with tow and leaves, wire and arsenic soap. He sent him out to Africa to help Charles John Anderson, who had by then discovered Lake Ngami and the river Okavango. Axel Ericson saw Anderson, aged forty, die in 1867. Axel dug his grave with an axe and a tin pan in the hard clay between two trees, and covered it with thorny bushes to protect it from wild animals. It was in Ovamboland near the Angolan border. Months later Anderson's wife got his last letter: 'When you receive this letter, you'll know that my bones are growing white in a distant wilderness.'

They left the museum, where Ericson's zebra mangust and porcupine were drying up in cases poor of oxygen. They took the file, and went down to the custom-house in the harbour. The railings along the quayside were washed by green water, and ice-floes splashed against the shore. At the brewery there was a café, where beer was served direct from the barrel. There were red-faced men peering out at Lake Vänern, as if the Flying Dutchman was taking in its sails out there.

It was easy to imagine Ericson amid the official yellow buildings with grey velvety carpets on the stairs, and the carriage wheels glistening against the cobble stones. He loved animals, in spite of being a butcher's son. When he travelled by hackney-coach, he made sure the horse was well groomed, and if the coachman lashed the horse's backs with his whip, he would immediately hit the coachman with a cane on his back. If he objected, Ericson would reply: 'So, you don't like it either?'

His letters revealed nostalgia: 'I prefer the inner regions of South Africa,' he wrote on August 6th, 1891, 'where I can do my ornithological research and studies among my black servants, far away from the rush and business problems of the civilized world ...'

'And yet he came back to visit,' Jenny said. 'I can read it here. He wanted to show the people of Vänersborg what had become of him. But they wouldn't believe him. Afri'ca, his mother pronounced it, not knowing where it was. You're a dreamer, she said, you're imagining Charles's wain with the wheels at the top. He had to accept that, in front of his mother, he had never travelled at all. His letters from Botswana arrived after him, and seemed to confirm to his mother that he was really a gamekeeper in a neighbouring village.

'It was probably the same in Botswana, when he spoke of Vänersborg. He was someone who came from a place a few miles away, maybe from Mafeking, travelling from one sparsely populated area to another.'

They had a sandwich in a cafeteria, looking at the people passing by, and watching the town's signboards: Shoes Post Office Ironmonger Carpets. It was the year when children wore tartan plastic trousers and navy woollen hats with a large pom-pom on top, red like an apple.

This was his last appearance on behalf of SAS. He would then go with Jenny to Skåne for one of her commissions. He noticed more than ever, how he constructed visions and cemented them with facts. He used his own imagination and desire; neither authentic, as they had no documentary proof of experience on the spot. He wanted to try out his authority and see how far it could take him, how much the words could disguise. But the feeling was his own, and the listeners seemed to identify with him. He brought out his file of facts at the coffee.

Things could be true and yet not good, a philosopher had consoled him once. Truth did not enrich experience and imagination, but kicked the spirit out with dry, precise facts.

73

Afterwards they went to the Freemasons' restaurant, and ordered herrings and Akvavit.

'We've learnt so much about people we haven't even met,' Jenny said.

'How do you mean?'

'Like your father and Axel Ericson. Here we are, travelling from one Swedish provincial town to another, and discovering fates in South America and Africa. In the museum I kept thinking of Gertrude.'

'So did I.'

And then he told her how he had thought of the honey-bird Ericson brought home, and the child Gertrude would bring.

Axel Ericson was the third guest at the table. The file lay opened between their plates. They saw his birds surrounded by their true colours, saw Tidström drawing diagrams on a blackboard, and Gertrude jolting along in a jeep through the scents of mignonette, which she loved.

Botswana and Namibia were blank pages to Ericson's unhistoric eyes. He could leave his stamp there. The old one-horse carriage was the cot of his apprentice years in Sweden, and for short trips in Africa he would use a similar vehicle. The large wheels spun slowly along the roads, unnoticeably changing into steppes. It jolted here and there with the gusts of wind, and when the wind died out, the horse would start panting with sweat running down the furrows of his face. Then thunder came, and the stuffy afternoon seemed to explode. Ericson drove the horse as hard as he had the heart to, and had a nip of brandy from his flask.

The predecessors' landmarks could sometimes be seen from his carriage. His face was lean, with a brown beard like a cloud round his chin. He would pass a farm, a man behind a couple of oxen, another in a deck-chair on the veranda, and their gestures meant: no vacancies, or: please help yourself. Dinner was laid at one end of a huge timber table. A servant brought a pail of fresh water to wash his clothes.

He travelled through deserted villages, and saw the white smokes from grass fires. The thunder was discharged; a wild animal roared in the mountains. The wind went through the thorny thicket, like waves tossed against a pier. Suddenly the rain came loose from the clouds. Thus the cattle avoided slaughter.

74

In his letters Ericson appeared irresponsible and unattached towards other people, that is, with no more responsibility than what he gave himself. His demands and motives were hard to define. Maybe he wanted one day to give an account in front of the bourgeoisie of his home town, although he knew they could neither estimate his achievements nor distinguish the areas which he had been the first to cross from the ones which he had passed only as a marauder.

He watched and imagined a lot about the country around him which later proved right. And if he did not become famous, he had heard the breakers off Walvis Bay, and seen the huge boulders in Damaraland. He had seen himself both as a merchant and as a tool of Fate: a deserter from civilization to 'the free and easy life in inner regions of South Africa, where they eat to live, and do not live to eat.'

Axel Ericson occasionally wrote about this yearning which would make him languid. He felt thirsty and limp: the yearning was a feverish ague, and he had to lie down, close his eyes and imagine other places. He listened to flies buzzing without moving a finger, he could smell grass fires, see the flames fluttering like streamers in the wind created by the fire. Destruction and transition: actions multiplying. His head became a termite-hill with no clear direction.

The contents of his yearning were not mentioned. In writing he was not very open-hearted. He lacked ideas to use as tools. The things were what they seemed to be: hard and square. The trees grew with their roots down towards the subsoil water, and turned their leaves towards the sun. The rest was just distortions and labyrinths.

Did he miss the presence of a woman? Not one of the natives, whose language he did not speak, but somebody who belonged to his irrevocable past, to a world that was really alien but could still be imagined, when he was lying there still and languid, as in a tomb, watching his life pass by.

Or was it Vänersborg: the Sunday school, the deer with tufts by the hooves hanging on hooks over the saw-dusted marble floor, the limping organ-player breathing like bellows, the sign saying By Royal Appointment, the service-berries and the moss and the little glass of sulphuric acid that kept the damp out of the double glazing, the sound of laundry batlets from the river . . .?

The fragments of letters left nothing but gaps. The documentation was poor; many messages had disappeared.

When the sandstorm went across the savanna and the steppe country which was half desert, there was a cruel and uncontrollable spirit living in it, who tore and pulled at him, gave him tired stinging eyes and the inclination to lie down under sacks to avoid the creaking and whizzing, the melody of hopelessness, which blunted his feelings, smothered his resolutions, and ravaged his powers.

When Axel Ericson died, fifty-four years old, in Damaraland, his servants buried him. The first night they kept watch for the hyenas. Then they dispersed. They deserted the man who could no longer protect them.

The message about his death reached Vänersborg six months later. Little canal steamers, after reloading in Gothenburg, shipped animals from Ericson for years, well into the twentieth century. Some of them were already conserved, whereas others were merely drawn by him. The custom's official and the biology teacher were the recipients, and it was to them like receiving greetings from an extinguished planet, carried on light waves through an immense vacuum.

A zebra mongoose and a Nubian cat were put into glass cases, increasing the numbers in the limited space. There were apparently ordinary finches and sparrows, which might recently have migrated from the county. Discreet foster homes were arranged for these on farms in the Kinne district in exchange for well-curbs, churns and bridal hats for the Museum of Swedish Folklore. But Ericson's fauna could be found everywhere, and the bridal gifts from the district, kneading-troughs, and motley skirts, long formed part of the African ethnography department, which surprised nobody.

When Jenny and Jan left the restaurant, the moon was shining, the snow thawing, and the clouds drifting. In one house they looked into the drawing-room, where there were velvet shields on the walls with thousands of little badges on them. A white woven drape with a brown wood-grouse flapping its wings covered a door. On an old-fashioned radio the waveband gleamed. A man sat by a table, among hyacinth bulbs and white begonias, glueing: stamps, newspaper cuttings . . . He was watched by a stuffed owl.

'That one doesn't look Swedish,' Jenny said.

They walked on past some grey buildings, which had managed to hide away from the Co-op and the dredgers.

'In there there are lots of honey badgers and grey-footed squirrels,' Jenny suggested. 'Their glass eyes gleam in the dark. All this town is invaded by Ericson's animals. Night-jars and field-mice hide behind the second edition of the Scandinavian Encyclopaedia. If you look at letter L, you'll get a lemon finch in your hand.'

The silence was soft, a quilt of fur and down. A light smell of chloride came sweeping towards them. Jan breathed deeply.

'We're walking inside a huge glass case,' he said. 'The kind museum official has provided it with a couple of stars to make us feel at home. What's that sad song you're humming?'

'An English nursery rhyme,' Jenny said. 'I was thinking of the sun-birds.' She sang:

'Their wings are cut, and they cannot fly,

On Christmas Day in the morning.'

They had taken a room overnight not far from Residens Street. They sat on their beds looking at each other and the carpet, where they could imagine a discontinued pattern of dwarfed firs. The curtains were bright green. Before drawing them, Jan looked down on the street at Hermes the messenger service, Comrade the bicycle shop, and a firm of accountants. The snow was falling, wet, near freezing point.

The town was quiet under the stars. It was a peaceful pocket on the boisterous body of the Earth; an appendix running the risk of an operation.

'This is a happy period of my life,' JB said. 'That's why I can imagine others so easily.'

Jenny nodded, and joined her fingers with his. They were close to each other. Time was suspended in the air, and repeated moments that had been lived before, maybe other people's, maybe theirs, a long time ago.

She lay down on the bedspread. After half a minute she was fast asleep – that was one of her characteristics. She let go of his hand and was alone. He woke her up, as she screamed.

'I fell asleep,' she said. 'I had a dream you went to Botswana.' She put her fists to her eyes and said thoughtfully: 'Look Jan, I don't ever want to reduce your freedom. If you do something for me, against your own will, it would make me indebted to you, and you would feel restricted by me. It would lead us

77

nowhere. Then I'd be happier without you. I want you to be always happy.'

'So what do you mean? I lean on you only as long as you're there.' He noticed that he had told her this before. 'We must see clearly what we're drawing each other into. Nothing should give you a nasty surprise. Least of all you yourself.'

They clung together, as if straws for each other.

'I understand why Ericson came back here so seldom, though he probably wanted to come more often,' Jenny said later. 'There's a kind of innocence prevalent only in people who have never travelled. You can never return to them. There are journeys which there is no point in describing.'

He found nothing to say. They looked at each other, suddenly mute, as if it had become impossible for them to tell all the things that they ought to tell. They felt there was another story lying in ambush for them, and they had to get past, with noiseless steps, and without turning round.

THE CALABASH

They woke up with their room smelling of smoke. Jan went up to the window, and saw a white cloud in the sky in the direction of the museum and the High School. It stuck to a roof, and then a black cloud arose. They got dressed, and went out. It was almost morning, but still dark.

'I'm sure the sun-birds are on fire,' Jan said to Jenny, 'and all the letters, along with the bear hunter's spinning rod.'

It was a men's outfitters a few streets away. Sparks were dancing in the snow. A male dummy had caught fire, flames licked his trousers and got hold of a handkerchief in his pocket. His hips melted away like a muddy river.

A book and stationery shop next door, specializing in religious books, had not yet been reached by the flames. A fireman took a stone and threw it through the shop window. The circulation of air let the fire jump in and occupy the premises. It found the shelves with cameras and film, which exploded

78

and melted with dull puffs. The novels were next. The firemen waited until the flames touched the backs of the books. Then they applied the hose and swept all the books down onto the floor, where they dissolved into a wet porridge of paper-pulp and unspeakable words.

When destruction had reached the total value of the insurance sum, the fire seemed to calm down.

In the shop window of the men's outfitters there was a huge copy of Rembrandt's gladiator in a golden helmet: a fire captain from hell. A male dummy, whose facial features had melted to feminine softness, leant naturally exhausted against a wall.

The owner of the stationery shop suddenly came out of his shop, with a sooty face, and dressed in a dark suit. 'In an hour's time I'll start selling fire damaged goods,' he said to Jan and Jenny. 'Low prices.'

JB was surprised at his presence of mind. Maybe he ought to buy a few eight hundred piece jigsaw puzzles, which the man had under his arm: The Water-Lily Lake, The Kitchen, Vanity Fair. Some pieces were probably singed round the edges, and would be difficult to piece together.

'Are you going to rebuild?' he asked the owner.

'I'll see about that. The Town Council could rent the lot for a car park, but it won't be empty for too long.'

'The life of generations gone in a flash,' Jenny said. 'You can't help watching it, because it will soon be forgotten.'

'Heaven and earth shall burn . . . but there was something in the song which did not burn.'

'I'm glad I haven't got a house. But you have.'

'I don't feel I have,' JB said. 'The Water Palace was created by those who lived there before me. I'm not very concerned about having a place of my own.'

'Most people are. I'm at home at Nybro Quay, I wouldn't want to change it for anything. Yet it will be pulled down in due course. It's too near the City Centre.'

Later on in the morning they returned the reference material they had borrowed from the museum, and continued south by train. The domestic air routes did not include Skåne.

In Kristianstad they met Jenny's friend Veronica. She was a lawyer with the County Council financial department. She was engaged in locating homes and factories.

The landscape changed every year, she said, new products were found, and people moved about. It was a large jigsaw puzzle that could never be completed. Taking out a piece, you found it showed something unexpected, and then you had to start again from the beginning.

JB said he felt the regional plans aimed at giving people as great a distance as possible to commute, to make sure that they had no time to react to either the regional plans or anything else they were subjected to. They should go through life in a tired fog. 'It's not too bad in a small town,' Veronica said, 'but people here often live on opposing impulses. They are aggressive, and yet want to please everybody. They want to triumph but fear real competition. The worst problem is that so few of them have any real job satisfaction.'

'Will they have to lash us to drive us together?' JB said. 'Men have their experiences in the military service, and women their ordeals in the maternity wards. Some people thought they lived for the first time during the Blitz in the London underground stations. That's the attraction of submitting, which allows the situation to get the better of you.'

'People who exploit their working hours, also exploit their leisure time,' Veronica said. 'Self-confidence at work makes socializing easier.'

'A person with a dynamic self-knowledge,' Jenny said, 'can attract new experiences and develop in that way. If you're not responsible for your station in life, you can experience neither success nor defeat. If people are unhappy at work, or amass in the suburbs, they easily become indifferent. They watch when other people are assaulted in the street.'

'Who is dynamic?' JB asked.

'The person who moves his positions according to new challenges,' Jenny suggested.

Veronica lived in an area with angular moats and ponds, the remains of old fortifications. She rented the top floor of a private house, where the ground floor was occupied by a widow who spent a great deal of the year with her daughter in Gothenburg. She had plenty of space and her own kitchen. They were spending the night in one of her rooms.

Jenny walked over to the County Hall to meet the architect who supervised unit plans. JB took a walk in the town. His mac was stained with dirt from various cities. He thought of times not long ago, when he could have walked anywhere just to see Jenny for a few minutes. He saw an old blackened Norwegian stove thrown out in a backyard, and winter laundry hanging pale and fluffy from frost: flannel pyjamas, long underwear, net tights, and thick socks.

On the postcards in his file of facts there was never snow. Jenny had made a journey with him to project summer onto the white screen of winter.

Within him his happiness was racing with something else: a wondering awe that they had so much time, a sweep of memories of all those hours he had spent missing her at his job, alone, with Gertrude, or other people. And yet he liked to remember the places of his yearnings, as these were connected with Jenny too.

The sun was so low at the opening of a street that he could have stretched out his hand to roll it up into a gateway. At some traffic-lights he waited next to a car, and heard the weather forecast: In White Bank and Helgoland Bay, moderate or strong north-easterly winds with showers of snow and bad visibility.

His job was finished. He did not have to give any more lectures. He was at the end of a series of themes which had been debated in Swedish towns for decades: Fairy-tales for people hungry for education, about missionaries who never returned, about Livingstone, Bellman and Lincoln, about suffragettes and inventors, about the possibilities of life in outer space, about the malaria fly and the extinction of the blue whale.

On days like this he felt available, open to meetings without an appointment. His loved one was at a conference, and he himself did not have to go out shopping. He thought the houses had human features, even the corners of the mouth of the transformer seemed to twitch like lightning. He felt like nudging other people on the pavement, smile at them and exchange some words. He was open to them, providing the world looked the same to them, not inaccessible and secretive, closed or conspiratorial, chasing them with a raised whip.

There were other days, he knew, when he felt threatened and had to clam up, or he would flow off towards other people like an egg when the membrane bursts in the frying-pan and it runs out in all directions. He then clammed up in order to keep things he needed to cling to. That was a way of reducing them. Still, he held on to them with some distorted sense of self-preservation.

In a book called 'The Morning of The Magicians' he had read about an experiment. A monkey put his hand into a calabash full of peanuts, clenched its hand around the nuts, but could not pull it out again. The instinct to hold on to the food was stronger than the ability to release the hand. The monkey starved. It literally had its life in its hand.

JB bought a hot dog in the Square. The man at the hot dog stand turned out to be a Yugoslav. He had conquered a bastion, which was very difficult to reach in the Great Power of Sweden. Jan watched the tomato ketchup spurting out over the transparent skin of an unknown substance. He could feel an unchecked appetite for life, and an uncertain inclination to use it in a productive way.

He had a lot of parallel and instantaneous experience which balanced each other. His lips were lowered towards a nipple, and a mouse started to nibble behind the skirting-boards.

Like thin pipe smoke a white streak moved across the sky in the easterly wind. He could take a photo now, knowing that the present would soon be past, would soon be long ago.

'I've never loved anyone but . . .' Headlines at the bus station : an actress talking about her husband, who was also famous. Many people rushed to read the stimulating moving article about love protected by the words 'not' and 'never' against the rest of the world. You and only you. But you'll have to stay with me, and reward me for my exclusive taste, and be my unscratched jewel, glittering only for me. Of two people, only one remains.

Outside the Baptist Church a man stood looking around him. He looked wet, as if he had just been saved from drowning in the sea of salvation.

I'm not in the least afraid of Jenny, JB thought. Love would be impossible, if he felt threatened by her existence.

When he came back to Veronica's house, he met her and Jenny; they were angry and thoughtful, talking about a local shooting range, the gravel-pits nearby, and the airfield in the midst of the pastures at Sturup, where birds were abundant . . . Jenny said she felt like giving up. The policy of balance was being taken too far. Economy against ecology, death against life . . . Aiming for the happy medium, they ended up in limbo, a half-dead nothing; they gave you a hare tasting of rabbit.

'You mustn't give up,' Veronica said. 'Men expect the women not to infiltrate. Too many women are forced to live supported by men. They ought to make themselves indispensable in their own way, they should get the man to say: I can't live without you. But if a woman offers to take care of his job instead of his household, then she lets him down, as he builds his house only for her, to make her feel secure and well-favoured in her nursing profession. "Aren't you happy at home?" the man asks his woman, when she wants to work. "Aren't you happy at home?" the woman asks her husband, when he disappears with another woman. "What have I done to deserve this?" they both ask. Time for fresh discussions regarding agreements.'

'Air, more air,' Jenny said.

They walked round the moat while they talked. The ice was black with bubbles like fisheyes in it. JB stuck his foot out to burst the ice crust with the tip of his toe. Jenny threw some stones, which jingled on different notes and stayed out among the reeds where the ice was wrinkled like cloth. The finger-tips contracted. Veronica had bought an eel-pout stuffed with roe, and cooked dinner for all of them. It weighed five pounds, and they had some difficulty skinning it.

The head was discarded in the garbage. The remainder was cut into thick slices like a rack of meat. The huge liver was divided into equal portions. The eel-pout was poached in its own water. The harsh, complicatedly stale taste was gingered up with pepper and lemon, and the firmness of the flesh: the sole of the lakes.

'In June I start to get bored with the town,' Veronica said. 'I have a friend who has a boat in Åhus, but it's very windy outside the reefs, the water of Hanö Bay is cold, and there are no islands where you can go ashore.'

'What is this?' JB asked. 'A cigar cutter?'

'A stone remover. We'll use it for the morello cherries.'

She served the dark stewed berries ice-cold with whipped cream. The stones rattled against the edge of the plates.

Veronica had a resigned air about her – as if she had missed a turning-point. But her movements had a certain energy,

83

which contradicted that impression. A person who has given up would not be able to move so easily. She had a quick smile, as if she was really shy but at the same time used to frank discussions.

JB regarded independent women like her as brilliant throws of a dice, which companies and civil service departments dared not double. Therefore they turned into islands, some a little lonelier than others, and sometimes a little more bitter, an outline of the male unity, which flourished at the Rotary and Lions Clubs, at sports clubs and social gatherings.

'As a woman I have to prove all the time that I'm as good as a man,' Veronica said. 'The difference is greater in my spare time. The others are a group, they get up early and run round the water tower, take a sauna in somebody's house, and arrive at work red-faced and happy.'

'There is emotional blackmail going on,' Jenny said. 'We are told that we despise our femininity, want to beat men, and get bored at home. We must remember to please ourselves or society more than the men. We must not let ourselves be lured into security or enticed by significant looks indicating that we are promiscuous or frigid. No one would judge a man like that. But a female Head of Department is seen as a security risk, and the way our working life is constructed, she probably is. The moment the women start to use their liberation, the whole conception of society has to be re-thought.'

'You have to conquer a job or a position,' Veronica said, 'just like the hero of a bad short story conquers a woman. Tolerance, co-operation, everyday life – these things are not exciting.'

'As soon as somebody talks about men and women in general terms, you have to remember that they are talking about the different kinds of behaviour which they see around them. They see innate characteristics, where living conditions are at stake. They believe something is given to them by nature, when it is in fact created by human beings. They forget that everything can be changed and could look different.'

JB tried to feel the nape of Veronica's neck in his hand. It gave no particular signals. He was hardly conscious of his bad habit of using his hands as an invisible divining-rod. His palms smiled, and little waves of laughter danced ahead over his finger-tips. Such things just happened. An unreliable game. In an unsensuous way he liked Veronica's face, beautiful, thin, with dark eyes.

'I don't believe in what I'm doing as strongly as I used to,' Veronica said. 'The edges of my area are too blurred. It should be larger, or much smaller. I come across ideas which can be carried out on a very confined level, but they become impossible when they concern regions, with everything else that is involved there.'

'There are alternatives,' Jenny said, 'but the disadvantage is that they aren't quite real until we experience them. At least we shouldn't be afraid of exposing ourselves to them.'

'Alternatives,' Veronica said, 'mean that all the time there should be parallel ways of living together, going to school, and planning a city.'

'Yes,' Jenny said. 'If only people were not like driftwood, letting everything float away and blaming the course of life. At the same time they are so reluctant to change themselves. Only circumstances are allowed to change them, because that gives them a reason to complain.'

'If I could only tighten the screw a little bit more,' JB said, 'I would discover things I can't see now. Now I don't notice whether I have my picnic on the shaft of a well, or on a bed of lava.'

He felt that one day it would have to be released, and then he would see not one road but several, and they would all be equally clear. He would be able to see how many kinds of fern existed. He would be out of the forest.

'All the time I worry about participating in the making of a world where my children won't want to live,' Jenny said.

We have a child growing in Africa, JB thought. And he could see before him Jenny, Gertrude and himself securing a push-chair on the roof rack of his car and going off somewhere with a newly made person in the backseat.

The eel-pout was finished, and the morello cherries. They were sitting in the upper hallway. A staircase led down to the rooms Veronica did not have access to. They played an LP of Wolf Biermann, and then turned on the television. On the screen, in a cloud of grey particles, an ice-hockey puck was creating history. They turned it off.

'I had an aunt,' Veronica said, 'who when she was widowed,

became aware of the problems outside her own family. Every year she would send cards to the world's statesmen wishing them a Happy New Year.'

'There's a good reason for that,' JB said.

'She died later, during a television quiz programme.'

Veronica made the fire in the tiled stove, and they felt they were in a country inn. The reddish-brown rag rug went across the floor up to a well-worn folding table. The blind was blue-grey with bleached golden coils and marks made by the string.

Jenny struck a chord on the piano. It was so badly tuned that every note tried to imitate the whole scale.

The fire soughed. Time passed.

In a speech to thank Veronica, JB talked about poetic materialism, implying that one should be neither a consumer, nor a puritan. Break away from the need to consume. Enjoy hidden daily resources. Spread what they did not believe they had; it might be found. There were the seasons, the different lights of day round the window, the grained surface of the table, the lingering taste in the mouth from the bottom of the lake, and last summer's berries.

He saw Jenny's alert face, suddenly a bit triangular. His body felt tight, inebriated but still clear. Like when a fly settles down on your face and your cheek muscles twitch, although you hardly know it.

They chatted until late, and then Jenny and Jan went to bed. There was a high bed in the room with a rough crocheted bedspread.

'Veronica has a lover she goes away with for some time in the summer,' Jenny said. 'He is married. I wonder how often they meet. Many men are frightened of women in high positions.'

Jenny had brought a novel by Joseph Roth for the journey. It was called The Radetsky March. She read out a piece to JB in bed. Her hip was pressed tightly against his, and as she turned a page, he could feel her elbow on his shoulder.

'In those days, before the World War, at the time of the events which I am relating on these pages, it was not yet a matter of indifference whether a man was dead or alive. If somebody had departed from the earthly shores, his memory was not immediately obliterated by another. He left a void, and both the closer and the more distant witnesses of his

86

departure were silent whenever they saw this void. If fire
had destroyed a house in a street, the place was left vacant for
a long time. The walls came down slowly and deliberately,
and both nextdoor neighbours and casual passers-by saw the
site of the burnt house and remembered the shape and the
character it had had.'

That was where JB passed out. Without noticing Jenny continued: 'That was what it was like in those days. Whatever
grew needed a long time to grow, and whatever expired took
a long time to be forgotten. Whatever had been left its traces,
and in those days they lived in memories, as people nowadays live on the ability to forget quickly and effectively.'

SQUARE PUPILS

He had been out to the airport to see the management.
There were some people there, who he usually only com-
municated with by telex and radio. The hotel room in Malmö
was empty when he came back. He started to write a letter
to Jenny. He ordered some tea, and a red-headed waitress
brought a pot so stuffed with tea leaves that there was hardly
room for water. She stared at him blankly. He poured the tea
leaves down the lavatory, and rang for her again. Another
girl came to get the pot. He did not see her again.

'This is the room of freedom,' he wrote. 'I can see the long
streaks of light from the cars in the streets. The street-lamps
are moving, the whole town is moving – and that's how we
shall travel, that's how you shall come to me. I think life seems
as short as a year and filled with sensuality and matter. I dislike stability, I'd prefer living recklessly. Tomorrow night there
will be other people in our room, as we will be gone. Another
entry in the registration book. I feel like merging into the
December dusk, with the pigeons who form a crest on Karl
X Gustav in the square. I want to become nothing and be
nothing, neither good nor evil. I just want to exist as a large
eye in the middle of all this diversity. I feel like camouflaging

myself and becoming a stone, a tree, whatever is the most common and least obvious.

Words are so weak, they can't reach what I want to tell you, they can only suggest like rings on the water, never realizing whether it was a roach or the great flounder himself who dived. Strong verbs are needed to tell you how much I love you.'

He stood by the window trying to discern Jenny among the winter people in the square. Tenderness inside him swelled towards her like a tidal wave. He wanted to make an effort. He put the beds next to each other, and dragged the bedside tables across the floor. He was standing with a marble plate in his arms, when Jenny came in.

'Have you become a transport worker?' she asked, relieving him of his burden.

They were not inexhaustible, but they were two people who could create new situations for themselves. They told themselves that most of the things between them had not yet been invented.

He used her real name, the one her parents had given her, as he never used nicknames. He looked unobstructedly into her eyes. He put his hand over hers as he entered her. He stroked her pubic hair and laughed as, for a second, his fingers remembered a soft toy dog he had slept with as a child.

They tried to avoid the silliness of love: amulets and charms, diminutives, everything that made the greatness small and handy, bound in the freedom of palpable facts, secrets, domesticities; everything that could restrict strong feelings to private imagination, to a world of their own, consisting of toys and pretence.

'I'm really afraid of getting deeply involved,' Jenny said, 'but it's at least the best fear I've ever known. Meeting you has sharpened my senses. I think they'll work even if we get tired of one another.'

Somewhere the fibres of their roots started to twist round each other, fretting and supporting. Nothing was left to chance any more. They discarded the images they had invented, and started to see each other. You are the one I met, not the one I imagined. I don't own you, but we own something together.

They had now reached a more even level. Not the climax

and worry of the stolen seconds. Something went on without blurring the outlines or consuming the oxygen.

They had more time, but used it to stop themselves, to turn to each other and watch. They feared the sleepy happiness.

There were different pictures of love. One showed the absolute feeling once love had been stated, where nothing had to be questioned and no shadows were seen; everything followed a secure repeated pattern.

But there was another picture of love, which tried everything again, day by day. Promises were mistrusted, no continuity taken for granted. Every morning was a fresh start.

They wanted to dwell somewhere between these two extremes. Trust each other in the way friends do, and still be forced to the effort and awareness which you afford to your friends, if they are not tied to you by family relations or any other involuntary proximity.

'When you're in love,' Jenny said, 'the two meet: responsibility and recklessness, inside and outside. You're within reach of all experiences and, just as quickly, out of reach.'

'Love brightens up reality, even if there does not seem to be room for it.'

JB rubbed his head against her vagina, till he was wet up to the roots of his hair. She let her fingers pass over the bend of his knee, till pleasure rose inside him like heavy joy, and he found his way into the warmth under her low vault.

'When I cup my hand around your balls,' Jenny said, 'I feel you're coming right out of my arm, from my own hand into me.'

He hardly knew who of them came. Sometimes he would caress her until she reared herself with a loud cry, sometimes she would kiss his penis until he showered her shoulder.

'I just hope it can remain a game with you and not a game with words,' she said. People can change within each other's sight and get into unbalanced states, as we know. I hope the awareness between us will save us from feeling ignored, sad, or envious. The language joins together, and adds to our knowledge. It looks after the misunderstandings and the appearances. What has happened to us is a gift which must not be corroded or used for something else.

Thus they exchanged words and gestures. With memories and looks, references and images, they got into each other's stores and warehouses. They assumed each other's patterns and echos, tones of voice and sensitivities, and out of this the so called togetherness was born. They were congenial.

'My holiday is over,' Jenny said the next morning. 'I have to go home and get down to some serious work.'

'I'll come with you.'

'Stay if you like,' she said.

They were no freer than that. That was how free they were.

She feared that he might do too much for her sake; yet she also feared that he might feel he had to convince her of the opposite.

She then told him that in the Malmö museum she had seen a poster which had confused her greatly. It was many years ago.

'Let's go there,' JB said. 'We've got a couple of hours to spare before our flight.'

The museum was a part of Malmöhus Castle. They crossed the drawbridge, and entered the silent halls. A man with bright red cheeks looked like the boss: he was half running, and told the caretaker he was going to a meeting of the County Council.

At the end of a corridor they found the poster. It was as grey as the light outside. Jenny read out: ' "At night, in deepest darkness, their eyes allow them to discern objects unnoticeable to other eyes. The pupils of their eyes are thus conditioned, and the pupil, which should be round and black, is instead square and a glowing red colour like fire".'

'What animals are these?' Jan asked.

'They are not animals. They are heliophobes.'

These were people with black parents, although they were themselves of an incomparable white colour and indescribably beautiful. They had appeared at the Hotel Stadt Hamburg in Malmö more than a hundred years ago, and claimed to be the most beautiful people existing in those days, with skin like the whitest alabaster, silvery woolly hair, and white beards which gave them a majestic and serious appearance. Fine down like on the neck of a swan covered their eyebrows and eyelids. Their eyes could not take the daylight, so they lived many metres beneath the surface of the Earth.

On the picture of the poster the eyes looked matt. They

were said to have come from inner Africa, but where exactly was not mentioned. What language they spoke was not revealed either. It was in the days when Axel Ericson would run through Vänersborg with meat scraps to Lloyd the bear hunter. They were called heliophobes, as they shunned the light and the sun. Beside this, little was known about their activities. They did not want to give away their secrets to the rest of mankind.

They flew from Malmö, and landed at the enclosed Bromma airport.

'Hungry?' JB asked, as they stood in the Arrivals Hall.

'We had a nice dinner here once,' Jenny said. 'Klas Lundin found us out. It was a nice day.'

'Shall we go there?'

'Not today. We'll come back here.'

A bright yellow bus called Boel took them through the suburban landscape of low industrial buildings, the zone of lifeless nature, exploited soil and unorganized ground surfaces, which is often found around large cities. Near Solna they saw huge grey and bright blue facades, gleaming to the highest standard: the slum timed for the next generation.

They were alone in the bus which stopped at Sergel Square. The staircase of a derelict house stretched happily towards a cloud. They were in the centre of the capital.

For the first time Jenny came with him to the flat in Uppland Street. There were two letters on the door-mat.

'Gertrude's handwriting,' JB said.

He read the letters.

'Do you want to know how Gertrude is?'

'Does she send me her love?' was Jenny's counter question.

'No.'

'Then the letters are very private.'

'Marianne Tidström is coming home. Gertrude writes quite a bit about her loneliness, and how strange it is for her not to know what I'm doing every day.'

'But she doesn't send me her love?' Jenny repeated.

Her voice was impersonal. He did not reply, but went on reading out the letters.

'I don't mind if you want to go away,' Jenny interrupted him. 'Love can't pass away. I just wish there wasn't any virtue in waiting.'

91

'You won't have to wait. I don't know where I should go.'

Jenny headed for the door.

'Are you going?' JB said, surprised.

She looked sad. They were silent. It was like the spring of the wheel of luck stopping for a moment and hesitating. One could not tell how much was due to the obstacle, and how much to the power of the wheel being exhausted.

'I think you want to be alone to reply to her letters,' Jenny said.

Closing the door after her, he felt unjustly disappointed.

'I'm sitting here looking for a solution to our problem,' Gertrude wrote. 'Sometimes I believe I've found it, and feel as happy as a child finding a glass bead on the floor.

I don't know if I ever told you this: I was ten at the pension in Switzerland, and I broke my necklace. It consisted of little green glass beads; I thought it was chrysophrase. I crawled on the floor picking up the beads, which had gone everywhere. One got stuck in the rubber pattern on the sole of my sport shoes, and walked about with me for days.

A week later, when my necklace had already been restrung, I saw a gleam in the corner between my desk and the window niche. I ran there to get the green bead, undid the string of my necklace, and had a lot of trouble undoing the clasp. But when I wanted to put the bead on the string, it had no hole.

I weeped with surprise. It was unreal like a nightmare. I turned it in my hand. Then I put the necklace away, and never wore it again.

Only last year I realized that I had found a green glass ball of the type used in ink stands to keep the pen upright.

Time after time I think I can see the solution. I feel happy, but then I feel like one of those beads without a hole that does not fit in anywhere, can't be put on any string. And it doesn't console me that I know you must be unhappy too, at this stage.'

Jan Backman wrote back:

'A solution to what? Try to understand that I love the two of you. Jenny and I have been on a winter journey. On December 3rd, we started our tour around Swedish towns. It was a sunny, sparkling day, with the smoke from the factories as straight as ramrods. We took the train to Örebro . . .'

He wrote with an abundance of warmth, convinced that she would understand what Jenny had misunderstood. During the course of the night, images from their journey arose. He told her of his joy, forgetting that Gertrude was not only his sister.

CHRISTMAS CUSTOMS

They became very busy. The charter air-traffic reached its winter peak, and JB was fully occupied sending people into exile. Jenny was writing an official report.

Veronica came to see Jenny the week-end before Christmas. The three of them went up into the Kaknäs Tower, which was off season and had a cafeteria. They saw mainly their own faces in the window looking out on the world. The fog was tottering outside, and came down a bit further to obscure even the closest objects: coal supplies, cisterns, and grey water. Afterwards they skied through sparse forests. Nobody could remember such a snowy December.

After searching for a long time, they found the dogs' cemetery at Lidingö Bridge. The colour of the plastic flowers had come out onto the snow. Anybody could come here to bury Susy, Roy or Fido. 'God's Beautiful Creation, All We Had' was, according to the inscription on the tombstone, the name of an elderly sheepdog. Pete, the budgie, was asleep under a cross, blue like his own former colour. A St Bernhard had been consigned to a sarcophagus large enough to house a human family.

Klas Lundin lived in the neighbourhood. Hare tracks ran across the snow, which had not been cleared away for a day or so. They rang his bell, though it was obvious that he was not in. JB wondered whether he had gone away. In a day one could get far – all the way to Botswana, if one wanted to.

Then once more they were out on snow-free roads, with the salt rubbing on their skis.

They waved good-bye to Veronica at the railway station.

93

Shoes, bringing in sand off the streets, creaked against the stone slabs. There was brown slush in the streets. Down in the Old City alleyways the snow was still white and untouched; so fresh that it showed people's tracks for several metres: heels with V-marks, children's boots, and a bicycle drawing a serpentine pattern. They dived into the ground like mice, preparing a temporary home in a basement restaurant named after the quail, which, according to his book on birds, was seldom seen by people, although it was common in the south of Sweden.

Jan Backman picked Jenny up outside the Department of The Environment one day when her car was being serviced. Hoar-frost and snow concealed a pile of rubbish, the lavatory drains, and the gullies of refuse. The misery was powdered over. The snowed-up government departments were the most beautiful.

Within a couple of kilometres' radius from this Department were refuse dumps, car wrecks, pails, cans, rubber tyres, the indisposable plastic containers, assorted remains and waste; all this which is sometimes called the greatest national product of the world.

'Next to Kumla prison we've got the longest corridor in Sweden,' Jenny said. 'The department employs one thousand people, and we keep expanding. Everybody has suddenly got an environment programme. County councillors phone up just to be able to tell their friends that they have been in contact.'

Another day Jan ran through the Arrivals Hall at Arlanda to buy newspapers and exchange some words with the Hall Manager. He unexpectedly saw Jenny there, and stopped short. He was pale and about to faint. Then he noticed that she was not approaching the ticket counter, but a telephone booth. She soon came out again, and he rushed up to her. Jenny had no idea of his shock, or his relief. It was as if they had not seen each other for a long time. They chatted happily:

'I thought you were running away,' JB said. 'I'm prepared for everything.'

'I just wanted to surprise you. But they said at the tower that you were out.'

'How could I know you were here?'

'I didn't want you to know.'

He felt he was balancing her at the end of his finger-tips. If she fell off, she would be near the ground.

Jenny spent Christmas in Scheele Street with her mother and relatives. If she had taken JB, it would have seemed to them a matter of accomplishment. They did not want to provoke that image. For the first time, Jan was spending Christmas Eve on his own, and he looked forward to it. He had turned down an offer to spend Christmas with Eklund, the meteorologist, who knew that Gertrude was in Botswana but nothing else.

In the evening JB walked in the empty City Centre. He passed the hotel where Jenny had booked in after running away from John. A Christmas tree next to the porter's desk concealed the Coca-Cola machine. The merchandise in this area had changed from fishing equipment, pawn goods and mattresses to vibrators, films in the tobacconists' inner rooms and all sorts of pornographic paraphernalia. The hotel looked still quite respectable in these changed surroundings.

At a Post Office in Malmskillnad Street he sent a Christmas greetings telegram to Gertrude. Walking on, he reflected how the words would probably be distorted by many intermediate hands before they reached her.

The bus traffic was practically cancelled. A lonely group of youths went like a miniature cyclone through the unploughed streets. Under a tarpaulin on a demolition site there was a light: unknown men, stretching themselves out on old blankets sewn together, celebrated the birth of Christ.

The security men at Hay Square saw neither stars nor cleaners' lights gleaming along their way. The dawn was expected in a thousand years, and whatever happened, happened somewhere else. Around a completely empty kernel, the last rolling stones fell from the pressure of the snow into hollow depressions. The rest of the city spread out.

It was a city where one person in eight was a pensioner, often alone, living on carbohydrates in slum houses in the city with department stores and car parks. Those who already had plenty of money made more money on them.

When Jan came home the telephone rang.

'May I have a cab to Scheele Street,' somebody said in a loud voice.

Jan, at first not recognizing her voice, was prepared to hang

95

up. Then he understood, and ran down to start his car. A little while later they were on their way to Nybro Quay. Jenny said:

'I must get some of the smoke out of my clothes. Let's take a walk round Blasieholmen.'

Queen Victoria's Naval Home was closed for Christmas, but below the shed of the Waxholm Company there was a light in a ship. Silent gulls fluttered about like agitated angels. Ducks floated asleep on the greyish water. The beaks of the bald coots looked like white almonds in the middle of Christmas gingerbread.

They met a woman with a dachshund. They themselves were only airing their shadows. These walked on short leashes under the street-lamps, but between the luminous spots they ran ahead of or behind their masters.

The Great Church looked at them with its cold green eye. Jenny's car was parked at the petrol station. The statues had lost their shapes under the snow in the park by the National Museum. The Foster Brothers looked deep into each other's eyes, and had not discovered the youth who had eyes only for a turtle. Jenny and Jan took a firm grip of each other at the socle of The Wrestlers. They kissed each other's lips, rough from the cold. The tips of their noses were cold, but the tips of the tongues connected the warmth of their bodies.

JB liked Jenny's sparsely furnished flat. She seemed to live with little luggage, as free as a bachelor. The courtyard looked as it had done a hundred years ago: dust-bins, rusty spouts, and passages. In the other direction was the Strand with Christmas trees standing two by two on the balconies, symmetric and with the same lights. Jenny made tea, and poured some rum into it. A candle, as thick as an arm, was in the middle of the floor. They sat naked on the window-sill looking out. It was dark at Strand Hotel, and the Academy of Music was silent. The wet snow tipped into the bay was drifting on top of the water like winter plankton. Some church-bells chimed, but the rest were silent. In certain places time had stopped, so that it did not disturb people.

They could hear music from the flat below.

'When I went to mother's they started off with a drinking song,' Jenny said. 'Now they've reached the hymns.'

Jan noticed that the blue apothecary bottle with gold print

96

that John had broken, had been replaced by another, almost the same. He mentioned it.

'He broke it because he was jealous of us. I did not consider that a good enough reason for losing a medicine bottle, so I found another one. It was one of the few things I was attached to, and he knew it.'

Jan held the inside of her thin elbows, feeling the softness of her arm. He was swinging to and fro at the corner of her mouth.

On the bed under the open window they caressed each other gently but for a long time and fully, in places that were seldom caressed and forgotten because they were insignificant or insensitive. These places woke up happily, and happiness spread to all parts of their bodies. They were looking at each other all the time, sometimes laughing. They were lying on their sides with Jenny's kneecaps high up against his armpits. He let himself be lead under her protective skin, which closed around him. He was embedded in her. They did not move. He thought they had reached the same subterranean water.

Waking up on Christmas Day, they found a heap of snow as large as a gull on the old-fashioned oak parquet floor. Jenny cleared it away, but it left a dark stain, a winter trademark in the shape of a quill-feather.

No newspapers arrived that day, and in some places around the world there were truces. JB read. Jenny had work to do.

They gave each other a present. He was given a picture of an Anemone Vernalis, its petals shed, with funny hairy tentacles like a jelly-fish on land. She had bought it in an antique shop around the corner. JB would put it up in his office at Arlanda. These anemones grew on the barren rolling stone ridges around the airport.

'I've got something more practical for you,' he said.

He had bought a pair of rough tweed trousers in a men's outfitters behind the Dramatic Theatre. Then he had gone to a tailor's in Riddar Street, and booked an appointment for Jenny, because he was sure that the waist would have to be taken in.

They ate and slept together. Another day was made their common property. They did not speak much about Gertrude. JB thought they were happy.

THE PROTECTED AREA

One of the days between Christmas and New Year they went to the Water Palace. They had not been there on their own before. Jan wanted to show Jenny that nothing of his past or his possessions could stand in their way.

To him homes were exchangeable. He had as usual that autumn locked up the Water Palace for the winter season, and moved into town as if he were not returning there until the warm weather. This was a customary action of reassurance, but he did not really believe in it. He did not want any more from the house; it had served a couple of generations, given him a push. Now it was time to move on.

The Water Palace had once appeared to him as an extension of his body. A roofing-tile came down, and he would bury his head in his hands. A board came loose, and he grit his teeth. As the house creaked in the night, he thought of his old age. It was inscribed in him. He could leave it in peace, but sounds brought him back: the creaking of rowlocks, the rattling of a tin tub as water was poured over a flower bed, and the dragon-fly hovering like a helicopter over the quaking grass.

They parked their car on the headland, and walked the last bit. The snow filled up the bootlegs. Mice tracks led from all directions into the house, which crouched there like a spider in its web. Jan unlocked, and the scents of summer poured out of a bag that had held them captive. A couple of autumn leaves had blown in across the threshold, when Jan last locked the door. The scattered tea leaves on the draining-board were rat droppings.

Jan managed to get the Aga cooker alight with newspapers, limp from the damp air. Cold oozed out of the pores of the walls, covering every surface with dampness as they got the fire going. An iron pot had white garlands on the outside as if the frost had forced out the last residue of grease.

JB stood stock-still for a moment. The walls of the Water

Palace seemed like a leaking shell, enclosing desolation, uselessness, and summer passions with a trail of pain.

He was surprised at Jenny's detachment. She was walking about in beige skiing trousers, strapped under her soles with elastic. She spoke of cultural history where he saw nightmares, thunderstorms, and playful, absentminded embraces.

'So this is where you live,' she said smiling, with a shade of pity, he imagined.

'No, this is just a place I drifted through. The Water Palace belonged to others. They found shelter here, just far enough from the sea. They never repainted that door in regulation brown – and nor did we, Gertrude and I.'

Everything spoke of Gertrude so clearly that he withdrew a little from Jenny, from lack of habit or shyness. As adults he and Gertrude had spent their holidays at the Water Palace. They had rarely travelled. And yet they had changed so little of the original environment that they had taken over: the useless rubbish had been cleared out and a well drilled. But the old well was still there, silted up over the years, and now a frog pond which the frogs probably never left. In the winter the water in it did not freeze, and looking down into the well, you could see groups of fully grown frogs like embryos along the walls, awaiting the spring.

They had also had a water heater installed. Once – in their grandfather's day – a young girl would come in in the morning to leave a mug of hot shaving water on the bedside table. Who was she? Someone from a local smallholding since abandoned? Someone who would do anything for the extra income in the summer, and moreover, could have a bath in the wooden tub? What had been said about her when she left? A good worker, quick and neat. And then she was gone. The bathing-hut collapsed when a tank vessel once threw up a too heavy wash on the shore. It had lain there like an untidy pile of timber, until somebody chopped it up.

'Is there much left from your childhood?' Jenny asked.

'Most of it. But it's been there all the time, so it doesn't remind me of my childhood any more.'

He showed her some old match-boxes in a wall cupboard, Klondyke Coldrain's Matches, and producer gas matches. 'To be kept in the car, not in a pocket.'

And in the attic, he told her, was his old quilt in a clothes basket. His mother had embroidered a letter of the alphabet on each square. He could remember nights he spent reading them with his fingers, learning to recognize them. This quilt had been his ABC book. It was long after his mother's death.

The past, like a vine on the wall, clung to the unmingled present, which he and Gertrude had considered their property. And who can tell what belongs here or what belongs there, how it was then and how it is now? You cannot stop contamination, for you do not know from which shelf you get one thing, and from where you get another. Maybe the things were drag anchors, which kept you on the right keel, and stopped you deviating from the course? Jan might have a couple of things that he wanted to keep if he could. Sten Tidström had not unmoored completely when he went to Botswana; he still had his things in Stockholm, and they did not tie him down.

He thought about his father on another continent. He had left behind a three-legged monk's chair in dark stained birchwood with a green tasselled cushion, a hollow wooden Arctic loon afloat on the floor boards, and deep in a drawer a bunch of way-bills from the steamers of the turn of the century: '. . . admit to have taken aboard my vessel . . . and undertake, safe on arrival, to deliver the above goods in like condition to . . .'

Jan saw Noah's Ark, tossing on the sea of life, with all living creatures gathered under its deck in a sort of inaccessible and unclassifiable community. And then land had been sighted, and it had all been set down on a jetty, in like condition.

At the Water Palace with Jenny, he looked with sudden tenderness, mingled with disquiet, at the old furniture which had once been transported there by sea. Perhaps they were now losing their significance for ever, slipping out of the present. Perhaps they did not have a home there any more, as a truth can only be realized to be true where it belongs. Perhaps they were stray nomads, and could no more be responsible for the house where they had ended up.

One wall of the entrance hall was covered with nautical charts. JB traced the names and the fathom lines. The navigable channels were marked with dotted lines, and the land, empty of names, looked like a grey tundra.

Often when waiting for Gertrude to get ready, he had stood

there navigating with his eyes. Here were the limits for the protected area; and there the lines marking 'passage through this area at your own risk' ceased. Within the protected area where they lived, he had had to apply for permits for foreign visitors. That was not necessary any more. The area could only reveal that the military plants were not from this century.

Nothing was revealed by Jenny being there. The district simply had yet another secret added to it.

'Let's go out while the house warms up,' he said to Jenny.

The snow in the courtyard was flecked with soot. The western wind could have carried it from the Stockholm factories. Certain winds brought black snow. The red rose hips were topped by a white dollop. Jenny said : 'When it was early morning and hot and the gravel was dry, I stood here, saying that you and Gertrude loved each other. I was intruding here on you and Gertrude.'

'Yes,' he said. 'You're my intruder.'

'I mean I'm very happy and yet so sad for Gertrude that I could give it all up.'

He understood. The thought of Gertrude's sadness streaked their happiness like soot. Between his fingers he crumbled some grey bitter wormwood flowers sticking up dry through the snow.

'Let's make sure we don't get married,' Jenny said.

'That won't be too hard if we decide in good time.'

'For then, suddenly, one doesn't see the other. One asks oneself when the other one is coming, and also why he isn't coming, which is silly. Why should anyone come ?'

They did not know what living together continuously would be like. Perhaps they would give in to each other's wishes till these unnoticeably merged and ceased to be wishes. Perhaps they would listen into each other until their union seemed to be heart-felt and everlastingly joined together, and the words they needed to exchange for confirmation would only be words of extreme importance or extreme triviality.

Better than the achievement of such togetherness was the astonished knowledge of a common basis under the unknown. The experience of the closest proximity to the goal at the outset of the expedition, not at the end. They could bear to see each other denuded and exposed and to know each birth-mark, but they were too weak to live without the astonishment.

The outer world was tapping on the door, waves or ice-floes from the broken channel. The snow with half an inch of crust, suitable for a push-sledge. There were shades of pink and blue in the sky wanting to efface each other, like kitchen china worn out by years of washing and yet as new. The iron black catkins of the ash-trees anchored the afternoon.

JB investigated the flag-pole socket. One of the planks was rotten. He was lucky to discover it, because the pole could have fallen on the house in the first westerly storm. They loosened the screws, attacked the frozen ground with an iron bar, pulled the last supporting planks out of the ground, and let the pole fall the last bit. It lay flat on the snow. He needed to order some new timber. There was a retired carpenter living at Torsvik, but he did not know when it could be raised again.

'There it is now,' Jan said. 'It looks pathetic.'

'Here we sat last summer, Gertrude and I,' Jenny said. 'We had a lot to talk about. I hope we'll be able to do so again some day, without discussing you. It's terrifying that we could talk about you as two women who know every expression on your face and in your voice, and the cold and the warmth of your eyes. Through you we might end up as one person.'

'That would be to honour me too much,' JB said.

'No, it would be to make you an object which we two mother figures can't do without, because we can't get rid of our passions. That's nothing to aspire to.'

JB remembered Jenny at the summer party. He had described the place beforehand, and told her that she could go there on some occasion when he and Gertrude were away. Then she could see what it was like. He liked to imagine her walking alone through the rooms, outside the circles of Backman generations, yet attentive as if it really concerned her. Then he had fervently wished that he would be able to say: 'There's always a room waiting for you at the Water Palace.'

The skerries were silent at this time of the year, as though the era of motor-boats was yet to come. Once a day one could hear the helicopter that delivered mail to the outer islands. Bird cries rose in the silence. The future was germinating under the snow.

They walked out on the ice to the broken channel. The coast was steep and rocky with pine and fir trees, and inbetween, the bare winter graphics. Certain outlines were as anonymous as faces in a crowd: others as clear as people he had watched for a long time, due to the landings he had made, his moorings among stones and wild flowers, and rowing trips across the calm water reflecting the world.

Warm air bubbles were trapped in the ice. Cracks ran inside the blocks without reaching the surface, linking the bubbles and hollowing out air blisters. Under the ice waves clucked, blind and captive.

They stopped by the channel, and looked down into the depths. The floes rattled like shingle, swayed and chafed.

'Glad you're on my side,' JB said.

'If we end up on separate sides, we must remember to turn round quickly and look to the shore,' Jenny said.

A family far away on touring skates reminded Jan of the children of the previous summer, the plunderers he and Gertrude had rescued from a capsized boat. He told Jenny about them, how he had sneaked off to Monica's window when she was asleep, in a sudden desire to see her. He did not understand it, it must have had something to do with his missing Jenny. He considered the situation and found it different. Most things in him were brought out by events and meetings and he knew nothing in advance. What filled him with lust on one occasion, gave him only repletion on another. He could not explain it.

From the frozen waters they could see how the Water Palace formed part of the family of inner skerries. In one direction was the sea landscape belonging to the summer visitors, in the other the countryside. The farming community had been practically rationalized away. Spindly farm machinery lay rusting behind high barns with sparse upright wall planks and no more hay to be aired. The landscape was on one side intercepted by young trees, which pressed on closer and closer in serried batallions; on the other by private and terraced houses surrounding the recreational grounds. A few fishermen still cast their nets for herring, and caught eel-pout and whitefish in the ice-holes. It was a long way to schools and youth centres, but some eccentrics – peculiar only because they knew their craft, took snuff and spoke their own minds – stayed in their low-ceilinged cottages.

It was only a degree or so below freezing. Water washed up

on the rocks became icing. The grass in the crevices had been bent by the snow, but had one day got their springing power back and straightened up, leaving deep traces in the snow cover. Now they were upright again, dry and yellow.

Some mooring bridles on the rocks had been eroded by rust. When they gave way, the coastline might bend slightly.

In the distance dull explosions could be heard, followed by sharper bangs like axe blows, all of it caused by the ice. Snow had spread over the pansy flower beds and garden seats. In his mind's eye JB could replace the landscape with other images: snow on a city street with motorists on their way home from the bandy* final, snow on a deserted beach on the English channel with grey bunkers from the Second World War surrounded by buckthorn.

Supplies were short at the Water Palace: a bottle of Akvavit in the fridge, some orange rusks and pumpernickel in the larder, and in the cellar potatoes, some tins, fermented blackcurrant juice, and hissing bats. Things you think in the autumn ought to survive the winter. They got provisions from a village store near Torsvik. It had been closed for a while, when the grocer and his wife drove their old Hudson back and forth on the German motorways. They had come across a side-wind in Holland, and then returned with rosy cheeks, disappointed because they had not got more stamps in their passports in the new borderless Europe. Now they had filled their counter with ham, sausages, mincemeat, and herrings in plastic bags. In the deep freeze there were fish fingers with tartar sauce enclosed.

The winter had moved indoors. They spread out the sheets cool from the basement, on the radiators. Every chair and bed radiated lethal cold. JB took Jenny's sheepskin coat off its hanger. They fell over on the smooth lining. Jenny lay flat on her back, quickly undoing his clothing. She made the tip of his penis travel along the inner pocket of the coat, bluntly reading the name of a furrier in Stockholm. JB felt dizzy at the unexpected meeting between so much pounding overwhelming lust and the trade marks of everyday life. He groped his way into her letter-less darkness.

Jenny gave a jerk.

'What's wrong? Am I hurting you?' he murmured.

* Bandy is a popular Swedish wintersport (Translator's note)

104

'Look,' she said, pointing.

Together they put their heads close to the threadbare lino-leum, and discovered a frightened spectator under the sink unit. The mouse was still on its hind legs, its round telescope ears fixed towards them. When JB made an attempt to take Jenny's hand, which lay childishly open like a book that some-body fell asleep over and left, the mouse jumped and dis-appeared. They never found the mouse hole, but agreed it was a magic bat who had quickly closed his invisibility cloak.

The sky cleared for a while. The sun held a brief banquet before leaving long before its guests. The moon opened a red-rimmed eye over the Sandö light-house.

'Is someone walking across the moon at this moment?' JB asked.

'Not this week. I haven't heard of it.'

The outdoor temperature rose to freezing point. They made sad-faced snow sculptures. Above them a squirrel leaped from branch to branch, and lumps of snow fell noiselessly to the ground.

'It's nice to feel something so vigorous and so solemn,' Jenny said. 'My tummy is like a mortar. You're moving in there. I long for you again.'

He felt unworn. The house was easy to shake off; it would not come and get him. Everything was a loan. He knew the world was impossible to acquire, but possible to inhabit. No view alone could be adequate. The bright light from the fjord lit up the veranda, but it was one of many lights, and a contrast to many kinds of darkness.

'We'll soon be old,' Jenny said. 'We'll be seeing each other then as well. I'll be sitting in the yellow light of daffodils at my window, looking out – not here but in town. The young people are moving about. I'm having tea, picking some withered leaves from my potted plant.'

'Then you'll be very old.'

'You enter, but you don't feel like pulling up my blouse. You've started to smoke a pipe, you suck at that rather than at my breasts. And I'm considering getting a little dog.'

'Then I'll go to evening classes. Adult education has become education for the aged. I go there to meet girls I can really talk to. They are old and lively, and have eventually grown into their faces.'

'If the worst comes to the worst I wouldn't mind being with you for ever,' Jenny said.

She had put Gertrude's woollen jacket over her shoulders, because there was a draught through the rooms. For a moment JB thought she was Gertrude. Everything could repeat itself so easily? The same clothes, the same house, the same food. Nights and days in a Swedish landscape. The whole of life.

Gertrude and he had spun each other a cocoon of security. The Water Palace was their warm cover. Consuming fire and death bells pealing in the timber about disintegration and death – none of this concerned them. They could withdraw here to efface lines, forget failures, erase the tapes, listen to the lapping of water and the rustle of ferns.

You cannot see your own face however much you twist and turn. You see others. Yet JB never pretended that he knew Gertrude. Sometimes he was Gertrude, but while he pretended to be Gertrude and believed that he could sense what kind of person she was, she slipped off out of reach.

There was only the Water Palace for Gertrude, address Sweden, Europe, Earth, Universe. Up to the day when she left for Botswana. She had met other men before Jan, but she loved him. And so she stayed within the family circle. Jan was there to confirm her conception of her own person. What she had confirmed for him he did not know.

Somewhere there was an image that she dared not test against reality, a surprise that she dared not face. It seemed that, in her childhood, she had entered a room where dolls were seated dressed and stiff around a table, engaged in conversation, representing all the people she was to meet later on in life. She made friends with them from the beginning – they were there, and nothing was added.

Gertrude was alone now, but that was an optical illusion too. Many people liked her, and a human being was growing inside her. Land and sea do not have their separate domains : the sea is sustained by its bed, and the earth is fed by the sea. He wished she were all the things he could not see.

Passing the stairs to the attic, he suddenly sensed Gertrude's presence. He could hear her complaining :

'You wish for so much. But you don't wish it from me.'

He had been on his way out, and she on her way up, and they had stopped to exchange some words. The bannister was worn smooth, caressed by hands. He remembered the fingers of a madonna in a church somewhere, polished by the kisses of centuries.

Up there in the attic were the inscriptions of the peaks of his love, and the misty skylight they eventually wiped clean just to look into the unexplored so full of anxiety. There she had been the mystical and wild mistress of ceremonies for their initation rites, in order to abdicate at the bottom of the stairs in favour of milder dances – as long as he was her partner.

He could not relate this to Jenny the way it really was, because she could capture only occasional flashes of the shudder and the ecstacy, the delight and liberation, and the terrible closeness to Gertrude, his grown-up alien sister, naked in the light of the bulb in the attic of the Water Palace.

There were still penetrating lights shining in the store room of his memories. He had forgotten to turn out the light. For a moment he had stepped over the edge of reality, and now he wanted to go back, yet was afraid of the temptation. At times he thought he was there, at that moment, with Jenny who was both earth and air, responsibility and purity. But with Jenny he moved over a larger sensual area than the cramped hide-out in the attic.

He liked to think of the fact that Gertrude, the well-known person who had seen him since he was a child, did not know what he could be like with Jenny, free under the circus marquee.

He discussed with Jenny why they had tried to hide their love from Gertrude.

'The love between me and Gertrude was secret as well,' he said, 'only half of it was known. Nobody knew that we were brother and sister as well as lovers. In the eyes of society it is a criminal offence to be so close.'

'We were afraid of leaving Gertrude without a focal point,' Jenny said. 'She assumed that everything between you and her was durable and unchangeable.'

'Maybe we were considering ourselves, I regret it now.'

'When I left you in Uppland Street reading Gertrude's letters, I went home and washed my hair, and then I felt suddenly abandoned and disheartened. I cried and cried. I was afraid of myself.'

'How unnecessary,' JB said. 'I never transferred feelings from Gertrude to you, or vice versa.'

The sunset was streaked with jet smoke; then darkness fell, and in a sporting lodge far away red table lamps shone like in a hotel. The cold crackled in the walls, and the wind laid walls of snow around the boulders of the shore. They lit a fire, and the house became a snow lantern in the night, one of the last nights of the year. A lark sang in the Akvavit. Jan squeezed some drops of garlic on the unsweetened bread. Cod fillets and frozen prawns in a strongly seasoned fish stock. A bottle of Clos Gravet, as round and mellow as a Russian old woman. In the kitchen there were some old prints: Mine For Ever, The Poacher Found Out, and The Life Boat Leaves The Shore. In the lavatory there was an etching from the days of Adolf Oscar: The Temptation of St Anthony. With an obviously ephemeral chastity the grey-beard averted his gaze from the nude temptress. As soon as the door closed on him, he would be at her again.

Late one night JB had woken up in his room above the kitchen, hearing A. O. Backman and some of his guests singing 'I See The Stars Spreading Their Shimmering Light'. It was a rare song, and only in Norrköping with Jenny had he realized that this was the song of the Freemasons.

'This is where they lived,' JB said. 'Father and grandfather, people hoisting the flag, thinking the peace of the skerries was the best Sunday medicine'. During the week they worked for a highly productive future that was to asphalt the meadows and poison the seas. Factories with eternal shifts were to give work, money and housing to everyone. That vision was shared by socialists and bourgeoisie alike. The only destruction of the environment they knew of was the forests becoming over-grown, and the slagheaps being gradually covered by vegetation. A grimy town was a rich town, and a clean town a forgotten one. The smoke from the factory chimneys was the sales curve of welfare.'

An atlas from the golden age of Imperial geography was left in the book-case. In the cupboards nearer the ceiling congratulation cards and tennis score-books rustled. Notebooks held recipes, which had been passed from friend to friend: Aunt Pauline's Marrow, Ida Svenson's Asian Cucumber, Lisen's Apple Sauce, and Jenny's Gingerbread. Jenny who? Jan did not know.

Even the measures were unknown: three gills of water, five quarts of almonds, half a drachm of purified potash.

While they ate, Jenny tried to tell the almost orphaned Jan about the Sweden her parents had known, the land of promises: the scout promise, the Holy Communion promise, the wedding promise; promises of dependence which everybody knew would be broken. People kept watch on each other. Marriages gave the security of the bank vault. Children were objects to boast about; you waved their school reports. Vitality was awarded behind pastry boards and sewing machines, but condemned in strange beds. Woe betide the one who filled in his tax returns to the penny – he must be neurotic. Woe betide the one who did not try to cheat the bus conductor of a few pence if he could. Life, unique life, ran out in hour upon hour of gossip – and if you did not wish to join the hen party, you were either antisocial or at least a snob.

Jenny spoke with anger about the heartiness which is sometimes called bourgeois: family ideals, physical health, and boldness. Its other face was the covert violence, the lurking war. The wolf-like leer of a relative as she said: What will become of it? 'It' was a female curator they knew who wanted to marry her fiancé although he was an invalid after an aircrash. They had loved each other for years, when he had arms, legs and full bodily powers. And now? If they wanted children, the world was full of orphans. If they wanted physical pleasure, it might be there for them as well. But in matters concerning marriage and the replenishment of the earth, the cave man peers out, illiterate, blind, and understanding nothing. Above all he feels nothing.

'We'll have to join the guerilla,' Jenny said. 'We'll have our exercises nightly, to avoid becoming martyrs. By day we'll appear as civil servants, and may even be considered well dressed with varnished nails at the cocktail parties.'

She seemed suddenly distant.

'You look pale. Are you all right?' he asked.

'I can't finish my cocoa,' Jenny said. 'I feel Gertrude is here. I think I'll go back to Nybro Quay.'

'Have you gone mad?'

'I'm not jealous. I wish Gertrude would come home again. I like to think of her baby. I don't mind baby-sitting. But still . . . do you see? Or do you just find me whimsical?'

She said she was glad and yet a little frost-bitten. There were many questions she wanted to put to him, but something stopped her. She aimed ahead to a freedom she did not quite possess. It had nothing to do with him.

She stayed. They slept heavily that night. The cold was like a quilt over them. Berenice's hair fluttered in the direction of Aldebaran. When JB put his arm across her back, the Water Palace was just a place they had used as a camp on their winter journey: it had beds and tables and floors. The house had lost its individuality – it could not be dishonoured and could not seek revenge.

They were awakened by the tits pecking at the window putty. The streak of sunlight on the floor was small enough to be swept under the rug. The thawing snow had enlarged the tracks of the mice. An icy mist hovered over the channel.

He prepared the breakfast: bacon rashers dented like a giant's ear, eggs, and a pile of thin golden brown slices of toast, which seemed to be waiting to be bound into an ancient folio.

Jenny's hand rested lightly on his knee when he drove towards Stockholm. It moved towards his stomach. The warmth of her hand said nothing about her thoughts, but his penis answered her hand without being questioned.

'I'm glad I'm as old as I am,' she said. 'I may never desire another man so strongly again.'

Love has many faces. It smooths itself out, and makes itself transparent. Fires in large bogs suddenly dive below the surface and make you think they are extinguished, but they continue between subterranean tufts, digging down until suddenly the heat can be sensed again just beneath the surface.

He closed his legs around her hand, while they drove through surges of traffic, passing Nacka, over Danvik Bridge, and then along the jetties and stretches of water to Nybro Quay.

III

A FUNNEL IN THE EARTH

One night when Jan Backman was alone at home in Uppland Street, the door-bell rang. He opened the door with a surprised smile of welcome meant for Jenny. But Klas Lundin noticed it and entered, encouraged.

'I was on my way to see an early movie, but it was sold out,' he said. 'You happen to live in the area. Was it rude of me to come?'

'No,' JB replied. 'I knocked on your door just before Christmas. You weren't in.'

He did not mention that Jenny had been with him.

'Did you really come out to my place?' Klas said surprised.

He looked worried. Jan wondered if he had a reason for his visit, but said nothing. Klas spoke about old times, old anecdotes.

'Did you hear about the parson on his way to a family where the man had just died?'

'No.'

'He got lost and went to a neighbour's house, and this man had just had his bicycle stolen. Sorry about your loss, the parson said. Well, the neighbour replied, the air came out at the back and there was a leak at the front, so it wasn't much to lose. Just good for the children to practice on.

'I'm not much use either,' Klas continued, and sat down heavily on a chair.

JB thought of the night outside the art gallery. A wave of jealousy had swept over him at the thought of Gertrude making love to Klas and being pregnant by him. Now he felt some kind of peace.

'What else have you got to tell me?' he asked.

'I've agreed to guarantee a friend who has invented a remarkable camera shutter. I know nothing about these things, I did it to help him, and now he has suggested a lot of free advertising for his invention, to get the money back faster.

What is there to advertise? What can I tell people about? This calculable risk has probably cost me money, but our friendship will remain, together with a drinking problem for the unfortunate inventor.'

They entered the kitchen. JB opened a tin of herrings, and poured out some ice-cold Akvavit and beer for the two of them. It might make Klas more talkative. Klas had some kind of faded tenderness, a desire to be kind, and at the same time a desire to be near life with all its surprises and risks. In advertising he had taken chances only on the glossy surface, slipped occasionally, but happily got up again to continue in the same direction. Jan saw him as a big child, easily amused, resolutely lacking any regular methods. He was someone who had always, that very day, experienced something which he either loved or hated.

JB wondered how one's appearance changed if one knew something about someone, which he did not know that one knew.

'We've got one thing in common,' Klas said.

'Oh?' Jan said hesitantly, expecting to hear Gertrude's name.

'We both live in houses built at the turn of the century. You at the Water Palace, and I at Lidingö Bridge. Why is that?'

'It turned out that way. The tired blue twilights, perhaps.'

'Not at all. It was the era of adventure. Everywhere there were unknown and unexplored areas, but they were being discovered. Industrialism gave the tools to overpower the virginal earth. Now in retrospect it seems awful, but in those days it was lovely. What results!'

'Most people were marked by suffering, not by memories.'

'As always. However the rest: Gleaming steam engines, huge trunks, modernistic paintings, the revolution of poetry, technical optimism. Inventions galore.'

'The white renaissance, before all the edelweiss were picked and the orchids protected. Before the freedom of choice had grown to such an extent that the richest companies had to direct our wishes with expensive advertising.'

'For every crown spent in Sweden, thirty-three öre are spent on marketing. Have you seen any good advertising lately?'

Jan told him he had walked through the city at night, and noticed that a letter had fallen out of the wording on a neon sign on a house facade. It made the advertisement seem worrying and untrustworthy. At once he looked at it.

'You often don't understand what I'm trying to say,' Klas complained.

'That's possible,' Jan replied. 'But usually I do understand what you say.'

Then they sat quiet in the kitchen. Klas did not make any move to go. The bottle of Akvavit shone against the smooth oilcloth. JB thought for a moment of divorced men, of comradeship under the sign of decay.

He had had a defined image of Klas Lundin. He was good at arranging parties for his friends, was often asked out, did not compete, and would not get jealous. He tasted wine, went on skating tours on the clear ice of lakes, practised bowling and had friends everywhere. To his friends his existence was a pleasant but not necessary part of life. His cheerful manner was sometimes trying, and his optimism not always catching.

'What keeps you going?' Jan asked.

'The suspicion of being on the wrong track. I make money on consumer goods, by advertising the goods to be used as quickly as possible. Life should not be like that.'

His huge hand was resting on the table, half-open, like a bowl.

'Do you want to know how Gertrude is?' JB said.

Klas gave him a quick glance, and then did not move his eyes from Jan's. Jan remembered the game he played as a child, meeting someone's eyes without winking or turning your head. Klas looked pale.

'Is she all right?'

'I've had some letters from her,' Jan said. 'She is well – considering the circumstances.'

'What do you mean?'

Klas's eyes still had not left JB.

'She's feeling lonely. There are so many new things for her.'

'Could I read Gertrude's letters?'

'No. If she's got something to tell you, she'll write to you.'

That was the first time JB had seen Klas disconcerted.

'You said she's well?' he asked, after a while.

'Yes.'

'Marianne Tidström came back the other day.'

'I'd heard that she was coming.'

'I spoke to her. She says Gertrude is pregnant.'

'I know. She's pleased.'

'Is she?'

'Yes.'

'Is she all right?'

'You've asked me that a couple of times already, you know.'

Klas did not reply. JB thought two things could happen: the conversation would ebb in chatting, or they would have to touch on the truth, which no advertising slogans could make more easy to handle. Jan had the ball. For Klas's sake it might be better to talk, but he felt he would then let Gertrude, the absent one, down.

'I've got to tell you something,' Klas said eventually.

'Don't. I know everything.'

Then Klas's defences came down. He started to cry. JB felt unexpected tenderness for him. Klas was a deserted father. Gertrude had made him pregnant without informing him. She had violated him, and left him.

'Why didn't you tell me?' Klas asked. 'Don't you understand how important it is?'

'Gertrude didn't want me to talk about it. In the first place, this concerns her. At least that's how I've seen it so far.'

'Marianne said she was surprised that you didn't come down. How are things between you and Gertrude?'

Jan did not reply. He let Klas tell him. When he had met JB outside the art gallery a couple of months ago, and heard that Gertrude was in Botswana, he had thought that Gertrude loved him. He had been overcome by the thought, turned round, and left. His intestines had been squeezed together. He had thought of JB alone in Stockholm and wanted to get in touch with him, but he did not dare. The fact that Gertrude visited him deliberately and then went to Africa, indicated that she did not want to stay with Jan.

Klas was discussing this in a moving uncritical way, as if there was no room for unknown factors in the pattern. JB thought he ought to be more open to Klas, but he could not be open on Gertrude's behalf. He said:

'Gertrude was not herself during those weeks. You became the victim of an unhappy person's ability to make another person unhappy.'

116

'Of course not. I'm glad she came to me. She said nothing. Nor did I. It was mysterious and amazing.'

'You were used as a tool for something. She didn't want you to be involved.'

'There's a difference between using and being made use of. She wished me well.'

'It wasn't you she came to.'

'I don't mind your saying so. She was with me.'

It frightened JB that their group was growing like this. The child made them all a sort of family. And Marianne Tidström who was back in town – how much did she know? The circle was enlarging.

'There's just one thing I absolutely must know,' Klas Lundin said. He took a large carving-knife from the table, and scratched lightly on the formica top. Then he put the knife down.

'Is it your child?'

JB did not reply straight away. For a moment he was tempted to give a vague answer. Then Klas would have to pay for his turmoil and pain with continued uncertainty. Lacking footholds they would be more evenly matched.

'No,' he said.

'That was all I wanted to know. I just had to know. It's the only thing that counts for me.'

Now he had betrayed Gertrude. He would never be able to explain that.

'I should have been told,' Klas said.

'In the long run I didn't want to lie to you by keeping quiet. But being frank was Gertrude's business.'

'Most people like a few lies. They accept them as part of truth. And I'm sure there are lies which can add to your experience of life. In this case, however, you were trying to lock me out of something I needed.'

'How could I have known?' Jan said defensively.

'I've been in advertising long enough to know when I want the truth, and nothing but the truth.'

'You've had it,' Jan said.

'Yes, I know. I was going to play tennis tomorrow, but now I'm not going. I'll have to think.'

'Who do you play with?'

'A tea merchant, a Head of Department in the educational sector, and a doctor of medicine. Good company. Sauna afterwards with all the social gossip. You find out a lot. Oh God.'

With his fingers spread out over his face, Klas Lundin was looking into his new life opening in front of him. He could not meet it with his eyes uncovered.

JB's emotional confusion made him feel unfree, a hostage of Klas's newly awakened powers. He went up to the window to look at the peep-show across the street, where he used to watch a mother and her child. She would sit there alone drinking tea and smoking, perhaps doing a cross-word puzzle. He hoped that she had a quiet life outside the hustle of life, and that no one would appear who was her husband's mistress, her own sister, or her child's mother.

Down in Uppland Street the snow was dirty. The remains of a January fog clung to the window-panes. The cabs had stopped using their 'for hire' signs. In the Trade Union building at the street corner there was a light on in the ground floor of the tower. On the ground floor of the National Union was the largest merchant bank in the country. Klas was lumbering about like a happy and drunk St Bernhard dog. He obviously believed Jan shared his joy.

'How wonderful to be able to speak to you,' he said. 'I don't want to grab anything. I don't want to come between you and Gertrude.'

'You're not coming between us,' JB said. 'I'm causing the damage myself.'

'I've always admired Gertrude. And she wanted to have a child by me! This is the turning point of my life.'

Klas thought Gertrude had chosen him. Like a goddess she had descended to make him a member of a group where he had earlier only been able to join in on the fringe with Akvavit and his jolly moods and a veranda with a sea view. Did it not strike him that Gertrude had exploited him just as ruthless advertising exploits the ignorant and manageable public?

'Do you think Gertrude might deny me the responsibility that I would like to take?' Klas asked.

'Probably,' Jan said. 'But that will be her decision.'

'I have a brotherly feeling for Gertrude,' Klas assured him.

Jan thought he felt an electric shock through his body.

'I must write to her. To the child as well,' Klas continued, as if the child had already been born.

'I have given her secret away,' Jan said. 'Let me talk to her first.'

'Naturally,' Klas said, but JB was not sure he understood. 'I haven't felt anything like this since I was a child on Christmas Eve.'

'You already love Gertrude's child,' JB said. 'I want it to be loved by many people.'

Face to face in the night at Uppland Street, he wished to put everything right. The situation was nasty, but not the person involved. Klas for a long time had dwelt in his periphery. Now he was approaching, coming close, and was visible, not just a party-goer who had been at hand and lent his boat. An immovable truce prevailed in the kitchen. The level in the Akvavit bottle sank.

'You must be annoyed with me,' Klas said. 'Maybe you'd like to beat me up?'

'I haven't felt like beating anyone up since I saw a boy walking around with a living butterfly pinned to his sweater. It was a long time ago.'

'Suddenly I know,' Klas said. 'And you have known it all along.'

He went up to the tap, and washed his face briskly. JB handed him a towel.

'How are things with your wife?' he asked.

'She says I lack the imagination to realize how mad she is. Her illness is mainly a desire to be ill. She's not one of those who clean what is already clean. She wanted to get away from it all. I didn't stop her, she stopped herself. She's now living in a nursing home south of Stockholm.'

'I've never met her.'

'In ten years a woman can get inconceivable, especially if you live with her. In this case she needed less time to disappear among the enigmas. I suppose my way of life got her bad genes going. Who knows, as a farmer's wife she might have been all right.'

'You never know how you impress or get impressed,' JB said. 'That's impossible to grasp at the time for it. And afterwards you forget. Memories are blurred, guilt and innocence confound the arithmetic rules.'

'She slowly withdrew from me. Now she's in exile in the nursing home. I may never communicate with her again. But

I'm no better off with the women I've met since she disappeared. My emotions are too fickle. I burn and then I break.'

'Like your advertising. First a campaign, a lot of enthusiasm, and then you forget all about it.'

'Yes, it's awful. I look at a girl, she's pretty but silent. Suddenly I ask myself what we would have to say to each other in ten years' time. That's the end. I must push her away from me. Then, strangely, she will get serious about me.'

'You're afraid of responsibility.'

'Why should I be responsible for adults? I dust the chords off, quickly, pling plong, then I'm on my way to the next note. Not many women share my interests. I just think they look as if they did.'

'They don't like to sit with binoculars counting ships coming in to the free port? I can understand them.'

'No. But what if one of them blurts out: So many foreigners everywhere, isn't it awful? She's probably heard someone say it in the office. Shall I then start to teach her, or tell her to leave? I get so tired, and I think of all the others I can find. I don't force anyone to think only of me. I'm one of many to them as well. It's bloody difficult to explain, it's like finding yourself on the doctor's file, at first described as neurotic, promiscuous, without permanent emotional ties; then as artistic, free from bourgeois hang-ups, with a high IQ. It makes you understand that nobody could ever understand you. You feel sorry for yourself, or you start to work at getting some messages through.'

'Do you succeed?'

'Not always, and it's my own fault. But now it has to work.'

'Why?'

'The baby . . .'

'It's a good thing if you're one of the many people in favour of it.'

'All at once I can see many years ahead. I have a need to tell the unborn creature who I am, give it some publicity for life. Oh well, I'm drunk and sentimental, I'm sorry. That's why I can talk like this. You may be going through an awful time. There's so much I don't understand.'

'I've been drinking as well, and I don't understand very much. I feel too compliant. I find it rather astounding as well, but I'm not Gertrude's agent.'

Klas knew nothing about Gertrude's fern forests. His face contracted into many wrinkles when he laughed. Jan surmised a joke in each furrow. Yet he effaced his image of a merry boor.

He had known Klas as a man who did not need much space around him. He was a fertile surface, but now the shell had come loose around something elusive and emotional. JB was amazed that he had never caught a glimpse of the messenger from a silent modern power station before. He had been mistaken. Gertrude might have noticed it, when she went to see Klas at the extreme end of the perspective drawing and slept with him three nights running. She had brought out in Klas something that seemed to grow and flourish. They had somehow fertilized each other.

Gertrude's stomach was getting round, and Jan had not seen it. He remembered a pregnant woman on the bus that day, a thin freckled face with trusting eyes. It was probably nice to expect a baby, he had told himself. However, he was not created that way, but was one of the powerful ones entirely in other people's hands.

He tried to imagine the unknown child wriggling under Gertrude's extended abdominal membrane. She was no longer the agile playmate of his childhood with a flat stomach. She was a woman, and expected perhaps as much of him as Jenny ever did. He was gripped by fear: how would they keep their balance? How much did he have to give away?

He could feel a sort of dull spite against all of them, Klas, Gertrude, Jenny, a smouldering yearning for freedom, an inclination to run away. Some boys had once threatened to beat him up when he came to school the next day. He spent that day roaming around the streets, while the teacher phoned Mrs Tapper. When he came home at the right time he would neither tell them about the threat nor about his activities outside the school curriculum.

'I've had an easy life,' Klas said. 'I attended High School, and studied extra maths by a correspondence course. I learnt the odd thing here and there, but couldn't get them together. The intention of school was to keep things incoherent, unnecessary and useless, so they wouldn't be abused. Spare time was devoted to communal activities: chalk on the walls, stones thrown at windows, and shoplifting. No sweater was wide enough for the pipe cleaners, calendars, gloves; whatever was of little value to me.'

'So you were a happy child?'

'Yes. My parents seemed to be all right, the little I saw of them. I think it's because I'm a born optimist. I have a kind of reassurance, a secret bank safe, making me immune to a lot of depression.'

'Childhood is a nice experience to people who survive it,' Jan said.

Klas drank, and wandered across the squares of the kitchen floor. Jan's hands were trembling, but he tried to hide it. A kind of unreal cosy feeling mixed with worry and became opaque. The night was burning towards its end.

'I'm in advertising,' Klas went on. 'I know it's a quasi-world, a castle of cards and a barricade to reality, but I could still tell Gertrude's child about unpayable things, the bank in the clouds, the silver being exchanged there, and the value of the worthless. I had a tin plate inscribed with a publicity slogan for Singer sewing machines. Thinking of that I feel happy. It was given to me when I was five. It was my treasure, like the people living near a gold-field who had not met the coin civilization. When white people came, the natives were so astonished that they died. Have you ever felt anything like that?'

Jan mumbled something. He tried to protect himself, Gertrude and Jenny. He did not want Klas to know that he, as Gertrude's brother could claim only a very small amount of her. He and Jenny were the reason for the child. The turmoil was rising and sinking inside him, but Klas did not notice.

Now, after several months, some radical change had come over Klas – just like the time when Jan met Jenny. JB had given a lift to a strange woman, not knowing that she would become his great love. Gertrude was carrying an unknown creature, and Klas Lundin had been struck with love for the unknown.

Klas had achieved something with Gertrude which made her different to JB. Gertrude's and Jan's silent agreement had implied no children, if they wanted to live outside society's conventions and yet seemingly inside. Klas and Gertrude would be sharing an experience which JB was locked out of, regardless of Gertrude's feelings or lack of feelings for Klas. Or was it the other way round, perhaps: Gertrude, Jan and Jenny had all participated, and therefore had to include Klas in their circle. A man who had seen the trains passing him by could now suddenly climb into a carriage, because Marianne Tidström had spilled the beans. He had been very close to missing it all.

JB could see the end of his and Gertrude's parallel lives within the brackets of their family relations: they were getting different experiences, which could bring them closer together, or keep them apart. They could choose, but nothing was simple any more.

He could not find an emotion to fit in with his changing moods. He felt he was united with Klas in some kind of conspiracy, in a common experience of something concealed and hard to find: the child growing far away in Africa in a woman they were both very fond of, but who did not seem to need them very much.

'You will is growing in the forest,' Klas said. That's what I was told as a child. I went out to look for it, I wanted to keep my will in a flower-pot. My father had sung a song about it too.

I came home with a pathetic plant, which I planted in a pot. An older school-friend saw it one day, and said: You're crazy, you've picked a protected plant, you'll end up in prison. It was a protected orchid with funny tubers that stuck out like fingers. Frightened, I hid it in my wardrobe. It withered in there from lack of light, so I took it out and watered it in a hiding place. Then I saw it after a long time growing new shoots.

You could conclude from this that it was my own will that I was cultivating, but it wasn't: I wanted to achieve something with that very plant, But it had its own laws, was rebellious and submissive as it liked, and was its own housekeeper. It found some fertile soil, some goodness its fingers could seize, and reappeared from the shadows to become what it had been in the meadow where I picked it.

'You must keep words straight, or they will outgrow you,' he said eventually. 'That's what I'd like to tell my child when it starts exploring the world.'

Red and shattered, ecstatic in his new role, Klas Lundin left the flat in Uppland Street. Jan was sitting looking around the kitchen, as if Klas was lingering there. He had appeared and broken up the fantasy Jan thought they lived in, he himself, Jenny and Gertrude. Klas was a steam-roller from reality. From now on everything would be more complicated.

Who was he? Bit by bit you learnt something – like in the fine new encyclopaedias where you saw on one page man in the flesh, and then looking ahead, the different layers of tissue, until the last plate showed the skeleton.

That was the time to turn the pages back. You never saw the whole picture.

Jan was frightened by his rapid emotional changes. Different holds broke loose. He was on a slippery surface, and loneliness wrapped its icy ring around him. For the first time Jenny was on the outside.

He slept little the rest of the night. Jenny phoned him early to say good morning. In the aftermath of happy memories she told him how much she had enjoyed her evening with an American research couple. They had taken a trip in the snowy twilight, and had dinner at an inn. They seemed to think the same about most things, and ended up having a beer at her place. Jenny's experience was in contrast to his own, but he did not mind: he heard her voice, and all his fears burst. He felt thrilled and clean, as if he had cried all night.

He said: 'Klas Lundin came over. He asked about Gertrude.'

'Did he suspect anything?'

'Yes, he knows everything now. We had a long chat. It made me very upset.'

'Maybe you won't want to see me today then?'

'I'm already on my way over to you.'

He had coffee at Jenny's place before going to Arlanda. He could not see enough of her face and eyes; he wanted to reach everything in her. The contact was there, and the lines were unhurt. He borrowed power from her.

'What did Klas say?' Jenny asked.

'He said he had found his will. It's growing in Africa.'

WALL TO WALL

There was a telegram from Sten Tidström, Swaneng Hill School, Botswana. 'Worried about Gertrude,' it said. 'Can you come?'

Jan Backman did not waste a minute. Something inside him reacted quickly and instinctively, like the departure of the migratory birds. Tidström would not send a cry of distress without a good reason. Gertrude needed him.

He called the tower and the personnel office, and took three weeks' holiday. He packed five shirts, summer jeans, cotton slacks, and two pairs of pyjamas. He bought some razor blades and an old-fashioned razor. He got some traveller's cheques; the Botswana currency was South African rand. He could get a visa on arrival. The doctor of the Air-Traffic Department filled him up with inoculations. The girl behind the counter in the Departure Lounge filled in his staff ticket, 'non-endorsable, non-exchangeable'.

He assumed that Jenny would have the same view as he had regarding his sudden departure. Travelling to Gertrude could never mean that he was travelling away from Jenny, and he knew she would understand that. Distance and desisting had never affected their relationship, which was light-weight and free of custom's duty. She was in London attending an environmental conference, but was due back in a few days' time. Composing a letter and posting it from Arlanda was almost unnecessary, but he still did it. He adressed it to Nybro Quay.

I'm just doing what I have to do, he wrote. Imagine yourself in my position.

He sent a telegram to Gertrude telling her he would come for a couple of weeks' holiday. He said nothing about Sten's alarm. He drove out to Arlanda in a rush. He was on his way to see Gertrude. It was a long journey. He saw two girls waving to get a lift, but did not have the time to stop. He left his car in the car park for the Air-Traffic Department personnel. He quickly said good-bye to his friends at the tower and asked Eklund, the meteorologist, for the latest weather forecast. He was given a sheet indicating the chart positions. He put it in his wallet as a souvenir from the North: 'A westerly air current prevails across Götaland and Svealand. In the northern parts of Norrland snow is falling, gradually decreasing in the South. Progressing to fair. Ground winds SW varying W/15 knots. Gusting at the coastal regions. Cloud base 2000 feet. Visibility 20/30 kms. In the South scattered snow showers with visibility 5/10 kms and cloud base 700/1500 feet. Wind, 2000 feet, 27 knots. Lowest QNH 980 MB.'

It was a Sunday afternoon: The SAS airline had a weekly flight to East Africa. The calls followed each other: '. . . the departure of flight number SK 961 to Zurich, Athens, and Nairobi.' The faces of passengers, indifferent, unknown, and tanned beforehand. Some quick good-byes. A couple kissed each other through the glass wall of the transit hall, their noses pressed flat against the glass.

The snow plough moved to and fro on the runways. The slush had to be removed, or it would be sucked into the engines. The aircraft wings were sprayed against ice.

Jan Backman was not a traveller. He had several free trips due to him. He made sure other people got off all right, that was his profession. Now, for half a day and one night he would be travelling a distance that had taken Axel Ericson several months. He knew the pilot only by name. The thin ice crust of Öresund gave firm outlines to the shadow of the plane. He saw the wheels extended in the mirror of the ice, before shadow and object met at the short thud of the landing moment.

The earth curved below him as if touched by a wind from inside its kernel. He saw the blue planet in the long, cold space, a manned raft at the edge of an insignificant galaxy.

Over the Libyan desert he looked down from the cockpit at the burning oil towers of the Sahara desert: an inverted starry sky. The moon rose over the horizon that guided them at an altitude of 13,000 metres. It looked as though it had got stuck in a coin slot, and not gone in properly.

In the dim night light of the cabin the passengers were dozing, satisfied just from studying the menu, where each vegetable and potato was listed separately. JB unfolded a letter he had received from Sten Tidström at the same time as the telegram, although it had been sent a week earlier. He had only looked through it for factual details, but now he found it, as usual, full of Sten's reflections. He read it while they were flying over Sudan and Uganda :

'The comparison between us and them, the rich and the poor, in income per capita, does not tell everything. The comparison between rich and poor in the same environment tells more. In Africa and India the barber puts his chair under a tree to avoid the expense of a shop. A restaurant can be a stove in a house, but the food is served out of doors. The sun is free and can't be included in statistics, or in the consumption of coal and oil.

Comparisons, statistical as well as subjective, remain unsafe. You travel as you live : to expand the limits of your ego, or to get painfully aware of them. Also, to investigate your own and other people's mental and social inflexibility. People live under different guiding stars, thinking, sensing their existence in a different way, and exposed to temptations unknown to me.

Still, the threat is the same, the ultimate conditions. Radio waves travel quickly across the earth, like the three per cent who have ever been in an aeroplane. The earth is still larger than most people can imagine. In one part of the world half of the population, that is the women, have practically no rights at all. What we see as Swedish virtues are vices to others. Where we see order, others see chaos.

Travelling, you meet many people who expect the world to correspond to their expectations. If it does not, they want to change it. Some are seized by the stubborn eagerness of missionaries and helpers. Others begin to hate, and dream about a violent transposal. Different people have different social and personal visions of what is right and wrong. A battlefield of pressed people appears where they meet.

A missionary here reads Pascal about our conditions, so unfortunate, he says, that if we watched them closely we would be inconsolable for ever.'

In Nairobi JB transferred to East African Airways, and in Lusaka it transpired that the direct scheduled flight to the capital of Botswana had just been withdrawn. They blamed the lack of passengers, but the motive could have been political : South Africa preferred people to go to and fro from Botswana via Johannesburg.

A Dakota belonging to Botswana Airways jolted from Lusaka to Livingstone on the Rhodesian border, and then on to Botswana. JB sat in the tail, and had some difficulty balancing a glass of orange juice. Africa was below : forests and savanna land in greens, greys and brick red. Occasionally the natives' huts could be seen at the edge of a grass fire.

The aeroplane landed in Maun by the Okavango marshes. He was not able to go on to Francistown until the next day. He was in the same country as Gertrude, and yet had not completed half of his journey, judging by the time. Maun, indicated as a town on the map, had a petrol station, a small boarding-house, and a café hiring guides to people who wanted to take motorboat trips around the Okavango delta.

Rather than booking into a local hotel, JB decided to take a Land Rover out to the marshes nearby. Okavango, Charles John Anderson's discovery to the white world, was a nature reserve. Little villages with grass huts were half invisible in the low bush. The inhabitants would pull enough sweetcorn and millet out of the sandy soil to keep starvation at bay. Wild animals which attracted tourists to Africa, had not yet become extinct. Axel Ericson had bought cattle here and lost them, and now Sweden was busy with hydrological examinations in the marshland.

The passengers travelling by outboard motor along the river, terrified the herons, otters, hippopotamuses, and wart-hogs. The tourist camp was a communal dining-room in a long, narrow hut with tents to spend the night in. When the food was served, the cicadas came out, sounding like importunate restaurant musicians. The mosquitoes prepared for precision shots. An anonymous African made up a fire between stones, somebody served whisky in plastic mugs, and the knights of the white skin engaged in conversation.

One of them was their guide, who called himself a white hunter. One was a Dutch travelling salesman on holiday from Zambia. Two were business men from Johannesburg : lamps and cars. At the camp fire they thought they were back in the world of their forefathers : pathfinders and pioneers, armed with the mauser and God against the British imperialism, international communism and barbarous natives.

JB who carefully asked his way thought their nighttime conversation confirmed how the country, on all sides except for one kilometre of its boundary, bordered onto white race regimes. Most of the large farms were owned by whites living in South Africa, but administered by locals. He was told that half of all Botswana's savings were deposited in South Africa.

Their discussion ran to and fro, and eventually the white hunter emptied the last of the whisky, and called the Swede and the Dutchman hypocrites, because they criticized from a distance of thousands of miles.

'You're like the bombers above the clouds. You exploit from a distance, whilst pretending not to. You support a market system just like ours; the difference is not all that great.'

'You're encouraging your own destruction,' the Dutchman said. 'You don't know what you're doing.'

'We know. If you conquer a person, you can do one of three things: You can pick him up and treat him like a brother, you can kill him, or you can put your foot on his neck and keep it there for as long as you can, which is what we have done.'

'But what if he gets up?'

'Then people like you will be the first to go, and people like me the last.'

He disappeared out into the darkness. They could hear the splashing as he relieved himself of the whisky, and the thump when he fell headlong into the tent.

The next morning the plane took off from Maun to Francistown. It flew over a country as large as the West European continent, over a plateau a thousand metres high, and yet in the whole of the country there were hardly a million inhabitants. Gertrude and Sten were somewhere. The school where they worked was famous for its teaching methods. Gertrude was planning branch libraries in the province around Serowe, and looking after the renewal of equipment for the primary school. Jan tried to telephone her from Francistown, but she was not available, so he left a message.

He waited for the train at the Tati hotel, a white building opposite the station, and looked at the sign 'Meet Miss Francistown with Her Charming Smile at the Friday Dance'. Outside was the only asphalt road with a clothes shop and a couple of petrol stations.

The train for Palapye came from Bulawayo and was bound for Mafeking connecting with the mail steamer from Capetown to Southampton. The smoke swept past the windows, and an African wearing the white uniform of the Rhodesian Railways rang a bell for lunch. JB was alone in his compartment as the conductor, without asking him, had sold him a second class ticket. Africans travelled third or fourth class. The train stopped at every rail junction, and women came running up to sell baskets and rugs, bird pictures and macondi. Nobody bought anything; he heard someone say that the people with money were the South African miners going north, home, in the opposite direction. Good morning my friends, the children sang under the shady roofs at the little halts. They waved and smiled. He did not know what they meant by that. He waved and smiled back.

At Palapye station some people were waiting: an African in a stationmaster's uniform, a young man in khaki slacks, a white school-girl with plaits, an elderly broad-shouldered man who could be a missionary, and a pregnant woman. He had time to ask himself where Gertrude was, before realizing that it was her, and the memory of his girlishly thin sister was effaced. She looked very happy. It was several months since they had seen each other.

'I told you not to bounce about like that,' he said, as they got into her Land Rover. 'You may have a miscarriage.'

She held his hand, stroked his shoulders and arms, almost surprised to find him all in one piece.

'It's your first trip to Africa,' she said, as if she herself had lived there for years.

He laughed, not able to deny his astonishment, which was partly because of her.

'So you have eventually managed to travel a bit,' she said. 'You've had so many opportunities to travel free.'

'Whose car is it?' Jan asked.

'It belongs to the school. A Norwegian doctor usually drives it. I sometimes go with her to schools and dispensaries. It takes sixteen gallons of petrol, has reinforced suspension, and steel protection for the crankshaft and the gearbox. It can take anything.'

'I'm not going to buy it.'

'I thought you were interested in cars.'

'I've changed our old Volvo to a Peugeot,' JB said.

But Gertrude did not seem to listen.

'We're some kilometres north of the tropic of Capricorn,' she informed him.

She drove slowly. The road was bumpy and full of stones like a riverbed. It was as though the tide had retired a long time ago, and everybody had expected it to return, but it never did.

The Africans they met greeted them with a raised hand crying out something that meant: I have seen you. Gertrude said many people had learnt to recognize her.

The visibility over the savanna was obstructed by mounds of stones, as if a huge farmer at the end of the Ice Age had hacked them out of the fields. Looking at these monotonous plains with rugged bushes and a hot even wind, Jan remembered the Swedish landscape as a pasture with wild gooseberries and a horizon brought so close by the forest that it could be touched.

Gertrude told him that there had once been green forests in Botswana. The lightning set them on fire and singed them, so they were cut down. The soil became rootless and blew away. The compass pointed over land getting emptier all the time. And ever since the natives strolled about all their lives looking for water, waited for it for months, saw it looming like castles and fountains. They dreamed of fresh running water under the soil, which was as inaccessible as Heaven and eternal life.

Pula pula: rain. They liked repeating, Gertrude said. There was plenty of time to emphasize what was important, a great deal of their life was spent waiting. To them it was natural to say: 'My son my son; friends friends.'

'The spring crop, last year's grass . . . this is a land lacking a lot of words,' Gertrude said. 'The thistles are brown and dry, you don't know why, perhaps because it's February, because of the drought, because they're never green.'

The Land Rover rocked. A cluster of cacti were unpleasantly close. Jan thought the spikes looked like the long egg tubes of beetles he had watched at the Water Palace. Gertrude took his hand, and put it on her stomach. She was wearing a thin smock over a pair of blue jeans that had material added in the front to reach round her new waist.

'Like to feel?' she said.

JB let his hand rest with bent fingers, but she pressed it

flat against her belly. He felt surprised how tense and hard her belly was, a firm muscular barrier protecting the growing creature in there. It was a totally new sensation of her body. His hand was shy and withdrew.

Gertrude was six months pregnant. The child in her body belonged to him as well, to his physiognomy, just as well as to that of a stranger. A creature huddled up like a question mark, locked in like in an aeroplane with regulated air pressure, and not dependent on the heat and cold of the exterior world.

'It's strange,' he said, 'I'm past the average age of our civilization, and yet I have never before put my hand on the tummy of a pregnant woman.'

'Neither had I,' Gertrude said. 'At the hospital here they see children once a week. I've been examined there and have talked to other women. I've felt their embryos moving under my hand, and I had the same thought: there's something perverted about a society where this experience is kept away from you.'

She braked. A shy ant-bear, an aardvark, stalked across the road and managed to escape the front wheels.

'If you're lucky you'll feel the baby kicking,' Gertrude said.

Jan pressed down his palm.

'I think I can feel something,' he said, his mouth turning up by itself. 'But it could be the jeep jolting.'

'It's probably the baby,' Gertrude said.

She had a contented look on her face, as if she was about to tell a good story and was already pleased at its twist. Some drops of perspiration glittered on her upper lip. JB gently stroked them off with his little finger.

They stopped on the earthy road of iron-sand red like rust, wiped the wind-screen, and drank some water from a plastic flask. Eagles were swooping about, prying for rabbits and wild squirrels. A naked boy appeared from nowhere, and waited behind a bush for them to move on and leave something useful behind: a cigarette butt, a piece of string, or a can. JB gave him the *Observer* magazine, which he had read in the train. The naked eleven-year-old sat down to look at the adverts, where the whisky was served on silver trays, the tweed suit was tailor-made for the fox hunt, and elegant women leant against the bonnet of a Rolls Royce.

'I've thought a lot about you,' Gertrude said. 'I thought that maybe you were thinking of me at the same time. I've been pretending that you arrived by Land Rover, craunching the gravel. You knew where I lived.'

She was the old Gertrude with new looks. Knut Tapper and the revelation that they were brother and sister, Jenny and Klas Lundin, all seemed to be forgotten. These things had threatened to separate them; yet JB thought they were the things that made them really close. Gertrude apparently believed that he had whole-heartedly returned to him. Sten had done him an ill-favour with his telegram. Perhaps Gertrude needed to be at a distance from him, not near him, to find her own way to a reality that they could both recognize.

'What did you tell Sten?' he asked.

'Nothing. He hasn't asked me anything. I wouldn't get any closer to him if I told him. There are a lot of things to be cleared up first.'

'How's that to be done?'

'It depends on me. And on you, now you're here.'

But she did not mention Jenny, and did not even pretend that Sweden existed. He kept waiting for a word that could give him the opportunity to talk about Jenny. She was the reason why Gertrude had come out here. He waited in vain. Maybe nobody would mention Jenny here. He felt he was travelling on a false passport.

'What have you told the others here?'

'That you're my husband who has come on holiday to see me. What else? You are my husband, dear brother—don't look so stunned. You have my name, and I have yours.'

He could see before him the signpost at Uppland Street. The plain became narrow like a trawl-net. In it they were all floundering with their personal problems: Gertrude encircled him as if they were in their Stockholm flat. He wondered what Jenny was up to.

When they arrived at the school – a collection of bungalows, hovels and round huts a few miles from Serowe – Gertrude asked:

'Would you like to stay in my room or have your own?'

'I'd like my own.'

'Okay. You can have the one next to mine. Knock three times to assure me it's you.'

He wondered about her slightly confident tone of voice.

133

Gertrude's house was one of the first ones to be built; it was on the top of a ridge with a view in two directions. The school grounds extended over several acres with a farm, vegetable gardens, and irrigation canals. Down on the plain there were the newer staff houses, as well as dormitories, schoolrooms, and workshops for the students. That was where Sten Tidström lived.

When they entered Gertrude's room, he looked at the camp bed, the chest of drawers painted brown, and the chair, plastic to resist termites. Gertrude threw herself in his arms, and hugged him. He could feel her shape now, rounder and more mature, and he saw the lust laughing in her eyes. They kissed, and he was relieved that she was the way she was and at the same time a little bit frightened of her joy. He had travelled all that way to make her happy. He had seen himself as a brotherly comforter, and her broken down and grateful. Suddenly she turned her head away, whispering:

'You can't make love to me now.'

At that moment he had not even thought about it. He was mute and turned away. But she did not seem to notice.

The house had white plastered walls. They went out onto the little glass-sided porch. There she had put a bench, and a vase of wild flowers with some hardy plants looking like bitter and tufted vetch, but they were grown from bulbs. Closed shutters kept the house cool. Laundry was fluttering on a clothes line with bright plastic clothes-pegs. Gertrude pointed to a red painted garden table:

'This is where I sit and type on my IBM.'

'What do you type?'

'Progress reports. To assess what I've done. Like your tapes in the control tower. Then I write to you.'

'What about?'

'Telling you what it's like here, what we ought to do, and what you should do for me.'

'Yes, I'd like to know that.'

She squeezed little green limes, and poured the juice out for them in two glasses. He asked:

'Did you get my letters?'

'The account of your happy Swedish trip? Yes. You could have spared me that. It made me sad, terribly sad. I myself could hardly understand it. My face swelled up, Sten thought it was allergic fever. I suppose it was pregnancy depression.'

'We should never hide anything from each other, you said that yourself.'

'When I was really unhappy, Sten told me something about you that I had never known. He assumed I knew, he was surprised at my ignorance.'

'What was that?'

'That you applied to the Foreign Office as a trainee, and were not accepted.'

'Did I never tell you that? How strange.'

'You drank a lot of brandy with Sten afterwards, you were drunk and unhappy, and became sick. Some time later you applied for the job as air-traffic controller.'

'Another way to survey the world,' Jan said lightly.

'But you concealed it from me. Was it such a defeat?'

'I don't remember it like that.'

'If you had really loved me, you wouldn't have hesitated to tell me about it.'

'Sometimes one may keep quiet – but not because one wants to cheat. The person subjected to it still feels cheated. Consequently, people don't know each other. Sten doesn't know Marianne, you don't know me, Klas doesn't know you . . .'

He paused. He wanted to talk about Klas, but it was too soon. And Gertrude interrupted him:

'And do you think you know Jenny?'

'No,' he replied, undeliberately happy to hear her name pronounced.

'We have to guess. That is, we have to be bold. And now I think all my sadness is gone, for you are here, which means that nothing was in vain.'

She beamed at him. He dared not ask her what she was thinking.

Jan Backman stood outside Gertrude's house, looking out over the school grounds. Goats were getting up on their hind legs to reach the buds on the thorn bushes. The landscape was uniformly grey with burnt shadows over its back, and cacti as epaulets. The residential quarters were empty. They had all gone to work. Gertrude and the Norwegian doctor had left at six o'clock in the morning for Malapye, where they were building a new comprehensive school.

Jan discovered Sten Tidström walking up the hill. He was more tanned and had more furrows on his brow, but looked younger. He was wearing dirty jeans, an open grey shirt, and safari boots. He put his hands on Jan's shoulders, and JB somewhat awkwardly patted his elbows. He was scrutinized at arm's length, and then Sten said:

'It's nice to have you here. I went to a teachers' meeting in Tonota yesterday, so I couldn't be here to welcome you. It's strange to see you in this environment.'

'Well, I'm in Africa now, but I feel just as useless here,' JB said.

'We'll give you something to do, don't worry.'

'I read your letter in the plane coming here,' Jan said.

'You don't write very much to me. I have evenings when I enjoy writing. I sometimes feel isolated now Marianne and the children have left. I miss them more than I could have anticipated. The bodies of children, bathing them and having them climbing about in the evenings . . . Yet the days are full of discussions.'

'So you want to stay here?'

'Yes. My last months in Sweden I felt like a dried-up paint brush, lots of stiff paint, but no liquid to dissolve the stiff and tacky substance. I told Gertrude, and I believe she understood me. I wanted to become more flexible again, to glide across surfaces, useful and soft.'

The wind shook unripe fruit off the rugged trees; they looked like little green clementines, but were called marula and were used for brewing beer. The clouds were high and angular like stones split by blasting. JB flicked off a spider clinging to his shirt.

'Come with me to my office,' Sten said. 'It's a bit of a walk.'

The few cars belonging to the school were used for trips outside the Swaneng Hill area. They were Land Rovers and lorries. Otherwise they used bicycles, or walked. The bicycle wheels drew patterns like garlands in the bumpy sandy ground.

'This is the day nursery,' Sten said. 'The children interchange languages, Norwegian, English, Tswana, Zulu . . . A few of the parents are students, and the others are teachers.'

'What exactly do you do most of the time?'

'It varies. Most people here do different jobs. I teach book-keeping and budget planning. We use the school shop as a practical example. Arne, a Norwegian, manages the vegetable gardens, the dairy, the silo, and is enlarging the hen-run. Peter, an exiled white South African, teaches maths and is also re-sponsible for the plumbing and farm management. We all have one practical and one theoretical job. There is no spare time. We have a beer in some lonely bar in the Serowe area, and we meet in the evenings but mainly speak about work. Would you like to see one of the dormitories?'

The boys and girls lived in different houses, six to ten in each dormitory. A map of Botswana on one wall, the Beatles on another, with equal difficulties sticking to the mortar and burnt brick. An electric wire hung from the ceiling. The light often went out due to faults in the transformer, a sand storm, or a cross-beak that had bit into the power line where it joined the wall : an explosion, and the bird was sent back to the bush by an electric shock. There were no windows in the rooms, only mosquito nets, and the smell of drought, perspiration, and sandy skin. The schoolbooks were wrapped in brown paper; the sand crackled between paper and cover.

'They rise with the sun,' Sten said. 'The day starts with new jobs. Learning geometry and how to stake out the foundations for a hut. Two sides of the same problem. The most import-ant courses are those that involve problems of development and citizenship. They are there to make sure that no one is estranged from the less privileged. Education must not be a ladder. It is essential that they feel they belong with the others. That's why teachers and students do rough manual work together at least one day a week extending the school. The school grows at our pace. This is a good time – until we have to stop the expansion and move somewhere else.'

'How are the students doing?'

'More than half of those attending secondary school take their exams. But that's not the important thing. The aim of the school is to adjust the young to Botswana's situation. A person able to write must also be able to make cheese. A person able to make cheese should also be able to keep the records of the cheese production. A person selling cheese should be able to build his own house with the money he gets for the cheese. Many schools are still missionary schools. There are still three times more students taking scripture, rather than agriculture, as one of their exam subjects.'

There were barrels for rain water round the school and dormitory buildings. They were empty. Clouds were sailing across the sky, but they yielded no rain until they reached the sea. It always rained over the sea: the moisture attracted the moisture.

JB asked Sten about the teachers. Eighty-five per cent of the High School teachers were foreigners, and almost half the teachers were charity workers from various countries with no teacher's training.

'Botswana was a forgotten and useless part of the British Empire,' Sten said. 'England protected it against apartheid, but also against development. There is no money here; but dams, roads, hospitals and schools have to be built. People have to realize that this is essential for them; that they must work for nothing. Only then will they make bricks to build a house, and cut trees to keep the fires going in the brick ovens. Then discipline will be a natural result, and regulations will be unnecessary.'

They were in Sten's office with a desk painted in a military grey, concrete floor, and white plaster walls. The ceiling was not flush with the walls because of the heat; the wind blew straight in. The only ornament was a fragile-looking iron sculpture. When JB went up to admire it, it immediately leaped over to another wall. Sten seemed to be used to it.

138

'Is this a letter from Gertrude?' Jan said, pointing at a sheet of paper with her handwriting on it.

'It's her suggestions about a report on the clinic here.'

'Does she do these things as well?'

'She has to have a go at most things. We're all amateurs. The environment itself is our teacher. What we bring here from home is not worth much, unless it's transposed over and over.'

Sten spoke eagerly, but at the same time watched JB with an amused smile. It was as though he hardly expected Jan to grasp what was going on.

'Would you like to see Gertrude's draft? It gives a picture of the medical care in a developing nation.'

JB read the familiar handwriting:

'The main function of the clinic now is caring for the sick, but it should as well be prophylactic (maternal and child welfare, education, and innoculation). Drilling could be done to test for a well to supply the whole village. The sewage goes to the common ditch, and there is no septic tank. There are few lavatories with tops attached. Lavatory tops are sold for three rand (20Skr.) The water is taken from something like a road ditch. The bushes around the clinic have not been cut back; cattle feed and leave their muck there, and the dam is not enclosed. The walls are drying up. In the slime at the bottom are water-fleas, half a centimetre long, carrying a parasite which enters the human body and settles in the lymphatic vessels.

At the clinic a surplus of taps and sink units in stainless steel. The doors fit badly, and many ought to be readjusted, instead of the weights now being used.

Most babies are still delivered at home. In the wards patients with contagious diseases, who should be in isolation, are placed together with the maternity cases. Tetanus is common, most cases are babies under one year old, whose umbilical cord was cut with dirty tools. Sometimes rancid butter has been applied to the child's navel. Stab or shot wounds and snake bites are rare. Injuries caused by sticks are common during holidays after men have been fighting.'

'Gertrude and I are doing this together,' Sten said. 'We hope to get some money from a students' collection in Sweden.'

'Do you co-operate a lot?' JB asked.

'Not really. Gertrude has her work, but we have built a house together with some of the other teachers: a white plaster building to be used as a guest-house for visiting parents. Marianne helped as well.'

Tidström was silent and looked at Jan.

'You were worried about Gertrude,' JB said.

'I guessed she had some reason to be depressed. I thought only you could make her happy. And I knew it wouldn't cost you too much to get a flight out here.'

'It was my fault that she was depressed.'

Sten let his words pass by and went on: 'She offered to help a West German girl make a sociological report on a residential area of Francistown. She's overdoing it, she's very tired. She was always so punctual, but is now never on time any more. She replies in a weird way to things you say. I thought she was sailing off somewhere. For long periods we never saw her, Marianne and I.'

'I haven't had time to see Marianne,' JB said apologetically. 'I was told she was back in Stockholm.'

'Marianne suddenly made up her mind. I think she was right to return to Sweden, and I think you were wrong sending Gertrude here on her own.'

'I never sent Gertrude anywhere. As I said: It was my fault that she was depressed. You've heard about Jenny, haven't you?'

'Is that what you call the child?' Sten said.

JB at first did not know what to say. Was it a challenge, or a joke?

'Jenny's last name is Jeger. She is thirty-six, and the head of her section at the Department of The Environment,' he said as if he was launching an appeal for her on the radio. 'She is a woman I love.'

'Something in your letters from the control tower made me suspect this. They indicated that in different ways the two of us had experienced something that was new and important. I never quite understood what it could be.'

'I would have liked to be more straight-forward,' Jan said and felt even now a happy tension in his stomach after having spoken Jenny's name.

'So Jenny is a woman you love,' Sten said. 'And who is Gertrude?'

'I still love her,' Jan said. 'She is expecting a baby, but it's not mine. A lot of this story is unfortunate, but no disaster has struck yet.'

'Gertrude doesn't say very much. Yet I think I can understand her well. Are you in the midst of leaving her?'

'I don't know if she wants to keep me the way I am now. She was so immensely pleased to see me yesterday, but I don't think it's me she sees. With pure will power she's trying to move me back by magic to the past. Maybe she's trying to forget about Jenny. She ought to grasp reality. Can you help me?'

'I've tried to talk to her. She says reality is going on between you two. She smiles slightly, as if I could be ruined by knowing too much.'

'Now you know that this reality has got a leak,' Jan said. 'That is Jenny. And Gertrude came here to get some firm ground beneath her feet.'

'Had I known more I might not have called for you,' Sten said.

'I could have coped with her sorrow, but her happiness makes me embarrassed. I can understand that she hasn't told you anything, because she left Sweden to spare her feelings. She wants the baby to belong to her, Jenny and me. At least that's what she said.'

'Whose child is it?'

'I'll leave that to Gertrude to tell you.'

'All this that you're telling me comes over me like a sand-drift,' Sten said. 'I feel like huddling up, I've been overcome by an undefensible sleepy feeling. We must talk more about this some other time.' He was silent. Suddenly he got up and put his arm round Jan's back. Thanks to that, the silence felt neither cold nor reproaching.

'Let's talk about something else,' Sten said. 'Yesterday I did something I never used to do. I shot rabbits. We've built a tannery, and also use the skins to make fur bedspreads for the children to sleep under in the winter. There were once many hunters here. Some drew new curves of altitudes and rivers on the map, and were called explorers.'

'Have you heard of Axel Ericson? Hunter and collector of wild creatures in the nineteenth century.'

'Did he live here?'

'Yes. Died in Namibia. It was all the same area in those days.'

'Explorers seldom returned to Sweden,' Sven said. 'There was no time, and no inclination. These days we go home to die. We go out on short contracts.'

'Have you ever considered staying on infinitely?'

'It's too early to tell. When I go to bed I hear unknown voices outside the house, speaking languages I can't understand, and laughing in a way they never laugh with me. Instead of feeling a foreigner I already look back here nostalgically, although I haven't even left yet.'

'It's hard to understand this for a newcomer like me.'

'There are no postcards of this place. It's almost impossible to show other people what it's like. The first few months I took a lot of photos, but I got bored. You know no more of the world here in Botswana, than the mediaeval map drawers who let the Earth end in flames in the South and darkness in the North, while a dragon and a virgin posed at the ultimate abysses where currents broke out from unpredicted depths.'

Here they had something in common to talk about: Sten trusted in the firm belief that people would always carry evidence and experience further. As a business man in Stockholm he was a servant of continuity. In bomb-proof caves all over the world microfilm was stored as souvenirs from the era of tradition, family trees and permanent inhabitation.

Jan remembered how the depths were marked on the maps: a thickening curtain of very fine lines in ink. And like an undulation it blew across their faces: the dizziness on steep hills, an unnoticeable confusion soon conquered.

'Are you happier here?' Jan asked as they left the house.

'Maybe. I can move more quickly and more easily. I wish Marianne had felt the same as Gertrude. We're higher above the sea than in Stockholm. But Africa has settled on my shoulder like a hawking falcon, I can feel its claws go through the material into my skin. It weighs me down sometimes, and won't fly to get me things.'

'Easy and heavy,' Jan said, 'you're contradicting yourself.'

'Yes, I am contradicting myself.'

Sten Tidström picked up a handful of sand from the ground.

'Throw it against the wind,' he said. 'All you can do, hoping that it won't all blow back on your face.'

142

THE LIMITS OF DARKNESS

'That's Gertrude coming in her jeep,' Sten said.

JB could not understand how he could recognize her at such a distance. A man with light blonde hair sat next to her. He got out of the car awkwardly, as if he had been travelling under great tension. He watched them without smiling. Suddenly a couple of teachers and some of the students appeared. It was the lunch break. They gathered around the newcomer.

'I found him at the station,' Gertrude said in Swedish to Jan and Sten. 'He comes from the dark interior. He doesn't know what to do. I thought he might as well stay with us while he makes his plans.'

'My name is Dave Griffiths,' he said.

'He needs some food and a bath,' Gertrude said.

JB noticed her firm behaviour. If she mastered things that were beyond him, which her dissertation on ferns had already proved – he might as well not worry too much about her.'

'You seem at home in these surroundings,' he said.

'Of course I'm at home. You're here.'

A little while later Sten called to them: 'Gertrude's passenger's got something he wants to tell us. I suggest we go and sit in the dining-room and listen to him.'

The Headmaster had gone to a conference in the capital. A young Irishman was the Deputy Headmaster. The teachers were seldom over thirty. One had trained as a craftsman in Sweden, another had been convicted to five years' imprisonment in South Africa for having encouraged sabotage of the power lines, and a third was a Jewish actor who had had problems getting jobs in England. From different directions they had streamed in over the brown and light green plains around Serowe.

The nurse had come up from the clinic, and sat down next to the matron. Ten students from the primary school entered. They all sat down around the large table.

Dave Griffiths, nineteen years old, had arrived on the mail train from South Africa and got off at Palapye, having heard of the Swaneng Hill School as a place for indoctrination against apartheid. The school had been founded by a white South African refugee, and blacks who had fled after the Sharpville massacre had been taught there. It was infamous on the side of the border that he came from.

Dave had replied six months earlier to an advert in Wales recruiting policemen for South Africa: free fare and a guaranteed future: no unemployment threatened the profession.

'My mum thought it would give me some discipline and deportment. She's a widow and still lives in Wales. I arrived two months early for the training course, so I was put into the service straight away, stationed in a Natal village . . .'

He stopped hesitantly.

'I don't know how to tell you this. I wish I were a journalist, but I've just deserted my job. Many people at home will think I've missed a good chance for the future. I'm afraid I might see it like that myself one day, if I'm unsuccessful. But what I saw was too bloody bad. I didn't know there were things like that in a – in a so called civilized country.'

'You tell us,' the Irishman said.

'Even on the first day they gave me a .38 Smith and Wesson revolver with five bullets. I thought it was strange. But then I soon stopped being surprised. A constable told me he had put out a cigarette in the palm of an African. His friend said: "How could you? You shouldn't touch a Jew with a butt, and you do it with a Kaffir." At the station they often daydreamed about destroying the black race. A constable imitated a dirty grotesque African until in the end we wanted to see the African dead, yes, kill him in the most ghastly possible way. Another wanted to fill the new Verwoer dam with sulphuric acid and force the black people to march into it. One imagined he was standing with a submachine gun in front of an enclosed African crowd.'

'When dreams like that become waking and calculating dreams, the laws of terror go through,' somebody said.

'Between themselves they were kind, kind to me too. They had a focus for their hatred, they could ease the pressure when they liked. Sergeant Oosthuisen at the station was well-known for quick results. Once he arrested the whole non-white staff in a warehouse where some whisky had been stolen. Each one of the forty men was examined individually, which meant they were tortured till they confessed, and eventually twelve of them were taken to court.

'Sometimes they wanted to amuse themselves. An African who had been seized because he had one gram of marijuana was to be examined. He was taken to a room large enough for all of us. They undressed him. They tied a piece of string around his balls while he cried for mercy. A bench was placed upside down in the middle of the room. The other end was tied to the bench. A police dog with a long rope at the collar was let in. The rope was fixed at the other end of the bench. The hands of the prisoner were tied behind his back. When the policeman holding the dog loosened the rope, the dog wanted to attack the African who then had to take a step back pulling the bench with him. The diversion lasted for an hour or so, but I managed to get out.'

Dave Griffiths spoke monotonously, looking at the others almost appealingly, as if impressing on them how serious his story was. He used helpless gestures where words would not do. All the time there was a void he had to fill.

'On another occasion I saw a man almost strangled. A rope was thrown over a rafter of a roof and tied around his neck. Four men pulled at the other end until he hung above the ground, while a fifth pulled his legs. Occasionally they let him down to breath, and then the torture continued.'

'You didn't object?' somebody said.

'It was impossible, especially for a recruit. I tried to spend most of my time out on patrol where I could be human. At the station I would hear the screams from the rooms where non-whites were examined. I couldn't take that.'

Gertrude passed her hand across her eyes, but there were no tears there. Peter, the exiled mathematics teacher also put his hand across his face, mumbling: 'It happens all the time. When I was there and now. It won't stop. It's the night of the soul.'

'I thought it would be rather like military service,' Dave said. 'A job that had to be done. I was poor. To stay all my life in the coal-mining slums at home seemed so pointless. And then this . . . it was hell.'

'You survived,' Sten said.

'In the end I feared I'd become like them. I had to get away at any cost.'

'If you had known, you'd never have gone,' somebody said.

'Some people choose the job because they know what it's like,' Peter said. 'They enjoy it.'

'I was at an ordinary peaceful station in Natal. There is less crime committed there than anywhere else in South Africa, according to the statistics. But I saw the real crimes.'

He spoke in a slow country accent. It was obvious that everybody believed him. He was not an informer who would report back to South Africa about rebellious activities and ideas at the school. Besides, there were no secrets. Swaneng was only dangerous as an example, not for what happened on the surface.

'After two months I was transferred to the Railway Police College in Kaalfontein outside Johannesburg, on the way to Pretoria. As a police student I was permitted to buy and carry a weapon also off duty. The recruits at the college were eighteen years old, and all carried guns. Our first shooting lesson was given by a sergeant called van den Bergh who said: "When you shoot at a Kaffir, shoot to kill and tell the judge you aimed at his legs, but he fell over just as you fired. Shooting at a white person, you fire a shot of warning, and then aim at his legs – if you absolutely have to."

'During shooting exercises we were encouraged to imagine we were shooting Kaffirs, especially the ones we disliked: a rude gardening boy, or a politician like Mandela or Sobukwe.

'An army officer lecturing to us said: "The days are gone when we beat the non-whites up in the street. That is nowadays the task of the police".

'Soldiers sometimes joined the Police Force at weekends to find an outlet for their need to beat Africans.'

Griffiths either looked into one person's eyes for a long time, or talked into the wall as if the room was empty. He continued:

'Train and mine disasters almost always happened only to black people. The one comment I heard was: Good, some Kaffirs less. And we were only trained to be railway policemen; we were not trained to control riots, we were spared the rough work. One day we were called into the great hall of the college. The Transport Minister Ben Schoeman was expected on a visit. An African cleaner was still in the hall when we entered. He had to run the gauntlet, was beaten, kicked, pounded with truncheons and ridiculed. The thought of a Minister having to see such a vermin was obviously unbearable.

'I got pissed out of my mind a couple of times. After two months at the school I bought my leave for sixty rand. I didn't want to be a Railway Policeman. I had a pass that allowed me to travel free on the railways. I took the train here. Nobody stopped me.'

'No,' Peter said. 'Nobody stops a South African policeman coming here.'

'South Africa is our neighbour,' Sten Tidström said to JB. 'We have to keep good neutral relations. We're a small state in the shadow of a big one.'

JB noticed that Sten said 'we' of Botswana. Dave Griffiths wiped the sweat off his forehead as if he had a temperature. The Deputy Headmaster asked him what he wanted to do. He wished to find a job with a good salary and eventually get to Australia or Canada. If he joined a building or mechanical group at the school he would be given food and lodgings, but no money. Several people advised him to go on to Kenya. He had a return ticket with half of the fare prepaid, which he could use. Botswana's Police Corps still had close and unpermitted contacts with the South African, so it could mean risks both for him and the school if he stayed.

'I know that all he tells is true,' Peter said. 'Still it is as though there was no truth to tell. In South Africa the ordinary whites try to live without thinking, which is wonderful to them. Then life is past, it's evening, they have slept all along, and it's too late to do anything about it at all.'

'They're not meant to either,' somebody said. 'The new laws give the secret police the power to conceal what happens. The whites will sit by their swimming-pools, saying: we knew nothing, we noticed nothing. The government has granted their consciences early retirement. That makes life easier for them.'

They were silent. Dave seemed unhappy. Somebody got up to go. An African in ragged khaki shorts suddenly appeared in the doorway. He pointed towards the yard.

'My daughter . . .'

Gertrude was closest to the exit. Jan followed her out. A

twelve-year-old girl had been pricked by thorns, and her foot had swollen up to twice its normal size.

'The plants are wilder here than the animals,' Gertrude said to JB. She helped the girl into the Land Rover. Jan had hesitated about what to do, and was again surprised at Gertrude's confidence. Her movements were swift, as if her pregnancy did not bother her at all.

'There was nobody in the clinic,' the girl's father said. He had waited for an hour or so. They discovered they had extended their lunch break because of Griffiths. They must hurry if they were to save the life of the girl. Africans could die so suddenly – malnutrition gave them bad resistance. It made children die from measles or diptheria as quickly as if somebody just deleted their names on their birth certificates.

The African nurse, who kept the keys for the medicine cabinets, sat in the car with Sten, and some other person who was going in the same direction. The father, who did not belong to the school, returned to his fields. For a little while JB and Dave were alone outside the dining-room, and looked at each other: two outsiders amid the everyday life of Botswana.

A couple of moonflowers, scented with vanilla, suddenly came loose from their bush, and blew off like light paper petals.

'Are they planted here?' JB asked.

'Suppose so,' Dave replied. 'I don't know.'

He had been in Africa for four months – about the same time as Gertrude.

'Is Gertrude your wife?' he asked.

JB hesitated. Should he stick to the usual version, the one he had grown into, which seemed to him to have a deeper truth? 'I'd say so,' he said. 'We're together.'

He knew the distance from Griffith's police station in Natal to the Water Palace, but Dave's experience too had a side to it which concerned him alone: what was he to do with his life after having seen this? Sten returned.

'The girl has total blood-poisoning. They gave her penicillin injections. She was all awake, although she probably had a temperature of a hundred and five. Her pulse was fluttering so they could hardly count it.'

'There they were waiting while we were listening to accounts of other people's nightmares,' JB said.

They looked out over their immediate surroundings: sandy

148

paths between the houses and huts, tangled grass, and thistles with white and yellow flowers.

'The plants are sparse here,' Sten said. 'They don't reach each other. The seeds are waiting for a dog's fur to sweep past them. The sheep catch them in their wool, women by the hem of their dress, squirrels carry them on their tail, and the wind stirs them up.'

Everything was sparse: stones, houses, greenery – but enclosed between Heaven and Earth, with walls of air, dancing inside one's head. The midsummer heat was like a membrane over the skin. The rains did not usually come until the end of March.

'Is it possible to phone Sweden from here?' JB asked Sten.

Jenny was to return home that day.

'It's difficult, and it will cost you a fortune. It's better not to communicate too much. Be patient. Well, I say that just as a general rule.'

Jan still sent a telegram about his yearning. It was brief. He did not sign it, but had to put the sender's address. A couple of hours later an African messenger left a copy on Gertrude's doorstep. JB did not know that it was the custom of Cable and Wireless. Gertrude automatically opened it. Then she gave it to JB.

'Did Jenny ask you to cable her?'

'No. We never promised each other anything.'

'You promised me a lot of things.'

He did not remember that. A feeling of self-evidence beyond promises had reigned between them, and the continuity remained. They could leave each other, but never be rid of each other.

'Your smile when you arrived lit me like a lamp,' she said. 'But it was directed towards Jenny.'

'No,' he said. 'I smiled to you. Try to see me as the person I am – for better or worse.'

'I have thought of all the times when I have woken up happy to see you. I didn't realize that you were somewhere else. It has terrified me. I can feel like a weed that ought to be removed, something that doesn't fit in. At the same time I know you experience things you might as well experience with me.'

'No,' he said. 'I have underestimated you if you can't accept the truth. You, my sister, ought to know that experiences look

149

alike from afar, like horses on a road. But they are different. They are not small change.'

'You wanted different experiences. Knowing where both of us stand is more important to me: that was my radical experience. You want to rob me of that. But you can't make me change. I want you to remember me as one single face, and remember that it is because of you that I'm here.'

She slowly passed her hands across her stomach, as if the child were really theirs.

Again he realized how for many years they had lived like two cogs, incessantly touching each other, without any play: that was how they had built up their life, closely and exactly. All the things that had then supported them were now an obstacle for one of them. He was surprised it was him. She should have been the one to find new paths, the older sister with her allure and lawlessness. He would never know how he would then have been transformed.

He looked at her face, where a certain stiffness lay like a strange make-up since Jenny's name had been mentioned. He loved her and they were together. He was suddenly filled with hope: as if his and Jenny's love was strong enough to bear anything, and his and Gertrude's so vulnerable that it had to be spared.

'I haven't exchanged you for Jenny,' JB said. 'I love both of you. I shall never in my life get the two of you mixed up. You think you're a sketch I've thrown away to make another draft. But somewhere you're etched into me, and no one can efface that.'

Towards the evening they were told that the girl with the blood-poisoning was allergic to penicillin. She had fallen into a coma after the treatment, and they did not know whether she would pull through, as her general condition was weak. She had eight brothers and sisters.

'If I had nine children and one of them died,' Gertrude said, 'the lives of the other eight wouldn't console me.'

'Do you think the girl will make it?' JB asked.

'They'll let us know in due course. You see – there is hardly time to listen to other people's experiences here. There's so much happening all the time. The landscape is monotonous, but not the everyday life.'

What Dave had told them lingered in the atmosphere that

day. A party planned to welcome JB was put off. They all had an early night.

Dave spent the night in Gertrude's house as they had promised him. JB suspected that his big sister had calculated that if Dave was given the room where he had spent his first night, he would have to move into her room to sleep.

That was exactly what happened. In Gertrude's room there was a chair, a basin, and paperback books on a shelf. Hardly anything indicated that it was Gertrude who lived there. She had brought some research matter from Sweden, but no personal belongings; Jan found Faegri-Iversen's text book on Pollen Analysis.

'Are there ferns in Botswana as well?' he asked.

'Many kinds. You find them everywhere.'

Letters, jewellery, souvenirs – she had brought none of these. The child lay in her womb as in a saucepan; she did not control the temperature herself.

'I've been feeling sorry for my body,' she said. 'My nipples have been hard, and you were far away. Yet I've been caressed inside.'

That night – with Dave sleeping heavily on the other side of the thin wall – they lay as they had done at the Water Palace: two spoons in a drawer. Gertrude had put the beds together, and JB held one arm heavily around her breasts. Gertrude said:

'I'm telling myself you love me for as long as you're here. That's why you're here. And I'm only concerned with the moments when you're here.'

Jan again was stunned at her bold tone of voice.

'If I had a magic net in the forest,' she continued, 'I would envelop you in that. Then you'd be with me, always in the net. I would treat you so well that you wouldn't find time to get tired or sad. You'd feel what I'm feeling.'

She laughed as if contradicting herself. She had left Sweden to prevent herself being caught in the net of emotions and habit.

'You must see me as the person I am,' he repeated.

'You mean I should see you as a beast. But I'm not that curious. I trust you. I prefer loving you in the dark to fearing you in daylight.'

She spoke into the warm bodily darkness of his armpit. She was soon breathing evenly, calm and satisfied.

They were all asleep, JB thought: Gertrude, the girl with blood-poisoning, the young police recruit with all his visions of torture, and the straight-forward Sten who would not let his private emotions confuse him.

He then dreamed about Jenny holding a wax candle over them. The little room lit up like a light bulb, and Jenny rushed off with a weird scream.

'You screamed something in your sleep last night,' Gertrude said as they had their morning tea.

But although Jan Backman asked her, she never told him what it was.

THE FLOATERS

Dave Griffith continued north with the mail train. JB moved his camp bed back. The girl allergic to penicillin was still unconscious. Gertrude received a letter from Marianne Tidström. At the weekend she went to work in the Francistown slums. Sten took JB on a sight-seeing tour of Botswana; they were to deliver tools and other necessities to a school building site, and a camp drilling wells.

'It's hard to find spare parts,' Sten said. 'An African farmer near Swaneng uses a Dutch name when ordering spares for his tractor, or he'd have to wait months longer.'

At dawn they loaded the Land Rover. The sun rose quickly like an escaped balloon. Swallows turned cart-wheels over the bushes, and far above it all was the cry of an eagle.

'I'd like to help out while I'm here,' JB said.

'Don't worry over Gertrude,' Sten said. 'I guess I was wrong. In dry hot continental climates like this infections heal more easily.'

They had packed pieces of machinery in old sacks with dirty flour dust and blurred aniline stamps: Lincoln Brothers, Gaborone.

'No rain today either,' Sten said. 'The ration of water is ten litres a day per person. Botswana has a special Minister for

Water. He dreams of a kingdom of greenery watered by deep wells, a flow combed out over the landscape by windmills until the fields are full of fourleafed clover.'

They drove east towards the railway. Outside the simplest huts – only dried clay without a supporting framework of stakes – old people were sitting doing wickerwork or stringing pumpkins. Sten said:

'I asked an old lady what security meant to her. She said she had thought a lot about it: the rains arriving when they should, nobody breaking her door open at daybreak, and being able to send her son with vegetables and beer to a relation knowing that he will arrive safely.'

They drove across flat countryside. To the East were the mountains of South Africa, and the mountain ridges of Rhodesia. Water ran down them like salt sandy tears down the cheek of a giant. It would soon dry up, but the traces remained.

In the vicinity of Francistown, foreign exploiters had in recent years discovered diamonds, nickel and copper in such quantities that it would pay off to extend the network of roads. The state of Botswana lacked money, but South Africa and multi-national companies arrived on the spot promising Botswana half the proceeds. The country was too small and too young to exploit its riches. A few thousand young people who had spent six years at school, but still not found profitable jobs, might be better off in the future. Yet the country would be robbed of natural assets which could be used in a wiser way.

A divided economy was created. In a state where most inhabitants were farmers and cattle breeders with their household wealth in kind, the miners became an elite, and their salaries formed standards. Prices rose, and the standard of the country was measured according to these. The fixing of maximum salaries to keep agriculture from being outdistanced, would favour the foreign companies, and then the miners' union would have to object.

The low level of economy in the country had its advantages, Sten said. No domineering elite, no escape to the cities. Only seventeen industrial companies employed more than nine workers. The salaried working class consisted of three thousand men, but twenty thousand worked in South Africa sending part of their salary home. Half the land was owned by the tribes themselves; they grew sweetcorn and sorghum, and fed their cattle there. In Botswana there were three times as many cows as people. The other half of the land was owned by the state, and mainly uninhabited like the Kalahari desert. Only four per cent of the country was private property.

The people owned little but their animals; a pair of trousers, two skirts, some ornaments, and sometimes enough money to travel by bus to a market-place. To them the upper class was the rest of the world. Their welfare could not be measured by the increase of their gross national product, which they did not notice, but by other values which increased their self-confidence and vital strength.

In three years as many people are born on this earth as the inhabitants of France, Italy, England, Holland and Belgium. The area of Botswana is as large as that of all these countries; but with hardly a million inhabitants, the country is so small that it cannot be really free, until its neighbours have their freedom too. 'No one trembles when we speak,' Seretse Khama, the president said. That was no reason to stay mute. But hardly anyone heard what the people said, as they were still too unclear, and too enigmatic.

Behind them history showed up all the other invisible peoples: those who built the pyramids, the dragon ships and the caravels; those who drowned at Trafalgar, perished in the rubber plantations and the concentration camps, disappeared in the oil war in Nigeria and in the name of Allah in Bangla Desh. They could not read or write, but now they had started to learn, and they taught each other. The world would cease to exist only in the way their upper classes envisaged it, and it was possible to influence and intervene. They were loaded with a special energy which did not show in the cash-books of the state, or in the statistics of the UN.

The car spread a trail of dust behind JB and Sten; they could be refugees escaping in a war film. Sometimes it seemed that the low hills on the horizon were reflected in the circular plain they enclosed. They saw fluttering shadows, dried out shore lines of a lake which might have once been here. Women with cans on their heads and babies on their backs stopped at the side of the road. Outside the huts clothes were drying on the prickles of thorn trees to keep the wind from donating them to the neighbour.

154

'This is the home of poverty,' Sten said. 'They carry it as a second skin. The annual income is on average two hundred kronor per capita. People don't look down at your tattered shoes. They look into your eyes: friend or foe? You have to retain somebody's gaze.'

They halted at a store, which was inside a shed. It was owned by an Indian who had a wart on his cheek like a brown gooseberry. There were a couple of sacks of corn flour and beans on the earth floor, materials and preservatives on a shelf, and bicarbonate and soap on another. There was a smell of perspiration, cow hide, corn flour, porridge, and monotony in a remote corner of the world. The Indian's means of transport was a mule and an open-sided wagon with a crooked branch as a connecting pole. He had sold out of Coca Cola and Fanta, so they had a cup of bark tea from the Cape Province. It tasted of withered leaves. They had half a bucket of water to wash their faces in, and lingered in the cool shade under a roof of rough leaves.

'What made the Indian choose this kind of life?' Sten said. 'Was he even worse off before? Was this his only choice? I've asked him, but he won't tell me anything. Indians here take care not to answer personal questions, as it doesn't pay off. I never heard him complain.'

'He either doesn't know what other places are like, or he does,' said JB. 'I think the only way to feel that you're not an ant, a mushroom, or a lichen, is to risk what's given to you, and take the chance at an alternative on the side. But also you have to understand those who do not choose to change, who won't take a chance at unknown and dangerous things. I admit the driving force in my own case: the same old battle of striving to fill myself up to the brim.

'I've realized what's so attractive to you in the school programme,' JB said. 'To create a keen feeling for work without any need of competition; a sense of self-respect that has no one else as a measuring rod.'

'Yes,' Sten said. 'The need here is for fertile soil for new patterns of action. But there's little time. It's too late to believe we're children gathering to watch the fire-flies in the twilight. You can't pull your bed curtains, and wash the world off your hands. This is no place for a privileged unbiased observer of events.'

'Where is that place? Not at my instrument panel at Arlanda. I don't survey events there, and I'm not unbiased.'

'You can be all right for a while with mechanics and routine, but that's not possible here.'

'Not in Sweden either. You think I'm sitting comfortably and safely in my glass tower. A couple of months ago we had a serious accident nearby in the woods. Did you read about it? The surviving air hostess cried for help. I heard her on my earphones when mechanics and routine failed. I can still hear her.'

Sten did not reply, and for a second Jan thought he had been speaking quietly to himself.

They continued towards Mahalapye. Sten drove fast. He kept his eyes on one thing while he talked about something else. The people he worked with seemed to reflect characteristics of traits within himself. He represented or integrated them. It gave him a kind of balance. The outside world had all the time left its imprints on him, and JB found that through Sten he gained knowledge of life without having to assemble it face to face on the field.

JB could be surprised at Sten Tidström. He had left his Stockholm company for Botswana. He had let Marianne and the children return to Sweden, assuming that was what they wished. His intentions were good. He lacked personal vanity. He thought reality could be changed, not by charity, but by making charity grow.

In the 1950s he had believed in the free world. Its freedom turned out to be rich nations consuming while the others starved, on the pretence that the poor somehow deserved to be poor. Therefore, the smaller cake suited them better: 'cut your coat according to your cloth', his father innocently said. The larger cake remained, and from that pieces were cut, called financial aid for developing nations: an invention of the rich nations to insure against the nightmare of a violent revolt. But there was no reason to believe that a sound economy made countries more democratic. Neither could democracy guarantee world peace more than any other system. If someone wanted to support the rights of the multitude to control their own lives, he had to do it with a different kind of conviction.

'The larger and more powerful a country is,' Sten said, 'the more essential it is to limit and distribute the power, and play the men in power against each other. There are socialists of aptitudes different from mine, who see it in a different way, who find a strong organizing hand beneficient. But I'm not religious, and I've had enough of patriarchs.'

They jolted along a road that allowed them to go exactly sixty kilometres an hour, or the jolting would be unbearable. Sten kept sharing his thoughts with JB:

'The dogmas of western capitalism have to be prized out: fear of poverty is a necessary driving force; poor people are lazy; equality is a fairy tale; capitalism and competition are the most effective ways to create welfare and freedom. There is an increasing distance between the desires and expectations of the third world and the ideas the rich world has about its needs.

I'm thinking of Sweden with its swift, anxiously glittering mirrors of time, the suspicious provincial minds, all the negative energy spilt with such talent, and each with a fragment of his own pompous truth . . . The claim all the time for something to happen.'

'I don't think everybody feels like that,' JB said.

'History moves slowly down here, like a hippopotamus in the mud. You don't notice it. A slow movement which gathers strength in itself. Then suddenly, with the final jerk of his head, the hippopotamus will upset the boat.'

'We don't know for sure what powers are forming our world,' JB said. 'Neither here nor in Europe. The mortar between the old bricks of history is crumbled to pieces more quickly in places where we least suspect it.'

'I feel less terrified here,' Sten said. 'In Sweden I had a clean conscience from carrying a feeling of guilt, and I found I functioned very well alongside what I could really achieve. But it was no good. Here I don't have to live on borrowed time. I wish Marianne could understand.'

After a couple of hours' driving they were in Mahalapye. Swaneng's professional gang of house construction and installation workers were erecting a new comprehensive school. There were also young people training as apprentices in the trade. Fifteen Swaneng girls were clearing land for a vegetable garden. Another group was experimenting making bricks with new mixtures of clay. Before the construction began, they had all discussed its purpose and agreed on it. Thus ideology and long time vision entered the picture. Each working group then decided for itself, and acted in the way it thought most effective.

Decades ago young men had gone out on long hunting trips, or served as soldiers. They walked away as children, and came back as men. Now in the same tradition they went to Johannesburg, worked there for a couple of years, returned with enough money to buy a bride, settled down and got married – if they ever got away from the mines. That was another kind of initiation rite. They returned with raincoats and umbrellas, sunglasses and cocked hats. Years later they met other men from some other tribe who had been in the same camp at the same time, and then they reminisced and discussed how awful the place had been, in the way old soldiers remember the toil and the dirt: now it's all over.

The mines were like a military tenure establishment, an institution to support them; now they tried to replace them in a more meaningful way, and give the young people professional knowledge and ability to identify with the problems of the country. They would otherwise drift towards the future without knowing their destination – like before, on the slave ships, where people were alone, without relations, and therefore jumped overboard or faded away. Recognizing people is the one security in life, and extending this recognition beyond the borders of the tribe . . .

Sten and JB unloaded the polythene pipes they had brought. These were to link the school with a water tank standing on spindly legs on a little hill three hundred metres away. Ditches were dug in the ground which looked like flaking slate. They started to work at once. The school was to be finished in two weeks' time with five class-rooms, outdoor lavatories, a laboratory, a teachers' house, and a football pitch. The water would have to run by then.

The schools following in the tradition of Swaneng Hill let their teaching focus on the immediate environment. There was no attraction in the freedom to train as a paleontologist or a Latin teacher in a country where knowledge of fertilizing techniques could give thousands of people a better kind of life. In the colonial days higher education had been a forbidden fruit. After almost ten years of independence, more than two thousand students had attended the comprehensive school, and a couple of hundred the High School. That was still not enough to excel in exclusive subjects. It would be some time before Serowe had traffic lights, and even longer before the history of learning, Gertrude's subject, could be studied there.

Being practical and down to earth was not enough. The right stimuli and the proper milieu had to be found as well. In the shade of a tree somebody surrounded by family and friends took every piece of his old sewing-machine out onto a cloth, vehemently teaching them, spurred on and criticized by them. Suddenly many more people knew how a sewing-machine worked.

When the foreign helpers came with their money and architects' drawings, and let people on the spot take care of the job, the result was envy and fatigue rather than pride. The inhabitants of each village had to achieve their own results, however slow the process. They had had enough of prototypes.

'You learn to work with them, not for them,' Sten said. 'But if I am to leave tomorrow, does it matter what I do? I've told myself that, but the longer I stay, the more I see the opposite view: since I may not stay much longer, I must consider whatever I do. I can't put the blame on someone else. Somehow I have to take responsibility for whatever I do. For it's the demands of this society that give a context to my actions. If they weren't there, the experiences would remain, but out of all context. Swaneng is a collective community, but I've never felt effaced there, since I carry part of the responsibility.' The day was hot, the air steamy and warm, and sticky like a pan of stock. JB was in the working team shovelling earth over the black polythene hose.

'This is Julius, and that's Dzwanda,' Sten said. Two boys raised their faces glistening with sweat towards him, and smiled. A third person who was levelling the bottom of the trench with a pickaxe, was a girl. They exchanged words between them, and laughed aloud.

'What's so funny?' JB asked.

'Impossible to explain,' the girl replied.

He thought of Jenny. They had a private laugh too. Lacking a telephone he picked up a dry morello stone he carried in his pocket, and let his fingers tap a message. There was a world further away, he would have been different if he had been in it from the start. He would have been different had he survived Hiroshima instead of living only in Stockholm. Many fingerprints could not be found on his body.

He had dreaded having to accept his fate, and realizing that he had been given a certain square of the world. In order to live, he had to keep other people's lives open to his. He did not want to be rootless, but neither did he want to give the impression that he had already been cast for his part, the only one.

JB and Sten worked tightly following each other. Stones and earth were protecting the pipes against feeding cattle, cars and rodents. Jan said he had never laid down pipes at the Water Palace, but in this place it seemed right that everybody should be able to build his own house. They started to talk about their backgrounds, and Sten told him that he was born four years before his parents got married. They left him as a foster child in a working class family in the South of Stockholm. His parents lived nearby, but never came to see him. Then they got some money and the opportunity to get married, so they moved into a large flat at Kungsholmen, put the piano along the drawing-room wall, and hung family portraits on the others, together with a dry salmon which was his father's one pride of nature. It was then convenient for them graciously to take the child back to grow up with the anxious narrow-minded bourgeoisie who mainly thought about other people's opinions. To many people still living and working this was not too long ago: in the early Thirties.

'Habit is strong here as well,' Sten said, 'but poverty makes it understandable. The cowardice of the kind my parents displayed I find hard to forgive. The workers' family was paid the money owing to them, and never seen again.'

Sten and JB continued to the camp drilling wells some twenty kilometres away. A group of Scandinavians worked there twelve hours a day, drilling four metres. After a hundred metres they had met a sufficient amount of water for a hand pump. They had a lorry with a corroded exhaust pipe, a radio transmitter, and a couple of tents.

When the drilling machine was not going, the unusual silence of a high plateau far away from the sea prevailed. A species of hardy water gathering plants grew there with pistils like twisted wire, and thin lemon yellow flowers shining with a special glow in the shadow of the clouds. They survived sun and insects. Their white roots were uncovered, but not gnawed by animals. It was hard to pull them out of the sand, and they did not die. They were always there, even after fires.

'I hope you've brought bread and dried meat,' a driller said. 'Herring and Akvavit would be too much to expect, I suppose. By the way, in the Francistown supermarket they've had a burglary. The thieves wore shorts, and oiled the rest of their bodies. They slid out of everybody's hands, and disappeared into the night. Nobody dared follow them. I found a thief in my room when I stayed at Tati, but he farted so terribly I had to let him go.'

'Look at the ground here!' another exclaimed. 'Destroyed by cows and goats. The whole district is gnawed to pieces. Yet there are antelopes and buffaloes here, all sorts of hoofed animals. They multiply faster and have more meat than the tame cattle. They make long journeys across the savanna, keeping grass and bushes alive. But people won't move until the ground is eaten bare. That's Africa's misfortune. And influencing the people – that is politics and teaching that nobody wants to engage in seriously. Meanwhile they imagine that the diamond finds will save the country.'

'Have you got anything to drink?' JB asked.

There was a paraffin fridge on the lorry. He got a glass, and let the ice-cold water flush his gums. As he closed his eyes, a curtain as red as a currant remained. Then the heat could return, and he took the whole sun in his mouth.

He found that the landscape overpowered him. Some days had now passed; he was out with Sten; it was easy not to think of Gertrude. The movements of the light, the course of the sun, the smell of the peat fires, the rough paths, the prickles and the leaves, the occupations of the people – all this filled him up so completely that he felt he had nothing left of his own.

He saw the sparse vegetation, originally manifold, now exhausted by cultivation. The restrictions gave good yields on a short-term basis, but no fertile soil. The soil blew away, the life-giving surface became thinner and thinner. Yet a low, gnarled acacia tree managed to get its water from the invisible and live on : bees would soon buzz around the white flowers.

The well drillers had cut silver thorns, and placed them like rolls of barbed wire round their camp of tents in case hyenas showed up at night. But they had not noticed any rapacious beasts in the area. After a short twilight the moon rose, and Sten said:

'It's as red as the fly-agarics that grow on the path to Taheiti. Sometimes I miss the damp smell of last year's leaves and pine needles glued together. Drought smells less.'

'Don't you ever wake up thinking you're in Sweden?' JB asked.

'Sometimes I go to sleep in the midday heat, and get woken up by a bird and the mumble of voices. I know I'm here and know what I've left, but for a moment I can suddenly feel the exhaust fumes of the rush hour between the pale plaster facades of the Vasa district, and the smell of a chemist's shop with wet snow on the floor. However, I immediately travel here in a transit of smells, land in Karthoum, and feel myself drawn into the undescribably heavy sweet smell of charcoal burning, and the warm earth which is Africa at night.'

JB left the area of the tent. The night's seams were fraying: the interior of stars was glistening. He looked up towards the breathing galaxies. Nearer the earth was the savanna, gnawed by desert and yet looking like a piece of the world which had not yet realized its potentials; an unborn streak, an undeveloped time.

Eventually he pushed aside the curtains of his private life, and met a piece of Africa face to face. He felt carried by a sort of gratitude that all this existed. Yet he had read so much about it.

He remembered that one of the country's explorers, Charles John Anderson from the province of Älvsborg had described how strange, stimulating and upsetting it was to discover something you had long known only by reports:

'When the natives who marched in front of my caravan got to the top of one of these ridges, they would stop short, and point ahead of them crying: "Ngami! Ngami!" In a moment I was with them. In the distance not very far away, there was in front of me an immense mirror of water, limited only by the horizon. My first impression of this sight was strange. I had long been prepared for this event, but was now almost overcome by it. It was a mixture of bliss and pain. My temples pounded, and my heart beat so hard that I had to dismount, and lean against a tree until my extreme reaction had calmed down.'

They slept in their own tent, which they had brought in the Land Rover. Getting up at daybreak, they found the landscape changed; the ground seemed to be covered by fresh snow. They stopped amazed at the opening of the tent. Sten had never seen this before. In the white blanket of snow they could see tracks of a badger, a thrush, and an antelope. One of the well drillers came up and told them what it was.

The snow was the remains of the starter threads of tens of thousands of little spiders who had taken off in the quiet of the morning. They were carried by the air current which rose when the Earth was warmed by the sun. They reached the stratosphere, and floated around the Earth on the back of the trade-winds. Only few of them ever found new places of abode.

NOT QUITE YET

Life at the school continued much as usual, more eventful for Gertrude and Sten than for Jan, who found himself counting the days until he would see Jenny again. This gave him a feeling of ingratitude to Africa and his sister.

Some kilometres north-east was a neighbour, a white Scottish born farmer aged about sixty, called Henry Douglas, with Mary his wife. He had saved a dusty bottle of vintage champagne from the christening of a grand-child, and he invited Jan and Gertrude Backman and Sten Tidström to his home. The latter two he had met when he sold fruit to the school. He had also, contrary to his own commercial interests, given some students instructions in the pruning and grafting of citrus trees.

When they arrived he was standing by the beehives among the gnarled grape-fruit trees: a tall broad-shouldered man with a humble appearance in a landscape where he had spent twenty years. He had adjusted, but not inside. He and Botswana could neither part nor meet. He had introduced chestnut trees, which were his pride.

He turned to JB the newcomer, talking about Africa as if everything depended on it. But sometimes he would see Africa as a contrast to Scotland, which made the continent less incomprehensible to Jan. Henry Douglas did not seem to expect an answer.

They walked along the wall where blackened grape-vines showed that the farmer had once tried viniculture, down to the cattle pond in the valley. They saw the tracks of elands; in one direction the grazing land was copper brown and stiff with clay, and in the other direction there were irrigated fields of ground-nuts and sweetcorn. Henry pointed to the farm-workers.

'Would you want to work like that from morning to night for a couple of rand? I can't see how they can, or want to. And they are supposed to be ruling our country.'

Again he did not seem to expect any comments. The low paid workers had themselves to blame : they were out of earshot.

The guests approached the house, recoiling at their own shadows on the white plaster wall. Dinner was early, as the journey home was long. A servant cleaned the dust off their shoes, and handed them warm damp towels for their faces. The rooms were all on the ground floor. The first floor was taken up by water tanks to keep the taps going.

Henry's wife Mary sailed through the rooms in a red silk dress, rustling like an auxiliary engine. She was small, tanned, and furrowed; she would have looked good in a pair of trousers. A smell of medications lingered round her like a memory of illnesses suffered. On the couch a permanent hollow marked her throne.

'How nice of you to come! I need a little chat for an hour or so. Henry, you see, works on the farm all day long . . .'

'I'm here now. I'm going to join you,' the farmer protested.

'Of course you're here, Henry, no one denies that. But as soon as we're alone again you'll very likely disappear. Our guests can't very well know what you'll be doing then. And let's not bore them by talking about it. But I could do with some small-talk and gossip to keep me going, not even you would begrudge me that, would you Henry?'

Her voice bubbled like soda water. Henry served drinks and

never stopped asking what they wanted. Eventually they were all landed with enormous gins in their hands, unable to remember what they had originally asked for.

Jan looked around. The dining-table was made of walnut from the Cape. A cabinet with glass doors contained handbooks on live-stock and agriculture, books which were school prizes, Stevenson's novels and Kipling's stories. An ancestor looked down from a painting like an oil painting of Zeus.

'This is my faithful old philodendron,' she showed them. 'We brought it here. It will soon come of age.'

It already towered above her shoulder.

They sat down at the table. The house-maid in black and white, with black skin, brought the champagne. Henry removed the protective wire himself, and let the cork pop.

'How festive,' Gertrude said in a low voice.

'It reminds you of so much,' said Mary.

And while she carried on talking, JB closed his eyes and saw white mushrooms in a park with elms and larches; he could smell jasmine in the warm wind, and hear the creaking of oars. So far from Botswana, and yet that scene might exist only a short distance away – in South Africa. That was the way it had turned out.

His thoughts were shattered by Mary's voice pitched higher than before:

'Really! Congratulations! Let's toast the little one on his way.'

She stared fixedly at Gertrude's stomach, and JB saw his half-sister quickly putting her arms protectively around the unknown one.

While the others mumbled their agreement, Mary threw in some good advice:

'Go home in good time. I don't trust the hygiene here. It may be all right for the natives, but we are a little more delicate, aren't we?'

As Jan was bracing himself against the impending interrogation, Mary plunged over to the servant problem:

'We call her Bado Kidogo. It's Swahili for "not quite yet". She doesn't understand that, we wouldn't want to hurt her. But that's what she replies in Tswana. Is dinner ready? When will the sun set? When is the train due? Has the milk gone bad? Are you pregnant? – "Not quite yet".'

'Sometimes we ask ourselves,' Henry said, 'what she'd say if we asked her whether she'd want to kill us.'

'We wouldn't ask,' Mary said. 'That would be unkind.'

They dined on steak from one of their own herd, followed by peach halves swimming in kirsch, and like people drowning, occasionally floating up to the surface of the glass bowl.

'We used to keep peacocks. They got on well with the guinea-fowl,' Mary said.

'It didn't work in the long run,' Henry said. 'The natives were frightened. They say peacocks will pick babies' eyes out. Pick them out like peas. One day my white peacock was snared and strangled, but left in its run. I didn't know what to believe.'

'It made a nice casserole,' Mary put in. 'But my God it's difficult to find pickled onions here.'

They then had tea at a low mahogany table. JB timidly stared down into his cup, where each leaf was swelling separately. Mary made the tea on a hot-plate; she warmed the pot, and then poured in the boiling water in a careful English manner. On the table there was a silver snake with red garnet eyes, as if nature did not provide enough snakes.

Mary and Henry in their conversation referred to topics they had touched on before. The guests remained uninitiated, and failed to understand the purpose of their presence. They felt superfluous, as if they were peeping undiscovered in through a window. And that was Botswana, JB thought. The whites were such a small percentage that the blacks looked at their everyday life when they had a chance, but without fear and envy. The threat was the whites on the other side of the border.

'Whom did you say you met in Francistown?' Mary asked.

'I don't know her name,' Henry replied, 'I just said she reminded me of Bertha.'

'Oh Bertha. I'd rather not think of her.'

'Why not?'

'She left without a word. Not a word to thank me. Not the slightest comment.'

'She dared not.'

'Dared what?'

'She didn't say anything because she didn't think she could.'

'By the way, do you know where this key comes from?'

'It winds up the alarm clock. Put it in the bowl with the hairpins.'

They both spoke in loud brittle voices, as if they never listened to each other. Mary did not speak while chewing, but even that was done under evil-boding mumbling: brm mm brm . . . When JB inserted a question, nobody heard it. However loud he spoke, he still could not reach the proper wavelength. When he had been talking for quite a while just to confirm that nobody paid attention, Mary said to him:

'You must find us noisy.'

And Henry added:

'I like people who are quiet.'

In the bathroom there were rows of little bottles in crystal cut glass with scented health-bringing decoctions long since evaporated, and next to them a box of capsules of snake serum – fatal if they were mixed up. Thus they tamed Africa to obedience, but Africa defied them in other ways, and remained incomprehensible. This indisputable fact was part of their view on life, and their party game.

'We would like to be able to understand all the strange things that happen these days,' said Mary, 'but we really can't. It's like teaching new games to old dogs.'

'Tricks,' Henry said.

'Why?' said Mary. 'It's like teaching old horses new dances. We can't make it.'

'Then there's the problem of the poultry feed,' Henry said.

'You can't get any proper feed here,' Mary said. 'It was different at home. I don't find the eggs here good; they are not what I mean by country eggs, like we had at home in Scotland.'

'No,' Henry said. 'There's no goodness in the feed. The shells are as soft as lizards' eggs.'

'It's not all that bad,' Mary objected, 'but it's not the way it should. I once mentioned to a Dutch girl in Francistown how difficult it was to find good feed. Try the restaurant in Serowe, she said, it's not too expensive. She was thinking of food and I meant poultry feed.'

Mary laughed to herself for some time. The others sat in silence, happy to hear the hostess entertaining herself.

On the drawing-room wall there was a picture with a little brass plate on the frame: A Windy Day Outside Johannesburg, and a recent nautical chart of the Bay of Singapore, which looked like the Stockholm archipelago: the Brothers lighthouse could have been Sandö, but the symbols indicated a less secure area: frequent typhoons, and ammunition dumped in the sea. JB looked for the classic cartographer's sign of surrender in the face of topographical threats: hic dragones, dragons here.

'If the guerilla should stop here for a night,' Henry said, 'we couldn't expect much mercy.'

'Although we've been Liberals all our lives,' Mary said.

'We're not like the South Africans, but how should they know? They often don't know in which country they are. The borders are not marked. We ought to have a signpost: Decent whites live here. However, you wouldn't know who would then come trampling into your kitchen.'

'We've taken good care of you, Bado Kidogo, haven't we?' Mary said. The housemaid nodded and folded up the tablecloth. She went out, leaving an unexpected emptiness behind. Jan caught Sten's and Gertrude's eyes at the same time, feeling that in this house they were people of his kind. They saw the Douglas couple from the outside.

An island in Botswana, JB thought, which resembled many other islands he had seen before. To live a lie you had to be part of the lie yourself. Around Mary and Henry the house and savanna and desert were silent. They did not understand the language of the Africans buzzing like a threatening wind or like a distant rattle of rifles. The first whites arrived here at the turn of the century as hunters and trackers. They did not care who owned the land, as long as no huts could be seen. Perhaps Axel Ericson had descendants here – but they were probably not white, and therefore in little doubt as to where they belonged.

Henry was the pioneer who worked not for Botswana's future, or his own, but to justify himself in the eyes of the dead. In a country without a historical background he gathered around him his ancestors from Scotland, asking them to note how he had broken new ground, made the earth yield fruit, and extended the family domains. It was a hard life, harder than life on the Orkneys. It took its share of patience and decency.

He told them about a friend, a farmer who had lived nearer the Rhodesian border. He had waited three years in vain for good rains. They had to come, every year could not be an exception. He was forced to sell his corn and cattle to natives, and did not have enough money to go to the tobacco auction in Salisbury. He was sixty years old, and tired. He wrote for his son, asking him to come and take over the farm, or have it sold. When the son arrived at the house, he saw a shadow at the window. It was his father on his knees, staring out over the bush with dead open eyes. Next to him was the rifle he had dropped.

'That's not an unusual fate,' Henry said.

'That's what life is like,' Mary said. 'Not many people understand what our life is like.'

JB had had too many of Henry's gins. He had a stale taste in his mouth. He was unable to sever himself from all this, he was drawn into it, somehow recognizing it all. He felt he was in the basement of the Biological Museum among forgotten, badly stuffed animals no longer waiting to be given an airing.

He felt like being alone with his yearning for Jenny. Words to her were crowding in his head, and he was afraid they could be read on his lips. When he got out into the still cold of the evening, the earth moved under his feet like the deck of a ship, and the stars changed places. The moon bounced like a balloon on a string. Supporting himself on an invisible stick, he peed in the direction of a bush, and felt with pleasure how he became lighter.

There are so many other people I discern by loving you, he whispered towards Jenny in the darkness. The road is clear where it used to be obstructed. If I only had the tongue of an ant-eater to move deep inside your vagina . . . Then two ruby red dots were lit, and he suspected his voice had woken up the grey galago, a little half-monkey that lived in an acacia and fed on insects at night.

His mind was clear enough to sense the banquet of the scents: the withered grass, the spicy herbs, the dusty earth, and the stones giving off their stored heat . . . He was happy to exist in that world. And the sounds of the night enabled him to find a place in Botswana for Mary and Henry with all their noisy egocentric kindness, for the night was but one large frog's belly of noise, flutes, croaks, and death howls, where nothing escaped mixing and melting in this belly of darkness.

JB waited before joining the others, because he felt rather

absent-minded. He thought to himself that he, Sten and Gertrude would never have been invited to the farm, had they not been white. They were either governors socializing, or survivors after a shipwreck gathering on an island. He himself felt neither here nor there, but it was probably the way Mary and Henry saw it: they were left in peace in a deserted outpost of the former British Empire, and around them lingered the atmosphere of old stamps from countries which had long since changed their names.

On their way home the headlights of the jeep caught a warthog. It disappeared into the bush with its tail upright like a radio aerial in search of better stations.

ON THE ROCKS

'I don't know if you feel like listening, but I've got a lot to tell you.' Gertrude brought the Land Rover to a halt. They were on their way to the Francistown slums.

'I want to know everything,' Jan said. 'Tell me how you came here.'

They stopped by one of the rock formations which for no apparent reason rose here and there on the savanna. Boulders weathered smooth had been piled up on top of each other, and in the crevices odd bushes grew. Gertrude had prepared a picnic basket, and wrapped it in a plastic dust-cover. She led the way towards the top, and Jan walked beside her. It was like going ashore from the rowing-boat at the Water Palace, looking for shelter from the wind.

'I felt terribly lonely when I first arrived,' she said. 'The Francistown airfield looked like that at Ronneby. Sten couldn't come and meet me. Swaneng was several hundred kilometres away. I got a message to take a cab to Shashi River School. There were eight of us in the taxi; the others all Africans going in the same direction. I wasn't sure whether the driver took the shortest route, and I had to pay for all of us. Shashi looked unoccupied; a record-player was booming out of one of the largest huts, where the teachers were marking papers while having dinner. They didn't pay any attention to me; they were used to people spending the night there before travelling on. There weren't enough plates and mugs, so we ate in shifts. The water tasted rusty. Old newspapers were spread over the table where sauce and beer bottles had left their marks. I tried to read while I ate, as everybody was silent.

'In the room next door there was a meeting of the second form teachers. Each student's report was read out: Catherine has problems at home, does not get on with her brothers and sisters, is often depressed and lethargic, her hygiene is bad . . . That's how it went. I thought it sounded insulting. I didn't know how soon I'd get used to it all.

'I felt helpless and lost that night. I lay in my single hut – the others had retired to theirs. It was pitch black – the electricity was turned off. I felt so lonely I could have masturbated with my biro. You should have been near me then. The journey away from you had after all been a link between us, I had thought of you in the control tower, remembering that I had once known happiness with you.'

'I never told you to leave,' JB said.

Gertrude made a gesture, as if flicking off a mosquito.

'Well, then I came to Swaneng where everything was different. Sten was there, and this whole world he'd made his own, "soiled with unresolved problems", as he put it.'

The sun was strong. It fell on Gertrude's breasts which had grown fuller, on her yellow checked shirt and her faded jeans which were tight across her stomach. Her ankles were covered with scratches from thorns and stones. She looked the way she used to during the summers at the Water Palace, but less tanned, her face thinner and her skin drier.

'Do you want to know more?' she asked, looking at him with some kind of malice which made him clench his arms tighter around his knees.

'Yes,' he replied. 'That's what I came here for.'

'No, that's not so,' she said, calmly and emphatically.

Before he could protest, she continued:

'Don't think the last word has been said between you and me. You went on your Swedish tour. I had my life to live. I respond to other people too, my world doesn't stand and fall with you. I'm open in other directions, but I would like to give our relationship a chance to survive. Above all I wish we could find the way back to each other.'

'You've met someone else, and now you want to tell me about him,' Jan said. 'Is it Sten?'

He did not look at her. He looked towards the dried-up river-bed surrounded by acacias with their shady parasols. In September, spring in the southern hemisphere, they would blossom in a landscape of pale pastels.

'You know nothing,' Gertrude said with sudden sharpness. 'If you understood, life would be unbearable for you.'

At that point Jan thought she would tell him nothing. She had a secret, and wanted to show him that she could keep it alive by silence. But she said:

'His eyes had recently seen other things. Things that every man should be spared.'

'Who are you talking about?'

'He was making a journey too, but not like you between Borensberg and Kristianstad to convince people that the world was made for globetrotters.'

'Gertrude!' Jan exclaimed hurt.

'Perhaps it was common experiences that brought the two of us so close. Things like witnessing your home country occupied by a colonial power.'

She smiled with irony and pity, informing JB that he on his side had only sailed in still waters.

'He was a South African,' she said. 'He spoke good English, and had studied almost up to A-levels. In spite of his education he had been a lorry driver. The company preferred him to a white man, as they could legally pay him a tenth of the normal wages. His family were not allowed to live with him in Johannesburg – they were deported to a reservation. That's the way with African marriages in South Africa: they are split up from the start. The law rules against black people living together. As if all Africans were blood relations, and had to be kept from seeing each other and having children.'

Above them vultures stood out against the blue board of the sky. JB had unpacked the picnic, but not touched it yet: bread, goat's cheese, and slices of goat's meat. That was the monotonous diet of the country: shoulder of goat, lung of goat, heart of goat and leg of goat.

'He had to run away. If they'd only allowed his family

172

to live with him, he would have tried to live like the others, in spite of the apartheid. But he couldn't bear it, he had to leave. I could well understand him. He wasn't a hero, but since his life was ruined and lost anyway, he might as well give the rest of his life to the revolution. He joined the liberation movement to enable others to live together one day.'

'He seems to have been clear about his motives,' JB said.

'He'd seen enough not to bother seeing any more. He wanted action. He wasn't frightened any more.'

'I'm thinking of Dave Griffiths,' Jan said. 'He also had seen too much. But he had a private and reasonable existence to return to.'

'He spoke to me about racialism. He said many people refused to accept their humiliation. They'd rather break the peace than succumb to it – the condition of everyday terror which the rest of the world calls peace.'

'What was his name?' JB asked.

'He's called Amos Bamuto Mokela.'

'What was he doing?'

'Smuggling medicine across the border to South Africa. He stuffed his haversack full and travelled immense distances. Most couriers were impossible, he said, because they were superstitious and afraid of the dark. They feared animals and people outside their home district.'

'Where did he get the medicines from?' JB asked.

'A donation from the Swedish government. When I told him I was Swedish, he became surprisingly much more communicative. At first I didn't understand why. I could still have hurt him just as much. He carried vitamins, disinfectants, quinine, and morphine for anaesthesia. Just over the South African border there are a couple of very isolated detention camps patrolled mainly by helicopter. The internees come from other parts of the country, and speak different languages. The tents and shacks are not enclosed by fences, just desert; and there's a constant lack of water. That's where he was taking the medicine. The time for arms has not yet come.'

'How did you meet?'

'He was standing by the road hitch-hiking. You know how it is with hitch-hikers. I was alone, I had dropped Aina, the Norwegian doctor, at a surgery. He had a large haversack, and was dressed like everybody else. He hesitated, probably because

I was a white woman. He wanted to go as far south as possible. It took us a few hours to get to Swaneng. We had a break on the way, by a termite hill. He didn't want to come with me into a café. He didn't ask for water.'

'Did he really answer all your questions?'

'He said he had come on the ferry from Zambia, but later I realized that he stealthily crossed the river boundary not far from there. The ferry was under surveillance from the South African side, and he didn't want to be seen, although his papers were okay. He had travel documents issued in Botswana, forged, I suppose. When I told him quite a lot about myself and about Swaneng, which he had heard of, he told me a few things which I knew were true.'

A baobab tree stood with its roots pointing to the sky, wind-blown, silvery grey, and probably still alive. JB had some goat's meat, and handed some to Gertrude. He passed his hand gently along her upper arm in a protective gesture. Almost impercep-tibly, she withdrew it.

Browny-black hymenoptera with eyes on long sticks darted between the stones. A heron passed flying low, its wings ex-tended: a flying hunch-back.

'Amos had been inside like almost all black men. In the central prison in Pretoria he had been kept awake all night by the songs from the death corridor. Men waiting to be hanged at dawn, but not knowing which day, sang their way through weeks and months. Their battle songs with music borrowed from revivalist tunes and missionary hymns lingered in his ears longer than the screams from the tortured.'

'Experience like that is like apartheid,' Jan said. 'A wall between him and us.'

'Us?' Gertrude said. 'I'm not sure. He showed me a photo of the children's graves in the Transkei near the oceanic coast. They lay open, row after row, waiting for the children who would die in the next few days. In the camps that Amos visited things are much worse. Apathy kills off people. They suffer every deprivation. There is no postal service. He comes as a courier every other month, and that's all they have to look forward to. He is all they wait and hope for. He knows it, and it makes him hard to others.'

'To you as well?'

'I had myself to blame. Somehow I meant nothing at all to

him. "I belong there, in South Africa," he said. "Not with you. In this way I'm not serving my people." He would talk like that, he had several different voices. He knew that basically I could do nothing to help him. He didn't feel bitter about it, but I don't think he could trust unselfish outsiders, only those who had lived a life of apartheid as black people. He hoped more couriers would be joining soon. He had plans for a depot of provisions and medicines near the border.'

'The risks he took!' JB said.

'If he is caught, no one will object, and no one will ever know what happened to him. He'll be tortured to death – and possibly a statement will be issued that he committed suicide during interrogation. No one would believe in this information, and no one is meant to. It's a warning from the Secret Police that it could happen to anyone.'

While Gertrude talked, JB got up. Stiff and serious and dignified as a white man, he paced the boulder, which was as large as their drawing-room in Uppland Street. But before him, up and down the crevices and clefts, his shadow was dancing, black on the grey granite, as short and mobile as a clown. He sat down abruptly.

'Amos came with me to Swaneng,' Gertrude continued. 'I told them he was a Botswanan student on his way to Zambia who had heard of me from a Swedish missionary. No one asked any questions, they all had their own affairs to attend to. When we were on our own during the afternoon, he told me these things I've been telling you. He spoke in a low voice, but I heard it clearly. It was quiet around us. The animals were silent. The sunshine was painted on the ground. I let him stay with me, in the room you have.'

'And he stayed with you for two days?'

'We slept together, if that's what you want to know. I didn't do it out of compassion, but out of desire.'

He heard Gertrude's voice as footsteps can be heard in a distant corridor. For a moment he looked at her like a stranger. Her pupils shrank, but the irises were dark, and directed towards him like binoculars. An enigmatic smile moved her lips. Did she remember their pleasure, or was she too embarrassed to tell him? He had the same quick reminder from the depth of jealousy, as he had had seeing Klas Lundin at the art gallery in Stockholm.

He tried to get himself together to survey the situation, and drive the black thoughts away. He accused himself of being stingy with her – after all, he had wanted her to try and treasure everything. He could see before him Gertrude and Amos, with Gertrude's stomach less round than it was now, her face and her breasts. He had let her down, and therefore little mattered to her, her life was a short breath, and the warmth she was able to give did not have to be weighed against her duties to other people. She had climbed over her walls, he thought, on a practical African ladder, one that looked like a fern.

'It was easy. We wore down the despair between us. I wanted him to understand that I did not know either where I would be in a couple of months' time.'

That's now, Jan thought. You're here, with me.

But he could hardly believe it. Everything seemed so fragile between them, as if bitten by termites. A careless move, and something would be helplessly lost.

'I did it because I desired him,' she said. 'There are things I couldn't have done. I don't like wasting time on indignities. I like strong emotions – to be lifted up and sunk by them, at any cost.'

Critical situations brought out a certain strength in her: in the attic at the Water Palace, or when she contacted Klas Lundin. When reality sawed off her branch, she responded by planting another tree.

JB thought he had to try to understand her, or he would have forfeited the right to her confidence. What she had written about the ferns, about the limits of sight and the way travellers were restricted by their time and experiences – all this he had seen as a concealed appeal to make the world inaccessible beyond their kinship. However, what she had told him contradicted this.

'I don't think I'd have done it if Jenny hadn't existed,' Gertrude said. 'That's frightening. What must one go through in order to achieve freedom of action? He lay in my arms for one long night. In silence similarities prevail.'

The rock was damp under Jan's hands, as he listened. When he removed them, the colour of the granite had darkened, as if it was blushing.

'He wasn't a hunted animal,' Gertrude continued. 'He was

176

someone prepared to die for the self-evident truth. Something in him had probably died already, to enable him to go on living.'

'Did he realize that you were pregnant?'

'I knew you'd ask. I told him. I was four months gone, and it was hardly noticeable. For a moment I was lodging two people inside my body. I felt I protected them.'

JB thought of the child in her body: a stranger who knew nothing about seasons, latitudes or cultures; as willing to accept a stone cave as a skyscraper, ignorant of human attempts to sort out this conflict of life, which anyway to him would be merely a fragment of the past.

'He asked me to name the child after him – as a second name. Amos or Bamuto if I had a boy. Mokela if it was a girl, as it ends with an a. Bamuto means "he who came after the disasters".'

'Did you agree?'

'I'll do what he wanted.'

As she said this, Jan felt violently close to her, which dispelled his doubts. And he pointed out quietly to Klas and Amos that they could never have felt Gertrude's body as he did at that moment without even touching it or making a gesture towards it.

'I was very tired at that time,' Gertrude said. 'He was just as tired. We were thrown into a kind of clear inebriation, a sort of morphine for the body. With him I felt strangely awake, and the whole world seemed improvised. I gave him a lift to the station, he left on the mixed train, the train without mail-carriages, travelling fourth class. I gave him what money I had, and then I slept for fifteen hours and woke up happy. It seemed weeks since he'd left.'

'And how long ago is it now?'

'More than two months. He should be back by now. But I'm not expecting him. There are other routes. He may have been seized. I gave him my Swedish address.'

JB looked at her in amazement. They were not alike, nobody could ever suspect they were closely related. But their hands looked the same, hers were like his seen slightly contracted in a mirror.

'I didn't have to tell you this,' Gertrude said. 'You didn't tell me how you tried to join the Diplomatic Corps, or how you met Jenny. I don't know what else you have concealed from me.'

He wanted to say: his lack of knowledge of Gertrude's activities. In Stockholm he had been afraid of looking incredibly happy because of Jenny; instead he had become alien to Gertrude. One evening at the Water Palace she had looked at him in the mirror, appealingly and searchingly. He had pretended not to notice anything.

'Have you ever done anything important that you haven't told me about?' he asked instead. 'It was Jenny you told about the man on the shore who had fooled you with stories when you were a child.'

'Oh him, the first man to deceive me. Not as much as you, though. I'll think about it, and if I think of something, I'll let you know while you're still in Africa.'

A yellowish-green butterfly landed on Jan's knee. As it closed its wings, it seemed to disappear completely. The underside of its wings was the same colour as his khaki trousers.

'What are you thinking about?' Gertrude asked after a little while. 'You're so very quiet.'

'I remember once at the Water Palace when I came out from town and found you reading a book. You smiled and looked up at me, but kept your finger on the page you were reading. Do you understand? I'm only here for a short while, you'll soon set to all the other tasks waiting for you here.'

'You were there that time,' she answered. 'There were no obstacles. Love is as self-evident as the sun. It's supposed to make you warm, not blind. I enjoyed loving you. Now I'll go on loving you, although I don't enjoy it.'

THE DRY SEA

A herd of sheep, guarded by a dog and a naked boy with a stick, spread slowly like a swell as they continued. A skeleton lay there, weathered like driftwood. The sea itself had withdrawn, and the whole country was now looking for it.

178

Over the savanna a road meandered with reminders from various travellers: rusty kegs, memorial stones to colonial governors, and huts for spending the night in, gradually absorbed by the earth.

The sun with warm hands was heavy on their heads, like an intrusive adult. They were far apart, although the jeep tried to jolt them together.

'Not only you have changed,' Jan said resolutely. 'Our father has changed as well.'

Gertrude looked at him in surprise, and burst out laughing. JB noticed how the tension was leaving her too.

'You haven't met him, have you?' she said.

'Oh no. He stays on his continent. But does the name Harold Engblom ring a bell?'

'One of his old sailing mates?' Gertrude suggested.

'That's right. I met him in Norrköping.'

He related the new and so much more honourable version of A. O. Backman's resignation from the Foreign Office.

'Do you really believe in that?' Gertrude asked sceptically. 'I'm sure we know him better than that.'

'Don't you trust what I say?'

'I haven't always had reason to. People talk so much. We've had many ideas revised. He never cared about us. Don't try to change that picture.'

JB understood that she had put her foot against childhood injustice, and leant heavily against him. He realized surprised that he had shared her attitude. One should not be too quick to talk about truth; it changed as time went by. Had the image of the cool, affable father been her alibi to love her brother? And had she found their illegal relationship a burden, a sacrifice balanced only by permanent love? It had never weighed him down. Soon he would not know what he dared tell her.

Near Francistown the houses became denser and more variable. Huts were succeeded by white plastered low buildings with tin roofs, occasional shops with their wooden shutters open to display their goods, work-shops and warehouses where illegible signposts reminded you about the necessity of metal and rubber on the world market. Here as well goats fed everywhere, drifting into the middle of the town in flocks, ignorant and devastating like people. The grey earthy ground shone through the sparse remaining straws.

The Francistown slums had made Sten fear that Gertrude was overdoing things, and this was partly the reason for his cable. It had begun with her meeting Lotte Schneider who had studied social medicine in West Berlin, and organized nurseries there for the students. She was younger than Gertrude, and already had a degree in nutrition physiology. She had been given a grant to delineate a limited social environment where deficiency diseases resulted in a high infant mortality rate, although more variable food was available. She said she could not watch her own children choosing in the affluent western shops without trying to do something for the children in need.

Gertrude had met Lotte at Swaneng, and been told that she was going to Sweden in the late spring as part of a research exchange between the Berlin University and the Caroline Institute in Stockholm. Eventually she was to return to Germany to write her dissertation.

Gertrude seemed impressed and pleased to have made her acquaintance. Lotte told her about her two children. She had them by different men whom she did not live with, but who were both her friends.

She had asked Gertrude to come along when she went round interviewing people, inquiring how they used their houses, how the children were looked after and the households composed, what they grew, sold, or bought, and how jobs were distributed. Their eating habits were most important. Lotte spoke some Tswana, while Gertrude knew only the greetings and shopping phrases.

The interesting thing was finding out how a community had been formed without any authoritative control or planning. Nobody knew who owned the land. The residents themselves decided on the capacity and the density, built their own houses and formed their environment, learnt from each other's experience, co-operated with their neighbours, took care of their shacks, and kept an eye on each other. Their huts of clay and sun-dried bricks burst in the drought, were glued together by the rains, and torn down by the wind. Many families moved in and out of their short-lived homes. The housing changed incessantly like a large body changing position while asleep.

Here many well-known objects had different uses : An empty can could be more useful than a full one, for the contents were alien and dangerous, while the can was an expedient cooking-utensil. Curtains became blankets, and an oilskin was used as a roof: their own skin protected even against the heaviest rains. In the same way edible things were discarded or approved of. That's where we must pay attention, Gertrude said. How come they exclude the more nutritious parts, peel off the vitamins and let the bulk be the standard dish?

The wells, lavatories and vegetable gardens were commonly owned by the households. That kind of co-operation gave security but also caused conflicts, mainly when people moving into the area claimed rights to what was already shared by the residents. Pride and rules could be as inflexible as in the tribal days, but there were no more duels for the price of a bride. Instead, they argued like choleric house-owners over the empty oil kegs marking the end of each lot.

If this was a slum area, it was because the standard of living was at the lowest level of existence. The crime rate was low, however, and family life as solid as in the country. The tokens of real slum did not yet show. That was Lotte's and Gertrude's conclusion.

Still, life was hard, and people toiled. Gertrude had learnt it by force, because she had grown attached to one family, and started to help them. They were called Matsoe and were worse off than the others, apparently more tied to their tin shack with two retarded children, who might be the reason why they were more isolated from their environment. Gertrude had given her mattress to the smallest child who slept on the ground; the following week it was sold. She gave them a plastic bucket instead of the rusty one. But whatever she brought disappeared as if through a hole in the floor.

After a fortnight their home looked the same again: an incurably broken cane chair, torn blankets to sleep on, the large coffee can hanging on small chains over an open fire, where the corn-flour was cooked so hard that it could be eaten with their fingers without making them sticky. Sometimes there was some sauce in a broken enamelled bowl, into which they dipped pieces of the corn porridge.

'Their resistance to accepting help was a challenge,' said Gertrude. 'I couldn't give up.'

The man went to a pub and had beer on credit. Gertrude tried to get the elder son a job disembowelling entrails in a shop. He stuck it for a few days drawing chickens, but then got the sack and came back explaining that his future was in cutting out button-holes in shirt-collars at the textile factory. But for this he needed more than two years' schooling.

She gave vitamins to the youngest child, but it remained undernourished, maybe retarded. The parents did not realize something was wrong – life ran its strange course. The child looked at her with wonder and reproach, pointing her out as some incomprehensible creature from a different world.

She took on more and more, and her reward had been fleas, a bleeding which made her fear a miscarriage, and the family's gratitude because someone wanted to bother with them, although her aims seemed unclear.

JB listened to Gertrude's description of the Matsoe family in Francistown, while they drove on sandy roads through the sprawling town district where no house was more than one storey high, and the heavy pea-pods of the jakaranda trees hung over the houses of whites and Indians. The houses soon became smaller, home-built and sparse. Rags filled the cracks, or was it the backs of the family, leaning against the walls of the one room?

Gertrude was still talking, as she brought the jeep to a halt in front of one of the shacks in a long row. In the doorway the adults of the Matsoe family were standing, listening without understanding to a language sounding like a musical box. Gertrude got out and introduced JB – as what, he did not catch – but their faces were stiff. She then started to sweep the floor like a maid helping some disabled people.

'Why can't Mrs Matsoe clean the place herself?' JB asked. This middle-aged toothless woman sat smiling in a corner.

'Poverty,' Gertrude said, 'makes them lethargic. They haven't got the energy to do the most natural things. She doesn't understand any more what she ought to do. It's better outside the home.'

JB was alarmed by the misery. He had not chosen this family. And they seemed to suspect him of representing the authorities.

'They dislike me,' he complained.

'They like me because I'm pregnant,' Gertrude said. 'They say if I haven't got a place to live I can always come and live here. They're hospitable. When people hardly have enough to eat every day, every child and relation is welcome for a meal;

but as soon as they have enough food for a couple of days, they're more particular.'

JB thought he saw Gertrude change every day. He had the impression that she wanted to show him different facets of herself, now scaring him, and then enticing him.

Lotte Schneider appeared in rough safari shoes, jeans and a shoulder-bag. She was tall with broad shoulders and blonde hair she shook off her face. There was a firm gaze in her grey-green eyes.

'Officially these houses are illegal,' she said. 'If we make a sociological report there's a chance they might get recognized. Then we could start providing running water, and arranging for education and welfare work. On the other hand, there's the risk that the houses are pulled down. Then where should they go and live?'

'If they were given a modern house, it would be even more difficult for Mrs Matsoe to adjust,' Gertrude said. 'Men are more adaptable to new conditions. Women have to be attacked harder, their oppression is worse.'

'Yet they're on the pill and try the coil,' Lotte said. 'At least in this country their resistance to birth control is less than we expected. But it's hard for them to imagine that life could be different. What men and tradition have laid down is accepted as nature's own law. They don't ask: why is it like this? Their one question is: why doesn't it rain?'

The girls had a lot to do. JB felt superfluous. Nobody gave him any orders, he was excluded from their shop talk. They knew the practicalities, whilst he was a stranger from Sweden. They looked at him inquiringly. Gertrude seemed to create a gulf between them. He sensed that he and Gertrude were all the time trying out different intimacies and escape valves. They seldom seemed to be at the same stage at the same time.

'Is there anything I can do?' he finally asked.

'Yes,' Gertrude said. 'Look in my handbag in the jeep for a pair of scissors.'

One of the children had pulled down the fly-paper which Lotte had just hung up, and it had got stuck in his hair.

'Shall I bring the whole bag?'

'No, then someone will start playing with it. Better leave it.'

He looked through her things. He was on his own known territory.

Suddenly he looked down into Jenny's eyes. At first he was happy, then terrified.

'My darling, what are you doing here?' he whispered. It was a newspaper cutting, in which Jenny gave a warning about the woods around Born lake, the reservoir for Stockholm's drinking water, where they wanted to build houses and so threaten the water supply. He put it back. Gertrude had not forgotten more than this. He would have liked to see Jenny anywhere, but not a prisoner in Gertrude's handbag.

He quickly passed his fingertip over his back pocket, where his return ticket was sticking up. It was like touching Jenny. He often caught himself making this gesture in Botswana.

'Why do you carry Jenny's picture in your handbag?' he asked Gertrude, as he handed her the scissors.

'I must remind myself all the time that the incredulous is true.'

'Who do you really think I am?'

'Someone who travels across the world just to see me.'

Then he felt he could not stay there.

'I'll take a sight-seeing trip round the district,' he said quickly, waving the car-keys. 'I'll pick you up later.'

'Don't bother,' Gertrude said. 'The building gang can give me a lift back. Hope you can manage the car. This is not Uppland Street.'

JB had some difficulty getting it started. The two girls were standing in the doorway laughing, as he went off with violent jerks.

He avoided Gertrude's eyes. He was no longer sure what they said. How many masks did she have, and what was she like underneath them? In spite of their long talks, the unspoken seemed to set the balance.

Far away on the other side of the town he felt some anxiety. It was the darkness of the handbag around Jenny's picture. He longed for a message from her. Now the long line of excuses was finished: she had stayed on in London, the mail was slow. In other words, there had to be a letter from her waiting when he returned to the school. But he knew reality was indifferent to the fervour of his thought.

Slowing down on a bend, he got too near the roadside. One wheel got stuck in a rut, and the wheel shaft rested against the side. He could not get the car moving, and had to get out.

Thorns, drought and poor flowers; the air free of insects; the weaver's nest hanging like a brown speckled sock on a fruit tree.

He had never before driven on African roads. He saw dusk falling before him and himself remaining there. If Gertrude passed him in the building gang's lorry, would she see him, and would she stop? The sand dunes far away started to move towards him dragging the desert with them. Cattle wandered ahead trampling the plants.

He tried to make the rut larger with a claw wrench to give the wheels more room to move. Feeling weak, he sat down on the foot-plate, and watched some lizards move from sun to shadow, unable to control their own temperature, completely controlled by their environment. They found the shade of a stone or a large leaf, and lay there panting, their tongues fluttering like streamers.

He suffered from thirst: his mouth was chalkily dry, which made him think of the inedible Christmas crackers of his childhood. Again he imagined the savanna as an inland sea. He sat on a copsy seabed where stones looked like overgrown treasure chests, and the leaves that had recently been as dry as mummified strips, were now moist and green and moving slowly like algae. Plankton drifted across the grazing grounds, followed by cattle herds like huge whales making their way without a sound through the swaying sea-weed. Through the salty membranes of his eyes the air shimmered like water, and the trees extended their branches like umbrellas.

Wild pigeons appeared in town suits, black, grey and white, like a number of merchants after dinner on their unsteady way home. Their cooing sounds were scaring and melancholy. JB heard them as: die now, die now, die now . . .

Eventually he pulled himself together and thought of gathering stones to put in the rut. The wheels found a grip, the car shaft jerked, and he was able to drive again.

He thought of Gertrude. She did not say straight out what she meant. Did she want more protection or more freedom? He did not know. He told himself that he had changed at least as thoroughly as Gertrude. No wonder it frightened her. And his visit to Botswana? Was it a clumsy attempt to help which only made her weaker? Suddenly his problem was not protecting Gertrude, but keeping his feeling for her. Was it a necessity that one person grew less identifiable when you loved two? Gertrude had been a sea where no nautical chart was needed. Now the land had risen, and displacement gaps appeared. He no longer knew how to navigate. And Jenny was not at hand to answer any questions. Anyway, who knew if she wanted to?

When he saw an African hitch-hiker on the roadside, it occurred to him that it could be Amos. He picked him up, a young man dressed for a visit to town, but barefoot; he had left his shoes as pawn in a bar, he said. He got out after a mile or so, and disappeared into a village. JB felt a childish inclination to follow him and disappear too, into the darkness of a hut.

THE SURFACE OF FRACTURE

They talked through the late summer days of the southern hemisphere. They placed words individually with light bangs, like chessmen.

Botswana's plains shrunk. He felt snared by their private experiences. Gertrude thought she could isolate him between herself and the elements; there were few distractions here. He thought he had been nearer Africa in Axel Ericson's home town. The days dried away like stale bread. He needed sharper tools to cut them.

'Look, that's the girl they gave penicillin to,' he exclaimed. 'She pulled through.'

It was the sleepy intermediate part of the day. The children had their afternoon nap at the clinic. An old African called Cricket had taken a last swig at his bottle, and now slept by the roadside. The girl passed him alone with a bunch of swedes, apparently fully recovered.

'Yes,' Gertrude said. 'And we – will we pull through?'

JB felt impatient. Pull through . . . They sat next to each other. The sun reached them; the shadows blended behind their backs.

He suspected that her question was constantly changing its implication. He thought they had tried the most dangerous thing: to be close to each other all the time. Like children left out in the forest when they were young. She had taken care of him, shown him the edible berries, the outlook tower, and the stone altar. She had seduced him – a dance, a game. She had led him to the end of the world, and then they had gone back into the woods. Eventually he had started to show her a way out. And all this seemed to have been planned beforehand, at first through her strength, then his.

In Botswana JB felt possessed by a double vision. He had brought the Water Palace here, because Gertrude was here, and he forgot what grew in her for the past which reappeared in him. He was led to believe that she had not changed; but was also led to see her as a different person in a different country, closer to independence and creation than to erosion and obliteration.

He still tried to console her:

'You and I have been close since we were born. That's a strength no one can take away from us. Not even Sten knows we're brother and sister.'

She still appealed:

'We have our coarse skin in common, with a thin alien layer on top.'

'I came here because I suspected you were having a hard time,' he said.

'I don't think you know why you're here. You will eventually.'

Her superiority put him off. Their conversation became a mine field.

'We always suited one another hand in glove,' Gertrude said.

'We're gloves of the same hand,' he said.

They were sitting outside Gertrude's house, on a rough bench hewn from a tree-trunk. A calla blossomed white and stiff in a tin can.

'I don't want to sacrifice myself for you,' she said. 'I want to save something that belongs to us. That wouldn't be a sacrifice. I wish we could continue from where we left off.'

'You mean the Water Palace?'

'The Water Palace or Uppland Street, places of abode are of little consequence. But if you mean by the Water Palace a way of life where you and I are turned to each other, then that's what I wish.'

'You want me to give up Jenny?'

'I know you can't do it now. But I look forward to the future without her.'

'I was never bored with our way of life,' JB said. 'I wasn't looking for someone else. She just appeared. And now she's there. Jenny is a fact, and nobody could now describe a future with me not longing for her any more. I'm just afraid that your honesty concerning Jenny will force me to dislike you.'

'I'm glad you weren't bored with us. But what do you know about my endurance? Couldn't I have longed to get out?'

'Did you? Or do you say it just to pay me back?'

Gertrude told him that she had at one time fought a strong feeling of indifference to Jan.

'You didn't ask me what I did, or who I was with. But then one night when I came home after seeing The Knife in The Water, you were standing there with a hydrangea flower you had picked in a park. Do you remember? I thought you looked just like the boy I had once fallen in love with. I could feel something turning slowly inside me. And it all streamed out to meet you. I was happy I had subjected our love to a test.'

JB remembered that night. He had stood breathless outside Jenny's front door on the second or third floor at Nybro Quay, not knowing whether he was more afraid of being found out, or of remaining undiscovered. He had been so surprised at himself, that he had wanted to surprise Gertrude too. He could at any time recall the scent of wet soil, and the earth making its way like wedges under his nails. He had looked across his shoulder to make sure no policeman was around. He had felt himself trembling through those days and nights as if he were a tuning-fork struck by Jenny.

'I'm sorry I made you reveal what was between you and Jenny,' Gertrude said. 'If I hadn't all this might have passed, and we wouldn't have been sitting here. For at that time I also had someone else I longed for, and I didn't want to talk to you about him. I feared our words and agitation would water down the truth until it grew more dangerous and false.'

'Who was he?'

'It was Sten.'

JB felt a heel, as if Botswana were the deck of a ship. The

ballast moved a bit. He stood with his feet wide apart to receive revisions of the course.

'It all blew past,' Gertrude said, 'and now I like him without being affected by it.'

'That day when I drove to Stockholm and had left the key behind, you were at the Water Palace. You were often there.'

'Yes. You didn't seem to mind, you never asked me. I had to consider our situation out there.'

'That time,' JB said, 'I was more lonely than I understood. I spent the night in Sten's office, while you were brooding over him. How much did he know?'

'Not much. I don't usually drag other people into it. I only drag you in. Somehow I always thought you'd understand whatever I decided to do.'

'I'm surprised to hear you say that,' Jan said seriously. 'I don't trust your understanding that much.'

'Have you decided then?' she asked with a smile, stroking his cheek. JB felt ill at ease, reminded of elderly relatives committing a friendly outrage against him as a child. I ought to go home now, he thought.

But they went to have lunch at the canteen. They turned over the thick white plates, placed with the bottom up to keep the dust out. The cloth was stained and threadbare, and changed once a week. They had beetroot, rice, and boiled goat's meat. The lettuce leaves were dry, legible like a yellowed newspaper. The radio was always on for the news, and it was difficult to listen to someone else talking at the same time at the table. JB was pleased to have a break in his conversation with Gertrude.

Afterwards he went past the dispatch-box to look for mail. No letter from Jenny; she must be out of her mind. He saw no other reasons. Now there was no buffer between him and his yearnings. His worry over Jenny's silence grew in him as he spoke to Gertrude.

She gave him a couple of pages she had written, and said:

'You sent me honest reports on your Swedish tour. Here are some thoughts concerning us. Read this when you have time – there's no hurry. I want you to know what my life has been like.'

JB put the pages in the inner pocket of his suitcase.

The drought continued. The spider shortened his march

round the net. At the edge of the well there were beetle wings. The moonflowers waxed their last funnels. The wind hid from the heat in the bells of the aloes, loosening their petals from inside.

They all spared their strength. The skin was eaten into the soul. The vultures looked anybody in the eye.

Gertude said: 'I'm happy to have a baby by someone I don't know very well. Now I can register it as mine. I don't have to give the name of the father, and officially, you and I aren't married. The child doesn't have to confirm a secret.'

'What about when it's old enough to ask questions? What kind of image are you going to present to the child of its father?'

'I always thought the child would be yours and mine.'

As he did not reply, she added: 'And Jenny's.'

'There's another person you have to take into consideration.'

'There's no one else.'

'The natural father.'

'We'll leave him out of it. He'll never guess.'

'Klas knows all about it.'

Gertrude looked at him with an unrecognizable expression on her face. It did not go, and he had to exclaim:

'But my dear Gertrude, what's the matter? Say something.'

She kept staring and staring at him, as if she had seen a zombie.

'You've deceived me,' she whispered finally. 'It's inconceivable.'

'I think you've had enough secrets with other people.'

'He would never have had to know.'

'Marianne told him you were pregnant. He jumped to one of several possible conclusions. He came to me in despair. I couldn't hide what I knew.'

'To me he is dead and irrelevant.'

JB was upset at her refusal to see that love can possess anyone. She wanted to rest in a guiltless world of her own making. The benevolent Klas with all his fatherly eagerness was to her a threatening creature who would destroy everything.

'I came here partly to tell you that Klas is an upset father who suffers from being kept out of it,' Jan said. 'He's like a pregnant girl let down by the father of her child. You shouldn't disdain him. I did it too, easily, but not any more.'

'He has nothing to do with me.'

'But you've got something to do with him.'

'So he sent you?'

'No.'

'Then why did you come?'

'I don't know any more.'

She slapped him hard across the face. It was the first time in their life together. She looked furious.

'You deceived me for Klas. Therefore, I shall deceive you to Jenny.'

'How do you mean?'

'By telling her you're my brother.'

'She already knows that,' JB said.

Before he had time to say any more, she rushed out of the room. A few seconds later he heard the jeep start. He could not stop her. Just as he was considering calling on Sten to borrow a vehicle, Aina, the Norwegian doctor, passed by.

'Was that Gertrude leaving?'

'Yes.'

'Good. I promised to remind her that she had to go to Palapye.'

That statement calmed him down. He remembered the pages from her diary, took them out and started to read them. His cheek was still smarting.

CALENDAR DAYS

I left to prove my love for you: In fairy-tales they walk around the world, or count the stones of the king's court-yard before daybreak. I also left because I feared that my existence would otherwise become posthumous. Words like home, you, I, we, changed. I wanted to go through inverted travail – incorporating in my body some alien substance, sub-mitting myself to a force penetrating my muscles and blood, giving pain and forcing adjustment. In that way you would remain within me, whatever I did.

It's now December, that is midsummer in the southern hemisphere. The atmosphere is fresher than in Sweden, but thinner. I feel I can never breath deeply enough. The plants of the savanna may not attract enough oxygen. The high plateau is like a crumpled palm, slightly cupped to gather the rains when they come. A desert rose with pink petals is in blossom outside my house.

I've travelled by jeep to the local schools. Sten was keen to provide me with an assistant. The boy he sent with me only wanted to stop for a beer in every village. I soon learnt to find the way better on my own. The libraries have large gaps, the Encyclopaedia Britannica is far away. I have interesting discussions with the teachers. We plan smart libraries until the budget brings us back to earth.

I've been to see a dentist in Francistown. Dental care is free in Sweden when you're pregnant, but here I had to pay. The dentist was a Pole who had escaped from the Nazis, ended up in South Africa, disliked it, and become frightened. I've had a lot of goat's cheese and take iron tablets, I'm okay. A few months to go, hopefully, and it will be launched. I already laugh at it surreptitiously, I say to myself that it will come out of a hidden door with the longest death already behind it, a gentleman of the old school looking as though he belonged to a secret and unregistered order.

You must have a special kind of character to like it here. You can't live as a recipient or a television watcher. You have to find your own diversions. I don't miss the flow of information or the views on the world constantly changing like playing cards. In Stockholm I thought I was always in the shadow of new viaducts. Here in Botswana things are easier to grasp. People want porridge, blankets, letters, a football . . .

Thank you for your Christmas telegram. But it leaves so many things unanswered. How is life at Uppland Street? Do you ever think of me there? Have you changed anything? What do you see? What do you do? Do you take your work home? Does the telephone often ring? Do people ever ask for me? The loneliness here is easier to take, as I seldom see its opposite.

Would you like to hear about my bat? It snatches a mango fruit and hangs from an iron rod sticking out under my roof. It holds the fruit in its thumbs. Hanging by its feet, it doesn't get sticky as the mango juice drips directly down onto the ground. But when passing its water and excrements it keeps its feet down, to avoid tainting the body.

With one foot it presses its food into the hollows of its cheeks. It folds up its thin wing membrane into thousands of little folds, where air pockets are formed to conserve the warmth. It's got large brown eyes, a soft furry body, and a little dog's head with white tufts on the ears.

Life is wasted here. Cemeteries are rare. People are buried in their villages, children next to the hut where they were born. That's everyday life. To us death is exclusive and absent for as long as possible.

The first time I felt I was going to die, I was sitting on the edge of a sofa putting on red sandals. I went all sweaty. I was eleven and just about to play animal snaps with a girl, which was forbidden at the boarding school. I shall become unforgettable, I decided. And when my friend heard what I'd experienced, she took out the sweets she had got from home, sweets looking like wet morello cherries, and to my great surprise, gave them all to me.

We hear about the horrible things happening in South Africa. Just over the border two policemen hanged an African upside down in a tree, and slowly killed him with electric shocks. They were caught and given three months in prison. No compensation was given to the bereaved family. The man had forgotten to report his change of address. The judge thought the punishment was too drastic. The policemen didn't seem to understand.

A woman known by some people here was seized in her home by South African police who walked across the border without being stopped. She is a Botswana citizen. If she wanted to see her husband alive, she had to go with them to Mafeking. The man had driven his tractor on the wrong side of the unmarked boundary. He had wounds and bumps all over his body. A few months later she saw him again, with fresh wounds on his face. And he is still there.

Refugees pass, stay for a while, are put up in crowded rooms in Francistown and encouraged to continue north. A constant winter bivouac of life. They long for the final stamp on their passports, a thick and wonderful document to fill in page after page like tent pegs hammered into the ground. But they are given a grey piece of paper, a travel document of two pages, soon soiled by the fingers of suspicious border guards.

Today I read Seretse Khama's latest speech which we had already heard on the radio yesterday :

'Africa does not suffer alone. Neither has she special demands to be seen as the dark civilization. Events in Europe in the 30s and 40s, when almost two thousand years of white civilization – to borrow a phrase much used in certain South African circles – culminated in the extermination of six million Jews and the death of millions of other people, remind us of the fact that other parts of the world have had their share of human tragedy and mass devastation.

In the large and sombre register of the lack of humanity displayed by human beings, southern Africa has a special page. The moral question posed by South Africa is unique in the world, and remains a question of international opinion, implying suppression and injustice based on race and colour of skin. South Africa alone amongst sovereign states has created this institution.

If Africa can live without apartheid, we can only expect the western countries to do the same . . . but can anything be achieved by a policy of talks and communications from the western countries, whose friendship South Africa obviously values highly? I only mean, why does the West pretend they need South Africa any more than South Africa needs the West, when the opposite is the case?'

I've been to the Tidströms; ate potato dumplings and drank tea. Marianne has grown cucumber seeds on blotting paper, and then transplanted them in the garden. I don't think they'll grow. Sten was full of ideas. If he had a special talent, he would cultivate it. He said that in the old days our feelings of guilt were loaded by the fact that the past could never be undone, but had to be reconciled with. The children who worked, the cruelties of industrialization ... Now we extend on the surface instead, which involves contemporary global injustice that is unreachable in a way different from that of the past. The insensitivity gap there holds us back more than the hunger or the standard gap.

Maybe it's possible to start again, like rewinding a film from the end to the beginning; the fragments of the house are joined together, and the bomb finds its way back to the plane. All returns to its source. The painful present is absorbed by the past. The future is pure and untarnished. That is my dream.

I travelled on a desolate road at highest possible speed ...
I picked up an African; having access to a car, one must share it. Much has happened which I may never be able to make you understand. I slept for fifteen hours. I was happy. I didn't know I'd wake up to the letter about your journey with Jenny. I thought I wanted to hear your key in the door at Uppland Street, or see your face pass the kitchen window at the Water Palace, and I stood there knowing the night was ours and it had almost always been so and would remain so. It was unchangeable, it was part of our closeness that nobody could prize open. How could I believe it? How could I be so sure of us?

My little brother, you've found a treasure in the forest. Now you come running to show it to me. I'm sure it's very beautiful, but I only care about the hand that gives it to me.

Now I realize that I was always in that forest. It wasn't you, you're no God. The forest was there between you and me. I want to go back there. I fight my way through the shrubbery here, but as soon as I have pulled up the weeds they grow again, finally a patch of grass, an open bank, but when I rest there everything grows all around me: weeds, thorns, lianas, and prickly plants. I never have time to stop.

I've seen women selling macondi to the miners leaning out of the north bound trains on their way back to Malawi after a three year contract, with money and beautiful clothes, with silicosis and death in their bodies. I've heard Radio Rhodesia presenting its version of the evil of the world. I know what Tswana sounds like, and what development projects are. I've read twenty reports on the subject: why is a population census important to Botswana? I know the names of the students now: Beauty, Lovemore, Phillimon, Cornelius, Desire, Genesis, Osenotse, Batumelo.

A Botswana girl at the nursery patted my stomach, and gave me a painted wooden hare – for the baby. She hoped it would be a boy. I was too tired to protest. I hope it will have eyes, ears, a nose and a mouth and all the other things necessary for feeling and recognizing. That's all I hope. The child takes over where my life is ending. I want it to live and learn not to take life too seriously – rather like you.

All day in darkness. Your letter . . . your happiness which you expect me to understand. But you were happy for a long time when I didn't know why. That was the hardest thing. My jealousy which was to wither away here has reached subterranean water and been nourished. It frightens me and infuriates me. I wish I didn't have to bother with myself when there are so many other things to worry about.

Sten reproached me again for not coming to a meeting concerning library subsidies. There is a big hole in my memory. I'm trying not to think of you. That takes all my strength.

If I had a different picture of you, if I could see you as you are now, I might cease to identify with you. That would release me, or kill me. If I can't become another person, I want to be nobody.

I am woken up by the screeching of a cock, whose throat is cut by an African. The orbit of my yearning is too narrow. I went to Botswana on my own. It's not far enough. My map is too small. I long to be carried to another place like a seed carried under the hoofs of the antelope and not knowing where it's going.

In the drought my water is evaporating. So distant: a world that you *dare* be curious about. There is drought in my heart. The curare numbness of boredom. Indifference to the baby as well. I don't want to have it, it may have my features. Oh please, come and read to me about the book-fish.

There are memories that won't pass. They suddenly form into a little white tornado ravaging through my body.

What will remain of us? What can we look forward to? On the rim of the TV camera lense left behind on the moon and retrieved after a few weeks they found a streptococcus. It had survived the long nights on the moon, and found new chemical combinations to survive radiation and exposure. That's what I hope for: to survive a succession of moon nights in order to return to Earth and live in the green grass. I know what you'd say: experience itself is surviving; adjusting to new instruments. I only hope all this isn't unnecessary and pointless, this wear of the hub within me, which makes me just a flapping rag without a skeleton. After all you've done to me, you ought to provide the soil necessary for the strepto-coccus.

Today the cable arrived. You're coming after all. I feel I could hold my breath until you're here.

THE PIT

When JB finished reading he looked at his watch. Had Gertrude really gone where she should be going, or was she roving about on the roads? He felt how present anxiety prevented him feeling the pains of the diary. He went over to Sten to ask when Gertrude could be expected back.

'Later on in the evening. She's used to driving in the dark. Are you worried?'

'We quarrelled. Well, worse than that. She left in a state of fury.'

'In that case you'd better not be here when she returns. I mean it would be better for Gertrude, but that's not easily arranged.'

'My concern is too egotistical. I have to know that she's all right. I can't part from her like this.'

He walked around the school buildings, heard the children's voices from the nursery, saw a young teacher hurrying to-wards a classroom with a bundle of books. He soon went back to Sten.

'I have a wee whisky for you,' Sten said. 'This is a place of sheer puritanism. It's practically impossible to get hold of alcohol, and it's much too expensive. We have to live as close as possible to the level we're trying to abolish.'

They chatted for a while about this and that. JB debated whether in spite of everything, he should tell Sten about Klas

Lundin, but considered that this was up to Gertrude. If she returned. For the first time the thought struck him with unreal strength. From the diary he remembered her words about being nobody.

By and by Sten became restless too. They found an old Peugeot owned by one of the teachers, and borrowed it on the condition that they would not overtax it. They drove slowly towards Palapye. They asked for Gertrude. She had not shown up. They had waited for her in vain, and there was no telephone connection between them and Swaneng. A couple of uncomprehending faces turned to their upset faces. Here they were used to plans being hampered, and nobody had been worried. But their concern made itself felt, and questions and answers became more eager; also more confused.

'Come on,' Jan said. 'Let's go back.'

He was struck by a feeling that they might have passed her on their way there. She could have called out to them without being heard.

They went back the same way. Paths turned off from the road, leading to villages, clusters of houses, water tanks, or cattle ponds. The ground was flat and hard in the drought; they could take the car anywhere in this landscape, as long as they cruised between hillocks, bushes and stone blocks.

Sten tried to remember the topography of the road and its surroundings. It was dark. The stars had arranged themselves into mathematical calculations. They saw fires glowing outside some huts and stopped. Sten's Tswana was not fluent.

'Have you seen a car pass?' he asked two men who had just woken up. They nodded.

'What direction did it go in?'

They pointed towards Swaneng, as if Gertrude had been on her way back. But they nodded in reply to most questions, and Sten's unfamiliarity with the different tenses made JB suspect that the people of the village only confirmed that their own car was now turned with its bonnet towards Swaneng.

They went on. The road was too dry for the tyres to leave any tracks. In the thistle plants eyes gleamed like red rear lights. They followed a path leading to a dried out watercourse. The cows were inside their night-time enclosures of thorn. They were told at some huts where they inquired that the sound of an engine had been heard on one occasion. It was not necessarily Gertrude – there were other people who occasionally travelled between the railway and Serowe, and most of them had jeeps.

'The fact that she never went to Palapye doesn't mean that something has happened to her,' Sten said. 'She may have had an impulse to drive somewhere else just to be alone. She's not afraid of the dark. She wouldn't mind spending the night alone in the car.'

'She may want to scare me. That conversation had to cost something.'

'What were you quarrelling about?'

'I can't tell you. But it was all my fault.'

'I see.'

'She may have left the car somewhere out in the bush,' Jan said. 'She can see our headlights. She's laughing at us . . . no, she's not laughing.'

'She could be anywhere,' Sten said. 'But there aren't many roads to choose between.'

He drove slowly. In one place they saw that the sand bank by the edge of the road had been crossed by wheel tracks. They got out, and brought torches. Their eyes got accustomed to the light. It was not completely dark. A half moon was situated near the horizon. They heard the night-jars humming like huge insects stuck in a spider's web. It sounded sad when the notes sunk to signals hardly audible over the savanna.

The cardinal points were scrunched up. All was gathered here among termite hills and low boulders: pode and antipode joined together. His anxiety was too great for any thoughts, and living inside him like a swell. The stars rose and fell like wreckage in a surge.

He pointed his torch to the ground as if for support. The beam showed an old man's face with a pointed beard. Jan in fear fluttered with the light, and the face nodded. It was an old goat grazing in the night who had turned his yellow suspicious gaze at him. They stared at each other, and then JB began to walk towards the goat who replied with a snort.

When he came up to the goat, it took a gentle step aside. JB let the light fall on its white flanks which looked smaller in the dark. He felt that he was about to lose his balance. One foot sank in the softer soil, and he was forced down on his knees. Looking at the animal, he had not watched his step.

In a flash he remembered the mountain beetle the Arlanda meterologist had told him about: it fell down a ravine and came back after a couple of hundred years, frozen and well preserved. He cried:

'Sten! We're near a ravine. A goat almost pulled me down.'

'There are no ravines here.'

He then directed the beam on the ground, and saw that they were standing at the edge of a funnel shaped quarry.

'It's something else,' he said. 'It's deep.'

'We're probably near the sand pit,' Sten said, approaching.

They dislodged stones and heard how they fell, gathering more sand with them. Then it was silent. The silence made the darkness deeper. Gertrude might be at arm's length without them knowing it.

The torch had a small dispersion of light, and he could not see much at a time. He was suddenly physically frightened. Existence felt rough like the tongue of a rapacious beast, dark and narrow like the throat of a horse. He wanted to cry out for Gertrude, but dared not. The thought of her being there to reply made him equally frightened.

If she were dead, he thought, what would it mean? Awareness that his life would be worth so much less? She would take away a piece of him that he would never be able to find again, and give him a debt that he could neither live with nor cast aside.

Sten had reached him.

'Where is the sand pit?' Jan asked.

'Not far from the railway.'

'There are tracks here,' Jan said. 'Broken bushes and stems.'

'Then she is down there.'

He could see it before him: the wheels turning in the dark, and the petrol burning. For a moment he felt numb all over, turned into a stone which the world could turn and carry wherever it liked.

The sand pit had a long slope down, like a number of abrupt terraces. The climb down was easy. Then the light of Jan's torch bounced on the grey jeep. It was on its side. He was there quicker than he could explain.

The car was empty. He saw Gertrude lying some distance away from it. In the light he saw her pale face with her mouth half-open and eyes closed. They would take her dead body home, he thought. He felt paralyzed as if fear had been a poisoned arrow. At the same time he had the inclination to act quickly and sensibly, as if directed by some other intelligence.

Sten knelt by the body, shining the light across her. She had scratches on her face and shoulders. They saw no direct injuries. JB touching her blouse found blood stains, but soon realized it was his own blood. He had scratched himself on thorns : his arms were streaky.

'She's alive,' Sten said. 'I can feel her pulse.'

'The car skidded,' Jan said. 'I don't suppose it was intentional.'

'No. I'd be surprised. The Gertrude I know . . . but I don't know her. You don't know anyone, I've realized that.'

'If Gertrude is alive, the baby is still getting oxygen and nourishment,' JB said. 'But we don't know what knocks she's had.'

They were afraid to move her in case her back was injured, but there was nothing else to do. They had to get her away from there. They carried her as carefully as they could up to the car. She woke up, moaned, tossed her head and was unconscious again. The sound filled them with unreasonable joy.

'She's alive,' Sten said several times, as they carried her up the slope. Three hours had passed since they went out to look for her. Time was an invisible weave that Gertrude was tearing at in order to get out into something, or up from nothing.

All their efforts were concentrated on Gertrude. JB thought they created a magical circle around her. Everything had to work out right – like for the sleep-walker on the window-sill.

The school clinic had a sick-room. The African nurse lived next door, and they woke her up. Gertrude was placed on a hard surface. She remained unconscious. They told the nurse about the sand pit.

'If she pulls through she'll be lucky,' the nurse said.

JB went to get Aina, the only doctor at the school. In a moment she was down at the clinic, and started to examine Gertrude.

'No serious back injury, I shouldn't think,' she said. 'It's hard to tell now whether she's got any other injuries. You go to bed. I'll see to her now.'

Jan suddenly felt exhausted and thought he could fall asleep anywhere: the darkness would receive him and be a mattress where he did not leave any imprints.

Later that night the nurse came to his room and woke him up.

'Your wife is awake now,' she said. 'The baby is alive. They will both be all right. But she can't be disturbed now. Try to go back to sleep.'

Jan burst into tears of relief. He had not cried like that since he was a child. When the tears stopped he was dry and exhausted.

This was difficult Jenny, he said towards the ceiling. I wish I didn't have to face her.

THE ANT LION

Jan Backman woke up early remembering everything. The sun was red at the edge of the steppe. He wanted to tear the view down like a poster left up on the wall for too long.

A lizard wrote a nonchalant signature on the wall. On the ceiling a fly slept. He broke a spider's thread between the door handle and the bed, and went out. Under the pitch of the roof Gertrude's bats hung in a cluster like blackened bananas. Far away on the savanna he saw a grass fire creep along the ground like a worm. Antelopes, snakes and insects fled from the embrace of the elements.

He was spinning out time. His fear of facing Gertrude increased to anxiety. What would she say? He feared that something inside him would burst, jump up like a spring and hit her unfairly. It was his fault that she lay there. That was why he felt it an inhuman cowardice to want to put off the meeting.

Jenny was the only person to whom he would be able to confess his hesitation. Their openness was his breathing-pore. He checked that his flight ticket was still in his back pocket. He then went over to the clinic.

Walking between the white school buildings, he remembered an occasion at the Water Palace when they were children. He had just about strangled her, she had wanted him to, but adults who hurried to assist her did not understand, but separated them for many years to come. And she had buried him in the sand, just for fun, and he had not resisted until she put her foot on his chest and he had difficulty in breathing. She had laughed at the risks they took. It seemed to spur her on to approach the limits of danger. But now he felt himself left out of these games.

When JB entered the clinic, Aina was examining Gertrude. She pressed a stethoscope against Gertrude's stomach. Jan stopped in the doorway. Gertrude hardly seemed to notice him. He thought of the child, the unpredictable offspring inside her. It did not yet need her thoughts, just her breath and her nourishment. It had survived the fall. It was suspended in its embryonic water and did not notice the heavy sea.

Soon it would be crawling, laughing and imitating. It would turn a grain of gravel as if looking for its signature.

'It aches,' Gertrude said.

He saw her features stripped of her sensuality. The pain was like childish nakedness.

'You can stay with her,' Aina said to Jan. 'She has a light concussion and a lot of bruises and scratches. That's all I should think.'

He sat down on a chair by her bed. She gave him no comforting smile, but looked serious and dignified. Her eyes did not reproach him. They were silent. He now realized that they had reached some kind of an end. Soil erosion, resulting in denuded ground. If the humus was removed, it took many hundred years before something could grow again. By then they would long since be dead and part of the new soil.

'What actually happened?' he asked.

Gertrude watched him from a distance. He remembered scenes where he had waved at someone on an ocean liner, and suddenly was unable to see which of the pinsize heads he waved to.

'I didn't care how near the edge I drove. The sand pit was like a funnel in the earth. Down there was an ant lion waving his feelers, imbibing people who go too near the edge of the pit.'

'Don't you remember how it happened?'

'One headlight went out. I skidded somehow. For a moment I thought you were there as I slid about. You weren't, I suppose?'

'Of course not. What could I have done?'

'You could have calmed me down, and I could have driven more carefully. But now I know you make me insecure and weak rather than calm and strong.'

He had given her what he had to give, he told himself. That was insufficient. She no longer wanted understanding and adjustment between them at any cost; she preferred distance and independence. Maybe she would from now on resist the ant lion rather than just roll down the slope like a pebble.

'The child's all right,' she said. 'But something else died.'

'I think I know what you mean,' he replied.

Her face looked empty. He wondered what she had experienced. So much happened watched by nobody; like a door closing at the far end of a room. You found it inexplicable, because you were not there yourself.

'I never wanted to be jealous of you or Jenny,' Gertrude said. 'Remember that. It's something else. Our closeness is thinning out. I have to look so far away. I took the car out . . . to find out where the rope would break. I walked on it totally unconcerned before, knowing it would carry my weight. I didn't even see the rope. I don't know how I made my way.'

'Our experiences have changed us more than we wanted,' he said. 'We tried to lean heavily against each other. Then the balance was disturbed.'

He stopped himself. Obviously they were both frightened of the influence they had on each other. They had been brought to the verge of a catastrophe. Now they both wanted to get back safe and sound.

'When Klas left me that night, I thought only truth was good enough,' he said.

She looked at him like at a stranger.

'You can be as serious with others as you are with me,' she said. 'I'm trying to understand this. It has made you different. It may be a gain, it may be a loss, I don't know. But we're not brother and sister in the way we used to be.'

He looked out of the window. He thought their experiences

were being recorded with unknown instruments from inside a poppy's seed-vessel. Someone was sitting there registering the magnetic storms of human life through observatory apertures.

'Now I can understand the distance you wanted to create between us,' Gertrude said. 'Jenny was not enough. She was also to be let into our secret. You really wanted to be free of me. But you could have told me sooner. I'm surprised that you had to make such a long journey to see me just to get rid of me. I'm surprised, but I suppose it was necessary.'

A gleam of light was joined to the wall above her bed like an abstract painting. It then jumped down from its invisible hook. Outside, hoes with worn handles were leaned against the clinic walls. The men had left the tools outside as they had to come in to have a wound dressed, or a tablet for nausea or headache. Their mumbling voices and the sharp orders of the nurse reached Gertrude's ears. In there a cheap clock lived its radio-active hours, also ticking when you held your breath. He opened the framed mosquito net which was in the place of a window, and looked out over the Botswana countryside. He saw a finch.

'Can you hear it?' he asked.

'Yes. It squeaks like a pram,' Gertrude said, attempting to smile.

He was pleased that she replied. He was going back to Sweden as soon as possible. Perhaps in the future they might find a language they could both understand.

Gertrude had to stay in bed for a few days for the sake of the baby. She moved up to her own house. JB arranged his trip home. Once a week there was a flight to Zambia, and from there connections to Europe. Those days the wind whistled as usual in the thorn bushes, and rubbed the thorns against each other. It set the weaver's droopy nests swinging, and played ball with the yellow fruits of the wild tomatoes.

On his last evening in Botswana it eventually started to rain. They had waited a long time for rains, and yet they were not late. The clouds did not look like the ordinary stationary clouds; they had gathered to a riot at the horizon. Under them were black baskets like old-fashioned gas balloons relieving themselves of their load over the sparse vegetation of the savanna, where the drought had burnt its mark of ownership.

The cattle, whose mucous membranes had notified them of the arrival of the rainy season, returned to the watering-places long before they had had time to fill up. They had survived many dry months, but in spite of this it happened that at that stage, facing the silver thorn and the cracked clay, they would lie down to die, cheated at the watering-place.

That evening JB saw termites rising in pale swarms out of their cone shaped hills resembling the Botswana huts. The news of the wedding flight of the termites immediately reached animals and people. Near the starting range greedy toads gathered licking so many termites that they swelled like drums, and when their stomachs could take no more, they stuffed their mouths, wiping wings off from the corners.

The bats swished past with a high confined sound. Level with the tree tops the termites ended up on a round-about of robbers. The swift birds formed a circle, the more clumsy ones flying to and fro. Swallows and finches sometimes flew too low. JB heard the air hissing in their quill-feathers, and the click as a quarry swiftly collided with a beak.

To many it was a wakeful night. At the Africans' huts fires were lit to attract the insects. Children and adults sat there catching the termites and throwing them into saucepans of water. Wet-winged they were then sprinkled into frying-pans, cooked in their own fat, and eaten.

The atmosphere was merry like the beginning of the crayfish season in Sweden. JB was given a few termites. They tasted of pinewood and resin, reminding him of the devastated forests of Botswana.

Those who survived the wedding the same night cast off their wings into heaps that rustled like paper, and returned into the darkness of their hill to build and keep house for the next generation.

In the morning the air had a vibrating pureness, as if one raindrop had been blown up to a thin dome over the landscape.

Sten Tidström gave him a lift to the station in Palapye.

'Let's go on writing to each other,' Sten said. 'You'll be our man in Sweden.'

JB took the mail train north to Francistown, and a flight from there. He felt set to zero, deep frozen against his will. Jenny was storing his joy. He wanted to get inside her like getting into a warm house.

When they had broken through the clouds resting over southern Scandinavia, he saw Arlanda approaching, a little singeing spot in the large forest. The runways were salted and skiddy, Sweden had winter in March. Jan Backman persuaded the pilot of the DC8 to tell the control tower that he would be on duty the following day.

IV

BEHIND THE GLASS

A NIGHT OUT

Arlanda in the early morning, still grey – like changing from a colour film to black and white. On the runways aeroplanes were waiting with lights blinking for the starting signal. Figures and starting conditions were exchanged between the control tower and the planes. There was the occasional jest – forbidden according to the rules which allowed only duty messages. Some pilots noticed that Jan was back on duty after being absent for some time.

So did his friends in the tower, when the morning traffic had diminished and Christina brought the ten o'clock coffee.

'Thanks for letting me know that you were flying in,' Jansson said.

'It's on the tape, in case you hadn't appeared today. Did you go on a safari?'

'No,' Jan Backman said. 'I had enough of adventures as it was.'

'What was the coffee like?' Christina asked.

'Chicory.'

'What did the stars look like?' Eklund, the meteorologist, asked.

'The Plough evolved in a funny way.'

'Did you find out anything about the giraffes' blood pressure? What kind of huge pump drives their blood up through those necks?'

'Giraffes are extinct in Botswana.'

'Remember Hansson?' Christina said. 'The caretaker at the reptile house outside here? When we came in we found him staring at a boa. He said he was depressed – I think it was after the Tonkin Bay intermezzo – and then he had to feel that reptiles were wiser than people.'

'I remember,' JB said. 'I'm sorry the animals got caught in the fire. I didn't see any snakes in Botswana. What happened to Hansson, by the way?'

'Lorry driver,' Jansson said. 'However, aeroplanes will soon replace lorries. People don't understand this, and those who extend airports don't understand how enormous the scope will be. Lobsters alive from Alaska the same day. The next revolution will be a transport one. What were the cars like in Botswana?'

'They were few in number.'

'My Volkswagen van is bloody awful,' Jansson swore. 'To get the clutch down on the floor I have to turn my foot out. There's no space. Makes my knee ache for the rest of the day. What did you drive down there?'

Jan listened to the usual coffee talk, feeling as if he had not been far away. The others had hardly noticed his absence. But when he tried to tell them something they teased him. He felt like Axel Ericson at home for a short visit. Then one of them said:

'Someone called Jeger phoned you just after you'd left. We said you were in Botswana.'

'Oh you did? In Botswana?'

Outside the bulldozers and salt spreaders were at work. The little trolleys from the kitchen were being driven around with trays of cold roast beef, Lurpak butter, Danish Blue Cheese, bread to be heated mid-flight, and Danish pastries with hard grains of sugar in the folds.

A little while later JB went down to his office to dial Jenny's number again. He had phoned her at Nybro Quay all the previous night without getting a reply. Now he dialled the number of the Department of The Environment, only to be told that Jenny was still in London. He realized that she had telephoned Arlanda from there. Why had she not written to him? He felt a cold shiver run along his spine. Wet snow-flakes stuck to the window like moths.

He was given the number of the Department of The Environment in London, and booked a personal call. He was told that Jenny had gone to a congress outside the city. He had not heard from her for weeks. He did not know what to do.

As Christina entered, he sat perplexed in front of an unwritten memo.

'What's the matter? Would you like an Aspirin?'

'An Aspirin wouldn't help me.'

'I'll give you two then,' she said, and put them on his desk.

At six o'clock he had still not done much. Once an hour the telephonist called to say that Jenny Jeger was not available. It was as though she tried to persuade him that Jenny did not exist. He persevered and booked another call.

Christina opened the door slightly.

'I saw the light was on. How are you now?'

'The Aspirins weren't strong enough. I need something better. Would you like to have dinner with me?'

This time she said: 'Why not? I'll just give mummy a ring not to wait for me.'

On their way into Stockholm Christina told him about the old flat in Bonde Street where she lived with a younger brother and her mother who was a retired telephonist. It was a cheap and nice way to live, she said. Her fiancé often came to see them. He was training to be a land surveyor.

'He often stays the night at weekends. We all have breakfast together. It's not very liberated or very strange. It was different when I was younger.'

JB laughed at her.

'I'm twenty-eight,' Christina said. 'But imagine ten years ago. I remember what it was like when my sister lived at home. What a fuss about morality.'

'Did she survive it?'

'She's has more trouble than I have. Her marriage seems to be on the rocks. They live in a tower block in Jordbro.'

'That's where we could have ended up,' JB said. 'It was just about definite that the large airport should be there instead of Arlanda.'

'We want to live in the country,' Christina said. 'I'm getting like my grandma. To her the city is people going deaf from pile-drivers, and fainting from exhaust fumes. They smoke foreign grass in the tube, and strip in the coffee shops.'

'In a big city one should be able to find everything,' JB said. 'Grazing ground and yacht havens as well. Ideally one should be able to catch crayfish within the borders. I've heard someone say that a big city is a place where you should be able to buy artificial wound scabs. Underneath them you hide little razor blades to escape from prison.'

They had been given a table at the far end of the basement restaurant. JB felt he had to bend over to get into the dungeon. The sighs of the ghosts were drowned by the hum of merry town councillors celebrating a victory, which to other people looked like defeat.

'Suffering is fine when it's past,' JB said, pointing at a ring in the wall. 'This is where people perished in the old days.'

'I heard they used it for hoisting up the wine anchor,' Christina said.

'An optimistic view,' JB retorted. 'Let's stick to it and see what the house has to offer.'

He had taken Christina out to pass the evening without having to listen for the telephone. Christina was happy and witty. The conversation passed freely between them, both laughing as they caught or missed the words. He told Christina he felt happier than earlier on in the day. He indicated that somebody he missed very much had not phoned him. 'I realize you're not married any more,' Christina said with the voice of an expert. JB for a moment was embarrassed. She was at the beginning of something she hoped would last all her life. He himself had broken out of it, and created worry and despair. How much could she take of that truth?

'I've almost forgotten what it feels like,' Christina continued precociously, turning her large ring. 'Being in love was bloody awful.'

'But aren't you in love now?'

'Well yes, but it's different after a few years.'

JB thought of the short time he had known Jenny, and how he had believed that their quick moments were the points of balance both for the past and for the future. Now he was stranded in uncertainty.

'Don't worry about it,' Christina said in a motherly voice. 'Either she likes you and then it's all right, or she's had enough – and in that case, she wasn't much to lose.'

'Everybody must have their own freedom to come and go,' JB said, 'but that's easier to accept for yourself.'

They said no more about Jenny.

'Did you hear that Jansson's girl has come back from the home?' Christina asked. 'She's a drug addict. They love her whatever she does.'

'I had no idea about that.'

'Eklund's wife is having another baby. Their fourth.'

'How is it done?' JB said.

'What? Having children?'

'Do you know if women have to book a room in a good hospital?'

'I think the pre-natal clinic takes care of all those details.'

'But if the woman is abroad?'

'Then she has to write to ask the social security office. Eklund's eldest daughter could be the mother of the one they're expecting now.'

'There are so many things you never know about,' JB said. 'We're all so wrapped up in our own problems.'

'Just look at you and me,' Christina said. 'We've seen each other for four years and never said as much as tonight.'

They chatted until closing-time. JB walked Christina home.

She looked like a pale city girl in the night light. They said good-bye outside the little grey door at Bonde Street, which looked like the stage door of a theatre. She gave him a bear-hug, and for a moment he felt her body with the open jacket and the long rough knitted cardigan, her cold wintery cheek against his, and her hard hands on the back.

'Thanks for tonight,' she said. 'See you tomorrow.'

Nothing much has happened, but he felt secure thinking about her, and thinking that they could continue talking to each other the next day if they wanted to. It was windy, and the wind whistled around him as he walked back. The neon lights panted as if breathing. The chimneys of the Old City formed a barricade. The cars wiped out the dark with their headlights.

Nothing was present, everything was transitory. JB got the idea that someone was calling out among the clunking ice-floes, once, twice. He looked round for a life-buoy, but it was not in its place when needed. He leaned far over the rail. The shipwrecked rose quickly: a grey gull almost nudging his head.

'Jesus is arriving. Yes, with hammer and nails', he read on a lamp-post next to a poster about local meetings at the City Museum. A Finnish sailor came up to him, seized him by the collar and showered him with eager strings of words. JB released himself with a jerk to avoid getting involved with an argument in an unknown language. Just as incomprehensible – he thought – as his loving telegram to Jenny may have sounded if she had moved on to a different wave-length. He felt threatened by catastrophes. The Stockholm traffic was considerably thinning out while he was walking. An elderly lady passed him in Arsenal Street. They were alone in the area. He thought

215

that she looked at him with a sad smile: did she recognize him? In the old days he would have been a gentleman who doffed his hat and offered to escort her. Now he did not feel any safer than she did.

Not much later he was in Jenny's flat. He wondered when she had last been there. They had not been in touch for six weeks. In the hallway he stumbled over a pile of newspapers and letters. He imagined that he could hear her breathing evenly on the wide bed, and felt the joy somersaulting in his chest. But it was his own breath he heard.

He bent down to sort out her mail. He found his departing letter, and the telegram from Botswana, and put them in his pocket. His messages had not reached her. He could feel gravel rolling under his feet; his life was skidding in a curve.

He turned out the light, and looked out towards other black windows. He suspected there were many people like him: staring unseen at each other behind dark glossy windows.

Smoke belched out over the city. The houses appeared to hide rubbish burning stations starting after midnight to avoid the rules in force. So the sun would rise over a misty city as a red warning for storms.

He felt like getting up on the roof where they had made love, but he was stopped by the locked attic door. If he beat a drum roll on it, he would wake up the rest of the house. He waited for a while, went down again, and was seized by a naïve feeling that Jenny might have returned in the meantime. He listened by the door like the first time he met her; it was silent.

He then went slowly down the stairs, but his steps sounded so sad that he hurried on. No unknown person in the warmth of his flat would have to wonder who was the tragic creature on the stairs.

There were no taxis around. He found a night bus, empty with chocolate paper and cigarette packets on the floor, and a newspaper on the seat next to him. It took him up to the Vasa district.

THE FUNERAL SERVICE

I n the morning he lit the stove under the kettle, and tried to find time to wash up before the water boiled and the lid started making a noise. He scoured the draining board in the kitchen with Brillo, swept the floor around the garbage bin, and sprayed a green liquid on the finger-prints around the lock of the larder door. On top of the fridge a pink coating from some secret recipe was congealing. Sometimes he would fly through the rooms doing his chores, with joy and resolution under his brow. Now he felt the kitchen and the movements of his hands did not really belong to him.

He cleared out his provisions: onions sprouting, a packet of spaghetti suspiciously darkened, a tin of anchovies on its way to take off. In a corner of the larder he found some cans without labels. These were army rations delivered by Diana Game Products Ltd. to the Swedish Defence. JB had brought them back from his military service a long time ago, but they had remained unopened, as an analyst had proved the contents to be a mixture of badger, crow and fox meat.

He wrapped the lot in yesterday's newspaper, and then discovered an obituary saying that Christian Stoll had passed away peacefully, leaving behind Agnes Stoll. He started, as he had never thought he would have to read about it like this. Although the Stoll hardware shop was almost next door, he had not been there for months.

He walked over to find Mrs Stoll grinding coffee for herself. The ground beans fell into a wooden box, which she emptied into a flask. 'He had a stroke,' she said, her mouth curling down. 'He had high blood pressure. Suddenly it was all over. The funeral is today. Three days after his death, according to the rules.'

The bubbles were rising, slowly and hesitantly, until the whole amount of water defying the laws of gravity rose through the glass pipe. 'I've only got powdered cream,' she said. 'Every year the dairy gets a bit further away.'

She offered JB a simple cup made by Rosenthal, of which there were dozens on the shelves.

'I met Christian when he was twenty-one,' she said. 'I was twenty. It was in the summer. There won't be much to remember soon.'

The memories passed, peeled off like hotel labels on a suitcase.

'I've done my duty,' she went on. 'The invoices have been paid. I don't owe anybody anything. That's the only way: never to be in debt.'

'Are you going to sell the shop? I mean, sell the lease on certain conditions?'

'To whom?'

'Maybe a designer. Someone who would turn the premises into a studio, a silversmith's shop, some kind of workshop, a Russian café, or a sectarian bookshop.'

'I don't understand what you're talking about.'

JB missed Stoll. He could hear him humming like a bumblebee against a window pane, angry but powerless.

'They crossed his hands on his chest. They looked like two thin leaves. He had lost so much weight.'

She cried a little.

'Maybe I shouldn't ask,' JB said, 'but what are your plans now?'

'I'm going into a home in Tumba. They can look after my legs there. I can hardly stand on my feet any more. I don't want to think about it. Do you know the kind of people who live in Tumba?'

'No,' JB said. 'All I know is that they make bank-notes there.'

'I don't expect too many people at the funeral service. He occasionally went to the synagogue in St Paul's Street among the Black Jews: that was where we belonged. We never dared mix with the White Jews in Wahrendorff Street.'

Later in the day JB sent a cable to Jenny Jeger at the Department of The Environment in London: 'Give me some sign of life. Whatever you're up to ring me at Arlanda on Tuesday Wednesday Thursday or Friday between three and five.' It's a small world Jenny, he told himself. Interpol watch you. How people could stay away after all!

All the things he and Jenny had done together in Stockholm lived within him with all unnecessary details, with careless colours and a prehistoric presence he had never asked for. He felt like going back to her flat to take out an old sweater he had seen her wear the first week they knew each other. It smelt of her.

Instead he remained at Uppland Street. He was to have the night shift at Arlanda that day. He found a bottle of paint remover and used it for scraping the thick varnish off his desk, expecting a beautiful oak surface to appear. Something else much simpler appeared. Were desks ever made of fir? He had bought his at the army surplus store for next to nothing, as army men are no business men but professional consumers. He looked at his work in astonishment. Then he sat down at the desk, and began to write a letter to Jenny which he crumpled up immediately.

More than ever he felt that he lacked a definite way of thinking to hide behind or stick to. All parts of his life were open to revision, but he had not achieved a story, and who would grant him freedom from responsibility?

Jenny's and Gertrude's behaviour did not allow him to be himself. Somebody pulled at an invisible leash. He was trapped by his own feelings trying to fight them off, and the fight itself gave him a feeling of existing in the world, of having a place in the world, although it would not obey him. They probably felt the same.

The same afternoon he appeared at the funeral service in the Chapel of the Mosaic at the Northern Cemetery. The undecorated house with Hebrew lettering in gold on the cornices and the few people gathered, created a great loneliness around Christian Stoll's coffin. For a moment JB wished Gertrude had been there. She had known him as well.

Jan was the only man not to wear a hat. He had forgotten to bring his. They read some texts from the Bible, and an old member of the congregation sang a lamentation. The Linjeflyg Metropolitan approaching Bromma Airport erased a couple of verses from the Old Testament. The friends present pressed Mrs Stoll's hand. Then they dispersed.

JB left by a side path leading through a hedge to the protestant cemetery, where there were tombstones in all directions with very different shapes according to the tastes of the bereaved and the fashion of the time. By coincidence he found Mrs Tapper's low stone in dark granite, cared for by the cemetery administration and paid for by A. O. Backman. She was surrounded by a chemist, a sea captain and a widow like herself. JB had not been there since she died many years ago.

He went to the shop by the gates, and returned with a hyacinth. Coronets of peat-moss were on the other graves, and magpies stole pieces of them for their nests which they were already building for the spring. A damp mist rose over the grassy places of rest.

JB remained standing. He wanted to tell Jenny about his life with Mrs Tapper, the housekeeper at the Water Palace. He had been on a walk with her once when a magpie got stuck on a barbed wire fence. It was blinded by the snow and trapping itself to death. It was already dark, and they were on their way home.

'Leave it alone,' Mrs Tapper had said. 'It's had it already.'

She was afraid of animals, especially those he had touched and brought home. They wanted to be near her, but she thought they attacked her. He released the magpie, though it snapped at him in despair. He held the wings against its body until he could throw it into the air. Then it took off as if the stars were edible.

'It's flying towards a certain death,' Mrs Tapper said in a sombre voice.

She also had an introverted nature. She would go to weddings in Jacob's Church, sit at the end near the door crying to the notes of the wedding march. He remembered her going to a birthday party given by a relation, wearing a dress beige like artichoke hearts and thin like parachute silk. She had stood silently in front of the mirror fiddling with herself, her eyes looking into the distance as though she saw nobody at all. Her lips moved a bit as if she were trying to remember a folk song, something about a merry partridge.

When Jan came home again, Marianne Tidström phoned him.

'I had a letter from Sten saying you ought to be back. You must tell me about Botswana. Can I see you?'

'Yes of course,' Jan said.

'I want you to know that I've heard you and Gertrude are having a rough time,' went on Marianne.

'The last six months have been difficult,' JB said. 'I don't know if we can go on.'

'Did Sten talk a lot about me?'

'He only said you were tired and depressed about not being able to contribute. I can understand that. I felt the same, though in a different way.'

While he talked to Marianne, a naked woman tilted her venetian blinds in the house opposite, to keep people in the street from seeing her. For JB one storey above, the vision was clear. He could not take his eyes off her. She lay down with a stout man about fifty. She was somewhat younger and thinner. The man stayed mainly on his back, but she seemed happy and keen, caressing his hips, sitting on top of him, swinging one leg to and fro across his body. He was pleased and just passed his hand across her back. When JB had hung up after his call, he went on watching them. She took a few dance steps in front of him, smiling as if she was bold even daring to believe that she pleased him. Then she fetched a tray of coffee, they had a rest, and then started afresh.

Their bodies were not beautiful, but they seemed to enjoy themselves. Their actions were ordinary, but still attractive. JB felt a great tenderness towards them, but did not know how to use it. They were there across the street, within sight, and yet out of reach. The sunset was soon reflected in their blinds, leaving them hazy.

It was late in the day. For the remaining night shifts in March he had offered to do the radar control. He patted his trouser pocket, an old habit to check if his car keys were there. It was part of his identity, but they had been pushed aside by his erected penis.

He got out sandwiches, cereal and milk for a meal before his night work. The cereal packet rattled invitingly. He was prepared for anything. More than once he had poured the contents into a bowl to find, instead of food, warships and racing cars, balloons and coupons piling up, numerous but free of nutritive value. Meanwhile he read that a bowl of cereal from this packet together with unskimmed milk offered him one day's supply of calories and proteins, plus an inflatable lilo, a tricycle, and a play-pen.

He took off his jacket when he got to the radar control centre. The temperature was controlled, because the electrical apparatus could be damaged by temperature differentiations. The room was full of a slow buzzing, low-key noise from electronic machines, the teleprinter and the operator's directions on various frequencies.

At first he saw nothing but the weak circles of light, and the seemingly confused journeys of the aircrafts towards wider and wider circles. The man he relieved wrote in a log book. Jan Backman noted the time when he took over responsibility for the air-traffic.

His colleagues looked pale with deep sunk eyes in the indirect light. They had names for all the mobile dots. They had to know their exact speed the instant they appeared. The planes all received orders from the radar control centre: course instructions in figures, and compass directions. When a new plane appeared on the radar screen, it had to be immediately identified, given a course, a space, and then be placed on the waiting-list for landing, and have its circles described.

JB sat in front of the instrument screens. Every flash meant something he did not have time to interpret in words. Yet his manual exercises were carried out – the actions were the main things, not the implications, as the planes were not metaphysical birds, but swift vulnerable transport chambers.

The difficulty of a critical situation was to sharpen one's eyes and concentration instantaneously, and not let it be revealed in the voice. The orders had to be given in a neutral voice, or the pilot could be alarmed. The air-traffic controller often worked over-time. The shifts did not comply with other people's working hours. The control tower was one thing: the direct contact with the air, and the eye's own ability for surveillance. The radar control, however, was strenuous, especially in the morning and at night when the planes were crowding in the air space, and unbeknown to the passengers, had to circle around at several hundred kilometres per hour: a lot of identical light dots in the black glass.

Arlanda was an easy working environment compared to the large airports with their roundabouts and crossroads. Arlanda was a final destination. 'Current flight control data . . . decreasing traffic volume . . . northern watch area . . . change of course order for AF 306 . . .' The phrases, the terminology whirled to and fro. It all functioned. JB could toss about sleepless, wondering how collisions were avoided. They seldom

222

talked about it at work. If there was a narrow escape, nobody was told about it. But he racked his brain, and his eyes grew dry and red from the effort of really trying to see how it all had happened: what was already past. In the wood of his desk upstairs there was an eye. It stared at his face when he sat by the desk. It never winked in fear. He dared not leave a mug of coffee, or a sheet of paper on it. He took care never to blur the eye's vision.

THE SACK HOUSE

One night, returning from Arlanda, Jan Backman had difficulty finding his house. For one week it had been encased by scaffolding, and this day they had hung the sacking. The façade was concealed by straw grey shimmering drapings, gleaming in the street light. The demolition threat had all of a sudden been removed, and the house almost a hundred years old was no longer dilapidated. Better terms for borrowing money, and a scheme to charge repair expenses with the rent, had immediately made the house purposeful and solid. The slums of the city centre were delayed.

Now they picked the noses of the old mortar lions, and cleaned the furrowed skin of the pillar lady in the doorway. They wanted to restore the grained structure of the façade by polishing and blasting – however, they did it in the wrong way, attracting the soot of the air and fixing it better than before.

That night JB opened his window on to something looking like a wall half a metre away. He heard a taxi stopping, and the front door closing. The house was blind and silent inside its shroud. The furniture looked alien. As soon as he had sat down, he had to get up to find another position.

Inside the sacking the house had lost contact with the world about it and become a submarine. He opened the door onto the landing slightly. The front door had opaque glass with a clear lily-stalk in the middle. Through this he could see the lift light come on, casting up light in the shaft. As it passed he could see the person who had arrived in the cab: a woman stroking her hair and yawning at her reflection in the mirror – one of the fifteen tenants.

For the second night running he had the same dream: a stork, colourless, grey and mossy, drifted under the water in what looked like the Djurgårdsbrunn canal. The currents moved its wings. It had been dead for a long time, and could neither sink nor float. The neck bent forward. He was nearby watching it, and that was his fear.

His shouting woke him up to hours that could be divided into those when he thought of Jenny, and those when he was free of her, but even the freedom or emptiness had her outline. He waited: three to five o'clock p.m.

Who did Jenny think he was? He was bitter with himself for not having been able to articulate his love in a more convincing manner, and with Jenny for not daring to trust him even if he had not said a word. He had believed that there was an arc-light between them.

What was wrong with him? Maybe the inability to foresee the consequences of his actions. He preferred being elastic to being crushed. He feared the restlessness that overcame him whenever he rose from his senses to brood over the fates of other people without bothering to intervene. He saw himself ageing by the side of the action.

He walked around in what was one of his homes. Where were the places where the unworn feelings could spend the night? Where was the young Mozart now, where the flautist was heard the breathing between the notes?

He reiterated in his mind the expected phone call from Jenny. He had an old dream of the truth as a folded napkin: to serve the whole image quickly, before the eyes of the other person had time to freeze so that she heard only one word at a time.

The job routine itself was an advantage these days. JB realized how much he felt at home at Arlanda. At best he felt emancipated from his past; history was ahead of him, and his working place was at the same time a point of growth and a point of rest.

He was glad to have come closer to Christina. They did not exchange more words than before, but there was a new kind of warmth between them. One day she told him that her mother had gone to the Women's Liberation meeting at the

City Museum; another time she told him what her aunt had seen on an Old Age Pensioners' Club bus trip to the most modern suburbs of Stockholm.

The time limit had only one hour left to go when Jenny phoned. Then he had both the meteorologist and Jansson sitting next to him. JB felt his heart beating till it hurt, but his words were forcibly cool. Eventually the two realized that they were in the way, and withdrew to their places in the tower.

'Jenny!' Jan exclaimed. 'At last! Your voice . . . where are you? What are you doing?'

But Jenny was just as cool and self-controlled.

'Do you have people sitting around you as well?' JB asked. 'My intruders have just left.'

'No,' Jenny said. 'I'm sitting on the bed in the small attic I've borrowed. I'm all alone except for the pigeons, but they are behind my windows and bars. I'm very well. I'm sorry to hear you so upset.'

'But I haven't seen you since I don't know when. When are you coming home?'

'I can't tell you that,' Jenny said.

And he felt how he was brought back to reality with a thump, as if his life-line had been cut off.

'I have a lot of work to do at the moment,' Jenny said.

He felt like shaking her until the last vestige of her ladylike coolness fell off like old mortar. Underneath it she would be warm and laughing, full of caresses and impulses.

But she continued: 'They have formed a special committee for the purification of water, and an Englishman and I are the secretaries. They're more advanced here in dealing with certain problems.'

'For example, with the cooling problem,' Jan said.

'First of all I have to stay the rest of my time here. That's another fortnight.'

'A fortnight! Then I'll come over to see you. I have some more holiday time free. You can't be working all the time.'

'Sorry Jan,' she said, and he now heard a malicious tinge she had never used before. 'It doesn't suit me. Keep your holiday time for those who need it better.'

'You're trying to punish me for going to see Gertrude,' he complained. 'I assumed you'd understand.'

'I understood and I drew my own conclusions.'

'But you don't know everything.'

'No. I'm sure there's a lot to know.'

'Don't talk like that. Listen to me. Trust us.'

'You've got many slogans,' Jenny said. 'Mine has become: rather alone than exposed.'

'I see,' Jan said, without wanting to understand anything. 'But once we said: you must feel your freedom so strongly that you don't feel hurt when the loved one uses his.'

She was silent for a while.

'Did you hear?' Jan said.

'I did,' Jenny said, sounding sad rather than superior. 'Was that a rule that applied to only one of us? I'm using my freedom, and I advise you to enjoy yours.'

'It's unfair. I never wanted to leave you for a minute. I had to go.'

'I was told by other people,' Jenny said. 'I phoned you a long time ago.'

'A lot of things have happened since.'

'And more will happen, and now I think I have to hang up,' Jenny said lightly.

'I'm glad, for this was a terrible phone call. I think I'm dreaming.'

'I don't think so,' Jenny said, and he felt his behaviour noted in an official report. 'All the best, Jan.'

He mumbled good-bye when the receiver was put down at the other end.

He felt sick. He put his hand on the window pane. It was already open. Still he felt he was suffocating.

He had said nothing about Gertrude. His feelings for her and his departure from Botswana had nothing to do with Jenny. Gertrude had never been the centre of their life.

He was exposed to things he could not help, felt the responsibility for his actions yielding. His life was showered with forces impossible to master. Others had been through it before him, he thought, but that did not help him.

One hour later he was free for the day. The two messages from Jenny, which had been left unread in her flat, he sent to the Department of The Environment without any further greeting. He took his car to Skansen, parked it at the Nordic Museum, and strolled about at dusk in the sparsely falling snow with his collar turned up. The ducks and the white-feathered geese lay immobile on the paths. A quiet roe-deer rushed towards him, but turned aside at the last moment. It had escaped from its pen, but was caught by the larger fence around the park. It could not get back to its own family.

An illness, he thought, seeing bunches of herring flying through the air and down into open mouths with sharp teeth. It's an illness and she will recover; but he knew that nothing was certain.

There were few people on the Skansen mountain. Some thin girls in green keeper's uniforms passed with empty food buckets. He found the animals lived a life which reminded him of his own: enclosed, sad, and introspective, whirling around in each other's dead-end streets, making sudden false starts out into non-existent freedom, and becoming ill-tempered, introvert, and unpredictable.

The seals were modest and unambitious air-traffic controllers like himself, dutiful in their tasks but with various other interests. The owl tightened its ear tufts. It was very secretive: an unused reserve of talent.

The wild hogs grunted from their hogcote: don't overlook us, write our monographies. They rooted up the edible parts of life, not tickled by artificial consumer's needs.

The bisons watched him with frozen melancholy: just imagine yourself sitting there when you're as old as we are . . . Like people they probably experienced their alter ego quite often as a kernel in an alien body. I am somebody else, if it were not for this clumsy crumpled loose cover. I am really a very small creature.

In the ape house he found the animals imitating and defiant just like other people, and like them overcome by powerlessness, boredom and lewdness. Their faces expressed obvious doubts as to his importance. They exposed themselves to him as to an imaginary mirror. The orangutang hanging by the knuckles of his fingers, looked sadly at him for several minutes. Then he turned his head away to the sawdust strewn floor, and vomited until it splashed on Jan.

From one of the bell towers he looked out over the city. The sun had disappeared but left an oil stain in the western sky. The darkness was pushed back by the electric light on the ground. Some herons who were free to fly, although they lived at Skansen, stood in a row like a grey fence along the edge of a rock. The waves in Nybro Bay shimmered like a shoal released by the ice. Above the mine-sweeper's bridge at the Galär Wharf he saw the roof of Jenny's house.

He hoped the winter would pass like grouse in flight. An Easter storm would have to blow up to clear away the dry twigs. Then the winter respite would be over, snowdrops and crocuses would push out sprouts from nowhere, and the Insurance Company called New Life would start to pay out its policies.

The cold of the evening was rigid in his nostrils as he came out of the park. Outside the Biological Museum he saw the muscles of the bronze stallion trembling. He wanted to throw off Karl XV, the last king before motorism, who had mounted him in the false daybreak of historic romanticism.

JB took his car to Karla Square and parked it there. Instead of Strindberg's former house a new façade arose, which made pedestrians sick on their way to the supermarket on the ground floor. He saw raspberries dissolved in buckling marinade, or the inside of a smoke damaged lung. He turned his back on the nasty view, and sat down at a pizzeria with a bottle of wine and the evening paper. He had been given a vacant table in a corner. At the other tables sat young people who seemed to know each other and enjoy themselves.

He was suddenly annoyed with Jenny's behaviour, and considered he had a right to be. She robbed him of his happiness, but also renounced her own. He felt this in a moment of spiteful perceptiveness.

In the paper he found a statement by the public prosecutor: 'Sexual intercourse between half-brothers and sisters should not be considered a criminal offence.' Have we got as far as that, he thought, and remained sitting with the article. He and Gertrude from the beginning had swallowed their secret like a love potion. Their lives had then entered recognizable paths. Now they should have been ready to meet new values. He wondered if they had wanted to protect their love by avoiding all trouble with society, or if they had thought the secret itself more important – like an iron clamp deep inside keeping the different parts of a building together.

He suddenly discovered a well-known face – the author he had met at the art exhibition in Drottning Street last November. He stopped at Jan's table to tell him that he had

had a collection of prose poems published under the title of
The Glass Apple which, due to coterie mentality and the death
of this country's newspapers, had so far only been reviewed
by a horticultural publication.

'The glass apple? What do you mean by that?' JB asked.

'You apply codes at Arlanda,' he said. 'Don't we all?'

JB admitted this was true.

'And what can you do about it?'

'I undermine the language which conceals society, protects
its virtue and hides its dirt. When I've finished my cleaning,
the language will be hard to take in.'

'Then new codes will be created,' JB said. 'Will that enable
us to understand each other better?'

He then left his car for the night, and staggered through an
empty city. He thought he participated in a new kind of sack
race: the sack was over his head, but his legs just kept on
walking. At home he did not sleep a wink.

I ought to go over there to kiss her, he thought. She has
turned into an ice maid. She has to be thawed out from her
toes to her temples. She has told me that she doesn't want me.
What if it's true?

Then he wandered from one room into another, and for
the first time in many months he felt guilty about Gertrude.
His own fate was irrelevant. He had hurt her for something
worthless. The neighbours' clock told him that the night was
passing. The sacking hit the walls in the morning breeze without letting the light in.

SUNNY HILL

When Jan Backman's shift was over, the first spring winds
blew gently over his face. Once again he tried to remember that Jenny was out of reach. Within him there was unused joy
that he wanted to use only with her. He drove aimlessly about
on the roads, but found it a bad occupation. The snowbound
dust of the winter blew about freely. He expected to find a fire
in the next bend, but it was just a dusty cloud from a lorry.

At a newsagent on the outskirts of Södertälje he got out to phone Mrs Stoll. An unknown voice replied that she was at an old people's home called Sunny Hill near the centre of Tumba. JB turned his car round, and made his way toward the mint. But no old buildings were to be seen there; they were concealed by trees. He parked his car on the roadside, and had a look at the fatuous square in the centre of the town. A department store and a couple of banks shared the attention of the few strollers. A goldsmith cherishing weddings and fiftieth anniversaries exhibited the same kind of presents as JB had seen as a child. Maybe they were constantly exchanged, worked like a challenge cup at celebrations?

There was nobody there to show him the way: some children who did not speak Swedish, and an elderly man supported by a stick, who trembled so much that his speech was unintelligible. A verbal combat was being fought between two windows on the sixth floor in something JB took for Serbian. An outdated poster announced a comedy in the park called 'Summer Flirt', but he doubted that many people in this immigrant suburb would appreciate its twists, if there were any.

In a side street he found a branch library. There a long-haired girl in jeans knew where Sunny Hill was, and he soon parked his car outside some low yellow plaster buildings. He could not see any hill, and the sun was too cool for sun-bathing. A window had been left hesitantly ajar. Inside a wrinkled face, leaning at a suitable angle with closed eyelids, was greeting the Swedish spring.

A nurse went to get Mrs Stoll, as JB did not want to burst into her room. In the shop she had always been wearing a flowered overall. Now she was dressed in black with a pearl necklace and a brooch. Maybe she thought of her stay as one long party. She yawned and looked bored. Would they not let her go home soon?

To JB Mrs Stoll said she was pleased and surprised.

'Mr Backman comes instead of a son,' she said solemnly. 'This is my little room, please come in.'

JB sat down on a yellow varnished chair, watching the dark pines outside. Photographs with and without frames were crowded on a bookcase.

'This is my family,' Mrs Stoll said. 'I have all of them with me. This is Jüngli and the twins, one of them drowned at five;

the more talented one. Jüngli was lost in the war. This is our wedding photo. Stoll forgot to have his hair cut. He always talked about it. So annoying with a photo everybody wanted. And here's aunt Minnie who was a teacher, before she developed tuberculosis. Mr Hopf here helped us a lot, he was rich, very rich, but not really a good-hearted man. Oh, you know nothing, Mr Backman. You lead a calm and quiet life. I always see you with your little wife and your shopping bags.'

JB was amazed at this picture of his life. Then he asked how her legs were. Mrs Stoll gave him a comprehensive account. He opened his coat, feeling the sweat dripping down inside his shirt collar. He would have found it easier to hear about her leg wound, her ointments and bandages, if he had been treating her himself.

'And all day long they kill long-tailed ducks,' she went on to a different subject.

'Where?'

'The oil slicks in the Baltic. Thousands of them. An oil patch the size of a twopenny piece is enough to put them to death. It's better to kill them if there's nobody there to clean them.'

JB got up, and asked if they could have a look round the home together. Mrs Stoll took his arm, and off they went.

There was a lift, though it was only three floors. They saw the weaving room and the therapy department. A landing led off the staircase, different on each floor. On the top floor there was red furniture, upholstered and soft. The curtains had a fringe. A lonely lady in a peasant skirt was crocheting and smiling in this artificial nineteenth century world. She gave them a kind nod, but Mrs Stoll seemed frightened.

The floor below was in white and blue. Three ladies were sitting in high comfortable arm-chairs, not saying a word to each other. From the kitchen the light laughter of the staff could be heard. There life went on.

JB and Mrs Stoll returned to her room. The sun had moved. A girl in a white overall brought coffee and a saffron bun. 'This is not coffee,' Mrs Stoll said. 'I'm trying to teach them what coffee is, the coffee we had at home.'

'In the shop?'

No, to her home was Prague. She sat like a dignified bird in a cage politely watching her surroundings. She was passing through, though totally still. JB helped her with the earphones.

She did not hear him say good-bye, and she might not have remembered his words anyway.

He buttoned up his coat collar and went out to the car. The shadows were heavy and blue, like in lingering snow, but they rested directly on the ground. He felt stiff and aged. A soft layer between him and death had started to dry out. Something crumbled and burst. He remembered his father's old desk at the Water Palace, the black leather surface mellowing, and a tan, corky surface beginning to appear.

In that mood he telephoned Marianne Tidström to invite her to dinner at Cattelin. That was fine, her mother could baby-sit. He suddenly realized how spoilt he had been with warmth. He felt cold. The care he took when studying the menu seemed senile to him. He wanted to eat and drink his way to a fusible point which could solder together his scattered parts. However, he did not believe in the enterprise.

Raising his eyes, he saw Marianne at the doorway looking out over the tables in white cloths. She smoothed down her jersey dress and fiddled with her silver chain with the globe-shaped charm. They smiled at each other, a little embarrassed. The two of them had never been together on their own before, although they had known each other for years. They ordered bouillabaisse, and postponed the rest till later. After tasting the soup and agreeing on red wine, Marianne said:

'How is Gertrude?'

JB hesitated, which he found strange. Sten he could tell everything. Naturally it was all passed on to Marianne, though he hardly assumed it.

'We did not part enemies,' he said. 'So you see.'

'Well that's not much,' Marianne said. 'Will it pass, do you think?'

'I don't know. I fell in love with another woman. She doesn't want to see me now. Something went wrong. Meanwhile Gertrude and I have lost touch. Neither of us thinks it's too bad.'

'Yes,' Marianne said. 'I'm sure Gertrude does. Don't imagine she's just like you.'

'You don't know everything. She's expecting a baby by another man. She doesn't want to suffer with me. I think the two of us are happier free. We may see each other in a different and safer light.'

'Once you're at a distance, criticism sets in. Then you notice all sorts of things that didn't show when you were too close to discern it.'

'Are you afraid of being far away from Sten?' JB asked, as he did not want to talk any more about Gertrude.

'I staked everything on Sten. It sounds so silly. Like an investment or stock exchange speculation. He was a nice, free and different person. I suppose I used to be very hampered; my life was limited and secure. I always loved his ideas, his wild plans. Yet Africa was more than I could take.'

'Africa is a lot,' JB said. 'It's large and difficult. Don't reproach yourself too much.'

'I'm not reproaching myself,' Marianne said, looking into his eyes. 'It's Sten.'

Jan listened without saying much. At the moment when the plane took off from Botswana, Marianne told him, she felt an unusual kind of independence, a kind of freedom mixed with anger. It was her first trip towards a goal of her own since she married Sten. It was certainly an escape from something she had not been able to cope with, but it also meant facing her own difficulties and plans; things he could neither keep her away from nor help her with.

'At first I was just desperate and cried. The children began to comfort me. Martin is eleven now and Malin seven. When I saw how calm and motherly they were, I pulled myself together. We went to see my parents; they are retired and live in Strängnäs. Then we settled down in the flat in Mörby, and I went to see a vocational counsellor. It was like starting afresh. I knew I had to get myself a job, even if it meant working part-time as a secretary, or I would never make it. And what was worse: I'd never be able to face Sten again. At first I thought I had to be hard with him. Then I realized that if I was only strong, it would be all right.'

'So you got a job in an office?'

'No, the counsellor was a very sensible woman. She spared me several visits to a psychiatrist, I think. She asked me if I thought my husband would accept a job like that if he had to start again. I said no. She asked me if I was that much less intelligent than him. Or just lazier. Or whether I had to earn any money at all. Eventually she persuaded me to register at the university. So now I study law at home in the evenings.'

She looked at Jan exhilarated, as if she had told him of an amorous adventure.

'Fine,' he said. 'I thought you preferred weaving and embroidering.'

'Therapy,' Marianne said. 'I know a lot about it, because it was all I did the last few years before going to Africa. It felt like therapy to me as well. But I'm not ill, I'm not a convalescent. I've given the loom to my mother. She's staying with me and the children now. Half the day I help an old school-friend with her hire firm. We hire towels and overalls to a lot of shops and offices in the suburbs.'

JB looked at her in surprise. He remembered her face pale and sharp in the light of the cinema foyer. He and Gertrude had come out arm in arm. The four of them had chatted together before going back to Uppland Street for tea.

The woman opposite him seemed younger and more vivacious. Had Sten let her out of the narrow confines of her parents' home just to place her in a different cage? What would happen when he returned home?

'Do you think Sten will come back to Sweden?' she asked as if she had read his thoughts.

'I don't know. I think so. What if he doesn't? Will you go back?'

'No, not the way I feel now. Yet I know we need each other very much. Don't think I'm sitting here looking back at something past.'

She seemed almost shy to admit that she missed him. JB felt a wave of tenderness for these two people who had been driven together so hard. Did Sten know who Marianne was? Had he taken the time to stop and listen? Now Marianne was fighting for firm ground. She knew Sten would benefit from it as well.

He told her about Stoll's funeral, and Mrs Stoll at Sunny Hill's slope down to oblivion. The restaurant with its white table-cloths started to fill up with people. Waitresses with heavy trays of herrings pushed their way between the tables. Marianne talked about her girl-friend who was one of these laughing, easy-going characters that many people call cynical and superficial.

'Nobody knows what she's been through. Her mother died in a mental hospital, and she always worried about the symptoms appearing in herself and her brother as well. One day her house got burnt down. The insurance covered only half the value. Now she's married but refuses to have children. They're expecting to adopt an Indian boy any day.'

As soon as Marianne talked about things concerning her at that moment, in her different new kind of life, her face lit up. Sten and Botswana were shadows, a hope or a threat she pushed aside. Jan was pleased to leave the subject too. For this reason they felt as if they had met for the first time, two new people with a lot unsaid.

'My father was an accountant in a small provincial town. He didn't make much money. But it had to look good. We had a tiny three room flat, but inside those walls bulged the dream of an over-furnished seven room flat. The fringes of the rugs were combed, the floors overpolished. Mother cried nervously about the fine guests, while she folded napkins. I loved sitting on the floor with my head against her knees. Do you remember that world under the furniture that you later grew away from? The smell of dust and polish. The unpainted surfaces face down, the funny crossed saddle girth bands of the chairs. Sometimes I found the mark of a carpenter, or other pencil strokes which made sense only to the makers.

'All was strain and tension,' she continued. 'For what, I wondered later. Where did all those ambitions take them? Not until now can I see that this pressing bourgeois environment was just about to kill me. Sten came like a wind – but he lifted me up, and put me down again in another place. I wasn't kept floating for long . . .

'The day before yesterday I took the children to Kina Palace. When we got there it was raining. We had a long way to the bus stop, and when we got there the bus had left. Malin started to cry, and I was afraid she might catch cold. We took a cab all the way home; then we made hot chocolate and lit a fire although it was daylight. The children were exhilarated. I myself felt like a millionaire and very extravagant. To take a cab that distance. I'd never have done that before. Earning my own money means more to me than I ever believed it would.'

JB liked listening to her. The telephone call with Jenny and the ensuing silence had turned him upside down with emptiness. The earth fell out of the flower-pot, the piece of brick at the bottom fell out. Now he allowed himself to be filled by

Marianne's words. He was pleased that she could see herself from outside. He had not expected her to.

'Do you know how anything will work out?' she asked.

'No.'

Then she gave him an open and warm smile. He thought her eyes glistened like insects' wings, and he was smitten by obscure worry. When they got out into the alleys of the Old City, the full moon was shining like a replica of the clock face on the Great Church. They did not feel like going home. JB suggested a visit to Stampen Club where they played New Orleans jazz. It was smoky and crowded, so that they had to stand at the far end by the door. The music filled the whole room and set it all swinging, from the prams and the gramophone trumpets hanging on piano strings from the ceiling, to the old counter from a demolished chemist's shop and the bone frames of all these feet trampling on the worn wooden tiles.

To keep them from losing each other, JB put his hand on Marianne's shoulder. She leant towards him, her hair level with his nose. A man with two pints of beer pushed them, and Jan's hand happened to nudge her breast.

'I like it,' she said. 'Keep it there.'

He felt at home with her: she was Marianne, someone he had known over the years. There was nothing alien to spur him on. With the certainty that they would never hurt each other, he pulled her closer. He thought of nobody else, neither in the future nor in the past. They were here, now, in the crowd, and between their bodies another silent music started, which neither of them intended to quell.

The following morning they woke up at Uppland Street, and got dressed with an ordinary everyday feeling that they had neither expected nor asked for. As they had breakfast in the kitchen he longed to get out. He told himself this was due to the darkness inside the sacking which distorted the rhythm of the day. Marianne seemed more at home and in no hurry. It was not really an adventure; neither of them was being watched or had to get out by the back door.

As he drove to Arlanda, he thought to himself that she had helped him forget. Did he help her forget? Suddenly he remembered that several times that night she had whispered his name as they were making love. He had not been prepared for that. He had said nothing himself.

SHARED TIME

Relapse into winter. A March storm changed the landscape. Hail clattered over runways and denuded areas. After the hard winds of morning it was still again, and the light was greyish-blue as if painted with a pigeon's feather. The plain was covered by a threadbare blanket of snow.

On his way home from the airport, JB passed an ice-hockey rink swept clean and shiny under the row of light bulbs. Maybe it could be used once more. Then the football season would come, when thrushes pulled worms out of the hard stamped earth. But in the Bothnian Sea, the car radio said, ice-breakers still piloted ore ships through the packed ice.

On a round-about he noticed just ahead of him on the bend a car with one door not properly closed. He hooted. Several other motorists noticed and watched him angrily. A little girl, without a seat-belt, sat in the front seat next to the driver; he had looked at her hair in the slow traffic at the northern exit before discovering the door. He tried to drive up along the side of the car, but it was swept into another lane. It was impossible to change lanes, and he had to continue.

Would she fall out? Was his mind paralysed? It was his fault – and it was not. He could have caught them up, no, they were out of his sight, he would be booked for speeding and upset the other motorists till they collided.

Gertrude and Jenny – it was the same thing there. He hoped the head-wind would keep the door closed, so that no one would be hurt. He was on his way to meet Marianne at a pizzeria, but he could not find a parking space. The feeling of guilt over the girl in the car unexpectedly slid over to Sten Tidström. Would Sten detest him if he knew what he had done? Would Sten look at him and feel the physical disgust he had felt himself when he ran into Klas Lundin for the first time after Gertrude's departure? He suddenly felt cold all over. In the void after Gertrude and Jenny he felt exposed, but also dangerous to others, because he attached less value to them.

'I hope you're not doing anything to hurt someone else,' Marianne had said to emphasize the fact that she considered herself free. He could not really pretend he belonged to anyone.

He parked on an empty site, one of these sites too expensive for the city to build houses on. The former city centre consisted of a vacuum expecting to be filled with ideas. It was strange to be in a centre where the houses had disappeared. Magnificent rumours circulated about palmhouses and glass galleries in a southern style. They had talked about it for so long that some people imagined these subtropic miracles had once existed, maybe in a sunken Vineta over which gravel and refuse had been accumulating.

JB was late, but did not hurry. From a viaduct over Hamn Street he saw people milling far below on the pavements and temporary wooden bridges over the slopes and hollows of the rubble ridge. There was a jealous man, there a deserted young girl with a baby and its father with someone else. He groped with facts he knew nothing about. He himself was the most alien of them all. At the end of the Regering Street canyon of dusk Marianne was waiting for him. For whom? And why?

A group of youngsters brushed past him like a zebra herd. He ran against the tide like a refugee. The faces were wintery pale and empty. All around them rites were taking place in the night light. People who had quite a lot of possessions looked as if they had never enjoyed them less. Was their instinct somewhere telling them it was all wrong, and their lives could be greener and calmer? They had left their power in unknown office rooms, and their imagination. Now they took what was offered: the television, the discotheques; and the more old-fashioned dance palaces, the cinemas and the restaurants; the Klara porn clubs, the drug addicts' squats, the Finnish day-break sauna in Grev Ture Street . . .

He thought he looked just the same as usual, when he took Marianne by the elbow, saying:

'Sorry I'm so late. The car was being difficult, and I couldn't find a parking space.'

The pizzeria was crowded around them, young people eagerly talking, and chefs rattling plates. Marianne and Jan thoughtful. They spoke slowly, sometimes without hearing each other. They pushed a piece of bread to and fro across the table; a tram of loneliness.

They went to the cinema, and saw a film called Sunday Bloody Sunday. It had been made in London where Jenny was staying somewhere; he did not know where; and he saw her in Glenda Jackson. They had the same way of pulling a thick sweater down over their hips, the same fairly short hair; but Jenny probably did not have any boring Sundays; she was active and had friends. The shadows of boredom never caught up with her.

It filled him with joy that this had existed, although it was now past. He took Marianne's hand. Glenda Jackson made a move, and he let go of it. On the pavement of a London street, where Jenny might have walked, branches of trees drew clear patterns: the children played hop-scotch, and when they went out after breakfast the hop-scotch had moved forty-five degrees round the tree-trunk.

He hardly looked at Marianne. They sat there lit by other people's games. He understood the tenderness between the two men who embraced each other. Somewhere under layers of material his elbow met Marianne's. Easily – and yet it made his blood rush. Hesitation and worry disappeared for desire growing in the darkness of the cinema. The message was neither subtitled nor dubbed, but the meaning came across.

When JB hung up Marianne's coat in the hall, it ended up next to the winter coat Gertrude had not bothered to take to Botswana. Jan remembered the night in the gravel pit, her white face in the beam of the torch. It had been a narrow escape – she might never have needed the coat again. His desire for Marianne's body was new, but the situation old. For a moment he felt confused, like a card lost in an alien pack. The clothes were swinging, they were uninformed shells, decorations for ancient plays.

He kissed her square shoulders. It was easier to come near and love just a part of her. She was very thin; her ribs were obvious under his fingers, and her breasts small. It did not show that they had been sucked by two children. He wished he could fence off an area of her body and stay there.

'You asked me about Sten,' Marianne said a little later, when they were lying half-naked on top of Jan's and Gertrude's beds. 'I want to ask you about Gertrude.'

JB replied that he had not heard from her for a long time.

'It's hard to put into words,' Marianne said. 'It's about her and Sten.' Then she was silent again, and JB felt impatient and like throwing the words like planks across the morass. But he knew short-cuts were no good.

On another occasion Marianne said :

'I'm not jealous of them. Well I am really. That's probably exactly what I am.'

'What do you imagine?' Jan asked. 'That they sleep together? So do you and I.'

'I don't think that's the worst. I can see before me how they talk together. Gertrude's got a lot that I lack. She understands Sten better than I do. Now in retrospect I think that was a strong reason why I left Botswana – I couldn't stand seeing them walking, standing and sitting there in discussion. Wherever I went, they were there already. So completely innocent. You see, they're not in love with each other. They may be on the other side of love.'

She buried her face close to his. He thought she was laughing. Then he noticed that she was crying. She wanted comfort, but he was too tired to act as a comforter. Why should she be dependent on Sten's complete attention? She had just given him her declaration of independence. Did the expectations begin to mount up already? JB saw gaps between preconditioning, between male and female upbringing and their aims in life. Somewhere a loophole had occurred. What the actress said was not what the prompter whispered.

'They are close,' he said to fend her off. 'They always liked each other. That's all there is to it. Nothing to cry about.'

'They have a common language,' Marianne said. 'A language I never learnt.'

'Isn't it a good thing that some people understand each other, when so many don't seem able to?' asked JB.

'I envy Sten for being what he is. People like him so easily.'

They lay still next to each other, Marianne's hand occasionally sliding across his hips, weighing his penis and then letting go of it. He constantly felt he wanted to apologize to her, and tell her what he never said :

To be able to love you I have to exist myself, and have my own range of vision. So much ego is needed to hold other

240

people in it. Call it egotism if you like, but it must be the same for you? A heat zone within myself – where you can come in and grow under my roof. Now you're running towards me naked; I'm not afraid, just a little, for you. My fingertips start to live, but my heart-felt sincerity dwells far beneath the surface of the earth.

He wanted to go further, but could not:

I need to be lifted up; you want to be weighed down. What you want from me is not there for you exclusively, and I can't find what I want in you, although you would like to give it to me. Our bodies lead the way, but they can't take us there.

All he said was:

'Liberation is not having to be cheated any more by what feels good.'

'You're good at explaining,' Marianne said.

'Yes, but I'm not quite sure what I'm explaining.'

While Jenny's magical circle was still closed, he had been ruled by a strange power. He had wanted to be under its rule. This now happened against his will; his love had lost its command, and in the void no new orders came across. He longed to go to Arlanda while he got dressed and made tea in the kitchen.

'Do you want to get rid of me?' Marianne asked.

Then he felt sorry for her, and said she was welcome to stay the night. They had tea; JB tried to talk about Gertrude and Sten, but the words crowded unfamiliar in his mouth. He and Gertrude had never conversed with other people about each other.

'If you feel jealous, imagine what Sten would feel if he knew.'

'He doesn't care what I do,' Marianne said. 'He looks further afield, towards unbuilt cities and future generations. He doesn't really see me.'

'I like both you and Sten,' JB said. 'That's a problem, or may become one. Maybe we shouldn't see each other like this.'

'If you like,' Marianne said. 'It sounds very sensible.'

She put her hand on his arm, smiling indulgently, and the smile wiped out her words like a duster.

'I'd like to be able to meet both you and Sten after this,' JB mumbled.

'We're in the middle of something we never expected would

241

happen, and you're already talking about the aftermath. Aren't you a bit too premature?'

'I'm alone and confused,' JB said. 'I don't want you and me to get hurt by each other. You must understand that I have my focus elsewhere.'

'With the girl who doesn't want to see you any more?' Marianne asked. That was what he thought when he went to sleep with Marianne's head on his arm: That Jenny did not want to see him. That must not be the only reason to see Marianne.

Marianne, carefully and rather unobtrusively, made herself at home in Uppland Street. It felt strange to have her in the calm white rooms where so few upsetting scenes had taken place. He caught her with a photo of Gertrude that she had found in a drawer: Gertrude had moved, her face transparent, her smile broad and shimmering. He took it away from Marianne, and she was embarrassed.

'It isn't holy,' he apologized.

He felt punished by Gertrude's silence. It did not bring them any closer. The distance increased.

'Sometimes I have a compelling thought that Gertrude's child is Sten's,' Marianne said. 'Sten said in a letter the other day that it isn't yours.' Then JB told her about Klas Lundin and the child which Gertrude thought she needed as a focus when her life suddenly changed.

'I've known Gertrude for a long time,' he said. 'You build a house higher and higher without reinforcing the foundations. You trust them. You know skyscrapers: they float. That's all right. I moved most of myself over in the floating. I started to live in it. My plumb-line changed completely.'

He did not speak about Jenny, as he was afraid of showing self-pity. It was too much and too solemn, and thinking about it, he immediately felt hopeful: that must mean it was too great to perish? When Marianne arrived dusk had fallen. When she left it was just as dark. The sacking wrapped the house like a bandage. On the stairs the light was constantly on. They stopped and looked at the stone stairway. So many footsteps had trodden it that the fossils in the stone had slowly moved towards the edge, towards their firing-point.

In the dusky light of the sacking JB forgot to keep track of the hours, and for the first time ever arrived late at Arlanda.

Someone had telephoned him, and the person who had the shift before him had saved him by saying that he had to go and see to something. It was embarrassing. He considered himself as utterly reliable.

'Doesn't your mother ask any questions?' he asked when Marianne had stayed two nights running.

No, she did not. The children came home from school in the afternoon, and their grandmother looked after them if Marianne was not there. They were happy with an elderly person who had plenty of time for them.

Marianne scoured and cleaned the kitchen.

'What a mess.'

'I'll fix it in a minute,' he said insulted. 'I'm used to that kind of thing.'

She carried on with a resolute and angry look on her face, as if he had demanded her to do it. Still he hardly asked her to come. Only when he had not heard from her for a couple of days, did he phone her. She sounded happy and said he could be alone as much as he wanted; she could come and sit in a corner working. She brought her law books and stayed all night.

He went down to a snack bar to buy some take-away food. Coming back, he found Marianne curled up in a chair, her chin cupped in her hand, and a dimple in her cheek which showed up best when she was serious. She was totally still, lost in a world inaccessible to him.

'What are you doing?'

'Nothing,' she said. 'I like doing nothing when you're around.'

He stood there gazing at her so sharply that her outline became hazy, and he thought he could see her counter image, maybe Jenny. He thought that she ought to meet a young, inexperienced man who could give her the confidence she dared not give herself. He doubted that he really made her happy; and yet this somehow tied him to her: he wanted to find out what was going on.

He had received a letter from Sten: 'Marianne says in her letters that you've helped her a lot.'

'What have you told Sten?' he asked.

'That we're in touch. He doesn't ask for any more information. He hardly discusses his ideas with me. I'm just one of his minor dreams, while Botswana is the major. I had no Botswana to place against him.'

'Do you envy Sten for his job?'

'No, but I envy the fact that he has an alternative. The children need me. Sten's got his own world.'

'Sten may be more attached to the children than you think,' Jan said, remembering Sten's words about missing them.

'For a long time I didn't know that Sten was so fascinated by Africa. By the developing nations, by something so different from our life here. When we were there I remembered that I had often seen English books and magazines about Africa on his desk, and I felt he had deceived me for a long time, as I hadn't been able to interpret the clues before.'

There's only one kind of adultery, he told himself: not to have any more to give to the partner. In that sense he felt unfaithful, although he noticed that Marianne received something from him, which he did not even know what it was. Maybe he was the nearest thing to Sten that she could find.

He realised that Marianne had been smitten with anxiety that she might not have time to live. Behind her was the doubt that she had ever lived the kind of life she wanted. The past was lost, out of reach and immeasurable. What she had just found could not compete with it. New hope and old despair seldom succeeded in keeping an equilibrium.

As for himself he only wished that there would be a playful warmth between them; nothing else. But she wanted more, she wanted to talk, and she said he was easy to talk to.

'This family circle,' she said, 'bound for you by circumstances. Half the time you want to be inside, half the time break out of it. I can see how Sten and the children and myself try to create our own profile. Each one of us wants to protect his own spirit and not lose it in the big family mélange.'

She presented him with new glimpses from her life. When she met Sten, she was working as a bank trainee in Simrishamn for the summer. He was doing his military service nearby at the Ravlunda barracks, and was the first man in her life. Her father disapproved of the marriage. Marianne was studying economics, and her father who was paying for the studies wanted results. Sten saw her staggering under the demands, and made her give up her studies. That was his mistake. Children soon arrived. Marianne had no strong will of her own, and could not resist the temptation to assume the rôle of wife. It protected her against her parents. Sten was her life, and for that no education was necessary. He had chosen her, and so she must be all right as she was. But latent in her, invisible to Sten, was the terrified school-girl who was always to produce results. He had given her too heavy a burden by demanding nothing. The idyllic life was too much for her. Sometimes it felt like misery to be near this extrovert well-defined person, so certain of his ability to make her happy. JB was convinced that she thought of him as a man not nearly so interesting as Sten, but harmless and equal.

Jan showed Marianne a book covered in transparent cellophane paper which had come from a bookstand on a Paris quay. Sten had bought it for him when he was there at a microfilm conference. JB had never unpacked it. His French was poor, so he looked at it and left it there. It was more use unopened, as he would hover greedily around it trying to assess its thoughts. It was about time, different conceptions of time, and historic calendars – things they had often discussed, he and Sten, the era of flying and the time when Sweden was an agricultural nation.

'Let's have a look at it,' Marianne said. 'It's got pictures.'

'No,' he said, 'leave it. Let time pass.'

JB thought Marianne spent a lot of time in the bathroom. The water streamed; she was washing something. She had been there as a guest over the years, and knew how it all worked. One night he was on the verge of telling her that she did not have to be a housewife; she ought to think more about her studies. Then he heard her moaning, and ran over to her. She had upset a basket with dirty laundry to sort it for the washing machine. She had fallen down on the heap, and pressed her finger-nails into her calves. He fell down on his knees in front of her, and she leant her forehead against his stomach, supporting her hips with her hands.

'Are you all right?'

'I think I'm pregnant. No, that's not true, I just said so. It's a temptation you may not understand: to free yourself of everything, give up your studies for independence, and only become a mother.'

She suddenly opened the zip of his trousers.

'I've got to feel your warmth,' she mumbled.

And still soft he was in her mouth; she could take all from him, but he grew out of her. She had borrowed Gertrude's bathrobe, while she was washing her bra and tights. Her body was incredibly familiar under the material. It was more like habit than any stimulus, and yet bodies were so different when one got close to them. He did not think of her when she was not with him, and even now he saw other things before him : the windows of the Water Palace, Christina's smile . . . and he heard the flapping of the sacking. It shifted like sails, and the whole house sailed like a ship tacking.

There were no organized feelings. They were pervaded by memories and side glances which mingled and blended and were yeast for one another. His own thumbs were short; hers were longer and thinner, with little white spots on her nails. He passed his hand over her body, and saw them moving like shuttlecocks, but suddenly he saw only her, and he felt happy. His balls contracted like her nipples puckering under his fingers.

A feeling free of amazement, pain and happiness overcame him. Marianne was there. Different people could satisfy different kinds of hunger. He no longer dreamed about being everything for anyone.

They kissed for a long time, silently and violently. They did not have much to say about their feelings. Their meetings were easier if they touched each other's shoulders, stomachs and hips. Her body had no marks from her swimsuit. The soles of her feet were hard and brown like sand. He bit into them, and put her instep over his face. He then looked out, and saw the line between her buttocks bending slightly to the right at the top. He was filled with benevolence for the whole human creation, but dared not show it, as it was only to a certain extent connected with Marianne.

So much tenderness would be lost and homeless without bodies, he thought. He was glad she was no stranger, but someone he had exchanged words with over the years. He saw her ordinariness, and her deviations off course, all of which had brought them together. They had known each other for a long time, but not until they got undressed, could they talk seriously.

Letting her nipples dance up and down between his knuckles,

he thought it was strange that it was he who lived in his body, so concentrated and scattered. It might as well have been someone else: Jansson, the Linköping forester, the guerilla man Amos Bamuto Mokela. But only he – and possibly, according to some genetic disintegration theory, a piece of Gertrude.

Marianne's narrow vagina had opened to allow two children to pass through. Now he was immersed in it, and she pressed herself hard onto him and had several orgasms without his conscious assistance.

'It's so easy for us to kiss,' she said.

'It's free. You'll soon go back to Sten. We'll say good-bye. We'll meet again, in other ways. It doesn't really matter. We're not going to hurt anyone else.'

'It does matter,' she said. 'I want Sten to come back, but not just for me.'

His eyes found hers, but turned away. Her eyes looked too straight, gleamed at him too strongly, and he felt dishonest.

He had experienced love as a road to knowledge, as self-exploration and a stimulus for curiosity, and sex itself as a familiarity as long as it could come and go as it liked. He was also familiar with Marianne, but not curious enough. Maybe Jenny's phone call and his experiences in Botswana had deadened a nerve.

His activities with Marianne were a kind of waiting-game, without virtue and detachment. A dragon-fly's life, a spark, a fusion. Liquids communicating, emptying into each other, and evaporating. Experiences of a few minutes, followed by an eternity emptied of a vacuum. Somewhere within them a swell would continue, weaker and weaker, but never completely fading, into a fully revealing future.

They were still and close that night. The room was dark as if someone had drawn the curtains. They kept each other warm like sleepy squirrels in winter, and when they were too hot, they moved away from each other towards the edges of the bed.

He remembered his first meetings with Jenny, when every minute was dear, and they managed to squeeze food, chatter, walking and intercourse into a lunch-hour. With Marianne time had the usual run between the fixed stations of life.

The alarm went off before daybreak. He smoothed the sheets, and prepared himself for the early morning shift at Arlanda. He gave Marianne a lift to Mörby on white polished roads through the Lilljan Woods. Darkness was disappearing over the western horizon, and the variable light made one alert and disturbed after the long winter nights. There were patches of snow on the northern side, an inclined sun, and the melting snow flowing down a ski slope into a muddy lake with an icy crust in the middle.

Marianne quickly pulled her hair back until it pulled at her temples and left her forehead free.

'I now feel brave after having been a coward for so long,' she said. He had nothing to reply. Spring was coming; the thrushes sang in the woods. The pigs still rooted outdoors in the clay behind the Institute of Agriculture, but the new university buildings completely hemmed them in. How much would change? What recently had shape and a kind of permanence melted like an ice cone in a warm hand.

He dropped her off at the entrance to one of the copperclad tower blocks, which she entered at the same time as the newspaper man. The children would not wake up, and her mother asked no questions. She jumped out of the car like a distant acquaintance he had given a lift to. On his way to Arlanda he forgot what her body felt like against his. He could remember her words more easily than her nipples. He thought it would be wrong if someone felt jealous of them.

At Arlanda people were to be made redundant. Certain appointments were to be withdrawn, and some people to be transferred to different duties. Nobody seemed to know who would be affected. Christina told him her job was in jeopardy. JB was upset.

'You've been here for years. It's this mobile labour market; people move to and fro between sterile places without a home ground for anybody. People get aggressive and angular like orphans caressed by nobody, and never looked in the eye by anyone.

'I'll be all right,' Christina said. 'Hans, my fiancé, will soon be a surveyor.'

'I thought most of the land had already been surveyed,' JB said.

'In that case I can get a job as a visiting social worker. I've had temporary jobs doing that before. Twelve kronor per hour during the week, twenty-five at weekends. You clean, cook, read and talk to them. And listen. It's old spinsters and widows. They want to tell you things. What surprised me is that so many of them want to die. Those who realize that they will never get well again, who have arthritic knees and can't go out. Memories don't satisfy them.'

Christina had had her hair cut to a light-brown helmet. She wore beige corduroy trousers, and an Indian shirt with pink checks. He saw she was beautiful.

'Old maids and servants are the happiest ones,' she said. 'They're not half as frightened of the things that make their employers tremble. It's uncanny to see women's fear of power, men, violence; of anything unknown and impossible to penetrate.'

'I hope you'll stay,' Jan said. 'We need you here.'

He wanted to say something else, but the jet engines were switched on down on the ground below, and they drowned his thoughts.

At ten o'clock they had a pause at the same time as the traffic. Jansson played a game of houses with Christina, and JB relieved him. It gave enough excitement and an almost total emptiness: the clattering of the little pyramids, the few combinations, nothing to consider, no unnecessary delays, and easy to talk at the same time.

In the lift down to the office Christina asked him how he was. He evaded the question, but was pleased to hear it.

'Won't you come round for supper tonight?' she asked.

'Tonight?'

'I thought you might feel lonely.'

'I'd love to come,' he said.

In the afternoon he telephoned Klas Lundin to give him the news of Botswana. They agreed to meet at Klas's advertising agency just before the office closed. Klas's office was in a house built in between the wars, as the term was so far.

In the entrance hall there was a film poster for The Kiss of The Vampire, a collage of parking fines, and a faded Argentinian flag. JB knew the history of the latter: it had blown in the wind outside the Embassy, but had been blown down by a violent gust of summer wind just as Klas passed by. It threw itself in his arms like a man in distress, and since it was at sunset when it was to be taken down anyway, he had taken it home as a token that he would sometime in his life see Terra del Fuego. Blue and white like the Patagonian ice, JB thought, and remembered the Academy of Science and its portraits of Swedish ethnographers in fluffy furcoats and shiny faces posing in a confined artist's studio at Kungholmen.

Klas came up to him and hugged him.

'You don't have to tell me about Botswana,' he said. 'Everything seems to be all right.'

'All right?' JB said.

'Have a whisky. The glasses are a Christmas present from the company – I wouldn't have chosen them myself. Would you like something else?'

'I'd like one year when nothing happens,' JB said.

'Don't be silly. I've had a letter from Gertrude. Did you know? I thought she might have told you.'

'No.'

'She tells me what date the baby is due, and that she's booked a room at the maternity hospital. Isn't it incredible? She wanted me to know that she had made the necessary arrangements.'

Jan felt shattered, realizing that Gertrude had by-passed him. He still regarded himself as her next of kin.

'I don't know how you managed to change her mind,' Klas said, 'but just imagine how happy it has made me.'

Apparently he had no idea of the limits that Gertrude had been so near, when she thought of him regarding the child as his. JB said nothing; her resistance seemed to have passed now.

'I've bought a nice cot,' Klas said, and described something adjustable with balls and rattles attached.

'I think Gertrude would prefer something simpler.'

'It was so bloody nice to walk about there. I see everything in a different light now. At the cemetery the children from some nursery play, splashing in the clay from the graves. I watch their movements and study them more carefully than the ships by Lidingö Bridge. They are so near the ground.'

'Yes, that's strange,' Jan said, emptying his glass.

'Not any more. I'm finding it natural. You and I haven't cheated each other.'

'If anybody tried to cheat you, it's Gertrude.'

For Gertrude had gone out into society to rob a child to foster in their secret clan. Now the bubble had burst.

'We ought to have dinner together,' Klas said. 'This is worth celebrating.'

'I'm going out tonight,' Jan said.

'Pity. Do you see a lot of Marianne, by the way?'

'Sometimes. She is working and studying. Her mother looks after the children. Well, you know all that.'

'I've tried to phone her,' Klas said, 'but she's not there. That's a good sign. I'm sure it'll be all right. We'll all be happy.'

JB cringed under Klas's optimism. He caught a glimpse of himself in the entrance hall mirror: eyes red from lack of sleep the previous night, and then the whisky. He had turned into a heliophobe with square pupils and straight white hair. He would stand like that on a stage somewhere, and Jenny would come and see right through him. He looked out of the window to St John's cemetery. The children had disappeared, and the graves lay empty. He was not sufficient for Marianne. Klas frightened him. He was an aeroplane impatiently waiting for the starting signal. Once there had been an air route . . .

'What are you brooding about?' Klas rumbled, slapping him on the shoulder. 'For God's sake, you must make up your mind to enjoy life. It's nothing that comes to you.'

He drove across the southern parts of Stockholm and, stopping at the red lights at Renstierna's Street, he heard the first blackbird. All the motorists were waiting in first gear; it was hot and Jan had opened his side window. The sea was ice-free. He thought of the fact that it was now April.

When he arrived at Bonde Street, Christina opened the door, and there were her fiancé Hans, and her brother Thomas who was almost qualified as an engineer, and the mother, a retired telephonist: a commune. The flat was hideous, but Christina gave him and the surroundings an encouraging smile. He immediately liked the atmosphere, and felt like a lonely wrecked figure whose life-boat finds another ship.

Christina had changed into a light trouser-suit with a wide belt, size fourteen, he decided. Hans was a bit overweight, shorter than Christina, and to Jan unattractive. He had a ruddy complexion, and spoke with a Gothenburg accent. He made them all laugh, but afterwards Jan did not understand why.

'He writes terrific Christmas rhymes as well,' Christina said in an attempt to portray him. But she got no further.

They had pork chops and peas followed by meringue à la Reine which was all very rich. They ate off odd china plates. Only four plates remained from the mother's old wedding china. Thomas was responsible for the family budget, and would not permit any new purchases. He had a soft brown beard and cork sandals, good for the instep and spine. On the kitchen door Jan had seen a work schedule indicating the various tasks to be done by the members of the family every month.

After a while Hans disappeared. JB found him impolite, but it turned out he was washing up the kitchen.

'I would never have dared invite my boss,' Christina's mother said.

'I'm not really her boss,' Jan said.

'Who brings whom coffee? When Christina was a child I told her : never learn typing. You'll just get stuck in the office routine.'

'Mother always goes on like that,' Christina said. 'I tell her to be grateful that I'm not at the top of my career. Then I'd never have time to listen to her.'

'I saw the misery first-hand,' her mother said. 'The girls were sacked and disappeared. I've seen it all my life.'

She had been an active member of the union, and launched a campaign for equal pay at the GPO. She had seen the automation and the cancellation of the personal calls. Female professions meant they could sack without any consequences. It was assumed that there was a supporting husband in the background.

Christina's father had been a quiet man, employed by the tram company mainly on line number four. On quiet Sundays in the spring they would hear him ring the bell three times on the track where Bonde Street began. The sound was carried in through the open windows, and they knew the father was passing – like an astronaut the moment he enters the earth atmosphere. At home he behaved like a traveller tired of tearing about. In his final years he hardly budged.

'I like high ceilings,' Jan said.

'In Sofia comprehensive school I played hand-ball because my arms were so long,' Christina said.

She stretched them up. They reached half way to the ceiling.

'Your arms seem to be an average length,' Thomas said turning to Jan.

'I have some plants I must show you.'

Jan thought of hashish, but it was tomatoes that he grew in a bay window facing south, which had become like a green-house. Then they watched an old film with Bing Crosby and Bob Hope on television. JB and the mother sat in armchairs, Thomas astride a camel saddle; and Hans and Christina had curled up on a divan, supporting each other's back. The film was something about the US Navy during the Second World War.

'In those days they were friends,' the mother said. 'Now they don't speak any more. Bob is too much to the right, and Bing too much to the left. Vietnam separated them.'

'I wonder when the Secret Service will find out that I have a communist mother,' Christina said.

'In the Air-Traffic Department it's certainly not a credit,' JB said.

'In that case I've got something to blame if they sack me,' Christina said.

'When I lift the receiver I think it takes some time to get a line,' the mother said. 'I can see before me the SS trying to decipher my calls to Hansson the grocer: One pound of sausages, five packets of spinach – what could that mean?'

'Do you believe in violent changes,' Jan asked, 'rather than in agreements and negotiations?'

'I hope for new mutations. So far no one has willingly given up his privileges.'

There was a curtain hanging on wooden rings between the hall and the drawing-room, embroidered in herring-bone stitch. The blue material showed only here and there; the rest was covered by sparkling coloured wool. As JB drove home along the Katarina Road, he wondered who had embroidered it. He felt he was one of the family, and not knowing this was rather like amnesia.

When he entered his flat, the telephone rang. It's Marianne feeling lonely, he thought, or Klas who wants to celebrate. Five rings, then silence, then it rang again. He did not answer; the sacking hid him and the house. It's enough, they can look after themselves for just one night. Or was he too passive, like with the little girl at the round-about? It might be Jenny trying to phone him from London. It was too late to find out. The telephone was silent.

He soon tossed in his dreams, pinioned by reality. He had

few phobias, but bridges opening was one of them. They opened, and he could not stop his car. He drove up the bridge on rolling tyres that would not stop in front of the vertical slope. Then he fell into nothingness, between two ironhands raised in prayer. This time only the car was hurled into the water. He himself managed to apply the breaks.

We made it, Marianne said in the dream. We did not, he replied. She raised her hand, and he shrunk back. It's all right, I just want to play, she said in the same voice as Mrs Tapper when she apologized for a large happy dog. And Marianne with a large, heavy paw smoothed his facial features.

IN THE WAKE OF THE SWAN

'All is indestructible,' Eklund said. 'Our smallest constituents have been taken from stars that went out and crumbled to invisibility.'

It was the lunch hour on the meteorologist stage. He pointed at Jan Backman.

'You're an antiquity in a new synthesis. You were made of star material. You will be whisked around for ever. At the moment you're aware of your rôle in the universe. But then there are other incarnations . . .'

In the hot air inlet Eklund had an opened bottle of Chateau Gontier, and in the drawer of his desk, oranges and glucose tablets. Behind the Deutscher Wetterdienst and the meteorological journals there was more space with a range of weather-books on the northern lights and gelded hogs, duck's blood and drought, old superstitions with which he wanted to liven up the forecasts.

'When the large Donatis comet appeared over Stockholm in the autumn of 1858,' Eklund said, 'terrified crowds gathered at Observatory Hill. Some could watch the horrible celestial body with the observational instruments. According to aptitude some thought they saw the destruction of the world; others saw a steam engine on the southern main line.'

'Due to telescopic sight,' JB said.

These April days he went between Stockholm and Arlanda in an eventless routine. With his elbow he would wipe off the condensation on the inside of the wind-screen, but there was not much to be seen, just junipers looking like witches, and lorries amassed in the lay-bys. In the newspaper he looked at photos of the earth taken from the moon. How delicate it was, how easily it could be extinguished. Then he washed his car, longed for fresh berries, read about the genetic code, had coffee and rusks, slept away a third of the time, and forgot about most things.

'They used to sigh over the earth being flat,' JB said, 'saying what can we do about it, that's how it is, and it couldn't be any different. Now it's round and we say the same thing. If we didn't stop there, we'd probably gain new knowledge. The fact that the earth is round may be much less important than the fact that it's rough or perforated, or that it breathes or has an inclined axis.'

'No, nothing is what it is,' Eklund said. 'I wouldn't be surprised if, for example, drinks or stamps went up tomorrow.'

'You're right,' Jan said. 'Stamps are going up. That's why I'm posting a letter today. It's been lying around for some time.'

He wanted to get in touch with Jenny. It was hard to stay silent. Where was she? Somewhere in London. It was like seeing in the dark: you must not fix your gaze, but let it switch on and off in order to catch the sight of the objects you want to watch. If you let your eyes rest, it disappeared.

The SAS press officer joined them.

'I heard you were here,' he said to JB. 'I'm expecting some American journalists, and their plane is delayed. A member of your audience in Örebro claims that you were responsible for political propaganda in your lecture there. He's furious, and says that you warned people against visiting sunny countries with dictatorship.'

'I only recommended that they should travel further afield,' JB said. 'For the profit of the SAS.'

'Well, I don't care. Principally we fly anywhere as long as the corresponding airlines don't invade Arlanda. I'll write back to this man and tell him that his views have been passed on. Then it will sound as if we were impressed by them.'

The press officer left, and Eklund knocked his pipe against the edge of the desk.

255

'It's empty. I've given it up. The smoke affected my observations. Haven't you got any vices? Haven't you thought of changing your job?'

'What else is there to do these days?'

'That's it. That's why we sit here on top of each other, you and I, arranging our matinées and soirées behind the glass, while the elements perform their show.'

They looked out towards the fuel tanks, the radar screen on its concrete pillar, and the stores with Bibles, nappies, and mineral water. A Boeing 707 with chunky engines under its wings was landing. Somebody else looked after the domestic air-traffic control.

'I'll hang on here,' Eklund said. 'Can you see the lamp advert down by the exit? That's my motto: maximum yield of light, low costs for maintenance.'

'Many people say it's more important to choose your past than your future. You always had your interest in astronomy. Adjust the telescope for distances large enough, and it doesn't matter where you are yourself.'

Eklund poured the red wine into a paper mug. Drinking at work was prohibited, but the lunch hour turned the office into a restaurant. Some rolls had obtained their taste from a photocopy of yesterday's weather forecast.

'Mostly my world is as narrow as yours,' Eklund continued. 'Is visibility to the Kaknäs tower clear? No. By radar I find out about the precipitation within my two hundred kilometres circle, and draw it on my map. I look at the aneroid barometer, and reduce our forest millibar to sea level. Ten minutes later my map will be in Cairo, Rome or Moscow. Day after day the same thing. What happens in the meantime in the Swan constellation seven billion light-years away? There is a strong radio transmitter there. Other radio waves reach us from a distance of four and a half billion light-years. They make a pen draw the scale here on earth. The power that makes the crayon move left before our earth existed. I think of that, and then I think I ought to exchange Arlanda for Bromma, or bow on television and draw anticyclones on a map. It doesn't work.'

'I bought The Sea by Rachel Carson down in the Hall,' Jan told him. 'The oceans built while your radio waves travelled, could be poisoned in only a couple of generations. Humanity has got on to a blind track.'

He would have liked to discuss this with Jenny. Instead he read out to Eklund about the convoluta worms which live off a green alga they carry in their bodies. The alga needs sun to produce starch for food, and therefore the worms creep out of the sand when the tide ebbs. As the water rises, they dive down into the sand to avoid being washed out into deep water. If you leave them in an aquarium without the ebb and flow of the tides, they still spend their lives coming up from the sand twice a day to see the sunlight. They have no brain, but even in the alien environment of the aquarium they continue their habitual way of living because, Carson says, 'every fibre in their green little bodies remembers the rhythm of the distant sea.'

'We may be programmed in the same way,' the meteorologist said. 'We carry gestures and whims from the original seas, our heritage, our standard equipment. Then we were transferred into modern aquariums where our defence and our efforts are superfluous. Among all the finished products the will to create something is crushed, as well as the will to re-educate yourself and furnish your existence according to your own inclination and impulses. I live in a terraced house here in Märsta. That's okay, but I look at my neighbours living in tower blocks too square for their round gestures. Each flat is exactly the same. The result is a sort of self-effacement. Young families who for the first time are moving into a life of their own, find a flat where every function is built-in and catered for. They become submissive and passive, grasping fashion pictures and weekly magazines to stir up the surface. Pinioned people, exposed to the trespasses of the city planners.'

'Märsta has become a transit stage,' JB said, 'just like Arlanda.'

'To be able to identify with their environment, people must be able to have some control over it. In a fixed environment people become guests subjected to hard discipline. Living is acting and influencing. Without action there's no response.'

'What would you do about Märsta?' JB asked.

'A new area is being planned. Some of us living in Märsta and some of the people moving in are working on it together with architects and social workers. We want it to be an area that people want to develop and take on responsibility for. It's easy to find out how they want it: trees, holy and inviolable, low buildings with balconies overlooking a traffic-free street where everything happens; and the other side of the house preferably to parkland where children can make discoveries. The street is a place to meet, and a place for observation; while the back of the house is for peace and anonymity. Nurseries, nursery schools, and premises for leisure activities should be located in a square yard. They should all have a right to change the houses, and leave their imprint on them. The way it is now people flee to uncomfortable holiday homes, where their imagination can play around, and they can find an outlet for their arranging and creative abilities.'

JB ran up the stairs to the tower. Window-cleaners had been there to wash the windows. He suddenly worked in the house of clarity. Everything could be seen, except the shadows. Otherwise he suspected to see sprinkles of rain and soft lines of dirt – like the thin metal streaks showing in certain windows, probably part of an alarm system. Now they were gone, these threads keeping his house together. The invisible glass was left, tinting the sky softly green, and not letting in warmth or cold.

Jansson had 'flu and JB took over part of his shift. They were short of air-traffic controllers at that moment. Christina in turn looked after some of his office duties. He tried to find Jansson in the telephone directory : column after column with the same name. Nearby he found the name Jenny Jeger, which he had encircled with a biro a long time ago. He remained seated. A name among thousands. One person among nonentities.

In a few code letters and figures he could write a story about arrival and departure, but he had no contracted forms for the trip itself. Those who talked about man's basic conditions should stick to birth and death. There were no formulas for what lay in-between.

He thought of Gertrude and Jenny, and how they had changed because of something he had done. He had helped to provoke situations he could not live with. He saw before him Gertrude's face in Botswana, at first independent and arrogant; then etched in the torch light at her breakdown.

He and Jenny were two ordinary people who had created something unusual by meeting each other. Now he could not even rob her of her pride and unjustified jealousy. I have no truly passionate nature, he thought, I am not prepared to let my life be torn to pieces by passion. He was prepared to desist. Love would feel it, and go the long way around him.

Many things seemed to him so involved. He longed for the open, sensual calmness of the women's faces on the walls of Herculaneum, without all coquetry, prudence or fear. And he remembered an old riddle which A. O. Backman had pleased him with : Which is heavier, one pound of wool, or one pound of iron? Solution : Drop it on your feet, and you'll know. Such was love – sometimes as easy as could be, and sometimes un-bearable.

Was cowardice his most prominent feature?

The house in Uppland Street sighed inside its sacking. They had started to sandblast the façade. The dust came in. JB shook a rug out of the back window, although it was prohibited. He threw away a tooth brush, took out a new kitchen roll, and mended some fuses in a box. On the window-sill in the draw-ing-room he placed some thick candles. Though it was April outside, the winter solstice prevailed in the flat.

He went to a cinema matinée with Marianne and her children. Martin called him uncle Jan, Malin just you. They talked a lot about Sten, and admired JB for directing aircraft. They laughed hysterically at the film. They passed low whistles on two notes between them when they experienced a climax. They pressed their elbows into their knees, and put their chins on the row in front of them, on their way into the screen.

The film was called "Those Magnificent Men in Their Flying Machines". Marianne and Jan found it boring. JB told himself there was nothing for Sten to worry about. They had no euphoric moments to pay for.

Afterwards the children seemed depressed, as the ecstasy was extinguished. JB suggested hot chocolate or hot dogs, but they stayed listless by the side of the adults, and wanted to go home. They had talked about all of them going out to the Water Palace one Sunday. When they parted Jan took out his key-ring, took the simple key to the Water Palace off, and gave it to Marianne.

'Take this, and you can go out whenever you feel like it,' he said. 'The Water Palace is at your disposal.'

'What about you?' Marianne said.

'I have a spare key at home.'

Not until later did he understand that she had asked whether he was going with them.

In Kung Street Knut Tapper appeared out of the shadow of

the viaduct, the childhood friend who knew he and Gertrude were sister and brother, and had once tried to blackmail JB. Now he took Jan by the arm in a familiar manner, and did not let go of him until they came to Sture Square. Knut spoke verbosely of his job selling second-hand cars.

'You know there are times in life . . .'

He did not finish his sentence. JB made a gesture towards his wallet.

'No man, that's not it.'

He probably wanted to apologize for his previous behaviour, but could not get the words out. He wore a white military fur coat, and looked less dilapidated than before. He had a curious and suspicious streak which made Jan keep quiet about himself.

He went to the city library, and sat at a long table with a pile of books. The red covers had the same smell as in his childhood. He felt empty in an exhilarated way : there was no room for another great love, that would be a repetition. He had almost spied a plan drawn for his life. This was how it looked now, without any extra room or secrets. The limits were staked out. He borrowed The Era of The Mammals, The Armies of Night, and some ecological books. When he walked home, he noticed that the lime-trees had just been pruned. He took a branch back to Uppland Street.

The pram he had bought on an impulse a few weeks before he gave to a charity organization. Klas would look after Gertrude. He took a sack of Gertrude's clothes to the dry-cleaner. The clean clothes he hung in a plastic storage bag. She did not care much for clothes, she said. It made him upset to do this. The distance between him and Gertrude would increase.

He began writing a letter to her : 'I hear you've been in touch with Klas, I'm so glad. He seems very happy. If there's anything I can do for you, you know you can trust me as well.'

It was a short letter. After Botswana he was not sure of the effect that words might have.

There were few people he had ever been close to. He might be tied to the past, but it held a chance to explore the future. He wanted to find out where the rope was fastened, and how long it was. He must look for his answer in other people, and at the same time accept fate which had placed him like a railway carriage on a certain gauge of track with no possibility of trespassing across certain borders.

Occasionally he envied Gertrude and Jenny. They had chosen their world, and this might have made it more real. They were in the shadow. They saw a lot that they might never tell him. Had he been too submissive himself? He had not acted violently, had not fallen down the gravel pit, not got pregnant or hidden abroad in cold-blooded silence. So what was he doing? Fostering his heart, or greasing a propeller?

One day, on passing Nybro quay, he thought he saw a light in Jenny's flat. He had palpitations; she had come back. A few more steps, and the light went out. It was the reflection of the sky's light. He went back, and the phenomenon was repeated. This time nothing happened inside him; his senses had been warned.

The Arlanda Association had their annual dinner in the Kevinge Sky Room at the top of one of the copper houses at Mörby. It was part of their tradition to choose a location with a view, so that they could keep an eye on the local air-traffic. Whilst eating spring chicken, they looked out over the Hallon mountains, the Danderyd forests, the yellow façades of Henriksdal at sunset, and in its high cement bowl the radar ball, which located all flights over central Sweden.

JB saw from his end of the table the city spreading in blunt star points with dark fields and forests inbetween. He also looked into the fifteenth floor of the next building, and suddenly realized that it was Marianne's building. He had soon located the Tidström flat. Going up to the window, he saw Marianne some floors beneath him. She sat by the blue light of the television, and her mother was mending the zip of one of the children's windcheaters. He could have telephoned across to her, but he did not make himself known.

The following day there was a letter from Sten in the mail on his desk. It told him that the Mahalapye comprehensive school was now opened, but was on a huge coal field. What could they do about the coal except sell it to South Africa? And how would they get the necessary energy for mining unless they harnessed the water of the Okavango bog? Then what would happen to ecology and politics? The longer the coal could be left untouched the better, Sten thought. People seldom saw clearly the results of their actions.

One example of this was the fact that the hippopotamus had now been more or less wiped out from southern Africa. 'It provided whips and suitcases for the whites, and meat for the

261

blacks. It is only now that it has been discovered that it saved thousands of human lives. The parasitic worms giving bilharzia dwell in still waters. One catches it from washing one's hands in a clear lake, or from getting out of a car in the rainy season and stepping into a puddle. The bilharzia penetrates the skin and slowly brings death by exhaustion. Only the richest people can afford to have it cured. As long as the hippopotamuses stirred up the water, there was no bilharzia. The little shells that house the worms could not stick anywhere. Regarding nature as an enemy to be conquered, and not as an ally – that is the catastrophe of man.'

Sten also wrote that they had had a card from Dave Griffiths who was back in Wales; and Aina had taken care of a refugee who had been badly tortured before being set free. 'The evil of the powerful is the worst evil. Also over this dry sparse landscape the splinter bombs can fall – just because it happens to have this geographical location. Thousands of little splinters untraceable to X-ray, causing slow internal bleeding, or in more fortunate cases, a constant ache.

Facing this, I can feel all reason leaving me, and I see mankind as carriers of so much evil that I wish radioactive waves would sweep over us – not to kill, but to open up other ways of development by new combinations and mutations. That's my desperate dream : anything except this.'

He looked in vain for a greeting from Gertrude.

JB went out to the Water Palace alone to check that it was still there. He stayed for a few hours. He put a ladder up against a wall, and cleared the sticky leaves from the gutters in the eaves. The birds were building nests. The wheat-ear was a brick layer, and the wagtail and the robin fine carpenters. The warbling sounded as it should. They had practised in Africa. Around them was the first spring light, heavy from rain. The tree trunks were black and wet like forest snails. The moss woke up, and the ants started to move.

In the crevices and cracks, in the hide-outs, and in moist skin, life awoke. In the calm bays ice still lingered, but it was now breaking up piece by piece – with a jingle like keys when someone goes round in a large house unlocking the rooms one after another.

JB looked at the grey sky, listening for the trumpet calls of the cranes. He heard sounds he could not explain, as if someone was hitting a stick against the stones on the gravel path.

The wind rustled in the reeds. Far away a motor saw turned round slowly.

There were china fragments scattered among the pebbles on the shore. It was the same everywhere on the skerries. How did the glittering pieces get there? Who smashed all these cups and saucers? At the water's edge a flat-bellied roach floated up and down. A gull dived towards it, but changed its mind. The water lapped against some protruding rocks the way it does between the floorboards of a skiff being rowed.

On the veranda the furniture was still but expectant. On the kitchen table was a plastic cloth resembling real material. All was there. Gertrude laughed, cried and slept somewhere else. The child in her grew, waiting like the anemones under the brown elm leaves. Soon it would learn the ways the wind preferred, and succumb to them, just like the new grass that year.

JB pulled out a drawer, and saw peppercorns and crumbs collected in the white plastic department for cutlery. Behind the scales there was a purse of well-worn saffian leather with five compartments and a golden buckle, filled with emergency money and stamps.

He thought of Jenny a lot: the last time he was here had been with her. The hardly visible experience became to him inexhaustible: the first time he and Jenny had held the handle of a saucepan together; his hand on hers, a factual and deliberate gesture extended without any further comment. The saucepan was still there, returned by unexpected shortcuts, gleaming like the northern lights inexplicably passing across the sky.

If Jenny were dead, he would like to discuss her with everyone who had known her. He would love whoever had loved her. They would belong to the same union. In spite of her absence, she gave him a feeling of togetherness. He knew there were departments full of facts, statements, complete information, and series of speeches. Everything was unalterable, confirmed in diaries. These assessments regarding weights and measures he could not use. In the erogenous zones of his memory not even a square centimetre was neutral or unmined.

JB saw, when he left the Water Palace at dusk, a badger dressed in a striped waistcoat to protect him from death in the dark. He saw it surveying the nutritious assets of the area in a pedantic and greedy manner, with no unnecessary heavy thoughts.

A day or so later Jan took out of his desk drawer at Arlanda a letter to Jenny, which he had worked on from time to time making cuts and alterations. He had not posted it before the postage had gone up.

'I have a thought I will turn over in my mind,' he wrote, 'which is that all the time you want to come to me as much as I want to come to you. Don't think I'm flattering myself with the stickiness of the glue stick. We came to each other by our free will. Birds of a feather. The glue between us was a third component, something we could neither help nor control.

If you want to come to me now, why don't you? I think I know how you tick: My sudden departure scared you more than my feelings for Gertrude. Something inside you hurt, and you cursed yourself because it hurt. Unnecessarily. Somewhere you knew, and still know, that I would never want anything to hurt you, neither my actions or somebody else's. So there you were with your pride and fear. Now time passes, the mechanical time limping on with its long and its short hand. You know me well enough to know that I won't storm any barricades where I'm not welcome – that is my pride and fear.

I miss you in a way I can't describe. So I won't. I can just try to talk to you about lost opportunities – to experience, see, feel, taste, and laugh together. There is everyday work and sleep, boring tasks and great sorrows. I would like to take part in it all somewhere in your orbit.

Our love was not a sack that was filled and tied up. It was a reflection of the sun which could hit the ceiling, or fly through the window all over the city: it can jump up and sit on anybody and make the statues squint.

I've got nothing to show you that you can't see for yourself. I don't think I've got anything to teach you, but together we might grow a bit, as long as the earth holds on to our roots.'

He read what he had written. Would the words reach her, or was her visor lowered and her ears stuffed? He thought that she might feel the essential questions wandering down into her as into a pit where they would remain.

If he was no longer able to make himself understood, all hope was lost. In that case they had mistaken each other, and he had to admit that these things happen every day, and are not part of the deadly sins.

He slowly pushed the letter into the lockable desk drawer. It would remain unposted awaiting heavier words.

V

AFTER THE TEST PICTURE

THE UPPLAND MEADOWS

At eleven o'clock one Saturday afternoon the telephone on Jan Backman's desk rang. Lifting the receiver he saw the Finnair landing and the London plane taking off steeply with its trail of black exhaust fumes – like the marks of dirty children's fingers on a blue wall. It was the voice he had ceased to wait for.

'Jenny!' he exclaimed.

Then he could not think of any more to say, but repeated her name sheepishly.

'Is it possible that you're pleased?' she said in her ordinary voice.

'Yes, yes. Don't reproach yourself.'

They cut the introductory phrases and explanations. Their conversation was brief. Jenny promised to arrange a picnic and nice weather if he met her at one o'clock at Skånela church. He thought she could work wonders and promised to be there.

He sank back into his writing-chair with a pounding heart, and looked sternly at his watch. Its activity was loaded with a new implication. He emptied his pockets of old receipts, and dismissed the thoughts of wisdom and routine. He was filled with astonishment and mobility.

He had been just as happy when she phoned him from London. That time he had hit his head against a wall. He might be doing the same thing now. It didn't matter. The lawn below smelt of damp earth; something was bursting out. It was an eternal repetition and an immense piece of news. He did not mind hitting the wall: that would just be like hitting his head against her body.

He got up, jumped up and down, and was grateful that no one entered the room. His penis settled down, but his thoughts were crawling towards her in the narrow channel of time.

On his way out he hugged Christina. Surplus joy exuded. She smiled and said she realized everything was all right. He could

not say much, his mouth was too wide for vowels and con-
sonants. He was terrified at Jenny's powers. Thus shattered
he went to meet her at Skånela church.

She was there, and they held each other's hands and walked
in silence towards the church. His love for her was so strong
that he felt some kind of shyness, an impulse to hide and hold
back. All seemed new. The miracle was the unworn.

They saw nobody. Over the fields was a smell of rotting
silage spread in the morning. They kissed against a runic stone
built into the church wall. He did not know the world could be
so alive. Finally the key was in the lock. The stores were within reach.

It was not her body he described but her face and the light
in it, her eyelids and the lines under her eyes that contracted
when she laughed.

'I've got so much to explain to you,' Jenny said.

'Leave it for a while,' Jan said. 'We have plenty of time.'

Their feet left double tracks in the clay. Their bodies leaned
heavily against each other, picking up the rhythm and the
pace they had adopted during their winter journey.

'Time brought us here,' she said. 'To cowslips as small as my
little finger.'

She pointed at them in the grass of last year mown short
along the churchyard wall. They stood looking out over the
lakes and the meadows. A tractor aroused a flurry of gulls. A
couple of peewits turned in and out like black and white gloves
in the spring dance. JB could feel Jenny's breath against his
palm. He had no wishes. Although neither of them wanted to
leave, they continued in Jenny's car. Jenny had arrived from
London the night before and thought she had seen his sil-
houette in the tower. She had considered phoning him from the
hall.

'It wasn't me,' he said, 'it was Jansson. He probably would
have welcomed your call.'

'He looked like you. How easy it is to imagine something
you want to see.'

He quickly described his evening to her. He had walked
along Drottning Street with its shops open all night, seen his
reflection in the aluminium sides of the Culture House, and got
some papers from Alternative City in Bryggar Street. In a bar
in the old Klara Hall he had had a steak, and got colic from the

cole-slaw. The cloak-room attendant had recommended that he stay on for a while in order to have, in exchange for a membership fee, the total freedom with girls who knew no limits. He walked home along the Klara shore where the first crocus bloomed in the warmth of the exhaust fumes.

The small country roads were free from holiday traffic. The gravel was damp; no dusty clouds revealed them. In a bend far from human dwellings they met a fox who unhurriedly changed his route.

'Let's stop soon,' Jenny said. 'My vagina is grabbing the empty air. I long for you from the tips of my fingers. I don't know what I'd most like to do.'

They soon sat on a slope with blueberry shrubs and warbling blackbirds. Jenny shook a dusty blanket; the sun was warm but the ground cold. Early spring with wood anemones. Nothing yet mature or completed; everything growing into a different stage while the earth inclined its axis.

They hurriedly took off each other's clothes. Jenny looked as wantonly happy as if they had met by chance.

'I want to go on living as if a comet was heading towards us,' she said.

'As if?' JB said.

'Something is finished,' she said. 'But it's not over. I don't know how to express it.'

'What do you mean?' JB said worriedly. 'Maybe I'd better not know too much. Because I love you.'

'You do? Then we've got each other. With the extreme tip of your penis you should have known all along, and I with the inner fold of my vagina. I think I've come to grips with my yielding self-discipline. That's what's been hurting me, not you.'

'The worst thing is that whatever you do to me or however you behave, I'm able to understand it or find an excuse for it – from some kind of terrible identification. You point out my shortcomings, and I imagine I might have acted in the same way.'

'You mustn't. I don't want you to repeat my stupidities.'

She was naked now. Joy and lust arranged themselves in his body like at the beginning of a chess party. He smiled at her, happy to feel her breasts again. To prevent her from catching cold, he lay down on his back and she pressed him so hard to the earth that he felt its curve. He was still like a stone, she was his movement. He saw her smile towards the pale milky depth of the sky. A flock of starlings passed them aimlessly, as swiftly as some spots dancing before their eyes.

'I'd like to collect your sperm in a large leaf,' she said.

'It's too early in the year,' he said.

She pressed her ankles against his hips. He was amazed at the fact that they both had kept their hands, skin and outsides. She turned with his penis as her axis – they lay like the clock's hands showing ten past twelve during daylight. He liked to see her clearly. She sucked his forefinger and swallowed her saliva as if it were his sperm.

'Sometimes the inside of my eyes feel erogenous,' she said. 'Closing my eyes is enough.' When his back arched she let herself fall against him, her breasts nudging his lips, and far away he heard her crying something unintelligible which his whole body understood. She leapt off him and squatted next to him caressing his penis, every vein and spot with careful, conscientious tenderness.

It was still. They slowly tasted each other's lips feeling all the wet and warm surfaces cooling in the wind.

Then they got up and started to dance round together on the meagre soil of the pine forest. There was a soft southerly wind; they might never experience again such a warm day in April. Jan felt happier than he had ever thought possible.

He stopped Jenny's movement, put his arms around her hips and buttocks and pressed his face against her vagina which was wet and rough.

'Quiet,' she said.

'I'm not talking,' he mumbled to her interior.

She caressed his neck and pressed him against her. She raised her leg until the inside of her thigh rested against his cheek. 'Listen.'

Then he heard deep clarinet trills interspersed with long pauses. She pulled him out of her moisture and pointed: the curlews had arrived; they cut their way through the air with slightly bent swords.

They continued their journey through the unprecedented reality. Nothing looked exciting, but an electric microbe bounced up and down inside them telling them that the world could very well have a beginning and an end here in this area of Uppland. A large cloth was pulled together and kept in a steady grip. They were swinging securely in the folds.

The bushes were getting foliage, the buds would soon open, then wither, go to seed, and move. The Creator of it all apparently liked a certain amount of mobility.

It was the sparse season when nothing could be concealed in the wing. The lakes gleamed through the net curtains of the aspen trees, and the trees protected neither cottages nor stately homes from being seen.

Eventually they arrived at Rimbo. They parked on the railway yard at the same time as the train left for Stockholm East. The old Railway Hotel was now renamed. It was a white plastered house near the office of the local newspaper. The restaurant only served two dishes, rump steak and home-cured smoked salmon with creamed potatoes. Passing through the restaurant, they saw two men at different tables carefully trying these dishes. Their faces indicated that they would not mind changing their dishes.

'Home-cured?' JB said. 'In whose home?'

They took a room overlooking the railway where they opened up their picnic basket which was in fact a carrier bag. They took out an anchovy omelette, veal cutlets, hard boiled eggs, Jarlsberg cheese, and Danish rye bread. They placed a bottle of Bulgarian wine under the cold water tap.

'I'll soon get the feeling that we've been together all the time,' Jan said.

They sat with their backs against the end of the bedstead, looking out over the station yard, the workshops and the fields. A rusty red curtain fluttered in the open window.

'I loved you,' Jenny said. 'Even when denying it, I did. You should mistrust my anger but never my joy. Joy can't be pretended.'

'You might have suspected there was a letter from me waiting in Stockholm. How could you believe that I'd left without letting you know?'

'I might have understood a lot of things – had I wanted to,' Jenny admitted. 'But I was frightened. I suddenly saw it all in a different light. But now I know what you knew all along. You turned like a hare and then ran back to me. How could I be sure? I thought Gertrude was good enough for you. I didn't consider it a catastrophe if the two of you forgot about me and went on together. I blew at the sails of jealousy to get away, far away from you.'

'You mustn't,' Jan said. 'You mustn't rush me like that.'

'Suddenly you were gone. To me that was deceit or sincerity. I was afraid of the kind of love that could hurt me. My life is full enough without something to conquer that won't be conquered.'

'All I wanted to do was pay a duty call.'

'It's all my fault. I passed an air-trap, I felt sick, and I was shattered. I'm just explaining, I don't want to blame anybody. My parents, my job, society and the Establishment are all blameless.'

'I returned from Africa to tell you that I needed you more than I'd thought. And you were not there. When you phoned you sounded different. I don't want to pursue you with explanations. Our meeting-place was always half-way. You weren't there. So I withdrew as well.'

'The experiment seemed to me more dangerous than useful. I suspected your pity for Gertrude was greater than your love for me. Duty is usually more binding than lust. Tears reach further than laughter. I wish you'd love Gertrude with all your being, and I wouldn't have to.'

'So much unnecessary anxiety, so many stupid thoughts.' JB exclaimed.

'You're a masochist.'

'How can you say that? I escaped from something that gave me pain.'

'If you believe I'm not concerned about you you might as well believe I'm self-destructive. But I can't protect you from one thing: your own moods. They tinge the whole set until you don't know what play is being performed there.'

The wine level had sunk in their mugs. They crumpled up the tin-foil and paper, and walked hastily out through Rimbo's streets, past the book-shop and the ironmonger's, the post office and the bank, the snack bar with a discotheque on Saturdays, and the bingo posters guiding the population to the school-house which was empty at weekends.

They wandered across the meadows, avoiding the fields where new crops were growing, and the pastures protected by barbed wire. The sun cast a sidelight on the birch stems: white sheets with a blurred text. A tractor was parked for the night under an oak tree; the farmer was not expecting rain. At the back of a hen-house hens were crowding around the entrance hole. The warmth of the air went down with the sun.

'It's fantastic that we're walking here,' Jenny said. 'I only just turned up my coat collar to keep the nightly wanderers in Oxford Street from seeing how I talked to you.'

They made their way alongside a lake through greenery still autumn red and across fields firm and dry. The buzzard had arrived. The titmouse sat in a hole in an ash. There were other birds there, but they were hidden. The light faded and slid over to another note.

They passed a lonely barn. It was easier to talk when they did not see each other too clearly. JB told her about Botswana and his hard time with Gertrude.

'Meanwhile you were in London nursing your jealousy like a nasty plant,' he said. 'You didn't know how wrong you were. Something between me and Gertrude was lost when she realized that you and I had no secrets. Don't reproach yourself. Unspoken demands and hidden clauses appeared. The person I've grown into couldn't have lived with them.' He hardly discerned her features.

'There's nothing you can do to help,' he continued. 'I sometimes feel that you, like Gertrude, like to give directions. But love is not theatre. It grows according to its kind.'

The stars came out like nails in the asphalted cardboard above them. The lamp outside the front door of a cottage allowed them to see each other. They stopped and kissed against a tree trunk, pressing themselves together, feeling their worries leave without catching their scent.

'You've had a horrible time,' Jenny said. 'I'm ashamed.'

But he wanted no pity. Joy stretched its rainbow across the anticyclones.

'I'd never longed for you more or less because of Gertrude's actions,' JB said. 'But there, in Botswana . . . I felt this yearning for you which was almost panicky. Gertrude and I had talked ourselves down to the very skeleton of emotion. It gave us a vicious grin.'

Jenny was silent, but held him so tight that she almost tried to lift him off the ground. JB went on :

'At a moment like that your whole existence is naked and aimless around you. You're super-conscious. I stared back at myself wherever I looked. I'd never want those weeks back. I wonder how Gertrude and I shall ever be able to meet without reminding each other of the horrors.'

After another kilometre Jenny said:

'I wrote to Gertrude from London. Before you left.'

'She never told me,' JB said surprised.

'I told her we could have been close friends, had we not loved the same man. It sounded like the old story but it was true. I hope it was a warm and open letter, for where Gertrude is concerned, all the time I have a hidden bugging device giving me critical comments.'

'Did she reply?'

'Not until you had left Botswana. She wrote that she could not return my sincerity. I had to accept there were things she could not discuss.'

'She writes to you and Klas,' Jan said. 'Not to me.'

They stopped by one of these large boulders which stick out of fields for no apparent reason, like the knee cap of a sleeping giant. There JB told her about Marianne Tidström, a woman Jenny had not met.

'Did you have a good time?' she asked, her voice filled with laughter.

'All I remember is that I missed you, not that I was with her.'

'So your secrets are always passed on. Between lovers there is the most shameless gossip.'

'That's one of the explanations for monogamy as a rule,' Jan suggested. 'Besides it probably varies. I can't expect to know everything however much I love you.'

'You'll probably find out anyway. To me it's almost like love's definition: to be able to discuss what's difficult to discuss. To dare dwell on forbidden ground.'

They went back across some scraggy rocks suitable for sheep grazing like in Botswana. An elk cracked some dry branches in a grove.

'We might be in central Africa,' Backman, the globetrotter said, 'in Axel Ericson's tracks. But we're in Uppland, within Arlanda's radar transmission.'

Jenny was wearing a sports jacket which had wide sleeves around her wrists, and he could tuck all his fingers in along her forearm to let them explore the darkness. With that touch, in their exchange of words and the silence of their breaths, he experienced truth, or rather a temporary invention beyond all catastrophes. JB told her about the well-drillers in Botswana, the school builders, the refugees from apartheid, the things that had been achieved and the things that remained to be done.

'We're stealing time to live,' he said. 'At the same time, in Rhodesia, white farmers kick Africans into a river full of crocodiles.'

Jenny asked him if he had seen Lennart Nilsson's micro photos of the inner ear. The little tufts of hair catch the sound, which is converted into an electric impulse that is transmitted to the brain. 'Those pictures give me hope,' she said. 'They are composed so genially and lovingly – imagine the loving and artistically perfect things we must be meant to listen to. The finely tuned mechanism is there, patiently waiting for better songs.'

At the hotel they moved the beds together, but then slept in only one of them. They rested like two ships moored for the night close together. Occasionally they moved in the pull from the underwater currents.

JB woke up early from a confused dream about the sacking suffocating the house in Uppland Street and Marianne pounding at the door to get in. He heard the lark singing on the other side of the narrow-gauge railway station through the window open to the province of Uppland. Jenny slept on her back, one foot against her knee, as if she were standing on one leg in her sleep. He watched her with a sense of excited security.

There was nothing in her he wanted to escape from or be without. He groped over her breasts. His fingers hardly noticed the difference between her nipple and the area around it, but eventually its teat stuck out indicating a centre point. He did not need to open her thighs. As he entered her, she put her arms and legs around him, and a little while later they slept on in the same position.

Then they went out into the light spring, along narrow roads where no traffic interrupted them, between houses and barns, between fields and hazel-trees. They stopped at random, sat down for a moment under a service-tree to read a map, and drank tea from their thermos where the tea leaves had extended to some botanic being again, and were not just dry merchandise.

They had lunch at a boarding-house where they were preparing for an eightieth birthday party. All they could get was
milk, bread and cold meats in a servants' room. In the dining-
rooms there were tulips on the tables and branches of juniper
on the floor. Their room had linoleum on the floor and a view
of the kitchen where they heard the servants talk.

'Hors d'oeuvre for seventy. I shall dream about pink salmon
and parsley.'

'There's a skin on the soup,' somebody shouted from the
stove.

'We'll take that off last thing. It keeps it warm,' the cook
said.

When they were leaving the landlady brought them their
coats, as the guests were arriving. They had to leave by the
kitchen door.

Traffic was growing dense around Uppsala. They drove round
the North of the city to the area around Jumkil church which
Jenny had worked on at the Department of The Environment.
They left the car outside a little school, and walked along the
trampled paths between Stone Age barrows.

They soon stood on the high bank of the Jumkil river; Jumkil
one of those water-courses that grope its way through history,
gushing out from underneath mossy mound, stopping to over-
flow into fields, saturating ridges and waving off wagtails,
rattling grey seed vessels, letting powerlines pass, resting in a
pocket, and noticing with blank surprise that no one has
scraped at the back of its mirror.

They were attracted by the stony pastures on the other side.
They went in by a silky grey gate. All was furnished and
decorated, ready for the first tenants; the sky extended between
oak groves with cloudy white stucco, junipers marking the
rooms, creating sections and wings. Taut grass was growing
into fitted carpets and, protected by the shrubberies, the
shadows deepened into hare-bell blue. In the drifts of oak
leaves the odd violet shone. They walked curiously from one
room to another. New halls opened out into the forest : the
cultivator's square fields, and also the pointed sectors of old
sea bays. They decided on a suitable drawing-room in green
and blue. Anonymous leaf buckles waited to become bluebells,
thistles, buttercups and fern. The wood anemones were still
knotty and reddish, another kind of the species from the

276

snowy white and pollen yellow which would wave the spring birthday telegram a week or so later. Among the frosty green juniper needles were plenty of pale berries. They could collect a dozen of blue shades, surprised that all these were called blue and that the net of the words had so few loops. Most things fell through the loop-holes, had no distinctive names, and were hard to catch.

JB took something out of his pocket.

'What's that?' Jenny asked.

'A morello stone from the time we had dinner with Veronica in Kristianstad. Whenever my fingertips felt it, I saw your face as it looked in that light. You were listening to Veronica, totally unaware of your appearance, not knowing I was admiring you.'

'Do you think it can grow?' Jenny asked.

'Let's plant it and wait. We can lie in its shadow.'

While Jan dug a suitable hole with his pocket-knife, Jenny looked in her handbag.

'Here you are,' she said.

It was a piece of an envelope. Its stamp had a Stockholm postmark with the date when he gave her a lift from Arlanda to Nybro Quay.

'I tore it off a letter in the mail on my desk that day. I told my secretary I had a relation who collected stamps. You know my childish urge to explain my actions sometimes.'

JB put the piece of paper in his wallet.

'Grow, grow, grow,' Jenny sang monotonously, pouring earth over the stone with her cupped hands. 'It won't hear me, it's already got its ears stuffed with earth. And you'll mislay that postage stamp. Fetiches and secret signs were never our scene.'

There was a motel outside Uppsala where JB unexpectedly stopped.

'What are we going to do?' Jenny asked. 'Are you hungry?'

While she went to the ladies' he booked a room. They had tournedos, charcoaled outside and raw inside. He hurried the meal. Jenny thought he wanted to get away, but he quickly pulled her along the corridor with its carpet and potted monstera to one of the rooms.

'You need a lot of bad morals,' he said, entering her so quickly that she resisted him.

'You haven't even asked me if I want to.'

After a while she said: 'I do want to. How did you know?'

Her face was under his. She looked at him, eyes wide-open. They gazed at each other in a steady, bold manner. A smile made her pupils shrink, and he said: 'Don't look like that. You'll make me come at once.'

Then she lifted both her face and her pelvis towards him, and he felt the muscles of her pupils closing even around his penis. And he said spontaneously: 'It's nice to make love to someone you love.' He slept with his head on her shoulder. Even in her sleep she held his waist tight.

When they awoke, Jan said:

'The car is just outside. Go and sit there while I pay the bill.'

They were happy and excited as they drove into Stockholm in the increasing afternoon traffic. Jenny thought she had been to the Wild West.

'We go from motel to motel,' she said, 'collecting silly stamps and chewing-gums bad for the teeth.'

They continued their imagining, and Jenny laughed till she sank down against his knee and the gear-lever, jeopardizing the journey.

'There's no limit to what we can do,' JB said. 'For example, you can come with me to the Town Hall in Södertälje to hear me talk about California.'

That night at Nybro Quay Jenny prepared a tea-tray and placed it at the end of the bed. They fell asleep, and Jan woke up in the middle of the night with his heel in the tea-strainer. He looked in wonder at the familiar surroundings, and put the tray silently on the floor. The light of the spring night over Nybro Quay shone into the room, making the shadows grey. A ship's siren sounded at the inlet. Cars sneaked past on soft rubber soles while their roofs mirrored the first green tinges of the parks.

He suddenly remembered his own car. He had left it under the limetrees at Skånela church.

He stretched himself out as near to Jenny as he could without waking her up. He looked at the stucco above their heads, wondering whether it looked like dogs or lions. A crack was taking sudden turns across the ceiling, but it didn't worry him. Above was the attic and the roof where they had made love. Above the roof was the sky. There was no end to the roof that had protected them. And home was any place where they met.

He looked back on their Uppland journey in the sunny wind. A well-known landscape – and yet it filled him with the same curiosity and wonder as the canopy of the blue sky. The flight of the curlews, the shadow of the barrows, the hardness of a lump of soil . . . If the experience of all these things could change men, he thought, the days on earth would be different.

PM FOR CLOSE RELATIONS

Jan Backman and Jenny Jeger were having lunch in one of the staff dining-rooms at the South Hospital. Jenny had some friends who worked there with system analysis, and they were carrying out an investigation. They were researchers in their mid-thirties, top of their year at their universities with secure careers ahead. They had high salaries, lived in terraced houses along Ed Bay, contributed to the Social Medicine Journal, and called themselves data processor, Master of Science and system analyst.

They planned man's future, while Jenny was busy with that of nature. Over lunch they discussed how much one man is allowed to cost. The proportion of the population who were working in Sweden kept decreasing. The production of nappies for adults would eventually surpass that of babies' nappies. The average expectancy of life stagnated, as money and machinery to keep the oldest citizens alive were lacking.

'Many things are never discussed,' Jan said. 'We don't even know about them.'

'The suicidal precipice is showing,' Jenny said. 'Insoluble problems are concealed as part of man's self-preservation instinct. The questions of over-population and air pollution did not appear until there was at least a theoretical chance to control them.'

'Doctors are used to preserving life,' said one of the researchers. 'They pick the best method of treatment. They don't ask about the price. But one method cures ninety per cent of the sick at the cost of one hundred kronor, while another cures ninety-nine per cent at the cost of ten thousand. The one per cent that dies costs millions. How can we press the taxpayers to produce a greater effort? How can we inform people that they should sacrifice their standards for the benefit of the old and sick?'

'How much am I prepared to give for my mother's kidney disease?' one investigator said, sucking his pipe. 'I know she'd be prepared to give anything for my life. Three years' salary, three years of total self-denial? It was easier in the old days when illness struck from Above. Now it depends on me. Few people want responsibility, and nor do the doctors. So we must have a policy: we can afford the cheap treatment. But every ten patients die. It has to be said.'

'The money comes from those who work,' the analyst said. 'Those who suffer from disease are often old and non-productive. They're worth less in the large household. We don't want to be a burden, the old people say. Now we have to take their word for it.'

'The doctors don't like to decide about it,' a young bearded man said. 'But lung machines are quietly turned off and the drip is stopped. It happens every day.'

'A vicious circle,' Jan said. 'Society is responsible for a lot of the wear and tear, the diseases and the accidents. Then we must question whether it can afford to repair the damage.'

'It's also a new social attitude that's brought about the problems of old age,' the researcher said. 'Wherever we look we're squeezed between cause and effect. But the worst thing is the fact that you're not allowed to talk about it. A lurking declaration of incapacity; a blurred democracy.'

The junior doctors, medical students and nurses pressed buttons for the dish of today. The hospital was bursting at its concrete seams. There was a faint smell of scouring powder, of chemical cleansers. It was strange to get out into the fresh air. Along the Ring Road walked people whose production results determined the lives of sick people. The whole city was like a factory. They all had invisible tags around their necks with today's price on them. They moved amongst each other, programmed by wishes and compulsions, on their way to meet hunger and emotional death, insecure and in search of protection, insecure and thus easy to handle, easy to tempt with advertising and propaganda. JB saw a society that wanted people to work for riches rather than for welfare.

They walked behind the hospital down towards Årsta Bay. There the city disappeared, and they moved in the maze between supported covered boats, their eyes level with the keels and propellers. The boats were dreams awakening, supposed to carry people across the waters. But the seabed was invisible even at a metre deep. There were black-listed fish, and fish suffocated in the sulphureous pockets of the provincial depths. The surface glittering in the sun was a dancing floor over a water forest turning into a desert.

At Årsta Bay on the shore there was a row of shacks with windows and shutters. They were the resthouses of the boat-owners where they could stay in the summer. One was equipped with a wrought iron chandelier, a bed, a chest of drawers, and a gas ring. A green painted shed with fragile furniture was open on Sundays only, and from there coffee was served to people under the chestnut trees.

Further down towards the Hammarby lock there was a three storey building where bricks showed through broken plaster. It had monstrous verandas in a Russian style. Now the house which had once been so pompous had a desolate air. The waterside curved here, birches stretched their roots into the water, and the garden smelt of earth and compost. By the bridge there was a white boat with white edges and a slightly cupped deck. The black waves of Lake Mälaren lapped against the rusty lock gate.

'I can't accept that progression and development should be as uncontrollable as volcano eruptions, earthquakes and old age,' Jenny said. 'Do countries produce weapons like these bushes produce currants? I feel they do, but yet my freedom means my chance to curb it.' She pointed to the tiny cottages at the Eriksdal Grove, the oldest summer cottages in Stockholm. The spring farming routine was starting there. They drilled the soil for the potatoes, and pruned the raspberry canes. Across the water was Årsta Forest with its inaccessible precipices, and closer to the lake were the loading quays of the Wine and Spirits Centre, where tankers moored with Bordeaux Vieux lapping inside.

'Remember Lövsta rubbish dump?' Jenny said.

'Yes. That was one of the first times you offered me to Gertrude.'

'The ashes and the soil of all this refuse will eventually become another large leisure centre with a walk along the waterside and bathing places, and the rubbish mountain will become a ski-slope. The soil will be fertile, with hazel and sloe, foxglove and cowslip.'

'Will it be long?' JB asked. 'I'd like to walk with you in that park.'

They still had another hour, and took the car to café Heimdal. Those who ate pork pancakes at three kronor fifty had tables with red checked plastic cloths, but they had just coffee, served by a motherly woman. There were old age pensioners there, and a few workers from a building-site nearby.

JB listened to the conversation of the old people around them:

'I've spent sixty years sitting here and you haven't even got your feet wet.'

'Your hands are just as dirty.'

'Are you asleep in the middle of the day?'

'I brought some pork dumpling home with me.'

'One day they'll come to get you, although you haven't done any harm. Except being a bit poorly.'

Jan hoped they would all be able to stay at Heimdal. They lead a dangerous life. More than death they feared the day when the last nanny would put them in a bathtub and calm their worry with a voice people used for pets.

'I've got to talk to you about my job,' said Jenny. 'I brood a lot over it. I've become hesitant. Sitting up there at the Department in Solna, I have a view different from our Uppland meadows. I can see our terrible age: the masses of refuse we do nothing about, the devastation of the forests, the pollution of the Baltic, the threat for the ground water . . .'

'Your life is more exposed than mine,' JB said. 'But don't assume that anything has been decided beforehand.'

'No. There are other alternatives to the given ones. But sometimes a choice has to be made. Then you head for the middle course. That's the crooked mean of democracy: adjustment, consideration, balance. There are truths that can ruin the balance, but we don't listen to those, unless they contradict each other. Then we can point out the paradox and go on. You search your way to intersection of interests. Compliance, not truth, is the point aimed at. Many interests are confused. It's suspected that the intersection is elsewhere but can't be expressed.'

'I think it's possible to rebel and yet remain faithful,' JB said.

'It may be a question of aptitude,' said Jenny.

'They are to cut down those limes in the yard,' said an old man at the table next to theirs.

'Where?'

'In Bonde Street. They want to make an underground store-room. But we are twenty studio flats who object, and we pay the landlord four thousand crowns every month. He has to consider that.'

JB thought of Christina. She lived a street or so from there.

'Give me a stale bun and something for the birds,' the old man said, and was given a plastic bag by the motherly woman. 'Back to the couch. Sleep well you too.'

'In London,' Jenny said, and Jan felt how the name gave him fine stings like nettles, 'I wrote a memorandum that I wanted to circulate at the Department of The Environment. It was pessimistic and oppositional. I wrote it instead of applying for leave. I'd like to discuss it with you.'

'We'll do it tonight,' Jan said. 'You have to go now.'

'Tonight, tonight . . .' Jenny hummed. 'Are we really to meet again so soon? We live in abundance.'

She grabbed his arm as they got out in the street. Her smile sparkled and warmed. All the winter stiffness waiting in him thawed.

'I'd like to pull you into the nearest doorway,' JB said. 'I could think of doing anything with you.'

Through the slow stream of traffic, under a sky promising hail showers, they drove in wordless proximity. It was two o'clock. The working day wanted them, but they were still engaged in their secret party.

Jenny dropped him off. He had not been to the flat in Uppland Street for four days. He went up to get his newspapers and mail. There was a letter from Gertrude there. It had arrived the same day as Jenny phoned. He felt uneasy, but neither from fear nor expectation. Joy all the time built its bridge span inside him. On that bridge Gertrude, like hundreds of other people, walked.

Gertrude wrote to tell him that she had booked a flight which was to arrive in Stockholm on the twenty-ninth of April. 'Take us down with care,' she wrote. In the empty kitchen he smiled at her soft tone. Klas would be there to meet her. He had arranged a bedsitter for her for the time being. He then wanted her to come and live in his house.

'I wouldn't even think of it,' Gertrude wrote. 'I may get to the point where I can like him, but so far I feel only benign tolerance. I shall never want to move in with him because of the baby. That would be wrong both for him and the Unborn. What I want more than anything else I won't tell anyone.'

JB looked at his watch. He had another half hour's respite before he had to set out for Arlanda. He quickly made up his mind. He got up on the kitchen ladder and got the largest suitcase down from one of the many high cupboards, filled it with shirts, sweaters, a lounge suit and some books. He then got together the few remaining personal possessions he could see around him and put them in a laundry basket in his wardrobe. He phoned the caretaker and asked him to arrange for a cleaner.

He wrote Gertrude a couple of lines telling her that the flat was empty now. Why couldn't she come and live there? The façade will be newly painted yellow to honour you and the baby, he wrote. Where he was going himself he did not say. Sleeping far away from Jenny had, by force, become a boring habit. Having her within arm's reach and leg's width was unusual. He felt he needed to practise that experience. Like an old silver spoon it would thus avoid getting tarnished.

Marianne was on the phone when he arrived at Arlanda. She had phoned before, and he had told her that he was very busy and would ring back in an hour. That was four days ago, she informed him. She sounded angry and hurt. He suspected he had been more of a valve to her than he had intended. She had had a letter from Sten saying Gertrude was expected in Stockholm. Now she connected Gertrude's homecoming with his hesitation to see her. He tried to say something that was both true and kind. He thought she would appreciate hearing what had really happened. So he told her about Jenny; that she had come back, and that they were living together. Marianne was silent. Then she said:

'You could have told me that straight away. It would have spared me a lot of yearning.'

She hung up before he had time to reply.

Late that night he was back at Nybro Quay. Jenny was hidden by a reading lamp, looking through photocopies as he entered. She made a funny grimace when she saw his bulging suitcase and the pile of his raincoat, sports jacket and winter coat which filled her entrance hall.

'Is there accommodation here for a homeless man?' JB asked.

'You can stay here for the time being,' Jenny replied.

Her indifference did not seem natural.

'Tell me something which is not for the time being.'

'It's a small flat,' she said.

'We'll have parties on the roof. Besides I'm hungry.'

'No food tonight. I bought an amaryllis bulb for the last of my money.'

'We can always make onion soup,' Jan suggested.

But Jenny put the bulb in a pot which JB thought large enough to hold a tree. She put it in one of the windows overlooking Nybro Bay. Jenny described how its pink trumpets of petals and green leaves would fill the whole bay-window. It smelt of spring farming, she thought, as she bent over it to see the ferry returning from its first night tour between the Dramatic Theatre and the Old City.

JB put some parmesan cheese on the remains of a large sausage, and put it in the oven. Jenny lit a candle on the glossy plastic cloth on the kitchen table.

'Now let's talk about you,' he said. 'This is the first time I hear you hesitate about your job.'

'We live in a society of balance,' Jenny said. 'We've been forced to become weighers at the Department of The Environment. I'm interested in application and practical results, as much as in the ideas behind them. That's why the job suited me. But I've been holding the scales for long enough, and cheated with the weights. Now I want to stand on one of the scales to see if it has any effect. What one person does naturally doesn't mean much. You have to join groups, parties. Great things are at stake. We're forced to compromises which are defeat for the future, you know the list. One union wants employment, one branch wants to expand, the Conservatives defend the ground values, and the county councils want tax money.'

'You're a political institution, so you must consider all those votes,' JB said.

'The basic ecological principle is to give everybody the best possible biophysical environment without always having to consider what he might earn or lose by it financially or socially. We've gone far towards that attitude in Sweden.'

Jenny spoke in dry words, but he could see the winds blowing green. She had put a bunch of dill in a jug to keep. He didn't eat it.

'There are enough people with the genuine will to solve the problems,' Jenny continued. 'There are many people with the power to stop the problems from being solved. People, organizations, parties; who dares take the responsibility? The opium grower, the tobacco producer, the city planner, the architect, the aeroplane designer, the army general, the bomber pilot – they are all involved. But others are always to blame. Give people a very small share of the decision making and the action, and they'll feel free of responsibility: it wasn't up to them.'

'Circulation must again be made a beautiful word,' JB said. 'The rising curve an ugly word. New valuations give new patterns of activity. And I believe people realize all the time that other values can balance certain material privations we're forced to.'

'You have to be able to use society, and also to protect yourself against it,' Jenny said. 'Never complain but protest. Never assume you're powerless or an object. It's not consumption that measures our standard, but the possibility of action, to be active, and to change conditions.

'The Department of The Environment ought to wash away the dust of DDT and gold off the present and describe the future, the foreseeable future and the one we can hardly envisage,' JB said.

'Politicians and business management work on a short-term basis. They need to show quick results. Other people often imagine they make decisions for life, but they don't. And the unborn can't vote. They won't receive a nice heritage. The

286

original sins have returned to Earth. If we look at the demands of the *whole* society . . . That's our permanent phrase at work. Society and nature are not opposites. If we don't do something quickly about nature, we'll soon lose society.

'I read today that in the USA a baby is born every twelve seconds and a car every five,' JB said. 'They both need space to live in. The road building programme in the USA eats up two acres of countryside every minute. The asphalted ground gives no oxygen. Three fourths of the Earth is sea. Half of its land surface can't be populated. The rest is half a metre of fertile surface soil with another metre underneath : our existence depends on this.'

It was their first meeting at home. JB had moved in with his luggage, but it was an evening in the middle of something like a long extended week-day : neither unlimited time nor stolen seconds. Jenny took out a file on a new investigation from her brief-case. 'Industries destructive to the environment are recommended to move to the East Coast. The west winds will then blow the dangerous fumes away from Sweden. The sulphuric acid will fall into the Baltic, which will then deteriorate as a result. The fumes will blow on to Finland and Russia – serves them right.'

'You can't blame the Department for that,' JB said. 'Your place of work will be neither stronger nor more resistant if you leave.'

'But how can I be of any use to the Department of The Environment the way it appears? How much can be changed and how radically? Maybe I'll just grow stupid and credulous myself?'

'What are your alternatives?' Jan asked.

'They're in the fog and mist. They aren't quite real.'

'In bad visibility you trust radar and routine. Don't rush it.'

'I've kept myself from rushing now for a year.'

She told him that the Department of The Environment had been refused a grant of five million kronor for research in the Baltic.

'I want to point out that there are other ways to live,' she continued. 'Freedom should be leisure and not redundance. Many types of work are nothing but exhausting and unnecessary and not worth the increased standard which is sometimes the consequence. The Uppland meadows should be accessible to all of us.'

The thick candle had been burning for a long time. The wick now floating in a lake of candle-wax had died and left a slight smell. Jenny kept on talking. Her face was white. The sounds of the city faded.

'Come on,' JB said. 'We've got to get some sleep.'

FREEDOM OF AND FOR

The days were light and dry. Jenny felt that she was already about to leave the Department of The Environment. At the same time she read about doctors who were cleaning up ditches, and MA's who were advised to work in garages or supermarkets. The academic course, which had previously been a safe route to the large motorway of a career, could now lead anywhere in the topography. The dreams of the future lay wrecked there.

This worried Jenny. Jan tried to advise her as well as he could. He was pleased by the confidence she had in his solutions to her problems. However, he felt assured that she would never let herself be persuaded against her will.

'Take some leave of absence,' he suggested. 'Live on my salary for a while. Our rent is low. We don't pay much for clothes and entertainment.'

'We live well,' Jenny said.

'The menu doesn't make the party,' Jan said. 'The lines of your palm inebriate me.'

'That's all right,' Jenny said soberly. 'At heart I approve of Women's Lib; I fear that some of my freedom and self-confidence comes from my salary. It doesn't sound good, but it's true.'

JB had seen her as a person who made quick decisions. Now he saw her wavering. During their discussions they drove here and there on the periphery of the city. Late one afternoon they went out to Lidingö. The farm appeared through the greenery, blackbirds imitated each other, and in the distance floated the demagnization station of Värtan.

'What's your main demand from society?' asked Jenny.

'The same as from life,' he replied. 'To give me important experiences.'

They were standing at the far end of the fragile pier at Lidingö throwing stones into the water, which was muddy and smelt of foreign ports. The ships passed by after having sneaked past Klas Lundin's garden and been noted in his unofficial register. In the empty sports restaurant cloakroom there was a slot-machine. For twenty-five öre you could compete with yourself. That was the only sport that remained here. But the mural on one wall showed how the Gåshaga Cape had been full of bathers in striped swimsuits in the Twenties. The opposite wall depicted winter sports with couples skating in the distance with skating sails. Girls skated on the edge in ankle-length skirts. Gentlemen in furcoats and ladies with muffs watched the performance on the ice with their binoculars.

The waiter had hastily pulled on a white coat. He served them a set tea which seemed to have been ready for days. The à la carte menu was as large as a sheet; yet they wondered who would find the place.

'When I went over to see my mother last night,' Jenny said, 'I thought a lot about you and me. Now we can feel freedom and togetherness at the same time. That's ideal. Soon it may be one thing or another.'

'There are so many different kinds of freedom,' Jan said. 'The freedom to escape, to submit, to gain experience, to take out a claim for a small area.'

'The freedom to be weak demands strength,' said Jenny, 'and trust on your own resources in the middle of dependence. You don't want to be lonely, and not unfree.'

'But I don't feel lonely,' Jan interrupted her. 'And not tied. With you I feel more myself than ever.'

'We shall all be lonely. You and I and Gertrude. A long period will suddenly be over. That's how I felt last night. The pieces of the puzzle are sometimes separated, and darkness shows between them. Getting used to the darkness is freedom as well.'

There was a Jenny who existed in other contexts and replied to questions he never put to her. Her gaze could stiffen like glass, and her voice be as factual as that of an accountant. When she felt her margins narrowing, a spiteful and head-strong streak appeared in her which could hurt other people: an unreasonable impulse to neglect compromises, consider-ations, various pressures. She wanted to hurl herself into a wild dream. Her sense of responsibility fought against this. A dialogue was going on inside her. It sometimes deteriorated into a fight, she complained.

They went north and ended up at Sättsjö shore near a valley with red cottages that had slanting roofs: that was the way they used to look all over the archipelago. A woodpecker screamed. Bogesund Castle appeared amongst the woods across the water.

Looking out over the fjord, as if she listened for something, Jenny balanced on planks placed across the shelving beach. An old age pensioner walked round his greenhouse looking into the water barrels. Gravel slipped under his shoes, the mossy apple trees, the ashes of burnt leaves . . . Jan sneaked up to her from behind and, without a sound, slowly kissed her neck. She put her arms up and seized his head.

'I think my life is parallel to the one I could live,' she said. 'I live in a world ruled by men and powers I can't get at. I feel like releasing myself, creating my own world; but then I may have to renounce someone I could share it with.'

'You speak so much about freedom,' Jan said. 'Freedom of what? Of me?'

'Freedom for you,' Jenny said. 'All the time for you.'

Unsure of what the public rights were, JB dug up a little birch-tree in the bilberry woods at Trolldalen. He planted it in a pot at Nybro Quay. Jenny put some wood anemones in a glass jar; bubbles formed round their reddish stems. Then Jan cleaned the windows: He wanted to see views.

'I had a letter from Gertrude,' he said. 'She's coming back. I wrote to her to say she can have Uppland Street to herself.'

'It's not true,' Jenny said. 'You probably had a letter from Gertrude and then moved in with me.'

'That's right.'

'Are you going to start being tactful with me?' Jenny said, her back to him. 'Then the end is near.'

JB turned her round with an iron grip on her shoulders, but her face was shiny.

'I'm telling you Jan Backman, that I can take whatever you do, but I won't stand what you only pretend to do.'

The following day they went looking for a toaster with continuous current. The old houses in Stockholm still did not have alternating current, and Jenny's house might be pulled down before it was changed; no one seemed to know anything about it. JB burned his fingers every morning on the steel wire handle of the toaster Jenny put on top of the gas stove to make toast for breakfast.

They had a Saturday off. On the building sites and in the deep pits in the city caterpillars and dredgers had stopped their movements. They had some difficulty finding an ironmonger. The little shops of Klara had moved.

They then went south through the suburbs built in the Thirties and Forties, through destroyed pine forests and hygienic social politics, seeing utopia turning into subtopia: blast stones filled the holes after trees that had been removed. Greenery soon concealed the sooty façades. In Skärholmen commerce and motorism dominated. The tower blocks stood silent on a hill slope, looking down over department stores: a newly varnished slum standing on the edge. The distress of the large families in tower blocks was the definition of a slum.

A valley yellow from yellow-stars-of-Bethlehem and celandine, led past a wild orchard and an ancient castle to the yellow Skärholmen manor, deserted by its last private owner as well as by the scouts. An elderly man lived in one wing and kept his dog on an unusually long line. The big house was unlocked, there was rubbish in the fireplace, and a plank of wood broken up on the floor. An avenue of trimmed lime and hazel-trees led down to a landing stage for steamboats, but there was no traffic any more.

At the shore were the remains of a cygnet, which had either died naturally or been taken by a fox. Its quill-feathers were spread over last year's decaying reeds. Suddenly a rain cloud passed Lake Mälaren; the sun kept shining and made each drop glitter. Grey horses grazed in the valley, runners from the local sports club passed them with distorted faces, and in a broken down garage hidden on the edge of the forest, somebody was trying out a starter motor.

They had tea at Lyran, a summer place with an outlook tower and windows resembling dice in yellow, green and red. A non-conformist was reading free literature whilst eating a cake. Mushrooms grew in the meadow outside.

Their joy had an absent-minded quality which was the opposite of apathy : impulses carried by the moment like gushes of water lifted by a straw. 'My sadness looks always the same,' Jenny said. 'But my love keeps entering new rooms.'

Gertrude was due back any day, and so Jenny and Jan went to Uppland Street to check that it had been cleaned. JB looked at the flat with the distant eyes of a stranger. The rooms suddenly looked smaller than he had imagined. The everlasting flowers in the bookcase had gathered dust. The door handle had a slight cover, like when one returns to town after the summer.

As they were about to leave, Jan saw Jenny take something out of her bag and put it on the hall table. He bent forward. It was a paper bag with clothes for a new-born baby.

'You weren't meant to see that,' she said. 'It's just something for Gertrude's baby.'

He then told her about the pram he had given away. Jenny reproached him. It should have been up to Gertrude to refuse the gift.

'The child should not suffer for what we have done,' Jenny said. 'It's at the beginning of something whose end we'll never see.'

The next day he phoned Klas Lundin. He knew that Klas was to meet Gertrude at Arlanda. He ought to have the keys in case Gertrude had not brought hers. They met at the flat in Uppland Street after office-hours.

'I'm happy I can take an interest in the child – with Gertrude's permission,' Klas said, at the same time triumphant and humble. JB thought it was a long time since they had had Akvavit together in the kitchen. That was before Botswana.

'My dear friend, you shouldn't stay away, I don't want to stand in your way.'

Klas hardly knew what to say.

'It's not what you think,' Jan said. 'I've moved in with the person I prefer to be with.'

'You're just as secretive as Gertrude,' Klas complained. 'I don't understand you.' And then he became eager and organizing: 'This will be the baby's room.'

He pointed to an area next to the kitchen, intended to be a maid's room. It was sometimes called Jan's office, though he seldom brought home any work. He saw a pile of inherited furniture from the Thirties.

'I ought to clear that out,' JB said.

'Don't worry about it,' Klas said. 'I'll see to it.'

And he described how the room would look.

'You'd better find out what Gertrude wants,' Jan warned him. 'She will surprise us with her own decisions. She may have a plan for her new life.'

It was his own fault that Klas walked about in his and Gertrude's flat pointing out a nursery, and that in Klas's eyes he was a deceived man. He found it amazing that this Klas was the father of Gertrude's child, but the absurdity of the situation stimulated him. He had never expected this, never expected Jenny either. The unexpected that he had not found in the Arlanda tower had occurred, over and over again. He discerned new patterns, as one event led to another in logical sentence. He saw no end, just felt he was moving.

'Gertrude has written to me again,' Klas said. 'A girl called Lotte Schneider is going to come and stay with her in a few weeks' time.'

A few days later JB parked his car outside the Arrivals Hall. He intended to meet Gertrude with Klas, but he was late. Before he got out of his car, he saw a heavy and different Gertrude being helped into a cab by Klas. Jan gesticulated to catch her attention, but she was speaking eagerly to Klas, only showing him her profile. She was wearing a rough knitted African shawl over her hair and shoulders. He did not recognize her luggage. He was concerned that they might meet somewhere in the world without recognizing each other. In the closeness of a thousand nights their features had been smoothed out and mingled like their breaths.

The worry worsened to sickness. Once, long ago, when Gertrude had told him that she was pregnant, an earthquake had erupted. One wave after another had reached him, and now was the time for the final outburst. The large stage of

Arlanda was askew. He grabbed the car door, feeling the wave continuing right through him into the landscape. After that he was on firm ground.

THE DAY MOON

'I miss the clouds,' Gertrude said. 'They're so different in Africa. I've photographed them. I call those pictures Africa. But jakaranda and moonflowers are nothing compared to wood anemones and sorrel.'

Jan and Gertrude Backman were on their way to the Water Palace. It was Walpurgis-night. She had asked him to take some furniture from Uppland Street to be stored at the summer house. She came with him. He made sure she did not lift any heavy objects.

There was a shyness between them. JB looked out of the windscreen. There's a cloud, he wanted to say, but it was the day moon like a white thumb print in the sky. As they passed a Co-op store, he saw the cigarette machines and said:

'Have you thought of something? We don't smoke.'

'No,' Gertrude said. 'We don't.'

Silence followed. It was one of the early spring days he remembered from far back. They were shorter now, the light steeper. He was getting a strange feeling of being a contemporary of the world after having long seen himself as somewhat younger. The yellow local buses had become red. Buildings made the landscape sterile. A motorway streamed through the nature reserves.

Gertrude was well. The child was pounding and kicking inside her, without any preconceived thoughts. It wanted to get out.

'It's strange to be back,' she said. 'I could imagine that here in the North we live in a world under occupation, cut off from the rest of the Earth. The rich are digging trenches, prepared to die for their comfort.'

'It's the same in Francistown,' JB said.

She told him of the growing slums. Francistown was a segregated town, the whites in houses, the blacks by the wayside, and Indians in between, with commerce in the middle. It might as well be South Africa.

'Fight for your standard, not for faith. And not just on land but in the air, on the water . . . The new religious wars. I thought I saw them clearly in Africa.'

'I understand you and Sten discussed it,' Jan said. 'How is he?'

'He's got a guilty conscience about Marianne, but I think he's glad she's in Stockholm.'

'He didn't manage to arrange for her among all those people he wanted to help and plan for.'

'The family business is too narrow for him,' Gertrude said.

She told him Lotte would soon join her with six year old Ua.

'I know,' Jan said. 'Klas told me.'

They arrived at the Water Palace. JB carried the furniture up to the attic. He stopped for a while in the dry air under the rafters, wiping the sweat off his upper lip. Through the small skylights he looked down upon the water: red streaks of felspar in the rock, crevices with heather and brown rain water, erratic stones with peat moss. There was a draught between the tiles. Moths lay like withered leaves on the floor. He could hear the starling squeaking under the tiles of the roof: the birds always returned.

Quickly, through the other end of the binoculars, he saw his life, with airy kilometres between here and then, a collected existence. Something released itself and approached his face across the distances. Was it the wrinkled sole of Gertrude's foot, or the pattern of triangles on the gravel: the bicycle tyres from the Trelleborg rubber factory whose tracks he used to follow the next day.

He met Gertrude in the courtyard, and they went down to the fjord. On the beams beneath the planks of the jetty were last summer's dried up bird droppings. Bilberries could also be seen, and the shimmering silver scales of bream or roach.

Leaning against the white wooden fence of the jetty weathered by rain and melting water, he remembered himself and Gertrude leaning against the reception desk in a seaside boarding-house on Jutland. Please register here. We give you bathing towels, we don't want you to take the ones in your room to the beach. Yet sand went up with them and trickled in their pyjamas. It was the time when they had begun to see each other again after the summers at the Water Palace. They were excited and a bit anxious that someone might recognize them and wonder. He remembered Gertrude's suntan lotion and her white swimsuit. The walls were thin, unsuitable for those who had nightmares or made love. They sent postcards and put their sweaty palms on the cards so that the biro did not work. One glassy August night they walked for miles along the sand-dunes setting fire to drift wood which had been lying on the sand for a long time.

He did not tell Gertrude. It was a memory without implications that had just appeared to him.

They heard the sound of a car engine, and before they had time to react with astonishment, a man walked across the headland and up the hill. They thought he was on his way to a masked ball, but the home-made pilot's uniform indicated that he was a flying photographer. He showed them a colour photograph which could be enlarged, mounted, and put on the wall. There was the house, the fjord, the rocks, the whole area. They did not buy anything; they had no wish to see the house from above. Gertrude looked for signs of life on the photo. Was she sitting on the jetty? It was desolate, the photograph must have been taken while she was in Africa.

'Just imagine that he came whilst we were here,' JB exclaimed after the photographer had left.

He started to mend the hydrophore. Then he turned on the bathroom taps.

At first the water flow was dark brown, a line of rust stuck around the basin. He looked at the peeling varnish on the lavatory seat, one of the wooden ones left. He ought to do something about it but did not know when. He did not know how things would develop.

In a boy's book which his grandfather, Gustaf Backman, the chemist and inventor, had probably brought there, JB found an explorer's map of the Water Palace. The book was The Black Robinson by Alfred Seguins, and the map drawn by himself a summer long ago with blurred circles and crosses: there was the camping place, the hovel, the wading place, the canoe, the hill where the porters turned, and the rock from where two islands could be seen in the North East. One point had no name to keep it from being identified by deceitful finders of the map. JB could no longer see this logic, as even a secret place marked with a circle was possible to find. It must have shown on the photograph the pilot wanted to sell.

By and by dusk fell, and they saw bonfires lit on the rocks protruding out into the fjord. One fire was so large that they thought it must be a house burning on a cape. The wind carried the smell of fire towards them. The sloe in bloom by the shores looked like stripes of foam.

'I realize I have to accept the so-called normal life,' Gertrude said. 'I'm not superstitious, I'm a realist; I dislike talking about the child at this stage. But if all goes well, Klas will have his share in it now that he knows. I'm looking forward to a life completely without glamour, but in retrospect even our life together was a clean floor, rough and hard-wearing. Sometimes I feel you helped me more when I cried than when you made me laugh.'

'Don't belie our past, even if you want to get rid of it,' JB said.

'Once upon a time I hardly knew Africa existed. And then you deceived me in a way I never thought possible, as . . .'

'As what?'

'As we were different from everybody else. We had special rules. You can do pretty awful things to yourself and others to prove that you're alive.'

'That goes for the two of us.'

'I begin to think there are many of your kind. At least more or less like you. And that opens up the world – though it robs it of meaning. Nothing scares me any more. That makes me frightened.'

Jan was pleased that they could speak to each other after all.

'Did you ever see Amos again?' he asked.

'Yes. He was more suspicious than the first time, he knows there are informers everywhere. Even in that respect we had the same experience. Still, he must have trusted me.'

'He meant a lot to you.'

'He made me feel that we may always be able to do what we want to do.'

They drove back to Stockholm. Jan looked round for the day moon, but like himself it was free from evening duty. He let Gertrude off at Uppland Street: without its sacking the house gleamed with new plaster in white and yellow. She had been invited by Klas to Lidingö Bridge, but had told him that she was not coming. She moved with care, slightly bent back by her weight: the child could arrive any week. She did not want Jan to come up with her.

He stayed in the car studying the headlines of the papers outside the newsagent, and the old sign: 'Advertisements for daily newspapers accepted.' He saw lights turned on upstairs. For a moment he thought he saw every object in the rooms with Gertrude's eyes, being who she was.

Then he went to Nybro Quay. He did not know whether Jenny would be there; she had so many friends. He did not mind waiting for her for a long time.

THE REFLECTION

The memory of Marianne's injured voice haunted Jan like sunburn. He kept talking to her in his mind, explaining and admonishing. He remembered something that had happened at school: he had leant across the space between his desk and the next to see if his friend was doing well in a math test. The teacher had assumed that he was trying to cheat. He had defended himself again and again. The teacher saw it from his angle. Innocent he brought home a letter to A. O. Backman with his first warning.

He dialled Marianne's number. It was a difficult conversation. She started to cry. He felt unhappy but found no words for it. When Marianne calmed down she said:

'I've had a letter from Sten which is so hard to interpret. I wish you'd read it and tell me what to do.'

He mentioned that he had had a letter from Sten as well. They decided to meet for an early lunch that day at the student restaurant in Frescati. They sat in the old farming museum under a lye washed ceiling in Swiss style. They talked through the noise of plates and voices, and looked out over the oaks saved at the edge of the Lilljans Woods.

Sten had written to Marianne: 'I've begun to doubt our situation.' In her loneliness she had misunderstood it. From Sten's letter to JB it was obvious that he doubted certain conditions at the school. Marianne asked to see the letter. She sat silently reading it for a long time. JB remembered Botswana: a boy playing the flute on a bicycle pump with holes in it, and the yellow aloe stalks along the railway to Rhodesia.

In his letter Sten had written that he wanted to concentrate on community development and practical studies; if the students learnt the western culture or not was irrelevant. But he had noticed a pressure on the school to train civil servants.

'About ninety per cent of the food grown in Botswana never passes out into commercial channels. It's eaten by the grower and his family. To give education and welfare to a child costs more than the family earns in cash in a whole lifetime. With half the population under sixteen, and an average life span of forty, there is not much time left for productive work.

Doubt does not mean despair, however. I just think I'm weaker and maybe less sound in judgement since my family left. Therefore I shall try to cut down my time here. I may even be able to return home this autumn. Marianne will naturally continue with her studies.'

'I'm happier than I can say that he's coming back,' Marianne said. 'And I'm happy to feel this happiness. I began to think I no longer needed him.'

She leant across the table, putting her forehead against his hand.

JB thought of the correct, almost stiff, Marianne he had known over the years. Now he knew her. She had assumed outlines which made him discern her in a way he never had when Sten was around.

He explained why he had not wanted to speak about Jenny before and said appealingly:

'You don't regret anything, do you?'

She showed him around the new university building: white corridors divided by gay flags, halls given their identity by fitted carpets in various colours, blinds of golden foil, and the library half-empty as it was one of the last days of the term. It was an anonymous house, with the main entrance almost concealed and not a sign to tell where you were.

JB said the students were no longer passive about the world they lived in. Still, school forced people to stake out a definite course much too soon. Students ought to start early, take a pause when they liked, mingle with people of all ages, and take no other final exam than that of senility and deterioration. Marianne talked about the difficulty of an adult student: combining old experience with new knowledge.

She had to rush off to a lecture, and cuddled him with childish softness.

On his way out to Arlanda he thought of the way bodies keep their memories without asking permission from feelings or reason. In the evening he took Jenny to the cinema. They saw a Truffaut film called Anne and Muriel, but it was sweet and shapeless like a worn lavender pillow. They could hardly stay in their seats from disappointment.

The May night was warm when they came out from the cinema, and they continued down towards Brunn Bay. They missed the road to Haga Palace, as it was concealed by the motorway. The next turning off the highway took them to the barracks of the Royal Engineers, which had recently been deserted. A gate was open, no guards could be seen. They went in under huge elms. 'Dining queue along the wall' a signpost said under the broken windowpanes of the canteen.

In a few nineteenth century houses sergeant majors and administrators had lived and grown beans and roses. The manor, formerly the officers' mess, was empty. On the exercise ground were the first camomiles of the year. The Crown had used these old buildings and saved nature which they could not afford to change. Neither could they afford to take away steam-boilers, rusty gun-carriages and used ammunition.

Down by Brunn Bay: a quay of blast stone, air-raid shelters concealed in the mountainside, and untouched shores. Across the water were the Bergian gardens with their caves, and the dilapidated poet's house which was closed. It could have been a lake many miles from the capital. A grebe flew past the reeds waiting under the surface. The roar of the traffic with its distant notes reminded them of a silence that did not exist.

'The surface water has improved,' Jenny said. 'We don't have the smell of rotten eggs when the ice breaks up. We'll soon be able to swim here.' He looked at her when she looked out over the shores, and again he knew that he would recognize her back all over Stockholm. He had often been wrong and about to embrace someone who was not her. Maybe that would have brought him onto contact with women who were like her. Her face got its special identity only when one came within a radius of twenty metres, with normal sight.

'What are you thinking of?' she said.

'Of all the meetings that never happen, of all human partnerships that don't. How we try to find reason in coincidence, and intention in chance.'

'Most people I know live at half speed,' Jenny said. 'I can understand drugs; waking the appetite for life. What makes you fall in love with life? A biological rhythm in harmony with the seasons – like the orchestra finding their melody after having tuned the instruments? Eyes complying.'

They stood in front of each other. They were rather tall. Like telephone poles, unconnected. But speech reached them. They were senses and words: taking and speaking, handling and conversing.

At the time when he met Jenny life had been only routine. He had lived with his arms crossed. From now on he wanted to create his own situations.

A guard with an Alsatian dog on a short leash appeared and asked them to leave. They then went down to Ling's grave outside the gates: his angular tombstone stood in shadow on a little hill, 1776 – 1839, and until recent years his relations had been buried under low grave-stones around him. Oaks and elms shaded them.

They sat down on a slab of stone and could still see the water of Brunn Bay between the dark tree trunks. Jenny said she wanted to tell him about something nasty that had happened to her one night in London.

She had been reading in bed until late. Early the next morning she had to attend a meeting. Stencilled papers were piled up on her desk. She did not have to turn out the lamp next to her on the floor – the light turned itself out. She sat up, leant on her elbow, and peeped out: the whole area was dark. A power cut or a broken electricity line. Then she fell asleep and thought for a long time she was dreaming. It is common in dreams to see a door handle move up and down and to feel that your voice refuses to cry out with authority: 'Who's there?' Only a pathetic squeak came out, and that woke her up properly. The handle wagged up and down. She thought she heard someone breathing outside.

'This someone,' Jenny continued, 'must have broken down the front door, where there was an entry phone, picked the lock of the heavy iron attic door, and then miraculously managed the two patent locks to my flat.'

When she realized her outcry had not reached the person, she decided to lie down and watch the whole thing. Her heart pounded so hard it hurt all the way to her finger tips. It seldom does in dreams.

'Why didn't you call the police?' Jan said sternly.

'Impossible. The telephone was in that very passage, between the bathroom and the kitchenette where this somebody was playing around with my handle.'

A girl in a mini skirt entered the room. Jenny saw her round knees gleaming of nylon in the grey light. She turned on a torch and pointed it directly at Jenny's desk. Then she went straight up to it, and started to tear the papers methodically into two pieces. She only took as many as she could manage : ten or twelve sheets at a time. When she had gone through the whole pile she looked to the side and met Jenny's gaze. She screamed and sank down on the floor in tears. Jenny put the torch on the desk. She asked the girl her name. But she just kept crying.

'At first I thought she was a drug addict and turned on,' Jenny said. 'It wasn't long ago that I tried to help a woman of my own age, well-groomed and well-dressed, in a bright red suit, sitting like a babbling fool on the pavement at twelve o'clock at night. But this girl then started a stuttering explanation, and I immediately heard that she was under the influence of uncontrollable emotions rather than alcohol and drugs.

She'd been a girl-friend of the young architect who owned the flat. He in turn was a friend of John's, which is why I was able to borrow it. He had left in such a hurry that he'd forgotten to ask for his key back from her. He'd forgotten other things too : for example to tell the girl that he enjoyed making love to her occasionally, but didn't love her and didn't consider himself responsible for her. She had been overcome by powerless despair and hate which directed itself alternately against herself and him.

'If we hadn't been so happy together,' she moaned several

times in the middle of her tears. 'He said we were so happy together.' That apparently was her criterion. Something between their bodies had worked well. But he had deceived the biological promise that she had felt in every embrace, and left as if she was nothing but a worrisome burden. 'We talked all through the night. When the sun came in, the light unexpectedly came on. I made her lie down on top of my bed. Then I had to leave.'

'You get involved in all sorts of things,' JB said worriedly. 'What happened next?'

'I was all right,' Jenny said. 'No, I wasn't; but I wasn't like her. That's beyond comparison. She disliked herself so intensely. This young man was the measure of her self-esteem. She had been judged: of no value. She was still there when I came back. She had slept for the first time in two months. I was furious when I heard about it. Maybe not with him, but with the situation: that even a superficial emotional involvement can cause such catastrophes when it's over.

For all over the world people are crying, being taken into mental hospitals or committing suicide, or having year-long depressions for the same reason: the love they trusted doesn't hold. Then not only the house of love falls down, but all they have, all they wear. Emptiness devours them, but without annihilating them. In the intercession they wriggle in a confined pain. The worst part of it being the sensible thought that they ought to be able to snap out of it with one single decisive step. But they can't. Something inside them has joined the side of the enemy and stops them; well, almost enjoys the pain.'

'Did you ever met her again?' JB asked.

'I phoned her a couple of times. She seemed embarrassed. Somehow I think the burglary in my flat was a kind of climax. She sounded calmer and more collected. She had gone to work for the first time in seven weeks. They didn't want to re-employ her there. I told her to contact the personnel department. It was a large car insurance company. The next time I phoned she said she'd been given her job back. She was pathetically grateful. She said she had nobody to talk to. In her circles these things weren't taken seriously, she said. Maybe more of them do than you think, I said. It wasn't long before the burglary that I had scattered the pieces of your photo in the Thames and was about to jump into it myself – yes, just to get them all together again. But I didn't want to tell her that.'

A cool night wind blew across Brunn Bay. The water shivered. They moved closer to each other.

'We've said many times that we're all right without each other,' Jan said. 'Now we can say that we're all right with each other. I read that eighty per cent of the prisoners returning from the Second World War got divorced. Eternal love could not survive a separation of three or five years. They had expected too much.'

'They had grown away from each other,' Jenny stated. 'They had been worried and hurt in different ways. Not everybody can use words as a binding agent. Too much was untold, and could never be reconstructed.'

'When I see people clinging to each other as if they were in distress, I tell myself their very closeness makes them hide something. Something they dare not face. But others say : look how brave they are to give everything.'

'I have practised both denial and denying myself,' Jenny said.

'I never was very good at it.'

'No, you were happier and kinder when you were immoral.'

'Now I'd like to practise intimacy. Jan, I need you so immensely.'

'Although you manage without me?'

'Of course. But I didn't say so.'

'I'm all right without most things too. I may be nearer a freezing-point than you. I sit there as a hibernating lizard waiting for the sunlight to touch the stone, too stiff with cold to look for warmth myself.'

'Then I'll come and breath on you,' Jenny said. 'I want you to be always quick and curious and playing with your tongue.'

He thought she was more beautiful than when he had met her at Chapman's and had his first dinner with her. She was serious in a new way, which made her happier than before. She also tried to explain to him, in other words, that she had found firm ground under her feet, and that every day was a newly discovered security.

'That's how I've been feeling all along,' JB said. 'You try to stake out the limits of your love as precisely as a surveyor. It can give so much, no more. It's like trying to plant an avenue in a forest.'

'I've always had a careful nature,' Jenny said. 'I laid a trail of crumbs to make sure I'd find my way out of the forest at the slightest danger. But the birds ate them. Now I'm at home in the wilderness, though I know it's very dangerous.'

'I ate the crumbs,' Jan said. 'I thought you'd left them there for me to eat.'

The maples were in blossom over the unenclosed grave-mound. Behind them in the trees were ringdoves talking in different words. A bat dived towards Jenny's white sweater.

Jan thought he was in a coalescence of variable conditions where no components were alien to each other. He spied into her face to see an explanation, but her smile was a reflection.

Brunn Bay was as still as a huge wash-tub. The night was still bright.

BROTHER AND SISTER IN THE FOREST

Jan Backman was reading The Radetsky March to avoid Jenny's threat to read it out loud. For once the radio was on while Jenny mended a tear in her coat lining. Among the news headlines he picked up phrases like devastating blaze, old house in the archipelago burnt down, Värmdö, a family called Backman. Dialling Gertrude's number, he thought of the Water Palace no longer existing. Nor was there a family called Backman, but that changed nothing. His sister cried inconsolably. She had tried to phone him before, but he had not been there. The police had phoned Uppland Street and asked to speak to him, as there was to be an inquiry. JB could not visualize the Water Palace in flames. He saw the house burning one early morning in Vänersborg, and the bookseller who wanted to sell damaged jigsaw puzzles.

'Do you want to go out there?' he asked.

'Why? There's nothing to be seen,' Gertrude replied listlessly.

He did not feel like going there himself. Apparently nothing had been saved, neither Robin Jouet's Journey and Adventures in The Brazilian Jungle nor the diary of Agnes Cecilia Backman, their grandmother. The volunteer fire brigade from Värmdö had been there and the old coastguard's boat. But they had been delayed; the Water Palace was hard to get at, situated on the headland, jutting out into the water like a little frequented ferry-station.

'How awful,' Jenny said. 'You've lost a large piece of your childhood. So many things that can never be recorded again.'

'You may grow up when your childhood passes,' JB said. Jenny held him tight; she seemed sadder than he was.

'It's too late now,' she said. 'I can't see you as a child, the sweet and silly photographs, toys and boys' books . . .'

'You'll have to be satisfied with the man I've grown into,' JB said.

They remained sitting in the twilight, while JB told her about the trips on the steamer, about his father and Mrs Tapper, episodes and people associated with the Water Palace – forgotten he thought, but they now reasserted themselves after losing their home.

The next afternoon he phoned Gertrude from Arlanda.

'How are you feeling? Are you upset?'

'I'm alarmingly calm these days,' Gertrude replied.

They agreed to go to the Water Palace. He phoned Jenny to ask her if she wanted to join them. He had a feeling of fear that he could not get rid of. But Jenny said Gertrude needed him. So brother and sister set out for a house that was no more.

'I'm glad I didn't have to go alone,' Gertrude said in the car. 'I feel so sentimental sometimes. Perhaps it's because of the baby. Last night I started to look for the key to the Water Palace. It was some time before I remembered I won't need it any more.'

'I lent it to Marianne,' Jan said. 'In case she wanted to go there with the children.'

'Didn't she want you to go along?'

'I couldn't.'

'Do you think she's been there recently?'

'In that case she would have said so.'

'Marianne is not a liberated woman,' Gertrude said 'I know you've been seeing her quite a lot. I wonder if she got involved

306

with you against her will. That could have given her a desire for revenge.'

'I'm surprised to hear you imply that Marianne set fire to the house. We know nothing about the cause of the fire.'

'People behave rationally only as long as everything goes more or less according to plan,' Gertrude said. 'When the pattern is disturbed other characteristics appear which have been concealed within them.'

The road looked the same. The path as well, through the bracken which was beginning to flourish, the green clusters of midsummer flowers, the rocks with saxifrage and wild-cherry gleaming like a glade in the fir forest. They were suddenly at the old parking place which they had driven to with the car loaded with heavy bags of provisions. There was a square the size of a car where the grass was darker and shorter. Some young rowans had been broken by the rampaging of firemen; and an old gatepost which had lost its gate a long time ago had been reduced to a stump.

They averted their eyes and saw a heron fly right over their garden and onto the forest with loud squawks: a trumpet in the sky.

'Did you see that? How extraordinary.'

Then they had to face the melodramatic sight, well-known from newspapers and news-reels: the sooty chimney, breast beams as black and bulbous as burnt rusks, some saturated mattresses, and a pile of furniture under a temporary tarpaulin. Of the room overlooking the fjord only a solitary window frame remained; through its glassless hole the water glittered happily unaware of the happenings on the shore. It was like facing a deathbed: something simple, yet inconceivable. New days produced by the night, but never the same. Impossible to take a step back. Impossible to make a new distribution. The key had no lock, the door no frame.

Gertrude picked up some iron rims. They belonged to a bucket they used to plant blue flowers in. The red maple tree looked withered. It had pounded its top branches against their bedroom window which had once been their father's.

'We shall have to let Adolf Oscar know,' JB said.

'Yes, he ought to know. But it probably won't affect him much.'

To JB too the Water Palace was in many ways consumed. All

that remained of the Sunday room of bygone summers was the low angular foundation walls with puddles of water inside them. They had arrived at the cooled site of the fire.

'Do you think the roots of these scorched plants are alive?' he asked. The wild vine, the comfrey, the honey-suckle, the delicate pale clematis next to the former back entrance: the juices might be drained from them, or they might be drowned from too much brackish water. They would not know for a long time.

Only a few pieces of furniture had been salvaged. Lamp stands, the electric stove and the frying-pans had survived in a soiled flaking condition. But they looked dead, and JB found them disgusting. They were the wreckage of the fire. Photographs, books, memos, old tax forms were obliterated, or lay like a paste under charred panelling with oily paint bubbles. He did not mourn them. The necessary data on citizens were no longer looked after by the individual himself, but stored in huge computer centres which were fireproof.

The cuckoo was heard in the East. The white tiled stove upstairs clung to the chimney-breast. The flag-pole lay deserted, glazed by the fire-engines. The water from the hoses had gathered in puddles and crevices.

JB could not help poking in the collapsed remains. His forehead became sooty as he wiped the sweat off his scalp. He hardly felt sad. So much of life is finished before it begins, he thought. You're embedded in it: a house, the looks of the people near you, concerns and habits. It's called security. The price you pay for it is consideration, time and adjustment. Then you look around deciding to make other places your home. He had long imagined that remarkable experiences befell other people and not him – matters were matched by a willingness to be ruthless and daring in larger contexts, if he only had a reason for it.

He found little in the rubble. Not much had survived the ordeal of the fire: a pair of plimsolls worn like slippery car tyres; something which had to be the yellow bread-bin from his childhood. He was surprised. He had seen fire as an old-fashioned, almost obsolete element.

'We got the Water Palace for nothing,' Gertrude said. 'We didn't have to work for it.'

'It disappeared just as it was to get an heir,' JB said.

'We ought to take the compensation in cash and share it,' Gertrude said.

'Which of us would want to build another house? We can sell the land any time.'

A stray cat came out of the currant bushes, and stalked round the site like a little inspector. They had nothing to give it.

'Perhaps he entered the house, and established a short-circuit,' JB said.

The cat rubbed silently against his legs, refusing to give evidence.

'What's saved may be only what Bengt and Monica dug down. If that was anything at all.'

Looking away from the site of the fire, he thought the Water Palace was still there, a hair's breadth from vision, and he turned his head a little bit further away. There was nothing in focus, but on the periphery his imagination grew.

'I'm sorry about the tapestry,' he said. 'It was expensive as well.' A lady had been astride a lion on their French tapestry. 'We'll soon be out of the forest', the motto said. Out on the wide open fields, locked out of the green landscape, lost in the unwoven. You could choose what you liked. They had often looked at it, and it changed its appearance according to the light – sometimes an Arcadian forest gathering oxygen in its lungs, sometimes brushwood with treacherously moving stems.

'We've got what we've got,' Gertrude said, turning her back on the devastation. He turned her round, put his arms around her, and they were quite still, just watching. Gertrude gave a quick sob.

'I've seen it and now it's over. I'm glad you brought me here today. I think that was the best remedy for my sadness. I never realized one has to forget and move on. I think one should try to go straight on. If I hadn't seen this, the image of how it might have looked would have haunted me.'

'What you imagine is often much worse than what you live through.'

They heard the whirr of gnats. A motor-boat sounded like a large insect. Pace enveloped them, life felt stripped, and Jan had a feeling of relief which he wanted to share with his sister.

'Come on,' he said. 'Let's go down to the water. The shore is still there and the waves.'

He thought her face was bonier than before, the outline tauter. She was tanned with some freckles at the bridge of her nose which he had not seen there before. He thought she was one of those who get thin and vital in their old age.

They left fresh foot-prints on the tabby sand. It squelched under their soles. They cautiously tried the sunbathing rock, but it was already cool; its coolness penetrated their clothes. Gertrude rested for a moment by his side, her head on his arm. A feeling of reconciliation spread its rings, extending the present.

The still coolness of the spring evening made everything natural and relaxed between them. He was happy that he was no longer afraid of her. She was Gertrude. She was his sister. She was the woman he had left for another. Yet there was warmth between them. It raised an invisible tent over them, keeping the dew away.

But the cold worried Gertrude. She wanted to continue round the boundary of the property. They were soon in the forest and no longer heard the waves and ships. The evening light filtered through the venetian blinds of the pine branches. The fog drifted over a meadow occupied by young aspens. The wild orchids, the brother and sister orchids of the May meadows, gleamed in soft purple and white on the threshold of an overgrown field.

His yearning for his half-sister moved on familiar paths. To prove to her that the foundations remained, although the house had burnt down, he wanted to be near her. However, he remembered her arrogance in Botswana, and how easily she believed that Jenny was but a bad dream. 'I'm almost happy,' she said then. 'I never thought I'd ever be happy again. Caress me a little Jan. I feel it wouldn't be wrong. We're not taking anything from anyone.'

By that she wanted to say that she was not worried about Jenny or the baby which was almost fully grown inside her. When he took her nipple between his thumb and forefinger, milk oozed out. He tasted it gently with the tip of his tongue and rubbed the drops like oil into the skin of her high taut stomach.

Gertrude lay on a bed of their clothes. The blackbird sang, unsure of whether the sun was going up or down. The moon was in position early: the clouds blew past it – like cannon smoke in the olden days. Jan dipped himself carefully in her.

'Gertrude,' he said.

Her face beamed at him. Deeper down the enchantment showed and the seduction at their meeting in the attic, like a treasure waiting to be found by someone else.

'Come Jan,' she said. 'I'm not afraid.'

He was in her opening when he came. He did not recognize the landscape of her body, and was anxious not to push the baby.

'Just some Christening water on its head,' he said, helping her to get her clothes on. 'Hurry up! None of you must get cold.'

They walked hand in hand along the old mushroom paths. Their bodies cooled off.

'Look, the stone altar,' Gertrude cried.

It lay brooding and dark in a dewy meadow. Two boulders raised up next to each other, less than a yard apart, perhaps split by lightning, with the insides free of moss, as pale as palms. A fallen fir tree embedded it with its branches. Lichens and bracken could not conceal that the place was holy. JB thought he glimpsed something between the stones: a pair of gleaming eyes, or shivering whiskers. Then the vision was gone. As they came closer they saw the tracks of a badger or fox.

'Our cult place has become an ordinary residence,' Gertrude said excitedly. 'I shall think of the cubs being born here in the stony darkness when I'm in the maternity hospital.'

She was full of confidence. She had never worried about the labour.

'I'm thirty-nine and fairly childish,' she said. 'I think the body can be childish too, in a good way, I mean soft and supple. And I believe it will be a boy. From the way it kicks. Men need to move about more.'

'The chances of a boy are greater,' Jan said. 'But the mortality of boys is higher and their life span shorter, regardless of the facts that some of them kill each other. They are badly equipped.'

'I'm sure it will be all right. This child had a funny start, but now it's had your blessing, and everything will be all right.'

She laughed and stroked his shoulders hastily. JB looked

pryingly into his sister's face: did she interpret this evening's embrace in a different way from him?

Then she said:

'I like you and Jenny better now. I don't feel afraid of meeting you.'

A little while later she was the one to suggest that they go back. It was getting dark as they drove towards Stockholm. Charles's Wain was emerging from one of the Milky Way ditches. The sky was full of reflex tapes; distant wanderers on the wrong side of the road.

'You needn't worry,' she said as he dropped her off at Uppland Street. 'You've relieved me of a burden.'

When JB got home, Jenny was in her usual armchair. She seldom ran out to greet him. She lifted her face and looked him straight in the eye. He stood still, smiling down at her.

'She's happier now,' he said.

'That's fine,' Jenny replied, touching his hand slightly.

When he did not move, she asked him what was the matter.

'It was all very strange,' he said. 'Not what I had imagined, and maybe not what you think. Would you like to hear about it?'

'Is it serious? Does it affect us in any way?'

'No,' Jan said quickly. 'Nothing affects us.'

'All right,' Jenny said with a laugh. 'In that case we'll talk about it some other time. I've got a lot to do.'

But he still lingered next to her, and she said inquiringly:
'Jan?'

'I just want to stand here watching you for a while,' he said. 'I'm so immensely glad that you exist.'

THE ARRIVAL

At the end of May Gertrude gave birth to a boy at the Central Maternity Hospital in Lilljans Woods. She named him Emile Bamuto Backman – Emile because she liked the name, and Bamuto to keep the promise to her friend, the South

African guerilla man. Bamuto meant: he who came after the disasters.

On arrival, Emile Bamuto Backman was fifty centimetres long and weighed three kilos and one hundred grammes. The labour was no more difficult than normal and took place between six and twelve p.m.

'If I had paused two minutes longer, he'd have had a different birthday,' Gertrude said later.

It was Lotte who rang JB that night to tell him that everything had gone well. He had not been able to sleep after he had heard that Gertrude had gone to the hospital. He and Jenny went for a drive. Jenny asked him to stop and ran out to break off a branch of sloe illegally in the park by the mouth of the canal.

'Now I've shed some blood for him too,' she said, showing the scratch from a thorn.

The following morning, on his way to Arlanda, JB went up to see Gertrude and Emile, who was just given his first drops of sugared water from a bottle. The baby lay huddled like a tree-frog in a towel. His eyebrows were faint like faded pencil lines, the irises dark smoky blue with speckles of mica. He had an adult and calm contemplative look on his face. JB thought he recognized Adolf Oscar's straight determined nose; from a distance in space and feeling he cast his shadow over the baby's profile.

Too new to be allowed even milk, Emile fell asleep with a slight grunt. He lowered his heavy eyelids having had his need satisfied, perhaps happy to be alive. He slept, and future experience was within him waiting to be released. There was explosive power in the tranquil body; he seemed older than them.

Gertrude shared the room with two other women whose babies were five days old and looked already robust and grown-up beside the new-born. 'It was more painful than I had imagined,' Gertrude said. 'And yet mine was considered easy.'

As soon as she had heard the midwife say that it was a boy, she had thought: at least he won't have to go through this.

She told JB that only close relations were allowed to be present during the labour. Klas could have come, had she demanded it. But Lotte who had had two children and knew a lot about relaxation techniques had not been allowed in. The mother could not decide.

JB stood by Gertrude's window on the fifth floor looking out over the Lilljans Woods, the old fort used by the cavalry of the staff company, the gasometer and the tall chimneys. He had passed his first evening here with Jenny after they had seen Les Enfants Du Paradis at the Bostock. He had been born in this house himself like hundreds of thousands of others. It was a baby manufacturing factory, worn and yellow plastered. He remembered his heart beating with excitement when he came back to Stockholm after the summer vacation, or just arrived on the train and saw the skyline of the city. Now the city had become a noisy slum where the cars drew pedestrians underground. It was strange to think of all the things that had been sacrificed: recognition, continuity, human standards slaughtered in the long nights of bureaucracy.

Perhaps Emile would grow up in this city which was still habitable in places, especially in the summer. But he might as well choose different places of abode. Jan's and Gertrude's parents had had a more static concept of their children's life: from the Maternity Hospital to the Northern Cemetery past the proper areas of the city. Since then the world had shrunk and the domicile been extended. JB tried to imagine Emile in Botswana at the turn of the next century, or in a women's commune in West Berlin where his Swedish accent would correspond to the broken Swedish of the refugee children in Jan's schools in the Forties.

Emile Bamuto woke up. He looked around him, in no way revealing what he saw – nothing, perhaps. Eventually a face emerged from the wall, or the wall from the house, or the house from the world. Something assumed a shape to distinguish it from other things – like a green butterfly taking off from a green leaf. Then the eyes started to work and wonder at the same time. For a long time to come Emile would regard the world as an annex to himself. He would sometimes leave the main building in order to inspect the wings.

'I'll let him turn over every stone and every cushion on the couch,' Gertrude said. 'Carry what is fragile, handle what is dangerous. He'll learn to be careful only by feeling and trying for himself.'

'Good,' JB said. 'Make him familiar with the world, and he'll feel at home even when he's grown out of his home.'

He felt like telling Emile about the air, the water and the earth. Above all about the air which carried the green glow of the acacias, let bats fly, and got the waves to write codes on the water's blackboard. The air was the landlord of light, carried it and kept it from falling between walls of fog into the dark well of winter.

Jan saw Emile Bamuto clenching his fists in a grip they hardly suspected. He sounded like a little starling. In the middle of other people's time he had found his own.

In the reception JB met Klas Lundin who was already tiptoeing. He had spent the night at Uppland Street looking after Lotte's daughter, and was furious that Lotte had not been allowed in during the labour. He had some flowers in his hand and did not give himself time for many words.

In the woods the bird-cherry tree was in blossom. On a shady pile of stones at the back of the hospital there were rows of brown buckler still low, with brown spore-cases on the leaves : they belonged to Gertrude's ferns. A good season and a difficult year to be born into. A golden era for domesday prophets and spiritual healers, as people were worried by the cruelty and vulgarity of an abundant society behaving wastefully and greedily rather than economically and generously.

Here and there in the world the war of the rich raged against the poor, and the war of the poor against their own people. But Sweden's shores were untouched by everything except summer houses, waste oil, power stations and pulp factories. The Baltic was dying. Gentlemen from the Town Planning Office had in mind a motorway through Lilljans Woods past the Ugglevik spring, but it might never materialize. The lack of ready money temporarily fended off both evil and great deeds. Powerlessness was the ashamed and unfamiliar expression on the face of power.

The politicians had promised the citizens that they would dwell with them in paradise. Expectations were thus raised high, but however high the standard of living became, the differences in level remained. To aim for expansion rather than distribution was to ignore the fact that the surface of the earth remained the same.

'Hate capitalism, love man', was written in chalk on the

fence round a sportsground. Step into the lives of others, Emile, Jan Backman thought, identify with them, but don't believe that anyone can carry you on his shoulders through life. Somebody may lift you to a vantage point and then drop you again in the mire. Try to make considerations on the basis of what you know, but don't use the apology that you know too little. Distrust whoever says that no sacrifice is in vain. There is no ultimate explanation and no inner formula between which you can hang your hammock.

Jan visited Gertrude twice more. That way he was able to see Lotte again. He liked her and understood how she had grown so close to Gertrude.

Gertrude showed him the plastic tag with the baby's birth code tied round her wrist. She and Emile had been given one each the moment he appeared.

She did not have to wear it any more, but did not want to part from it.

'I keep pulling up my sleeve to look at it,' she said. 'I believe it's my watch.'

THE INN

One evening Klas Lundin telephoned to invite Jenny and Jan to his house the following Friday night. Gertrude is coming as well, he said, and Emile Bamuto of course, and Marianne. It will be a party for Emile, to introduce him to his family, Klas added excitedly.

JB accepted the invitation without asking Jenny. Klas knew how to arrange parties.

'It will be strange to sit there watching you,' Jenny said.

'But you will come, won't you?' Jan said appealingly.

She was silent.

'Yes, of course I will,' she said, making up her mind. 'We're civilized human beings.'

Then they had other things to think about. A potato in the oven exploded with a bang. Opening the oven door they found fine particles of starch on the baking trays and inner walls. It looked like hoar frost in the heat. They sprinkled rough salt on the others. The chives were cut directly from the pot. Jenny got some beer and herrings from the fridge.

They heard whistles from the quay below, as a Dutch liner got ready to cast anchor. The summer tourists were arriving in the city.

'We could go to Amsterdam,' JB said.

'We can do many things. We have to be very selective.'

They thought that the world with all its unseen things was open to them. They could repeat their happiness in many countries. The dream machine stopped there, and they were hesitant.

'Frankly,' Jenny said, 'I wanted to be boring and dutiful, and spend all July and August in London.'

'You must do what you like regardless of me.'

'I don't want to be parted from you either,' Jenny said.

'In that case I'll come with you whatever you decide to do,' Jan suggested.

'Don't be too hasty. I can work this summer at the new Department of The Environment in London. There is some kind of exchange scheme. I feel both tempted and hesitant. I'd be there as an expert of environmental protection, not as a Swedish civil servant. My loyalty is for the greenery, not for the blue and yellow.'

'Blue and yellow makes green,' JB said, 'but unfortunately only on palettes.'

'That's how my egotistical summer looks. You won't enjoy London in the heat of the summer.'

'You want to be in London and I want to be with you. I'll take my holiday and some days that are due to me for overtime.'

'Oh, Jan, it's almost too good. We could stay in the attic . . .'

'I'll have dinner ready when you come home from work. If you need a chauffeur or a gravel counter I'll be at your service.'

'It will be a strange summer for you.'

'It will be the first time for ten years that I won't go to the Water Palace. Sometimes I grieve over the fact that you and I didn't spend any summer days there alone.'

'The house wanted to be alone with its memories of you and

Gertrude,' Jenny said. 'It withdrew into oblivion when the changes were too great.'

'It wasn't protected by its name either. Chateau d'eau, the French name for a watertank, a combatant of fire.'

Thus they decided about the summer, the first they were free to meet as they liked.

On the day that they were invited to Klas's, Jenny telephoned Arlanda to say that she was going to see Gertrude. She wanted to see the baby calmly and peacefully before the party.

'There's no point in you coming with me,' she said. 'I'm pleased that Gertrude wants to receive me. I'd like to talk to her alone.'

Hanging up, Jan felt like a baffled outsider. The postboy brought a pile of official letters to his desk. In the middle of the brown official pile with few stamps but many franking marks, a post-card gleamed. He was so surprised at the picture that it took him some time to find out who had sent it.

A melancholic caricature of the burnt tapestry at the Water Palace met his gaze. A girl in a nightgown half-asleep rode on an old shaggy wolf. The animal could have been taken from the collection in Vänersborg. So could its companion, a mongrel dog exhausted by chasing rabbits in the sparse Finnish pine forests. Hugo Sieberg 1895, it said at the bottom right-hand corner of the painting. Turning the card over he read Christina in large curly letters.

She was on holiday in Finland with her fiancé. Tidily written lines told him about the Saima Canal, the mosquitoes and the cloudberry liqueur. She wrote that her mother had often talked about him, and that they all ought to see each other again soon. 'Your girl-friend as well', she added.

He stuck the card to the wall by the window with cellotape. The lion which was maybe a wolf, or a sick musk-ox, stubbornly strode towards him with his sleeping white lady. 'We'll soon be out of the forest,' JB said to himself half-aloud.

'What are you saying?' asked the meteorologist who habitually sneaked around without a sound. 'And what is that moth-eaten monster on your wall?'

'Can't you see it's a lion with a lady on its back? It's an old mythological picture. It's got a motto which says: We'll soon be out of the forest.'

318

'I can't see a motto,' said Eklund sullenly. 'The animal appears to be an unidentified trotting creature.'

'I've had a post-card from Christina,' Jan said insulted.

'So have I. One with an aeroplane on. What a joke.'

He must tell Gertrude about the post-card, he thought. He was happy about Christina's consideration. He would soon show Jenny the old flat in Bonde Street, and have new household tricks demonstrated by the jolly fiancé.

When he came home time suddenly passed slowly. Jenny did not come back. He looked for her out of the window, and then concentrated on a pile of unread daily papers. At seven o'clock the telephone rang.

'Time passed so quickly while we were talking,' Jenny said. 'We're going there directly in my car. Go down to the street, and we'll pick you up.'

Therefore he had to travel in the back seat with Emile Bamuto on his lap. A bag with nappies and changes of clothes was next to Jenny in the front. Gertrude was at his side. His eyes met Jenny's in the rear mirror. They were full of questions and indications he could not interpret. He smiled at her and looked at the boy.

'It's the smallest baby I've ever held in my arms,' he said.

His eyes met two bluish-black ones that seemed bottomless. Sometimes they were fixed on him, not on his eyes but on his nose or cheeks. He touched his face to wipe off a mosquito or fly. The child kept taking in his gestures inch by inch. When he gave him his forefinger, Emile Bamuto grabbed it hard.

'You can pull him up until he hangs in the air,' Gertrude said. 'They have terribly strong hands.'

JB did not feel like experimenting. He solemnly kept his fingers still. Two lives involved in each other.

'I didn't know it was so much from the beginning,' Gertrude said. 'We can talk quite well to each other. He understands everything. He smiles a little and rubs his nose. That's when he's thinking. I must sound terribly childish.'

'He likes music,' she went on. 'I bought a tape recorder to tape reports and impressions for Lotte. Now I only use it for playing string quartets. He prefers Mozart.'

Both Jenny and JB laughed out loud at that. And Gertrude joined them.

'Klas plays to him too,' she defended herself.

'I didn't know Klas could play an instrument,' JB said.

'As a student he was a jazz musician. He has tuned an old square piano on the veranda and moved it further into the house. It needs an even temperature.'

They turned off into Klas's newly raked court-yard named The Inn, because the Lidingö Bridge Inn was his closest neighbour. His house was a summer house built in the 1890s. Across the water the sun was reflected in the windows of the Lidingö tower blocks. The factory smoke was dark when the air was warm, but higher up in the sky a couple of clouds were splashed like milk.

Klas and Marianne were standing on the steps. Klas was wearing an open Indian shirt in blue and green. He looked happier and more carefree than before. He boasted about being slim and tanned.

'Children harden,' he said. 'Emile is better than squash.'

'You can't do much with the poor little thing,' Marianne said. 'If my memory is right he sleeps most of the time.'

'You can't imagine what he wants,' Klas said. 'Walks in the pram. Little things that have to be chased in boutiques and special shops. Did you know that nappies are half the price in the large packs? That there are fifteen different kinds of ointments for the bottom? That he prefers blue teats to yellow ones?'

They laughed at his eagerness until Emile Bamuto woke up and started to cry. Klas took him away from Jan and shook him carefully.

'My little bumble-bee,' he said. 'Are you humming?'

The strong dark voice cut off the screams. Emile burped. They stood around watching him – a very small hub in the adults' wheel.

'I wonder where Martin is hiding, I promised him some champagne,' Marianne said, thus informing them that there were other children in the world.

They walked around looking at the viola cornuta and doronicum, at the Turk's caps stretching their clubs high, and the half-open lilac in dark violet and greenish-white. Suddenly Martin appeared at lethal speed on an old bicycle. He was wearing faded jeans and a slouch-hat which he refused to be parted from. He swayed in between them, and at the last moment was prevented from giving Emile Bamuto a push in his

PVC cradle which Klas was swinging to and fro in his hands.

The heat was dense between the few ash-trees. Tadpoles whirled in the ditch water. Ribs of cirrus clouds rose above the horizon like a fence against the night. The summer had become resident.

'What an unusually early summer,' Klas said. 'I think we're approaching a continental climate.'

'There are a few places in Sweden that still have a continental climate,' Gertrude said. 'Feather-grass from the Bronze Age steppes, troll strawberries in the shadow of barrows . . .'

Klas showed Martin a gear lever from the number seven tram which had run between Vanadis Square and Oakhill. He had found it one night, and though it had been used in the mid-Sixties, it was evidence of an era as distant as that of the three-masted sailing ships.

It was Friday night. On the fairway old-fashioned motor-boats passed with cabins dark in the dusk, and sailing boats with navy blue awnings; the gulls shunned shades of blue. They heard the sound of crashing glasses, as somebody at the inn dropped a tray.

'That reminds me of the champagne!' Klas shouted.

He left Emile on the grass, and disappeared into the house. Soon he was standing by the garden table easing off the first cork. It exploded into the chestnut tree, sending down a shower of white blossom like the feathers from a shot gull.

Martin gaped in admiration. A mood of magic and ease took them in. Emile had a drop of wine from Gertrude's little finger. Laughter welled up within him, and burst from his lips.

'The pram's in the boot,' Jenny said remembering.

While the others went in to help Klas with the meal, although he assured them it was all ready, Jenny took a lonely walk with Emile Bamuto in the pram.

Klas had arranged branches of bird-cherry in one vase and sloe in another. Buttercups and veronica on the table; simple white plates on a rough linen cloth. A seafood salad gleamed pink and yellow with shrimps, mussels and eggs. Celery stalks crunched like the crust on the snow. On the veranda there was a cane table with a carafe of lemonade and a basket of ginger-bread. They had a bumpy, uneven texture. Country wine was poured from moist ceramic jugs into thick tumblers. Klas's face was red, and his thick nicotine-stained fingers moved

L
321

rapidly among the dishes. Marianne pinched a withered leaf off the geranium in the window, saying:

'You've arranged it all so beautifully.'

'It's for Emile. It's for Emile.' Klas repeated.

'But we're here as well,' Marianne complained.

'You're all my children,' Klas promised.

His bear-hugging gesture made the wrought-iron chandelier, which had just been lit, swing. Candle wax splashed over the sea green carpet, and the host disappeared into the kitchen, hissing like a rocket.

Jenny entered when the others were ready to sit down at the table. JB felt excited at seeing her, and fell into a singular mood. Abyss and summer meadow were joined together.

'Emile is asleep outside,' Jenny said.

'Did you remember the pram's brake and the mosquito net?' Gertrude asked.

'I put on the brake, but I forgot the mosquito net.' Gertrude got up and went out. She soon returned and reported that the object of the ceremony was well under his white veil.

'In the old days parents were afraid to boast about their children,' Klas said. 'It was not considered the done thing. Yet they exaggerated to the other extreme and were critical, narrow-minded; worse than others around them.'

'The fear of the gods' revenge, of hubris,' Jenny said. 'At least you haven't got that.'

'He has taught me much already,' Klas said. 'And besides, he's so beautiful.'

Then Jenny told them that she had been attacked during her walk by an elderly lady who liked children. She had looked at the pink elephant next to Emile and asked:

'How old is she?'

When Jenny insisted that the baby was a boy, the lady said angrily:

'Of course it's a girl. She's got a pink teddy bear.'

'It's an elephant,' Jenny said.

'Well I suppose you know what you've got. Have you got any milk?'

'Not a drop,' Jenny had complained.

'Well in that case I'm glad it was one of the bad kind,' the lady stated.

'It's a boy, he has milk every day, I'm not his mother, and

there's no difference between boys and girls,' Jenny had said in rapid succession. This was too much for the lady who had walked off, muttering and shaking her head :

'Doesn't know the difference between boys and girls, and denies that she's the baby's mother. What's to become of the world?'

'I'll introduce them to each other properly tomorrow,' Klas said worriedly. 'She's an unimpeachable woman, she helps me with the garden.'

The twilight grew darker, as if someone was dripping ink into clear water. Temporary blackness rose from the sea. The evening song and the morning call of the blackbird would meet, since the summer night was so short.

Klas delivered a speech to Emile Bamuto, expressing the wish that he would be able to realize that nothing was static and given, but that everything was stamped by hidden contradictions and thus open to changes. He hoped that Emile would have the ability to be most surprised at things entirely expected, and the will to hear a story over and over again to get astonished at things he already knew. Finally, he hoped that Emile would learn what produced the best food on Earth : like a sailor ship-wrecked on a desert island eventually finding the edible roots.

Afterwards a fire was lit in the tiled stove. Gertrude rested on her side on an antique sofa with the baby curled up in the angle between her thighs and her stomach. She had recently fed it, the whole of one breast and some of the other.

'The DDT content has gone down a little,' she said. 'Lotte had girl-friends who stopped breast-feeding immediately and gave substitute milk instead when they learnt about the DDT in breast milk. But they could never get the exact figures on the risks involved. The storage ought to be less in Botswana than in Germany and Sweden. I also read about some unfortunate ingredients in the substitute milk. So what can one do? Stop feeding them completely?'

'And then there are the psychological aspects,' Marianne added. 'The security, the closeness. Maybe one thing balances out the other?'

'Secure but poisoned you grow up in an insecure world which has to use all its resources to detoxicate itself,' Gertrude said.

323

She stroked the child's bottom, round in his nappies. The thin legs stuck out like sprouts from his beetroot red suit. Marianne was sitting in front of the fire. Martin, copying the baby's example, had huddled up next to her. He was reading an old Bill book. Klas and Jan were telling Jenny about Taheiti.

'We'll soon be together again,' Marianne said, and told them that Sten was going to return in the autumn.

'But what about his great project,' Gertrude exclaimed, and Jan thought it sounded like a reproach. 'Does everybody have to give way, adjust . . .'

'He's coming home to be with me and the children,' Marianne said abruptly.

'But –' Gertrude began.

Then she was silent, probing Jan's eyes.

'Sten is not degrading himself,' JB said. 'He's just taking new courses.'

The bats started to dance over the skating ice of the windows. Gertrude wanted to go home, but Emile Bamuto slept and she did not want to disturb him. The conversation meandered between summer plans and legal studies, the oppression of women in Western Germany and Botswana rain songs.

'Hush,' Klas said, pointing.

Gertrude had fallen asleep on her sofa with one arm under her head and one around Emile Bamuto. JB put two chairs in front of them. Gertrude started as the legs of the chairs scraped against the floor, and she held the baby tighter.

They began tip-toeing about and whispering good-bye. Klas cuddled both Marianne and Jenny for a long time. Their objections were almost inaudible, from consideration. He waved and shooed them off to their car. His house shone like a lantern among the trees. The inn was dark and closed. The real inn, Jenny thought, was Klas's house.

They dropped off Marianne and Martin in Mörby, and then drove towards the city along asphalt roads, damp in the night.

'We're alone, eventually,' JB said. 'How did you get on with Gertrude?'

'The two of us hadn't met since that day at the Academy of Science, before she went to Botswana. We didn't say much then, and the few things we said were probably noble rather than true.'

'Were you any more honest this time?' Jan asked.

'We took care to say only things we could substantiate. But the situation is different, Gertrude herself is different. Don't you notice it? She's got a new kind of frankness.'

'So what did you talk about?'

'About Emile, about Francistown, about the position of researchers in Sweden today . . . She spoke about her new life, the loneliness and the strength of it. She said if she'd stayed in Stockholm, a lot of things would have been different, but she now thinks what happened could just as well have been her own choice. We can still talk easily about a wide range of things.'

The sunrise was already gleaming in the golden crowns of the City Hall. The pigeons had Tegel Hill to themselves. They had adapted the colour of their feathers to the exhaust fumes of the cars. The white and reddish-brown type from the days of trams and trolley-buses had become rarer and rarer.

'Let's go to Riddarholmen,' Jenny said. 'Everything there must be quite still on a night like this.'

It was their last night together in Stockholm. Jenny was leaving for London in two days' time, and Jan was going to join her after a week.

They walked hand in hand in the warm darkness. Jenny's sandals clattered against the cobble-stones. Aspen shoots and mayweed clung to the banks. A couple of tennis courts lay surprisingly within the shadow of the Ministeries. The star The Fox had shown for a while at Klas's place, but had now disappeared into its burrow.

In an alley they stopped in front of the secretive metal plaque on the foundation-stone.

'Sweden's standard elevation,' Jenny read. 'But didn't it say Stockholm's the last time we were here?'

'We must have been mistaken in the dark,' JB said.

They went through the gateway, where there was no door or lock. It was a year since they had wandered about here.

'In those days our elevations were few and stolen,' Jan said. 'I'm happier now.'

'I'd rather reach standard depth with you,' Jenny said, 'Than elevations without you. You help me to endure everyday life. Our vertigo feels good for me.'

Jan pulled her close. He said that he was amazed at all the

sleeping Stockholmers; once again they had the city to themselves. Riddarholmen was like an unheated drawing-room in a
country-house – you did not enter it without specific reasons,
such as when the vicar came to call, or when a corpse was laid
out.

Roses and catmint were in bloom under the thick walls. It
was too early yet for bees and flies. The odd car passed by on
the bridges. It was quieter than during the days when palaces
were privately owned. They slammed the car doors and left.
The gulls flew up with complaining noises, and spread out
over the Stream. The light coloured feathers on their breast
caught the morning sun and dispersed it around them.

THE WATER TOWER

The first ray of sunlight moved from the Baltic coast slowly
in over the Uppland Plain, informing the landscape of a
new day. The buttons on the instrument panel twinkled in-
gratiatingly to Jan Backman. Nothing in particular was happening within vision; he was only concerned with the local
visibility. He looked at the cracks in the asphalt below, the
low lights along the runways, and a blazing pile of rubbish
for the fire brigade to practise on. He thought he heard the
soporific notes of the planes as they took off or landed, but it
was Jansson humming the advertising melody of an American
airline: 'There's somebody up there who loves you.'

Later in the morning the planes were queuing up in the air.
They had to be a thousand metres apart, as they came down to
land. They hovered over the northern sector of the airfield,
which was the emptiest part, and were directed to their runways by the radar. Most of the planes were freighters, arriving
with loads of early fruit and vegetables, and taking off again
loaded with spare parts for cars and machinery.

The planes were fairly anonymous to Jan Backman. He
rarely saw the crew list with its information, the report on the
load weight, or the fuel consumption chart. Occasionally a

plane was delayed by orders for it to be reloaded. The weight of the fuel, mail sacks and luggage had to be distributed in a certain way, depending in turn on the number of passengers it carried.

Out here his working self dwelt and lived together with his other self, like a child's top with its coloured sections mingling together into all possible colour variations when the top spun: blue here, yellow there, and now green; the colours blending together, separating, dispersing, and then reassembling.

'The moon is not a satellite planet of the Earth, but an independent twin planet,' the meteorologist stated, closing one of his trade journals.

'And what are twin planets?' Jansson asked.

'Those which are so close in the sky that they appear to be one,' Eklund replied. 'There might still be large distances between them.'

Christina brought in some coffee. Just as usual.

'All our information is about the past,' Eklund continued, 'sent to us from distant stars that we can see with our own eyes on a clear night. This knowledge has been travelling for hundreds of years – what we know about our nearest nebula, Andromeda, is what it was like two million years ago. We must be satisfied with old newspapers.'

'You look happy,' Christina said to Jan.

'I am happy.'

'I think you have an ability to get through most things unscathed, though you're so old.'

They found it easy to talk. He had told her how insecure he felt regarding the future of his job. She was in the same position: not discarded but a bit bored with the cosy routine. At the same time she had the threat of being made redundant.

'I'm going to stay with Jenny in London for a while,' JB said. 'We'll see what happens next. Nobody has given me notice yet. We can leave on our own initiative if we find an alternative way to live.'

He wrote to Jenny about what he felt and thought, without any hindrance. If they had been subjected to censorship, they could have told each other lots of things within the huge bracket of weather reports: the air pressures, the winds, the terminology used to describe precipitation, and maps – what the whole country listens to every night in a way that they do not adhere to other sermons. New situations within the repetitive framework.

'An inventor,' Eklund said, reading a newspaper article about patents that had been applied for, 'is a man bringing out things that don't exist, and then proving that they have existed all along. He sees them first, then he invents them to make other people see them.'

'You mean there are no inventions,' JB said, 'only inventors, who don't assume that other people must have already seen what they see.'

Jan Backman and Jenny Jeger exchanged a few letters while Jenny was at the DOE, the Department of The Environment in London. JB wrote:

'Don't include me in your doubts about existence, but use me as a grinder of your emotions to keep them sharp. I think people around me have achieved a specific gravity, a density which I must not harm. Only to you, strangely enough, can I write this.'

Jenny wrote:

'I wonder how Gertrude is, and Lotte and Klas and Marianne. I know Emile Bamuto is well. Perhaps we, from short-sighted perspective, will be able to tell ourselves that most things worked out all right in the end. We didn't want to hurt anyone, though we knew we did. I haven't had any new attacks of mistrust, or any desire to keep my distance. I feel like one of the wise virgins, one of the trusting ones, who will keep oil in her lamp and wave it in the darkness of large western cities, to make sure you'll find me.

Imagine living like this: an inconceivable grace. I could pour sacks of words over the mystery of this experience, until I discover that the mystery is one single thread only a few millimetres long in the sack itself.

There is also this easily defined, undeserved fact: you exist. Even though there's a windy dirty sea between us, you're present and warm. The nights grow darker slowly. My antennae stretch towards the point where we shall meet in a week.'

JB wrote:

'I think our love enables us to discern each other completely. But since we don't know how to use this ability, we don't use it very much. I am satisfied just watching you.

You have given me a new superficiality of depth : the art of caressing has got to do with surfaces. And the art of loving existence is daring to walk on the water, which is another surface.

Good night. I cup my hands over your eyes to give you a canopy to sleep under.'

Jan read Jenny's letter, and replied to it whilst eating in a restaurant. It had the atmosphere of a private dining-room. People knew each other. The waitress asked a couple of her friends to stay behind and help with the washing up. She told them about the man who collected the restaurant refuse to return it to the consumer cycle. It became pigs' food and fertilizer instead of ashes. It was also profitable because of all the silver cutlery he found at the same time.

JB felt light around the head. He had had a haircut before going to the restaurant in a barber's shop with high ceilings and a tiled stove, managed by a stern elderly woman who had sat him down on an ordinary wooden chair. He had wanted a new hairstyle. By the time he left, she had nearly shorn all his hair off.

He wrote to Jenny about feeling at home in the centre of the city. Some parts of it were destroyed by geometrical nonsense, but other parts had become nicer. The boroughs of Vasa and Östermalm were not so grey any more. At Jenny's building a restaurant had opened between the messenger service and the racket workshop. The Stockholm of his childhood had had more lift shafts and dark stairways. He had stood on stairs with friends, and when chased by a boys' gang had run up all the stairs in one of the old council houses. They had thought they would press him against the locked attic door. But he knew there were green mountains up there on the fifth floor, mountains forgotten and never blasted, and he ran across them and down the stairs of another house. They could never catch him in that area.

In Jenny's letter he caught glimpses of her work :

'Every civilization, according to its ability, has been a plunderer. Our technical era is forceful : sound barriers are broken through, atoms are split, marketing is aggressive, we compete for life. All our ethics aim to master and conquer our environment. Although the social awareness has increased, the child labour of the Victorian times still exists in distant places, with our suppliers of raw material: South Africa, Bolivia . . .

I've made friends with a social anthropologist, Mary Deale. She compares the battle for the environment with the battle against slavery some hundred years ago. Those who won that battle also managed to change man's opinion of himself. In the same way the battle for the environment will change our opinion of nature. Time is ready. Slaves in the nineteenth century were getting more expensive than employed workers; that's why the campaign succeeded with its slogans about our common humanity. The public opinion against slavery was not directed against industry, but against its irresponsible, self-sufficient and impractical way of working. Same thing today. Let the bear exist and teach us how to survive by hibernating. Let the peregrine falcon fly: it catches fifteen mice a day. Learn from the penguins how to orientate yourself on huge ice-floes, and from the mountain gorilla how to lead an honest life. Make sure they don't perish. The migratory birds may have an ability to fly by the stars which human beings have all lost. That may be the reason for our dissatisfaction and sense of destruction, which we take out on nature and animals.

If we can find methods not to destroy our environment, we should also find a way not to annihilate each other.'

Jenny's letter ended:

'I can see you here, as I lie in my bed. You're standing in the kitchenette making tea. Your naked back is not very tanned, and your pyjama bottoms have some difficulty staying up on your slim hips.

You move quietly and lightly. You're not one of those who rattle and ramble. If you spill something, you immediately wipe it up. If we forget to buy something we need, you have a trick of making everything appetizing: even one crust each with marmalade.

I long for your arms. They're cool on the insides and warmed by the sun on top. Our legs are the same length and twist like ropes when we're asleep. But I dare not think of that now.

When you listen to somebody, the whole of your face is intent. Sometimes you forget to shut your mouth. Still, you never look silly. Whoever talks feels rewarded: you don't miss a word.

If I open up the skylight, which is quite sooty and stained by birds, there is a sunny square on the floor. You can leave the tray there, and there'll also be room for the two of us. Now that you've turned round and come towards me, your pyjama bottoms have fallen down and only your penis keeps them up.

If I don't stop writing now the tea will get cold, both the imaginary tea and the real version in a cup next to me.

I won't go on telling time to pass quickly: I want to wait for you, counting every second, one by one.'

JB took the Radetsky March to a bookbinder's, because it was falling to pieces. The bookbinder was going on holiday: JB could pick it up in September. He told himself with astonishment that there was an autumn ahead of them, of which he knew little.

Gertrude and Lotte also made him ponder about the future. He passed through a cemetery on his way to see them. There was a tombstone for a sail-maker, one for a poet who considered tears sweeter than laughter, and another for a trade union leader who had studied to be an astronomer. The light fell in between the branches of the limes and chestnuts, a variable source of light opening and shutting, with the brightness of the green shining between the trunks. He sat down on a brown painted iron bench with The Cemetery Administration inscribed on it. He felt at the same time indifferent to and involved with the activities of the city. He perceived the smells, and heard the sound of traffic and voices.

Then he went up to his old flat. Gertrude, Lotte, Emile and Ua had been out to look for flowers and wild strawberries in the Järva Plain, but been told to leave by the quarry men. Emile Bamuto was lying on his back in his cot, propelling with his legs. Jan saw the light falling in from the side onto the baby's eyes, like the sun shining onto spring ice.

'It's so beautiful here,' JB said, looking at the clean white walls.

'Jan,' Gertrude exclaimed. 'You never usually say things like that.'

The flat looked empty, as some things had been put away, and Gertrude had taken what she thought was unnecessary clutter to Oxfam. Ua's things were scattered around. Lotte used the maid's room for her office, and from there they heard the rattling of her typewriter. Proofs and stencilled reports were sent to her from West Berlin for suggestions of various lines to take for women's liberation. In Western Germany women were discriminated against in a way that was unthinkable in Sweden. Lotte interviewed Swedish researchers involved in the rôles of the sexes. Her real field was nutrition physiology. She had a research grant from the Caroline Institute to complete the investigation she had started in Francistown.

JB thought the flat was eventually being used. Gertrude looked around. 'It won't be like this for ever, but it's nice now that it works for all of us. I hope to have a security of my own when Lotte and Ua don't live here any more. I'll spend a lot of time with Emile. I had nobody when I was a child – sometimes Mrs Tapper, matrons, teachers, or friends. People appeared, warned me, and then disappeared.' She was dicing meat and potatoes for her large family. JB helped her with the onions. They were alone in the kitchen. He told her that he was going to London.

'I could see before me that Jenny was a comet in our life,' Gertrude said. 'She came too close, burnt and singed, but steered out into cosmos again. It may hurt you if I say that I still see her rôle like that. The difference is only that it doesn't change anything for me now. Only for you. I don't feel relieved any more if it happens, only worried about your reactions. A wedge was driven in, and I became more distant. Sometimes you see things more clearly at a distance. If you are too close you don't discover anything. I would never have stepped back deliberately to watch you.'

'You mean to say you're finding me unsympathetic?' Jan said.

'You're silly and silly again,' Gertrude said, laughing at him. 'I like you so much, but now I've got you at more than arm's length. My hands are not so eager to reach you. I expect something else will happen to me.'

'I've made a lot of mistakes,' JB said. 'I know it, and it's been difficult.'

'Difficult or easy,' Gertrude said. 'You've had a great experience.'

'I'm right in the middle of it,' JB mumbled with the need to defend his and Jenny's love.

'My experience seemed to turn out as one single minus. But that was wrong. In the void I've started to sense my own outlines. When you weren't there for me to gaze at, I saw a lot of things you had concealed, deliberately or not. Even if I wanted to, I couldn't get back into that narrow circle again.'

So little time had passed, he thought, when calculated in months and years. Yet a lot of things had happened. Beginning, middle and end: lazy measures. Gertrude had left her prison of radial projection drawing. She now saw a different city, a different drawing.

He was surprised to find that he could understand her so deeply without wanting to be with her.

'I know who set fire to it,' the voice on the telephone said.

JB felt more baffled than threatened. It was a call from the bookshelf in the room he had had as a boy, which had come loose in its old age, and been connected with the Arlanda tower.

The voice continued:

'It could be nice to know, I mean. And the box . . . You'd like to have that back, wouldn't you?'

He now realized who was talking. It was the girl that he and Gertrude had rescued last summer when she and her brother were found drifting on the keel of their overturned boat.

'Hallo Monica,' he said calmly. 'What do you want?'

'It's like I say. Don't you believe it? Come to the Vanadis pool, and I'll tell you more.'

When he did not reply, he could hear a whispering discussion going on at the other end. Then the voice came back:

'Tomorrow between twelve and one p.m. North side of the pool.'

She hung up. Jan casually cried hallo into the singing forest of the telephone network. Then he went back to his work, but he occasionally heard the hoarse teenage voice, oscillating between rudeness and shyness. What could the children know about the fire? Had they taken the box with the commercial and personal documents of A. O. Backman, which he and Gertrude lost a whole year ago?

When he went to see Gertrude in the evening, he wanted to tell her about the phone call. However, she forestalled it by saying that the police investigation was now finished: there had been a short-circuit in the old electrical wiring in the dining-room. The brown oak leaf wall-paper had nourished the sparks, the accidental fire became a fact, and the lion and his rider never got out of their forest. In other words the first part of Monica's evidence was false. She and her brother knew nothing about the cause of the fire, although they might have seen it from the shore, and maybe even taken the canoe across to poke around at the site of the fire, finding something.

Jan decided not to worry Gertrude with any of this. The mood of Uppland Street, a mood of active workshop and happy nursery did not call for ghost stories. Klas went singing through the rooms with Emile Bamuto expertly placed on his shoulder. The brownish-blue gaze of the baby bounced on the furniture, faces and piles of paper. Ua jumped about following Klas, grimacing and proudly crying out:

'Er lacht! Er lacht!'

'Suddenly the boy has got ancestors,' Klas said.

This thought had not occurred to Jan. He had cared little for his ancestors. They had never made contact.

'My grandfather was a temperance reformer,' Klas said. 'He drank a lot to keep the fire going. Fight for Peace was the name of the order. It died with him. My father sorted bank invoices in the daytime, studied poetry in the evenings, and wrote his own lays. An excellent state of ill-health kept him upright until he was ninety a few years ago. By then he was senile and started to abuse quotations. "Little elfs with rose-buds", he constantly mumbled.'

'Let's die when our time is up,' JB said, 'not years after the end of the party.'

Lotte was alone in the kitchen drinking coffee. Gertrude was audiotyping. Jan felt rather an outsider. He stood for a while in the kitchen doorway talking to Lotte.

'If there were as many fathers as mothers,' she said, 'day nurseries wouldn't be a problem.'

Klas gave Emile Bamuto to Jan, and he was surprised to feel how heavy the baby was – like expecting to get a puff-ball in your hand, but realizing that you are holding a dipstick. Soft warmth spread from the very small body. Emile exercised his fingers, and formed his mouth into unheard words. Jan had to take him to an empty room to be able to say something to him. He cupped his hands around Emile's soft skull, which pounded inside it as if the head was the eggshell around an eager bird.

Looking at numbers, there were more than enough people in the world. But never enough faces. The baby breathed inside his yellow towelling suit. His blood-vessels held a salty solution like sea water, and his skeleton held calcium from the oceans of the Cambrian period.

JB thought of the manufactured parts of the baby – like planks concealed in the trunk of a pine tree. The ear prepared to discern cushat calls, complaints, fire alarms, mouth-organs. Thirst which made the milk shimmer. He would soon try to taste the sunny spots on the floor; but he would soon leave them and progress out into the wide field.

Very soon – for time was short; all our written history was merely a pling of the Earth's clock. We recently squatted by the bluish abysses of the ice-field, not knowing how to cultivate land. Now we are forgetting it again.

He went down a few stairs, and looked through the back window at the firebrick wall covered in ivy. On the stairs fossils still lived. The wall was cool and rough. He ran his hands over the pink paint, which looked like stage make-up.

Somebody called his name. He turned round, and saw Gertrude standing in the doorway of the flat. She had stood there watching him. Now she smiled at his surprised face.

'What are you thinking of, Jan?'

'Nothing,' JB said. 'I was just looking out.'

'It's all so strange. Don't you agree?'

'Yes. I never stop being amazed.'

'I'm not annoyed with you,' Gertrude said.

She sounded like his sister had at the time of their summer holidays.

'I'm glad to hear that,' Jan said in an indistinct voice.

Then he went up two steps at a time and within seconds joined her.

He held her tight.

'Look after yourself well,' he said.

Over her shoulder he caught a glimpse of Ua on a tricycle, her legs going up past her ears like a cricket.

'I'm going back to the Academy of Science on the first of December,' Gertrude said.

'I'll see you before then,' JB said. 'I'm not emigrating.'

Then he left the house where he had lived for so many years that he knew that the sound of the front door closing could be heard after he had gone five steps along the pavement.

Entering the gates of the Vanadis pool, JB felt he was acting in a comical spy thriller. He had found a pair of sun-glasses which he seldom used, in the glove compartment of his car. He spied through these for Monica and Bengt in the crowd. Undressed, people seemed anonymous; identifiable only by the colour of their swimsuits. He found that there were a very large number of girls sun-bathing topless – until they turned round to reveal coarse bearded faces. JB listlessly lay down to sun-bathe on one of the inclined boards by what he hoped was the long northern side of the pool. He was not there to get a tan. He thought the sun ought to be made of papier-mâché; it was nothing but theatre, all of it. And Monica would probably not appear. She was busy at the moment, planning new deeds in a summer room on the northern side of Vindö Island.

Then a cold fishy hand was put on his naked back, and he started and dropped his sun-glasses. 'Don't be frightened,' Monica said without smiling. 'We're not going to hurt you.'

Bengt was standing behind her. They were one year older, which, however showed only in the girl. She had a tiny red bikini on. An area of white skin revealed that her ordinary swimsuit covered more of her. She was carrying a sun-yellow plastic bag. Her hair hung in wet streaks down towards her nipples, which had not yet relaxed after the cool bathe. Jan said they might as well tell him what they knew at once, as he did not have much time.

'It's not as easy as that,' Monica said.

'It could be worth a thousand kroner,' Bengt suggested.

Jan looked around at the hundreds of bathing Stockholmers. Who else, except him and the children had conversations like this? He laughed.

'Stop it now. That's enough. No more children's programmes.'

'What's the matter with you?' Monica said in a shrill voice. 'We know who set fire to the house. We've got the box.'

'But I'm not a buyer,' JB said. 'I too, know who set fire to it. You can keep the contents of the box. They're of no value.'

Brother and sister sat down close to each other on the empty deck-chair next to JB. They looked like deflated balloons. They looked lost. Bengt mumbled something into Monica's ear, and gave her a push in the back, but she was listless and kept saying:

'Oh come on. Why?'

Then she moved so close to Jan that he could see the freckles on her narrow shoulders, and the drops of water immobile on her brown thighs suitable for an advertising photo.

'Can't you be a sport?' she said in a totally different voice. 'We're in such a fix. If you come home with us, I'll tell you. There are too many listeners here. Bengt and I are alone in town. The others are at Vindö.'

The image of Monica, naked except for her bikini, in a bourgeois flat empty for the summer with white covers over the plush sofa, and the rugs rolled up like a pile of pancakes, flashed through Jan's mind. The scene had a scent of sunny skin and moth-balls. It stirred up the pot of memories. But then the director without warning changed the scene to JB pinioned in an arm-chair, robbed of his wallet and car key. Monica went towards the door, and said that their family was going abroad later that day. They were already at Arlanda. Bengt assured him that the telephone was out of order.

The sun was baking. A beach ball bounced on his legs, and woke him up from his James Bond fantasy. He looked straight into Monica's slanting blue eyes.

'I'm sorry you're in a fix,' he said. 'But knowing you, you've got yourselves to blame.'

'Well in that case,' said Monica, eager and appealing, 'let's say we'll put the box in a secret place. You go and get it, and then you can send us something, whatever you like, whatever you think it's worth.'

'You might as well give it to me straight away,' JB said, making a quick snatch at her yellow bathing bag.

'Stop it,' she snarled. 'What are you doing? Are you mad?'

She got up hurt. Bengt put a protective hand on her shoulder, and whispered something.

'Okay,' Monica said. 'Since we can't trust you we'll do this: we'll put the box under the bushes by the water tower. Go and look tonight, and you'll see.'

Before he had time to answer, they had disappeared into the crowd of bathers. Jan stretched out, letting the sun warm him

337

and calm him down. What was there in the box? He remembered having seen some yellowed sheets of paper that had often been folded. One of them was a document saying that A. O. Backman bequeathed the Water Palace with its grounds and inventories to his children, Gertrude and Jan.

If the brother and sister, Bengt and Monica, wanted to play at blackmail, they had there a hold on his and Gertrude's past. If they got into worse fixes later in life, they could be tempted by the thought. However, they had probably decided that he and Gertrude had done nothing illegal, and that was why they wanted to give the box back, hoping to receive a gratuity for their honesty.

Alternatively they might take out the valuable documents and return the box with only the special newspaper cuttings, old love letters and anything else it might hold. He suddenly remembered an ivory seal in shape of a dog with ruby red eyes. Had he been irresponsible not taking the children more seriously? He oscillated between fear and nonchalance as he had done the previous summer. They appealed somehow to his own childhood memories: he and Gertrude had also been a couple of children to whom grown-ups seldom listened, and never understood. Would his lack of sensitivity punish itself? Could it punish Gertrude again?

He himself felt fully insured by Jenny. He would be with her in London in two days' time. He imagined that nothing could happen to him before he met her again. He was in a blessed condition.

It was eleven o'clock when his night shift was over. There was not much to clear away on his desk. Jansson was already at his post in the tower. The night rested lightly against the greenery. He opened all the windows of his car, and travelled at walking pace on the empty motorway. The scent of cheese-rennet and honeysuckle wafted into his car, redolent of gardens and pasture land.

He had hardly given a thought to the children and their secret. However, turning off the main road, he realized that something inside him had all the time been urging him to make the nightly call to Vanadis Grove. He parked by St Stephen's Church and went into the empty and sombre park. He would not have done it unless he had known Jenny, he thought. He would have treated the cause in a more bureaucratic way.

338

The wide path crackled under his feet in the silence, and he thought that he heard the children giggling in a bush. He hurried on, looking around. Nobody followed him.

The Vanadis Grove was a green plateau which sloped steeply down towards the streets. A sign read: Beware of falling rocks. On the top of the plateau was the water tower, sealed like a prison, with an iron gate and thin bars over the windows.

JB went around the tower and found that the bushes grew against the wall only on the east side. He bent down at every protruding part of the building, and carefully groped with his hand. His fingers got hold of loose soil or something else: he dared not think of all the things that could be hidden under the couch-grass. Thorns caught onto his trousers. He stopped himself, blushing at the venture. The children had fooled him. But this also had its advantages for him, the cheated one: He was now, at one o'clock in the morning, watching Stockholm sleep under its roofs of copper and slate. A red streak portended the morning.

Another twenty-four hours, and he would take off and leave. Thanks to Jenny he felt at home everywhere. He might as well sleep on a park bench. He tried it, but the slats made his back sore. He took the car to Nybro Quay, parked under the chestnuts outside the National Museum, and rested a little later on the wide bed. Half asleep he longed for Jenny to put her leg across his hips.

Nobody could know where the box was. It cast forth a shadow of threatening revelations. He hoped that they would all be moving in the margins of light outside the domain of that shadow. Placed against a wall, he would be silent like a coward rather than admit that he had loved his sister.

Don't betray us! Don't deny us! Both appeals could not be adhered to. He knew that Gertrude would be stronger and more cunning about this. His own strength and cunning were sharpened where Jenny was concerned. She was his whet-stone and his stepping-stone.

By the time the alarm went off he had forgotten Monica, Bengt and the yellowed documents. Eventually it was time to get out the large suitcase.

While Jan Backman packed in the Nybro Quay flat, as eager as if he was preparing for his first journey, Stockholm on that day meant totally different things to other people. In the same locality millions of dramas were being enacted. Like his, they would all end tragically. Nobody described them. Nobody applauded. The gulls cried in a sun polished city, where the flags were hoisted for everybody and nobody.

IN A STRANGE CITY

Jan Backman was sitting by the desk in the window niche, drawing on the back of a paper bag. He first let a pencil draw soft outlines. Then he filled them in with red and blue. It was one of those pencils which are blue at one end and red at the other. Somewhere in the middle the two colours met without mingling. He sharpened it with a sheath-knife over the sink. The blue and red flakes gave their colour to little streams of water that disappeared out of sight. He drew a dragon coiling round a tower. The tower had glass windows; inside one of them he himself was sitting. On a ladder leant at a bold angle against the tower, Jenny climbed. She was wearing jeans and a shirt, cried something to him, and waved.

He put the drawing aside and leapt up, unhappy with the blue and red. He went out into the summer heat, past the grocery and the fishmonger's in Lambeth High Street, past the shoemaker's and the fire station which was also facing the Albert Embankment and the Thames. The attic where Jenny had lived before, which she had again borrowed from the young architect who was a friend of John Bringham's, was in Lambeth, near Old Paradise Street and Lambeth Walk, in a district where the housing was almost a slum and many blocks had been demolished to give room for the large approach roads from the southern suburbs.

JB liked walking about there in the day when he was alone. Jenny did not have far to walk to the Department of The Environment in a glass palace in Marsham Street; she crossed Lambeth Bridge and went past three streets into Westminster. From the attic windows they looked out on the nearest roofs towards the river and the Houses of Parliament. The traffic streaming along Lambeth Road towards Elephant and Castle never ceased. Transports of provisions rumbled past at daybreak. The trains from Waterloo Station passed at ground level. They got used to the noise, and the rent was low in this area near the Archbishop's park.

Opposite the Imperial War Museum he found a shop for office equipment, and returned with a set of felt-tipped pens of different colours. He set to his work again, and transferred the drawing to a page of a Swedish newspaper which he had read in the plane. He chose the page with employment adverts. The tower soon rose over its grey grainy texts, Jenny on her ladder, the dragon with its wide-open jaws. On the side of the dragon he wrote: The importance of Swedish unemployment.

He drew a bubble from Jenny's mouth: Come out, Jan. From his own mouth came the texted reply: To what?

The sun was laughing over it all. The yellow ink sunk into the black printer's ink and made the sunshine look polluted. At the horizon he drew an avenue of limes, at least he knew they were limes. Another person might have taken them for clover-leaves.

He stuck his drawing to the wall with cellotape. Jenny was surprised when she came home, breathless after running up the last staircase.

'Jan, I didn't know you could draw. That's me exactly, trying to pull my tummy in to look thin, and then sticking my chin out instead. And you look a bit stiff. You'd like to jump but dare not. That's obvious. But what shall we do, Jan?'

They sat for a long time at the desk, which was also their dining-table. The window was open. As he stuck out his hand, he could feel the thin sooty lichens on the roofing-tiles. Earlier on they had found the dry skeleton of a green grasshopper, and wondered how it had managed to get so high up. Some streets away they could see the Office for Lost Property for Greater London. Storey upon storey full of things that millions of people lost while travelling around the city. JB decided to go there one day.

'Right now, when I'm so happy with you,' he said, 'I feel it's important that I do something essential. The routine is not a reassuring, but merely a burden, a ballast. You have awakened some untried potential in me.'

'The situation on the market is not favourable for experiments,' Jenny said.

They did not get any further. The sun was sinking over the warm city.

'Come on,' Jenny said. 'It's easier to think on the move.'

So they went out on the pavements which the heat was deserting. The leaves of the elms were large and dark: night and shadow lived in their roughness. They heard their steps echoing along the Victoria Embankment towards Charing Cross Station. Covered passages and unlit nooks round the station took them into small streets with strange shops, theatrical agencies, tailor's shops for dolls, and workshops for dentures. They saw people pulling down the iron shutters and awnings, locking ingenious locks, and bolting their doors.

Around the vegetable market they waded through the refuse of the day: cabbage leaves and rhubarb stalks. The Covent Garden area was being evacuated. An acre there was worth a fortune, although the valuation was artificial: an acre was worth a way of living for those who lived and worked there.

'The Department of The Environment are more interested in the densely populated areas than in the countryside,' Jenny said. 'That skyscraper you can see all over the city is empty, built only on speculation. There should be laws to prevent this. Apart from that, the first attack should be directed towards the monotony of the suburbs, and secondly, the dirtying of the cities. The third aim is to keep historical cities and villages complete. A society where the gardening architect has as much influence as the economist, the Minister of The Environment said.'

'Phrases,' said JB.

'The ministries for transport, housing and local government have to report to the DOE. That's the interesting thing. Those responsible for the development of this country, have to confer with their superiors who are responsible for the environment. The economical and administrative power of the DOE by far surpasses that of the Swedish equivalent body.'

'Are they surprised to see a female delegate?' JB asked.

'Some of them, perhaps. They expect less from me, and at the same time demand more – both attitudes founded by contempt. Even from my superior position I can see how women's lives are often like the lives of the poor. The lives of the oppressed are similar. There won't be a change until the men see it as their life. But why should they share the misery?'

'Women are more easily accepted if they work for the environment or the developing nations,' JB said.

'Because these are new fields. Besides, women have always been connected with gardening and charity work.'

'I'd like to find a new kind of activity,' JB said. 'I'm afraid of deadlocks and stagnation. Have you got any ideas?'

'Not quite yet,' Jenny said. 'What makes you a good air-traffic controller is your ability to listen with a fixed gaze. Nor do you feel persecuted, unless someone is actually on your track. You don't imagine much yourself, but others can imagine things for you and about you.'

'I'm the one who takes you up and down when you fly away and return,' JB said. 'I like to think of that. But it's not enough.'

On lonely days in London he had occasionally longed to be back in the tower: a profession with great precision and small margins of freedom as long as the watch was on. At the same time London had helped him achieve something else. He saw an existence that did not need to be organized, interpreted or controlled. His attachment to habits yielded, although he had never been bored. A security screen was gone; he did not know whether he would ever be inside the glass again.

They took the tube for a bit and came up into a different area under a sky of contradicting water-colours. They passed a house built in the nineties. The façade was yellow and black; the windows had small panes. A mystical emblem over the gate attracted them. The marble stairway was cool. They read: The English-Speaking Union. Flower arrangements indicated that a congress was in progress. Jenny opened a double door. They saw about a hundred strangers with glasses and cocktail snacks in their hands. A girl in a black dress quickly gave them one glass of champagne each. JB headed for the exit, but Jenny took a glass.

'It's impolite to leave without having had a drink.'

Jan then made his way among the strangers, and laid hands on two miniature sandwiches with salmon. But when a lady of about fifty in a low-necked dress asked Jenny whether the introductory speech had not been a scandal, she wanted to laugh, and failed to find a reply.

'Absolutely,' JB said. 'Exactly what I thought.'

He then apologized, saying that they had to leave. They ran down the stairs and a few streets away. They stopped breathless by a private garden in Mayfair. Inside the flowerbeds was a playground. Two young mothers and two small children were swinging listlessly in the swings. The wind took them where it wanted. Nobody said anything. They looked like a family of bats, hung up for the night.

They did like most people: boiled their tea water on one of the two gas rings, let it brew till it was strong, and drank it with milk. They had agreed with the milkman on a pint daily. The postman put a letter to Jan in the tin cupboard in the entrance hall. That was unusual. Jenny's post was mostly sent to her at work. A hand-coloured postcard from her mother at her summer boarding house was so far the only message that had reached them from the outside world.

Jan let his gaze pass over the two full pages.

'From Gertrude. Love to you,' he mumbled. 'Emile Bamuto is well. He has been to the children care unit for a check-up. Gertrude drove out to a lake with him to bathe. That was daring.'

'So far he's just lying there,' Jenny said. 'He'll soon need a baby seat.'

Then they started to talk about a weekend trip they were planning. The letter lay by Jan's tea cup. He picked it up again when Jenny had left. He thought of all the housewives who heard the door close after their husbands, and then had another cuppa and grabbed the mail and the newspaper. If everybody had the same tight reins, a necessary laziness would disappear. Not saying that housewives had time to be lazy, but they often had the opportunity to stop and think about themselves and others, to feel and devote themselves to detail. The idea of sharing the breadwinning burden must be to save time for both men and women. This could then be utilized in timeless experiences – watching, pondering, being with the children, creating, laughing, chatting and socializing. Otherwise something valuable would be lost – a kind of oil to grease the social machinery.

Gertrude wrote that she had joined a group fighting to save the Baltic. Several scientists participated, some of whom she knew from the Academy. She had got new contacts. She did

344

not want to watch passively; Emile Bamuto and his generation demanded action.

She had let their father, Adolf Oscar Backman, now living in Brazil, know that he was a grandfather. She had written a brief note like an excerpt from the registrar's book : the name, date of birth, weight and length of the baby; the name, age and profession of the father. She had also mentioned that the Water Palace had burnt down. She had so far not received a reply.

JB wondered whether he should tell his father anything about his life : his happiness with Jenny, his leave of absence, his hesitation regarding his job. But even as a little boy he had decided that he had been sincere once too often. He preferred to be well-behaved and uninteresting, without any disturbing profiling.

He crossed the river to Tate Gallery. There was an exhibition there of Balthus, a Polish born Frenchman. The previous summer he had seen a couple of his paintings in Stockholm. It was impossible to forget these prepubertal girls with clear open eyes and breasts slightly rounded. He now saw again the gardens where the world began, and he stopped to watch them.

Aware of the fact that nothing is ever repeated, Balthus encircled the moment, and everything stopped in a frozen lack of balance. The girls had moved and breathed, but become intangible pictures. Or were they petrified only for as long as he watched them through the glass? Out of vision they would get their gestures back. And what would then happen, when the curtain was opened, and light streamed in; when the young girl awoke on her bed, and the child turned the page in the book he was reading?

The long acquaintance had not solved the enigma of the paintings. Living and dead eyes met. He was sensually moved by them. On a large picture children played in an empty Sunday street. The foliage of the leaves was well defined. It let in the light foreboding thunder. The effaced meetings of yesterday could not be found again. A little girl turned straight to the glass to meet the spectator's camera eye from the other side, to be blinded by life. And the artist himself, more tender than cruel, leaned over the fragile old lady and the tramp without shoes. It was a truce of life.

Jenny telephoned him from the DOE to say that she enjoyed living. And that was all he needed to know about her. He remembered the drawing from his physics classes: the effect of a magnetic field on a mobile current. Can you feel in the depth of your moisture how much I love you, he thought.

Yes, she could. For coming home, she found him there; she threw off her raincoat and everything else; the days were so hot. She hung naked from the door-post. Her waist was level with his face; he kissed her navel and hips, bent down putting his lips carefully to her vagina.

Then she sunk towards him, her arms straight. He received her naked. She slid down over him, open and wet. He staggered under his burden. As her toes reached the ground, he pressed her against the wall. Daylight fell in, making the pleasure sharp and clear. Inside her he was extended like an unborn child not knowing where his body ends, and another starts.

She caressed his hips and back.

'If you don't stop, I'll come,' he said.

But she did not stop, and her vagina squeezed him gently. Then he came in her like a flood running upstream, but up and down meant nothing any more; they were joined and suspended like a gyro compass.

'Still,' Jenny said. 'It's too lovely.' Jan held her so tight that her breasts were flat, and their ribs met. Jenny's lips blew warm words towards his neck.

They got dressed, and took the bus to a restaurant in a fragile boat on the Grand Union Canal. Since everybody wanted to see the view of Regent's Park, the boat had a list, and the glasses slid slowly starboard. The greenery extended in one direction: a savanna burnt in July and reminding him of Botswana; and in the distance cries and grunts from the beloved animals of the Zoo.

London was a green and crowded surface in north-western Europe. The saline wind seldom ceased, but blew the smoke out over the provinces. Even in the tube it was always windy. They travelled with the windows open and a draught. The trains seemed to go faster than in other cities.

'If I leave Arlanda, what could I do instead?' JB asked.

Neither Jenny nor the laughing gulls replied. One need in him exceeded many other needs: to be used. With Jenny he could set all he had at stake, and yet be convinced that there was a potential stored away somewhere which could help them if they grew tired. But he was not used sufficiently in his profession. If he increased or varied his few routine exercises, other people's lives would be jeopardized. The tune remained the same over the years; he liked it much but still wanted to get away.

'I could study again,' he said. 'But academics aren't that popular. I'm interested in meteorology. But that would imply bank loans, intense studies. What kind of job? The Broadcasting Corporation. The Air-Traffic Department. Back to the tower. That reminds me of something. Last winter before I left for Africa, Sven Viberg of the SAS mentioned to me that they need people at their Tokyo branch. I didn't find out about the details.'

'Then we could see each other for a few weeks in the year,' Jenny said.

'Provided we can have our holidays at the same time.'

'I couldn't take that,' Jan said resolutely.

'Nor could I,' Jenny said. 'We should have time to get more tired of each other first.'

'And if you leave the Department of The Environment . . .'

'We're already restricting each other with plans and contra-plans.'

'I ought to stick it for another year and see what you decide to do,' JB said. 'We can't be both at loose ends.'

They watched the people around them. Craftsmen, house-wives, civil servants, and children. They themselves had their rôles which many people could envy them. But they tossed and turned like snakes in outgrown skins.

Later on they walked on the straight gravel-paths in Regent's Park. The bridge across the lake had a fence of cast iron with blackened pine cones. An old man was asleep on a bench, but he would be all right, as it was warm outside, and not like Observatory Hill in November.

'We're actually living in the fifth glacial stage,' JB said, 'according to Eklund. The London tube trains run through a layer of tropical mud from the period when the Thames was a water-course surrounded by palm-trees. The fourth glacial stage oc-curred eighteen thousand years ago. Nothing much has changed since then: the vikings travelled on warm water between Iceland and Greenland, but Elisabeth I fried her oxen over an open fire on the ice on the Thames. The first forty years of our century were the warmest since the eleventh century.'

'I know,' Jenny said. 'It's slowly growing colder.'

They had come down to Baker Street. The moon, some time polluted by bacteriae from the Earth, showed over Soho. Jan stopped and blew into her hands.

A pale, still summer afternoon. The Thames still, and the sun a red turning disc. The smokes from the electric power station bent like ripe corn; they would soon glide down to mingle with exhaust fumes and coal smoke.

'It looks like Turner,' Jenny said.

They had made a quiet tour of the National Gallery, but soon became more interested in the air conditioning system and the degree of moisture than in Rubens.

They decided to examine the climate in the British Museum too. In one room a girl wearing jeans was lying on her tummy reading a paperback. On her back two dark-skinned children climbed. An old caretaker looked at the group, trying to look stern.

'Some years ago he would have told them to leave,' JB whispered. 'Now he doesn't know whether he has changed, or the attitude of society.'

'We've become a bit more human, I think,' Jenny said. 'Few people are afraid of postmasters, teachers and bus conductors. The fear and the class division are still there, but they have changed their positions.'

They smiled apologetically to the next caretaker, for their walking pace was an insult to the Ming vases and Hettitic grave miniatures. They actually used the museum, where the whole world had left their samples and souvenirs, as a shortcut to Russell Square. They were on their way to see John Bringham, Jenny's friend, who lived at Tavistock Place. The attic they rented did not provide many kitchen utensils. They needed a large saucepan, a colander, a cutting-board, and a sharp knife. Jenny thought it irresponsible to buy things she already had in Stockholm. She had called John who was glad to lend them these things. His bachelor flat had been well equipped. He now lived there with a girl of twenty-five, who wanted to be an interior decorator. She had brought a complete kitchen equipment, he said. They were welcome to whatever they needed.

JB yawned in the heat. People they met had taken off as much as they dared. An elderly gentleman was wearing linen shorts and a white hat. Apart from that he was naked.

Jan looked around him in the streets: research institutes, hotels, little squares with limes in blossom. Jenny had rushed along these streets on her way to a flat which she had at times called her home. John had been her London boy-friend. When she rang the bell, he had felt happy. If she came home before him, she had leant out of the window to look for him. His profile or way of moving had filled her with a feeling of security or closeness. That was how it had been.

As they went up the stairs, he took Jenny in a steady grip by the arm. She smiled and quickly put her forehead against his shoulder. They did not need many words, he told himself.

JB had never met John: they had seen each other from a distance the previous summer, pretending they did not. John, out of jealousy, had hated both Jan and Jenny.

Now he benignly showed them around in his large, bright two room flat. His girl-friend, Sheila, came out of the bathroom with her hair combed and bright lipstick. Her long straight hair was kept together by a silver ring on top of her head; from there it flowed without the slightest wave down towards her waist. JB wanted to ask her if she had ironed it.

John opened the French windows in the drawing-room. The sounds of traffic rose from Tavistock Place. The smell of cooking, and the voices of children playing, came from the ventilator in the kitchenette at the back of the house. There was a cross-draught, and they sat down in the hardly noticeable breeze with glasses of orange juice with ice. The mist glittered with unknown crystals.

'They have started to photograph the air in Sweden,' Jenny said. 'Only thirty per cent of the constituents are known. Woolly globes whirl around. The scientists can't explain them. Seeing them doesn't solve any enigmas.'

'The photo was taken in Sture Square,' said JB. 'A little square in the centre of Stockholm.'

'I know,' John interrupted him. 'I stayed nearby.'

Sheila wanted to know what Jan did in London.

'A strange question to ask a man,' JB said. 'I clean the house, and do the shopping, and make sure dinner is on the table when Jenny comes home from work.'

They all laughed.

'The fate of a houseman,' JB said. 'Everybody laughs at him.'

'Suppose it was serious,' Sheila said. 'It's more difficult for a man than for a woman to break out of his role. We are actually lucky: we can play over the whole range, and nobody lifts an eyebrow.'

'And nobody lifts our salary,' Jenny said quickly.

'Sheila is right,' John said. 'Here in England no man would dare to stay at home with the children. The women's lib over-exerted themselves with the suffrage bill.'

'The suffragettes had a definable goal to fight for,' Sheila said.

'Now everything flows. We've tried to progress with care. So now we fall between two stools.'

'The baby seat and the typing chair,' John said.

'I'm studying something which appears to be luxurious. But it isn't. Have you ever thought of all the things that have to be decorated and designed? The smallest café, pub, hairdresser's, supermarket. I hope to specialize in public waiting-rooms: doctor's surgeries, social security offices, children care units, chemist's shops . . . Places where people queue up and sit around staring into the air. The time spent queuing is wasted.'

'So what can be done?' JB asked.

'Colours, flowers, packs of newspapers, toys for the kids. Something to alert or annoy. Maybe pictures to challenge people, or political appeals. Screens telling them about something: the process of making coffee, the Stock Exchange speculations . . . How many people know what an anti-cyclone is?'

JB left Jenny outside the Department of The Environment at half past eight in the morning. She turned round on the stairs to wave at him. At the same time a gust of wind pulled up her short pleated skirt. She smiled and made a grimace, a comical expression on her face: she looked like a character actress playing an old lady. He laughed at her.

Going up Horseferry Road, he felt a tight yearning for her, as if an invisible string stretched between them. He had had to live without her for long periods because of his own actions and her decisions. Something had remained active between them. There was a language to use, a walking pace to fall into.

There was a zone of warmth which doubled and heated when they came close.

They had felt this before, or something like it, for a couple of other persons. Around him faces that meant a lot to others were concealed. They told him nothing now. In the future he might be able to see them again : a new profile, a different way of inclining the back and putting the feet down might make his heart race. He did not care to look for the unknown people. He lived in a present which ought not to be immobile, but could well have extended shopping-hours?

In Vauxhall Bridge Road he was stopped by a smell, mainly ammonia, reminding him of something. He heard the noise of copying-machines from the premises by a gateway, and understood that he was thinking of the smell of Sten Tidström's business in Stockholm. In the shop-window among architects' drawings and publicity prints, was a stencilled students' magazine, and the last annual report of the Anti-Slavery Society, a movement he did not think necessary any more. On the glass the slogan of the company was glued, saying 'You hint – we print.'

An errand-boy was sitting on the steps to the street eating fish and chips. He peered at JB with a foxy smile under a red fringe, but no conversation began. JB was pondering about the uses of a copying-machine. The literacy campaign in Botswana, written material for the schools, simple schemes for how to grow a vegetable garden. Sten knew about the needs down there, and he himself had learnt a great deal. Paper was cheaper in Sweden.

Walking on, he was formulating in his mind his next letter to Sten. He would not be back until October. Till then plans could be shaped and modified. He found the tower less threatening, if he could do this on the side.

At Victoria Station he bought a bunch of postcards of varying age and origin. Coming home he spread them out on the table. They formed an incomplete picture of the strange city where he now felt at home. On top, in the middle, he placed a corner of Hampstead Heath where Jenny and he had walked among old age pensioners and dogs. They had met a girl with a pram, and stopped to have a look at her baby. They had talked about Emile and about buying him something. Nothing had been bought. He decided to send this postcard to Gertrude.

He put the Tower in its place, and let Burlington Arcade border on an imagined Piccadilly. At the centre he placed the Thames at ebb. And in the South-East was a summer picture of Greenwich, as green as verdigris. A grey grainy old-fashioned photo showed the warehouses in their vicinity. Jenny and he had walked downstream along the South Bank one dark night, and like moths been attracted by the one light in the window-less alleyways that were as dark as in nightmares. It turned out to be a pub adjacent to the breweries and warehouses: blackened oak, windows of bottle glass, and a throng of little china dogs on the mantelpiece. They sang and drank beer and played darts. On the floor above they served lamb cutlets and fried plaice, and a house wine of a good year. They had sat on the wall benches until closing-time. They found it often easier to talk in an alien environment; no domestic distractions, but the words were sharp and clear, as if they had to say every-thing before leaving the restaurant.

One postcard showed a low house in Aldersgate Street: it was here that John Wesley, according to a plaque 'felt his heart strangely warmed'.

He put that aside.

He wrote to Gertrude and Emile: 'I'm sending you a greet-ing warm from the heat of July. Can see before me Uppland Street like a greenhouse: warmth and protection, but easy to look into. Send me a photo; my memory of Emile must be outdated already. He'll soon be ready for one of my talks abut the roof of the world, and the longest displacement gap.' He sent the Greenwich card to Sten. The old observatory was on its hill, and the nought meridian marked on the gravel-path – life's artificial stroke of twelve.

'Come soon to meet Jenny. I also need some vocational guidance. My tower is yielding. Visibility unclear from this hill, the observatory out of use like in Stockholm. What use could I be to society? Not much, I fear. I've got an idea.'

He did not want to say any more. He had to try his plans on Jenny first.

He sent the blurred view of the south bank of the Thames to Eklund, the meteorologist in the forecast room. 'The atmos-phere is saturated here, so the stars seem larger and redder. The Earth is round, Bethelgeuze a giant in Orion's queue, not an Arab without a visa who didn't pass the security barrier.

You were right in everything. But No sig – I doubt that.'

The most beautiful card – The Tower in the mist at day-break – was for Mrs Stoll. 'Dear Mrs Stoll, I'm spending the summer in London.' Then he hesitated. He wanted to tell her about Jenny. What could he say? That he was divorced and had remarried? That he was living with his girl-friend? The terms for the most important things were few and insufficient. Those who shaped the language had not foreseen much. The vocabulary itself became a chastity belt. The words served a social machinery which favoured law and order. The ecstasy, the caresses, and the new inventions, had to dwell outside the fence of letters, lawless and illiterate. So he wrote nothing about Jenny, but continued: 'There is often a temperature of thirty centigrades here. I have travelled back and forth on a double-decker. There is an excellent view from the top.' He stopped there, and wrote his name. He felt like the seven-year-old Jan writing a postcard to Mrs Tapper.

The picture of Burlington Arcade he had bought for Marianne. Shops and suspended flower-pots, gas-lamps converted for electricity, and a glass roof stained by the pigeons. 'Dear Marianne. We lead a warm attic life. I want you to be happy too. I'm trying to decide what to do in the autumn; the tower does not attract me any more. I'm bad at looking back and ahead, constantly devoured by the present. The children here have plastic satchels in yellow, blue and red. Do you think that might be something for Martin and Malin?' For Knut Tapper he selected the Thames at ebb with loaded barges: 'It's awful when good intentions are too late, but nice when evil thoughts do not reach you.'

He wrote no more, and he never sent that postcard.

THE VIEW

They fitted their summer holidays into some empty days in July in their calendar. The framework was a landscape of ridges, valleys and villages.

They travelled along the Thames, and turned off towards

353

Cirencester and Cotswold Hills. They were near the source of the river. Blackberry brambles showed in the bends. The berries were firm, still bitter. Bushes with honeysuckle in blossom stroked the green plate of the car. Wild roses shone like reflex tapes. Most of the time they drove slowly enough to see the rabbit outside its hole like a golfball on its way down.

The villages passed with low dark brick houses, Tudor cottages, churches, and tea shops. Jenny talked about extending man's views on his own potential. One had to look for new solutions to old problems, but, moreover, be aware of the new riddles. She spoke about the conservative self-preservation instinct, about the intense experiences that surpass the boundaries, and create gaps in the architecture, and lay the ground for social and psychological changes, exterior and interior, directed by knowledge as well as feelings.

Jan listened. At low speed he put his hand around her neck. He could feel the muscles of the words moving under the fingertips. They ran out of petrol climbing a hill, as they had forgotten to watch the meter. A farmer on the other side of the hedge sold them a couple of gallons. They stood there discussing the weather, the motorways which stole more and more of the province's fertile soil, about the lorries roaring through the old cities at night, making the foundations shake to pieces and over and over again driving into shop windows.

The farmer belonged to an older generation who were good at shaking their heads. He appeared to be a room full of echoes from their childhood, of religion and letters to the Editor, and of the beery complaint of the pubs. Young people doing nothing were as bad as the young people interfering and not appreciating the work of the older generation.

They went on, and JB could see in the rear mirror the clear blue door of the farmer's house, and a dwarf of terracotta who smiled in a shrubbery of rhododendron.

They stopped in a little village towards the evening by a sign announcing Bed & Breakfast. A wiry woman with swift movements received them. She managed a grocery and a petrol station in the house next door. There were sweet-peas in their room, light purple and dark red; the wallpaper had a rosy pattern, and the wooden ceiling was yellow. They felt welcome.

They let out some daddy-long-legs. From the kitchen came

354

the smell of steak and kidney pie. In a window niche were a couple of magazines and A Dictionary of Heroes. They discovered here that the house belonged to a little farm. The back looked out on open fields. Some cows were taken in for the night, driven by a sheepdog. On a hill there was a ruin with a gable sharp against the sky, and when they went out through the kitchen, the thin woman explained that her family had come from there in the seventeenth century, and moved a couple of hundred yards down to the village.

The sheepdog followed them a bit on their way. The night was as warm as the inside of a hand.

'I feel I could lean back into plain air without falling,' Jan said, meeting Jenny's eyes.

It was as though they had seamed a protective net long before they met and the performance began.

A pre-historic bird with pointed wings was sitting on the field clearing his throat. They discerned it on a white slab: the steps to a Druid temple, Jenny thought.

They suddenly had the feeling that they had left everything behind. Like leaving the luggage at the station when getting on the train.

They saw a satellite dribbling its way between the stars. A rocking torch cleverly keeping out of the way of the fixed lights.

'It can't be helped,' Jenny said.

'What?'

'The spoilt happiness I feel in spite of the condition of the world.'

The crickets around them talked about old times. They had been there almost always. Their habits had become nature's law: the sound of the crickets. Yet their existence was threatened, for the first time in a million years. Irrevocably.

Near the house they found a dead robin. Its creaking alarm clock had stopped. The beak was shiny, the short down on the head as light as dust. Its eyes two dark cough tablets.

'What killed it?'

'They saw another robin in our landlady's telly and didn't notice the window,' Jenny suggested.

'The Balthus effect,' JB mumbled.

They soon lay deep down in one of these warm English beds which rocked them away into nightmares. They woke scream-

355

ing in a pit. In the morning they saw the whitebeam turn the wrong sides of its leaves to the first wind: fish bellies in the sea of air. The short-grazed pastures gathered light. The odd park tree rose monumentally on a plinth of shadow.

Down in the courtyard an old man was peeling potatoes. He diced them and threw them into a tin pan which echoed with a sound that grew duller as it was filled. A faded rag rug was being aired. Cherry stones spat out, white and dried by the wind, were scattered over a garden table. The landlady served them dark tea, oat porridge and scones. They sat under a marine painting of a storm long outblown. A long dachshund begged for bread. It looked like a stuffed suitcase. Then they went out among the Cotswolds', some of the hills three hundred metres high, which was rare in southern England and the Midlands. There was dew and greenery there, the houses were sparse, and man could still walk on the ground. They left their car on a hill, or rather a protruding rock, which on the map was called Birdlip. They wandered casually into the grounds.

Near the road was an old limestone smithy. Its foundation was badger-legged, but mayweed and geranium had managed to grow between the stones; even there there was soil; the walls were powerless against the things that grew.

They climbed a hill. A pea picking machine rattled in a field, and they saw the turning-stone in the field with white marks from the harrow and the binder. Nobody had put his iron bar under it to lift it. It was a little bit too large, as grey and heavy as winter. It was one of these summer days which one knows are light and clear behind the mist. The spider had drawn his high voltage line between wild spiraea and ferns. The odd thread had fallen down and was no longer live.

Near a farm a cow walked anxiously on and off, rubbing against the fence. Then she lay down on her side, and before their eyes, had a calf, screaming only for a moment, as the calf slid out inside its membrane. The calf was on the grass, grey and curly, with white patches on its legs, and the hooves still soft. It looked like a little donkey, and showed its teeth. The cow watched and licked it. This was when one must not stick one's hand into the mouth of the calf, or it would not learn to shape its tongue around the teat. It got up tottering while the cow turned away to face the farmer who came running with rags and dry hay in his arms.

They walked in a circle around the top of the mountain. On the other side they looked in surprise out over a valley with two cities. They shimmered far below in the mist, with sweaty roofs and grainy smokes. Between them the pristine watercourse of the river glistened.

They were standing at a look-out point with a view over country and town, a place for surveillance and perception. But the heat and the glittering sun, the hay chaff in the air, the flies and other insects, pulled them down to a sphere closer to the ground. They found a plant with white flowers, but when Jenny bent down towards it, the flowers fluttered and disappeared into a hazel shrub : the hazel soon had the same flowers. A hillock turned out to be an ant-hill. With a thin layer of grass over their heads thousands of individuals were toiling there in the way that had been prescribed for them once and for all.

Jan took Jenny's hand and let go of it. They were surrounded by a smile, as hard to catch as the buzzing of the bees and the flashing of wings. They sat down on the ground, seeing the landscape extending in several directions. The sheep were immobile on a distant steep hill like light boulders that had fallen down and stopped. Fumitory, the dark pink weed, floated like low mist over the slope. The limestone houses were illuminated letters for life that had gone on for a long time. They thought they lay on the top of the hay wagon, nearest to the sun.

The past was there, stored in layers like the mountain they were standing on. And the future was a guest on his way to their table. They depended on the work of other people, people not yet born depended on them : Gertrude's child and other children.

'You can't find evidence against a dream,' Jenny said, 'not even the one of freedom.'

'Intense experiences risk becoming frozen blocks of memory,' Jan said. 'And an incredible experience becomes a story you get used to presenting in exactly the same way.'

'Watch that,' Jenny said. 'The outlook changes. There are many stories. Better try to see some of them yourself.'

He felt the smell of her armpit's salty sweat. He liked that smell. He saw the mountain denuded like worn mussel-shells. Then he looked at Jenny : her blouse had come out of her

357

trousers; he saw the skin of her waist, the light skin on her stomach. Her earthy elbow surrounded by blue chicory. Over the fields was a band of shadow and light like over the sea on clear summer days.

This was the earth of the surface, the zone of contact for the meetings of the skin, the life-bringing communications. The border area between the fire of the interior and the lack of oxygen of the stratosphere. Under the earth was the kingdom of moles. And in other places: air raid shelters, hollows for nuclear weapons, the preparations of death, the drive to extend the cemeteries, let the fire out, let the sputtering lava destroy the living cells.

JB thought about the road to Birdlip. He felt like trying the first caresses again, the slightest touch which had kept them satisfied for days. But before him he saw undeliberately Gertrude's alien face in Botswana. If feeling had a balance-sheet, he had been living on loans for a long time. The numbers above and below the line of suffering would never balance each other out. Yet he regretted nothing. Through love, he thought, he approached the inaccessible thing of another person's experience. It was not the only way, but the best. Only with others can one explore oneself. Alone one is un-intercepted. Through others one becomes someone different, and this new person one will eventually see as oneself.

Jenny had developed him: a blurred figure on a plate that she had made sharp. She had come to him from outside with a heat that he recognized as his own. And he had met her with the power he had borrowed from her. What they gave each other was unexpected and without demands.

Everything they had experienced existed as if they were still experiencing it: the bewitchment and the tremor of the skin, the slow ski-dive, the pleasure that would not be inscribed by the general magnetic rules, the expensive confusion, the readiness to suffer for the sake of a few moments, all this that had lasted for so long that it looked like wearing and every-day life.

When he started to tell Jenny about this, she did not reply. She was asleep on her side with her forehead pressed against his knee: two hard bodies weathered smooth meeting con-fidentially like the boulders around them.

He was surprised. He himself was as alert as ever. He could

not put his head on the grass worn by the wind and give his joy to the ground. But he leaned over her as if listening to her dreams. Storms might ravage in the loved one's head without a hair being touched on his own.

The harvesting machine was clattering further away. Voices rose from the fields. He cupped his hands over her sleep. He could feel her breath come and go against his palms. He stroked the air over her body : a vault like the first time at her front door at Nybro Quay. He didn't know her then. Now they knew a lot about each other, more than they imagined.

The light ripened like wheat. The sheep in the background started to move. An invisible shepherd drove them home. Jenny slept. He spied out over the landscape as her representative. He tried to penetrate the mist. Was there not a glitter of a car roof? Or a lake? He wanted her to see what she saw, and explain what he could not interpret. For yet another while they rested on the floor of the earth. What was consummated between them calmly awaited the unconsummated. He would soon wake her up.